A LOVE BEYOND THE STARS

JENNIFER CHIPMAN

For the girlies who watched Chris Pine as Captain Kirk and thought, "where do I get one of those?"

PLAYLIST

- Paradise - Coldplay
- You're On Your Own Kid - Taylor Swift
- Counting Stars - OneRepublic
- Stargazing - Myles Smith
- ocean eyes - Billie Eilish
- Satellite - Harry Styles
- Guilty as Sin? - Taylor Swift
- Too Sweet - Hozier
- Glimpse of Us - Joji
- illicit affairs - Taylor Swift
- Rewrite the Stars - Zac Efron, Zendaya
- All I Want - Kodaline
- Delicate - Taylor Swift
- eternal sunshine - Ariana Grande
- The Only Exception - Paramore
- Everything Has Changed - Taylor Swift, Ed Sheeran
- All of the Stars - Ed Sheeran
- Movement - Hozier
- Gravity - Sara Bareilles
- SLOW DANCING IN THE DARK - Joji
- Call It What You Want - Taylor Swift

CONTENTS

ONE
AURELIA

"*NOW PRESENTING, the graduating class of 3051...*" the announcer's voice boomed across the large room that boasted all the graduates of the UGSF's Flight School.

A day I'd been waiting for, counting down to for the last fifteen years. Ever since I was ten years old, I'd been dreaming of this moment: the day I crossed the stage and became a pilot for the *United Galactic Space Federation.* It was so close, I could almost taste it. Though, staring at the stars would pale compared to actually being *up* there.

"Aurelia Callisto!" The announcer, an older woman with white hair, called out my name, propelling me into motion across the stage.

This was it. My moment. The beginning of the rest of my life. At twenty-five years old, I hadn't accomplished a lot of the things on my list. But this was a start. The rest would come in time.

"Thank you," I said, tightly grasping hands with the Dean of the *Samuel D. Callisto Flight Academy.*

They'd named it after my father, one of the most famous pilots of this century, following his disappearance on his last mission when I was twelve. Thirteen years later, and the wound still stung. Most of all, because they never found out what happened to him, or how he met his end.

One day, I hoped to find out.

"Your father would have been so proud of you," Dean Baliss said.

Anderson Baliss was my dad's best friend, and I'd practically grown up around him and his family. His daughter was still one of my best friends.

I got choked up, trying to swallow the lump in my throat. "I appreciate it."

"We miss him every day."

I nodded, unable to say anything else.

There wasn't a way to describe that grief. It was a deep ache, a loss I felt every day. It wasn't something that could be summed up with kind words or well wishes.

He should have been here.

With my diploma in hand, I headed back to my seat, waiting for the rest of the graduates to walk before they would hand out our assignments.

Everyone had their own wishes for where they'd be stationed in the UGSF's fleet, from smaller crafts to the massive starship transports and space stations. I had bigger dreams. A *mission*. See the stars, travel to worlds unknown.

Follow in my dad's footsteps. Make him proud.

Once the last graduate had crossed the stage, taking his place back in the last row, Dean Baliss stepped back up to the podium.

"Congratulations to all of you. All of us here at the *Samuel D. Callisto Flight Academy* couldn't be more proud of our graduates, and we cannot wait to watch the amazing things our new pilots will do as you go out into the world. While some of you will stay closer to home, others will travel to worlds far beyond this galaxy. Beyond even the wildest reaches of the known universe."

A shiver ran down my spine just thinking about it.

"Now, as you all know, the last part of our graduation ceremony is receiving your assigned position. Though we did our best to comply with requests—" The dean's face formed into a frown. "—not all of them could be accommodated. However, we did our best to place each of you in a rank and on a ship we thought was befitting of your skill set." He nodded to the woman helping him as the large screen at the top of the stage flickered on. "Each graduating cadet's name will now be displayed on the screen with their assigned craft, in rank order. Please applaud as each name is announced."

All my years of schooling culminated in *this*. I crossed my fingers, and toes, like that would help me achieve my desired result. Though I'd already done everything I could, working my ass off every year, forgoing parties and relationships so I could focus on exams and simulations.

My name was the first one on the screen, in large, block letters.

Aurelia S. Callisto
Second Pilot, S.S. Octavia

My stomach sank. The *Octavia* was a smaller, older ship, mostly flying the same route between the space station outside of Earth's orbit and our colony on Mars to transport supplies. As the Second Pilot, I'd be the backup, flying the ship when the Head Pilot was otherwise occupied, off the ship, or needed relief. I already knew from all of my research that it was a two-year assignment.

There was no normal, not with space voyages, but I'd had my eyes on a research mission. Besides studying for graduation, my entire last semester had been spent scrutinizing every flight path, looking for the perfect one. I'd requested, well… it didn't matter now. The perfect mission, the perfect ship—neither of them was mine. I shook my head, like I was shaking away the idea. Best not to dwell on things that hadn't happened.

Instead, I pasted a smile on my face.

The rest of the ceremony was a blur, and then we were shuffled out of the room, all of us in our dress uniforms. I missed the comfort of my flight suit. I'd practically lived in it the last two years, despite only learning on flight simulators and airplanes. Neither were the real thing.

Besides, I'd be living in it day in and day out soon, as a pilot on an actual starship.

A grin split my face as a giddy feeling bubbled up through my system. *Hell yes.* I did it.

The crowd was full of loved ones congratulating their graduates, laughter and excitement and shrieks from those embracing their significant others.

All I had was—"Aurelia." My mom's voice brought my feet to a halt.

She looked so much older today, her sandy blonde hair brushed back into a low bun, the tight navy dress revealing just how much of my genes I'd gotten from her. I liked to imagine my father standing beside her, both of their faces beaming at me as I clutched my diploma in my hand, running into their open arms.

But just as quick as it came, the vision was gone, leaving my mom standing alone.

"Mom." Her hands cupped my face as my eyes flooded with tears.

"Congratulations, baby girl." She hugged me tight.

"Thanks for coming." I finally pulled out of our hug so I could look at her. We shared so many features—her curvy hips and that small, slightly upturned nose, but I'd gotten dad's coloring. His russet-brown hair. Though mine was a shade lighter than his, I still loved the reddish streaks in it.

"I wish your father was here," she said, resting her forehead against my own. It was like she knew what I was thinking about —because Elara Callisto had always been a bit of a mind reader. Or maybe it was just that she knew me too well.

"Me too."

"He'd never stop bragging about how proud he was of his

little girl if he was here." She tucked a strand of hair behind my ear.

"I know," I said, a laugh slipping from my lips as my smile grew wider. "He would have loved all of this. Boasting about me, seeing his buddies. Screaming about how I was number one."

He would have yelled for me till his voice grew hoarse. The thought brought a smile to my lips, even as I wiped a few beads of moisture from my eyes. The thought of never knowing what happened to him—never flying the same route—caused a sharp pain in my heart. I'd made a vow that first day at the academy, and I definitely wasn't going to break it now.

"How are you feeling?" she asked, and I knew she could sense some of my earlier disappointment. Yup, mind reader. Though she just called it her *mom-tuition*.

"Good. It might not be the assignment I wanted, but it's going to be amazing. I'll make sure of it." I gave a sharp nod. *It's going to be amazing* was my new mantra. Maybe if I repeated it enough times, it would be the truth.

"That's my girl," she said, squeezing my upper arm before letting me go to loop an arm through mine. "Now, what do you say we try to track down some food? I'm starving."

I laughed, following my mom towards the celebratory banquet, knowing that each step I took was one closer to my future.

Closer to a life amongst the stars.

ONE MONTH LATER...

I laid in my childhood bedroom, looking up at the constellations of LED stars my dad and I had installed when I was younger.

They were a perfect replica of the night sky above California, and I'd begged him for *weeks* to do them with me.

We'd finished them the night before he'd left on a six month mission, and they lit up my ceiling for years. I didn't have the heart to take them down, to patch the holes they left behind.

Soon, though, I'd be leaving all of this behind.

I'd moved out of my apartment today, getting ready for my mission. There was no point in paying credits when I wouldn't be on the planet for the next two years, so all of my furniture—what little I had—was now in storage, and the rest of the possessions I owned were now shoved in my closet.

Mom hadn't moved after we lost my dad. I thought this house would be too painful, that there would be too many memories here, but maybe that was the exact reason she hadn't left. Here, she felt close to him. Like she could almost pretend that he was still going to walk in that front door and come home to us.

I wished it was that easy. To pretend he'd just been on a long mission. Like when I was younger, and he'd open the door, and I'd raced into his arms every time.

But there was no coming back. Thirteen years had passed, and it was time to face the truth.

My communication device buzzed, startling me out of my thoughts. I scrambled to grab it off my nightstand, almost hitting myself in the face with it.

"Aurelia." Vice Admiral Rist's name popped up on my communicator, and I almost had to do a double take.

"Yes, Vice Admiral?"

A thousand thoughts flickered through my mind. *Why were they calling?*

Maybe the Federation had made a mistake. For a moment, I had a wave of anxiety. Had I forgotten to submit something? They'd let me graduate, of course, but what if I'd actually failed one of my final exams? It was a nightmare that kept waking me up at night.

6

"How are you doing?"

"Um. Good. You know. Getting ready to head out there for my commission."

It had only been a month since the ceremony, but it still felt like I was floating on air. I would have to report soon for my assignment, and I'd been trying to live it up before I headed up to the space station. Well—live it up as much as I normally did. Which often meant curling up on the couch next to my mom with a book in my hands, or grabbing dinner with the girls. I'd taken to a nightly walk along the beach, my favorite part of this house.

"Good, good. That's actually what I called to talk to you about. There's been a change in assignments." The words were stated so casually that I just blinked. Obviously, they couldn't see my face, since this was a voice call, but I still tried to mask my surprise.

"Okay…?" I held my breath, waiting to hear the words I'd only dreamed of. *It couldn't be…*

"The head pilot position on the *S.S. Paradise* just became available. Normally, I wouldn't offer it to someone just out of flight school, but the mission is scheduled to leave in a few days, and there's just not enough time to find someone else. I know that this was your requested assignment upon graduation." They took a brief pause. "In fact, it was the *only* commission you requested."

I was floored. *Flabbergasted.* Sure, some part of me had hoped that things would still work out, but I hadn't actually expected it to. Which was probably why the only words that escaped my lips were, "That's right." It had seemed crazy to put all of my eggs in one basket—even more so when I'd gotten a different assignment at graduation. Now… it felt like fate.

Or all of the stars aligning to take me exactly where I needed to go.

"Are you sure?"

"Well, you were top of your class, and I know if anyone can do it, you can."

"I—I don't know what to say." Mostly because I wasn't sure this wasn't a dream. I pinched my arm, smoothing over the sting on my skin. *Yep, not dreaming.*

"Say yes. The position is yours, if you accept it."

Obviously. How could I turn something like this down? It was my dream.

Being the head pilot on the S.S. Paradise was everything I'd ever worked towards. A position most people didn't earn for at least a few years after flight school. It was a five-year mission to the outer reaches of space, places humans used to only dream about exploring.

"Okay," I said, agreeing before they could change their mind. "I'd be honored. Of course I'll take it."

"That's what I like to hear. And just between us, Aurelia, you were always our favorite at the Academy. We know you're going to go far. Your father did too."

I closed my eyes, wondering if the reminders would ever get less painful. If they'd make me miss him less. "Thank you. I'll try to make you all proud."

After they gave me the details of the assignment, the boarding platform and everything I needed to know before departing for my mission in just *days,* we hung up the phone.

And… *Holy shit.* It was happening.

My dreams were coming true.

THE NIGHT SKY glimmered with stars, captivating me like it had each night since I was small. There was so much out there in the vastness of space, and I couldn't wait to explore it. My eyes trailed over the constellations as I leaned back against the sand.

The sun had long gone down, but I couldn't stop watching the sky as the sound of waves crashing against the beach filled my ears.

There wasn't a single other way I could imagine spending my last night on earth.

"Are you ready?" my best friend, Fionia, asked me.

I hold her gaze, even in the darkness. "Yeah. I've been waiting my whole life for this."

Tomorrow was my first day in the stars, a day I had only dreamed about.

The moon lit up her face, so even in the darkness, I could see Fia trying to hold back her tears. "I'll miss you so much."

"*Psh.* You'll forget about me so fast." I gave her a small smile, even though I hoped that wasn't true.

But five years was a long time to go with little to no contact. The chances of getting a satellite transmission to Earth from the far reaches of space was almost non-existent. Even if we could, those communications would be reserved for important messages—not for someone who was missing the people she'd left at home.

My best friend had gotten married this summer to her high school sweetheart, and I knew part of her decision had been so I could be there. For as long as I could remember, we'd done everything together: prom, first dates, saying goodbye to high school. We'd walked in to college arm and arm, even though we'd chosen wildly different fields of study. And then we'd graduated together too. Lia & Fia, two peas in a pod.

Besides flight school, this was the first thing I was really doing on my *own*. It was the reminder that from now on, everything I did would be by myself.

Her tone was light, but full of emotion. "Lia…"

"I know." Clasping our hands together, I squeezed hers tight.

I'd miss out on a lot of life by leaving. Of course I knew that. But I was fine with never getting married if I got to live my dream, following in my dad's footsteps. He'd been the greatest pilot our planet had ever known, and hopefully one day, they would say the same thing about me.

"Have you heard much about your new ship?"

I shook my head. "Just a few rumors about the captain, but I'm sure they're not true. But the ship's specs are incredible. And the recreation floor? *Wow.*"

"You're the only person I've ever known who'd get excited about the gym."

I'd always loved running. In some ways, I'd been running ever since my dad had died. Running towards something on the horizon that I wasn't quite aware of yet. Something beyond the stars.

"Do you think he's hot?"

"Who?" I blinked at her.

"The captain!"

I was slightly mortified. *"Fia*! He's going to be my boss. My *superior officer.*" As far as I was concerned, I wasn't allowed to even think he was hot.

"What? Is it so bad that I want you to be happy? Maybe you'll meet someone on the ship."

"Unlikely." My priorities for this mission definitely did *not* include falling in love. Absolutely not.

But, okay. I'd definitely peeked at the Captain's photo, and he was gorgeous. And ten years older than me, which made him off-limits in so many ways.

I'd heard about his reputation, though. That he was a little grumpy. Maybe everyone was just exaggerating? I didn't see how you could be the Captain of a massive starship like that and be unhappy.

Either way, I'd make the best of it. This mission was my first choice, and I wouldn't squander this opportunity. My dreams were coming true, even if I had to leave everyone I'd ever known and loved behind.

"Sorry I'm late," said Eliza as she dropped onto the sand next to me. "I brought wine to make up for it."

Eliza Baliss—the one and only daughter of Dean Baliss—and I had grown up together, but our friendship was forged like molten rock. When I'd lost my dad, she'd been my foundation that kept me from crumbling. She was a year older than me, but we'd spent most of my time in flight school together until she'd graduated the year before me.

"That's more like it," I said, throwing my arms around both girls. "In my favorite place with my favorite people."

Eliza waved the bottle of wine around. "We have to celebrate you leaving the planet, after all!" She popped the cork on the bottle.

"No wine for me," Fia said, a small smile tracking over her face.

"Fionia! You're not…" My eyes grew wide, flickering down to her abdomen.

She nodded, joy blossoming over her features. "It's really early, but… I'm so happy."

"And I'm going to miss all of it," I pouted, thinking about my mission. I'd known that life would move on without me—that my friends would get married and have babies all while I was in space—but this was the first time I really had to confront the idea.

Once, I'd imagined that future for myself too. A loving husband, a family—kids. But being a pilot, serving in space left little time to meet someone. Plus, leaving them behind wasn't in the cards for me. I couldn't risk anyone losing me like I'd lost my dad. It hurt too much.

"Hey, more for us," Eliza said with a shrug, drinking straight from the bottle. She handed it over to me, and I muttered a quick *what the hell* before taking a mouthful of the beverage.

"Everything is changing so fast," I said, staring up at the stars.

"The understatement of the *century*," Fionia remarked, letting her hand rest over her stomach. "We've got our whole lives ahead of us. Just think, five years is going to *fly* by." She turned to me.

I couldn't imagine it, and I hadn't even left yet.

"I don't know what's out there," Eliza said, "but I can't wait to find out."

I hugged my knees tighter as a shooting star dazzled its way through the sky, and I sent a wish up to the heavens.

That my mission would go well. That I'd find everything I was looking for.

Because tomorrow, like it or not, everything would change.

TWO
SYLAS

"CAPTAIN'S LOG. STAR DATE 05033051." I settled into my chair, adjusting the insignia on my new uniform. "The rest of the crew arrives today. I've spent the last few days inspecting the ship, getting acclimated to our new surroundings."

I'd never had so much time to thoroughly explore a vessel I'd been stationed on before, and I had to admit, I liked it. It had been informative, but what I enjoyed the most was the calm. The skeleton crew currently on the ship hadn't bothered me, and I'd found it relaxing. Though all of that peace would disappear as soon as my officers and the rest of the crew arrived. But a captain needed to know his ship, and finally, this one was all mine. Who could blame me for wanting to take the time to learn it *alone*?

"Tomorrow, we'll set out on our five-year mission to explore past the reaches of the known galaxy," I narrated, wondering if one day these logs would be in the historical records, like so many I'd studied in the past. "To search for planets lush with resources, rich with minerals—to find life. The Starship Paradise was designed for this, to travel beyond the stars. Taking us to places we could only dream about fifty years ago."

Paradise, also known as an *ideal or idyllic place or state*. That was the textbook definition, but somehow it was fitting for this ship, the culmination of over a thousand years of space travel development.

I paused my narration to look out at the space station the ship was docked at. Transports would arrive from the Earth's surface soon, carrying our passengers.

Including officers, crew, and families, we'd begin our maiden voyage with just over five hundred people on board. It was anyone's guess what we'd find out there, though I knew what the UGSF wanted. We faced land shortages, green spaces having to be protected as we humans continued to expand. Even after colonizing Mars, the world leaders were desperate. That pressure rested on my shoulders now.

I continued to narrate to my log, detailing the aims and some of my own personal goals.

"*Sylas!*" My silence ended, and I ended the recording with a wave as my first officer—and my younger sister—arrived on the bridge.

She'd joined me on the transport a few days ago, her new badge just as shiny as mine.

Kayle crossed her arms as she screeched to a halt in front of my chair. "Admiring your throne again, dear brother?"

I rolled my eyes. "Just breaking it in, Ky."

The white leather was soft under my fingertips, my chair still brand new. If I inhaled, I could still smell the new leather scent that reminded me of a new vehicle on Earth.

"Sure. That's what they all say. But I've caught you ogling it a few times…" Kayle didn't hide her smirk.

But she could make fun of me all she wanted—it was a nice chair.

"How long till everyone else comes on board?" I asked, glancing down at the communication device in her hands.

She was my executive officer, which made her first in line to take over command if anything should happen to me. Kayle would also be in charge of landing parties, overseeing all personnel on board the ship, and managing the ship's resources, in addition to assisting me in my personal duties.

"Just a few hours. Are you ready?"

"I was born ready," I said, not even a glimmer of a joke in my words.

Kayle gave me a serious look. "I know you were."

She turned, facing the large viewport as she leaned on the railing. Standing, I joined her.

"Think you'll have a problem treating me as your captain, not your brother?" I raised an eyebrow, looking over at her.

We shared the same face—the same dark brown hair, deep blue eyes, and the same slope of our nose, courtesy of our parents. The main difference besides our height, since I was a good four inches taller than her, was the small dusting of freckles along the bridge of her nose.

"Just because we haven't worked together before doesn't mean I can't treat you as my superior." My sister brushed her ponytail off her shoulder, adjusting the collar of her jumpsuit.

"Sure, sure. I'll believe it when I see it," I joked with her, nudging her with my elbow.

She raised her hand to her brow, mock saluting me. "Aye aye, *Captain* Kellar."

"Remind me why I chose you as my First Officer again?" I grumbled, rolling my eyes.

"Because I'm the best at my job. Plus, you love me."

I couldn't exactly argue with that. Because I did. She was the most important person in my life, and always had been.

"It's a good thing you're my sister, because I'm basically *required* to love you."

"You're insufferable."

A chuckle slipped from my lips. "Says the girl who bullied me into letting her come on a five-year journey."

"Bullied is a strong word, you know."

"Oh? What do you call it then?"

She punched me in the shoulder. "Hey. Not fair."

My lips twitched up, though I didn't quite smile. "Wouldn't have made you my first officer if I thought you couldn't do this."

Kayle was two years younger than me, though we'd grown up doing everything together, so people often mistook us for twins. We'd played sports together, argued over who got the newest copy of our favorite book series when it came out, and cleared hours and hours of video game levels together. At least, when we'd been able to afford all of those things.

When she'd graduated college two years behind me, she'd followed in my footsteps and joined the United Galactic Space Federation. Though I'd questioned what she was going to do with a communications degree, she'd more than proved herself, rising through the ranks to a Commander position faster than even I had.

I'd grumbled about it, but I was damn proud of her. And the decision on who would be my executive officer had come easy to me. I hadn't even considered anyone else.

"Didn't dream of doing it without you."

She was all I had left. I'd never leave her behind like our parents left us.

"What do you think we'll find out there?" Kayle asked, staring out the glass windows that ran along the front of the bridge.

"That's part of the excitement, isn't it? The adventure? The not knowing?"

Our mission would take us a few million light years away, utilizing brand new technology to travel through space faster than ever. They'd been developing it over the last fifteen years, using specific areas in space to warp through to other ends of the galaxy.

We were the first ship to test it out on a full-length mission.

No one had ever been that far into space, and it had only been loosely charted via high-powered telescopes. We would be the first humans to chart the space, to set foot on new planets. To journey to a new world, beyond the stars.

"Look at you, Captain Kellar. Sounding especially chipper today. That's so unlike you."

Resisting the urge to punch my sister, I grunted, staring out the window.

She was right, though—everything was about to change. At thirty-five years old, I'd finally gotten everything I'd been working towards all my life. My dream job. I was content with the life I had. There was no room for love or anyone else in it. I had my sister, and she was enough.

We stood in silence, watching the activity around the station. The stars flickered faintly in the background. Soon enough, we'd be in distant skies, and all of these would be a faint memory.

"I think I'm going to go run another lap around the rec floor," Kayle finally said. "Get rid of some of this jittery energy."

"Good idea." My fingers itched to pull back open my log. Maybe it was strange, but I liked the idea of having all of my thoughts collected somewhere. My legacy that would live on, even long after I was gone.

"You're going to stay here, aren't you?" She asked me, looking back from the door frame with her hands on her hips.

"Yes," I muttered under my breath. "Now, go."

She left me to the silence of the bridge, enjoying my last bit of quiet before the rest of the crew arrived.

"Here goes nothing," I said to myself, before hitting resume on my recording.

"EVERYONE'S READY, SY," Kayle said later, knocking on the door to my office. I'd retreated there when everyone else started boarding, finishing up some necessary paperwork before we'd set out in the morning.

After the crew got adjusted to being on the ship, our mission would officially begin.

I looked up, finding my sister in her dress uniform. It was strange to see her in the cobalt blue hue the command officers wore, but damn. "I'm proud of you. You know that, right?"

Our parents might not be around to tell her what a damn good person she'd become, but that was okay. I'd make up for it by making sure she knew every single day.

"Thanks, bro." She gave me a little wink, doing a twirl for me. "Looks good, doesn't it?"

We had a few different uniforms issued to us by the UGSF for daily wear, including a basic dark gray zippered jumpsuit, a flight suit for missions, and our dress uniforms, which consisted of a fitted top and black dress pants. All of them featured the color that denoted our department, and we wore our rank badge on top.

Standing up from my chair, I clasped a hand on her shoulder. "It looks great, *sis.*" I added the last word on the end to tease her, because I knew she only called me bro because she thought it annoyed me. In some ways, it did.

In other ways, she was my only family, and my best friend. I'd pretty much let her call me whatever she wanted, as long as it wasn't within the earshot of anyone else. I didn't need to be teased mercilessly for her childhood nickname for me, or the way she called me Sy. The kids in middle school had a field day with that one, and I'd been known as *Sy-Fi* for months. Little pricks.

But while they got to go home to their parents every night, it had just been Kayle and I, barely scraping by. Trying to make ends meet however we could.

So, yeah. I'd always let her get away with more than I should.

My sister cleared her throat. "Time to meet the crew."

I nodded, knowing I couldn't delay the inevitable. Soon, I'd be face to face with my officers.

Luckily, I'd hand picked most of them myself. My buddies

from college might have been good friends, but they were also *damn good* at what they did. And I'd had my selection of some of the finest researchers, medical officers, and bridge teams that the UGSF employed. Most of them had served with me during previous missions, which should have been reassuring, except...

"Is it bad that I'm nervous?" I asked, rubbing at my forehead. I'd never had to address my officers as the captain before.

She laughed. "You're gonna do fine."

"Well, *obviously*. This isn't my first day out of the academy. I know what I'm doing."

"I know you do."

No matter how confident I was, though, there was a hint of worry I was doing my best to keep locked down. Not that I would do a bad job, but that my crew wouldn't like me. Or some shit like that. My chest felt tight, and I took a deep breath. "How frowned upon would it be if I took a shot first?"

"Very." She handed me a bottle from the alcohol cart. "But I won't tell." My sister winked.

"Great," I said, taking a swig and grimacing at the taste as it went down. "What the hell did you give me?" Spinning the bottle around, I raised an eyebrow at the label on the bottle. "Blue absinthe, really?"

Kayle did her best to look innocent. "What, you don't like it? I thought it was your favorite."

She knew that I'd puked my guts out after drinking an entire bottle of it in college, and the smell still made me a little nauseous to this day. Plus, the color coming back up had been... awful.

"Thanks for that," I muttered, wiping my mouth off. "*Gross.*" I needed to scrape my tongue now.

She patted me on the back as we walked towards the door. "Anything for you."

"Time to go," I said, running my hands through my hair to smooth it back. "Got everything?"

She grabbed the large tablet from where she'd dropped it on the tabletop. "Yup. You?"

I flashed her a rare grin. "Absolutely. Let's go meet our crew, Commander Kellar."

"Aye, aye, Captain Kellar."

I rolled my eyes playfully, hiding the small smile by turning away from her and pressing the button to open the door.

Today, greeting my officers in person.

Tomorrow? Journeying beyond the stars.

THREE
AURELIA

WOAH. My eyes widened at the gleaming hull as we approached the docking station where the S.S. Paradise was currently docked.

The ship itself was sleek, all curved lines and white gleaming metal. During the last week, I'd inhaled every article and piece of information I could find about the ship, its floor-plans, and every spec or piece of technology they'd filled her up with. No expense had been spared. It had cutting edge technology suffi-cient enough to practically pilot *itself* through all the reaches of space. I'd been trained on a simulator version, but to be here—in front of the real thing—it took my breath away.

I still couldn't believe I was here.

As of tomorrow, I would officially be a UGSF Pilot. I'd be flying a *starship*, for crying out loud. I sucked in my squeal of excitement, not wanting to disturb the others surrounding me.

There were only twenty seats on the small craft, and there were a few small families on board, sending a jolt of envy through me. I'd begged my dad when I was younger to take me along, but back then, the ships weren't designed to house fami-lies. Everything was different now.

I shut my eyes, trying not to think about my father's last

mission again. About how much I missed him. *It's all for you, Dad*, I thought, hoping he was here with me somehow. I felt closer to him up here, where I could see the stars glittering outside my window. If I pretended, it was almost like he was here with me.

Looking out the glass, I let my eyes drift over the space station. Earth was still barely visible behind it. I mentally bid farewell to my home, welcoming the next part of my life.

The shuttle landed, smoothly locking onto the station. Once they opened the loading ramp, I quickly grabbed my bags and hurried off, heading into the main part of the space station.

My future was waiting.

THE CABIN I'd live in for the next five years of interplanetary space travel wasn't as big as my apartment back home on earth, but I'd get used to the bunk, eventually. At least it was a room by myself.

I was *here*. A grin lit up my face. "This is it, Aurelia," I said to myself, giving one more sweeping glance over the room. "This is your life now. The one you've dreamed about."

There was a desk underneath my bunk and a small dresser where I'd stowed the little clothing and personal effects I'd brought on board. A brand new data pad and communicator, both top of the line devices, rested on the small table opposite my bed. The little cow plushie my dad bought me when I was five sat next to my pillow. Even though I was probably *too old* to still carry something like that around, its presence made me feel a little lighter.

My new uniforms were all waiting for me in the closet, pops of dark purple peeking through. They'd been starched and pressed, with the officer's logo stitched on the sleeve, and there was one for every day of the week. The familiar sight of the gray jumpsuits I'd worn in flight school as well as flight suits hanging in my closet made my heart race.

Shedding the rest of my civilian clothes, I donned my officer's uniform, appreciating the block of purple that indicated my position. Most of the crew members who worked on the bridge would bear the same color, and I finished the ensemble with my shiny new badge with the UGSF's logo on it. It was a silver shield-like shape with three shooting stars in gold in the middle, featuring three gold dots to show my rank as a lieutenant.

Normally, graduates started out at a lower rank, but I would wear this badge with pride.

I pulled my hair back in a low bun, making sure I looked the part.

My eyes looked bright, standing out in the mirror as I gave myself one last look-over. As a kid, I'd always been made fun of for my heterochromia—one green eye from my father and one blue from my mother—but I'd stopped letting those comments bother me a long time ago. I always liked that I was different. That I carried bits of my parents with me always.

While I'd still spent my childhood playing with dolls and dreaming up fairytales of a grand romance, I'd also been looking up at the stars, waiting for my father to come home from his latest mission. Learning all of their names. As if committing the information to memory would make me closer to him.

You have the stars in your eyes; my dad used to whisper to me when he caught me staring at them. Like he knew just how badly I wanted to be up here.

Aurelia Serena Callisto, destined for the stars. Words he whispered to me as we watched shuttles launch into space, or from the beach near our house as he heaved me up into his arms. Words I'd never forget.

"Here I am, Dad," I whispered out the circular window that showed the dark vastness of space, our ship still docked at the space station. "Right where you always knew I'd be." I rested my hand against the thick glass, as if he could feel me there. *I hope you're proud of me.* A shiver ran through my body as I sent the thought out into the world.

That was why I was here, after all. To feel closer to my dad. To follow the same path he had. My fingers brushed over the flash drive I'd brought on board before tucking it into a drawer to keep it safe. If there was anything left, any remaining clues... I'd find them.

"All officers to the bridge for a briefing from the Captain," came through the ship's speaker.

"Well, that's my cue." I took one last look out the window, letting a small smile slip over my face.

Thanks for believing in me, Dad, I thought, pressing the button to open the electronic door. *I couldn't have done this without you.*

BY THE TIME I'd made it to the bridge, a handful of other officers had also arrived, standing in straight rows but mingling amongst themselves. Everyone was wearing their dress uniforms as well, cementing that I'd made the right decision by putting mine on. I breathed out a sigh of relief at not being the odd one out.

My eyes wandered around as I remained stationary, taking in the bridge. This was the place where I'd be spending most of my days—and likely some nights, as well. In some ways, it didn't differ from the ones I'd run hundreds of hours of simulation in, but in others, it was completely different. Maybe it was the thrum under my feet, the subtle vibrations of electricity that came from a vessel this size. It practically hummed in my ear, filling me with nervous energy.

I pasted a smile on my face, hoping my assimilation process went well. That I'd find a group of friends to spend the next few years with. It wasn't like I had another option if I didn't get along with the rest of the officers. Not that I ever had problems *making* friends—I was outgoing, considered myself to be a pretty cheerful person with a positive outlook—it was just that sometimes I had problems *keeping* friends. Fionia and Eliza had both been my friends for years, but other than that, I'd bounced between friend groups, never really finding where I belonged. But I'd left my best friends and the only home I'd ever known behind.

Not letting that fact weigh on me—I slid into formation, crossing my arms behind my back so I wouldn't fidget. Thankfully, my hair was up so I couldn't mess with it. It was my nervous habit, especially when I was in a new situation and didn't know anyone.

I stood between a girl with bright blue hair, and a tall blond man who flashed me a flirty grin.

"Hi," the girl next to me whispered, leaning over slightly. "I'm Astrid." Her dress uniform was white, instead of black, with a white cross patch opposite her rank badge. Four dots—a commander. "Chief Medical Officer," she confirmed.

"Hey. Aurelia—I'm the Head Pilot." I gave her a warm smile. "It's nice to meet you."

She grinned back. "I'm glad to see this room isn't *completely* full of testosterone."

There were two other women here—a redheaded girl with a face full of freckles, and a medium-skinned girl with dark brown hair. They both had different colored uniforms, though I didn't spend too much time studying their appearances, not wanting to stare.

"Too true." I let out a small giggle.

We'd all learned about Earth's history—about a time when women didn't even have rights in most countries. Now, women were in positions of power all across the world as well—and the federation was pushing more and more women into joining programs like mine. Fields that even fifty years ago were often male-dominated. Engineers, pilots, captains—the sky was the limit. Or, in this case, the stars.

The man next to me's eyes snapped to mine. "Wait, *you're* the new pilot?" He was in a red uniform—*engineering*.

I frowned. "Yes?"

He muttered under his breath, something that sounded a lot like, *he will not be thrilled about this.*

"Who's not going to—" I started, but then the automatic door slid open, and then a man with dark brown hair entered the room, stealing my breath.

Somehow, before I even saw his badge or the color of his uniform, I *knew* what position he occupied. It was something about the cocky confidence, how he strolled in here like he owned the damn ship we stood on. In some ways, he basically did. From the way he commanded the space, it was clear who he was.

Sylas Kellar. Captain of the S.S. Paradise.

Also known as… my new boss.

And my God, the photos I'd seen hadn't lied. He was handsome. A short beard covered his sharp jaw and chin, and I couldn't pull my eyes away from him. *Aurelia,* I mentally scolded myself. *Not the time. Do not salivate over your superior officer.*

Sure, nothing would ever come of it—but at least he was nice to look at, right?

I sucked in a breath, standing taller as our Captain's eyes drifted over us. The data pad in his hand lit up as he swiped across the screen, coming to a stop in front of all of us.

A woman stood behind him with a dark head of hair, wearing an identical uniform. *His first officer?* She had to be.

He looked up for a moment and glanced at all of us. We still stood in two rows, no one having taken their positions on the bridge yet.

"Hello, everyone." Finally, he spoke, and his voice was *deep.* In other situations, I might have found it sexy, like the narrator of an audio book that I'd put on to lull myself to sleep. "As you may already know, my name is Sylas Kellar, and I'll be your captain for our voyage aboard the *S.S. Paradise*. I've spent the last few days onboard, and I'm confident you'll all find her just as welcoming as I did."

He glanced at the woman by his side. The two looked similar —not quite *identical*, but up close, the familial resemblance was clear. A sister, if I'd had to guess. "This is Commander Kayle Kellar, who will serve as my First Officer."

She stepped forward slightly, the light reflecting off her badge. The deep blue of the uniform perfectly complimented her dark hair that she wore up in a high ponytail and her bright blue eyes. "Hi, gang." Kayle gave a slight wave of her hand, a smile lighting up her face. "I'm looking forward to getting to know all of you during our time on board. If you need anything, let me know. My brother here—" He shot her a look, and she rolled her eyes. "*Captain* Kellar and I are happy to help you as you get settled in to life onboard the Paradise."

He dipped his head in agreement. "I'm going to go through the assignments list to help put faces to names, and allow us all to get to know each other. After all, we will spend a lot of time in close quarters."

A lot of time in close quarters with him? I tugged at the collar of my uniform, feeling suddenly hot.

The screen in his hands came to life once again, but he hardly gave it a second glance. "Lieutenant Violet Alastair. Communications officer."

The brunette woman on the other side of Astrid, also wearing a purple outfit like mine, took half a step forward. "Here, sir."

He dipped his head in acknowledgment. "Your credentials are quite impressive. It's only your... what? Third year with the federation?" I wondered when she'd joined—right out of college? She was probably the same age as me, if that was the case.

"That's right." Her hair was secured into two low buns

behind her ears. "When I heard about this mission, I jumped at the chance for a transfer."

"Happy to have you." Captain Kellar didn't smile, tapping on his screen instead, as if familiarizing himself with all of us.

"Commander Astrid Loxley," He said, his eyes darting around the room before quickly landing on the girl beside me. "Chief Medical Officer."

She gave a small smile. "That's me." Her white uniform stood out amongst the gray and other colors, making her noticeable even without her bright hair color. I was a little obsessed with it, even though I loved my own russet locks. I'd always been too attached to my hair color to even think about changing it. Still, she rocked the blue.

"I understand you're one of the best doctors UGSF has."

She blushed a little, shaking her head. "Oh, I wouldn't say that, Captain."

"It's in your file," he mused, stating it all matter-of-fact. Like there was no way to dispute his claims, because they *were* true.

Standing in this room, surrounded by all these officers who were clearly the best of the best, I couldn't help but feel a little intimidated. Was this a mistake? *Why had Rist chosen me?* What did Sylas Kellar have about *me* on that manifest?

"Next is Commander Wren Navarro, our Chief of Security." The corner of his lips tilted up—almost a smile, but not quite. "I handpicked him to join our crew, and he'll also be serving as my Second."

Wren—a handsome man with tanned skin and tattoos that peeked out of his sleeves—gave us all a confident smirk. "Glad I could be of service, Cap."

Captain Kellar waved him off, continuing down his list. "Lieutenant Leo Sevyn is serving as our Chief Engineer, doing his best to repair the ship should anything happen."

"Yes, Captain." The handsome blond man beside me grinned, winking at the Captain's sister—who just rolled her eyes. "You can count on me."

"Who's left…" Another tap on the tablet, though there were only a few of us left who he hadn't already called. "Ah. Heading up our research department is Finley Cortez as Chief Science Officer. She's done quite remarkable work in her field of research already." He nodded. "Keep it up."

The freckled redhead with the green uniform wiggled her fingers. "Hey, everyone." Her Irish accent was noticeable as she spoke.

What Astrid had said to me before struck me again, and I really was glad this room had just as many women as men. We were five to four, not including the Ensigns and other, lower-ranked crew who would serve as replacements or backups, but I didn't feel like I'd have any issue with my voice being heard.

"Chief Navigator—Lieutenant Orion Hirsh." The dark-skinned man stood behind me, and I instantly gave him a small smile of acknowledgement, knowing we'd be sitting side by side. After all, our roles meant we would be working in tandem for the duration of the mission.

The Captain's face formed into a thin line as he looked down at his tablet. I looked around, noticing everyone else had been introduced. Which just left… *me*. The entire room went silent, and I couldn't help but think of Leo's words earlier. Was something wrong? Had he not been informed about the change in the position?

"You." His cold, barking voice called for attention as he took a step towards me. "What's your name?"

From this close, I could tell how tall he was, as every inch of his height towered over me. The way he was leering over me made me want to cower—back down, walk away—but I was my father's daughter. Straightening, I stood tall, proud.

"Captain." I gave him the sweetest smile I could muster up. "I'm Aurelia Callisto, sir." I jutted out my chin as my eyes met his, that smile not slipping.

His eyes were dark, *unfeeling*. His gaze seemed to settle over me, and I wondered if he was that displeased to be so cold with me. Would he find me unsatisfactory? I didn't know. Still, his eyes flickered in recognition, if only briefly.

"I'm the Head Pilot." Though that felt a little like stating the obvious, because how could he *not* know? "I got the call last week, and—"

"Hm." He grunted, cutting me off before sharing a look with his First Officer. "What happened with Vitto?"

The name sounded familiar, a UGSF pilot that had been in the headlines recently. Him dropping out of this mission was the only reason I was here. Damn, I wished I could send him a thank you note.

Kayle cleared her throat. "I believe there's a note in the file from Rist."

I opened my mouth to say something else—but closed it as I watched the two who seemed to share some sort of silent communication.

A frown filled his face as he turned back to me. "You've piloted before?"

"Well..." *Only if you counted flight school.* Which, I was guessing, he would *not.* I dipped my head. "Not exactly. This is my first commission, sir."

He cursed. The rest of the room was quiet—so still you could have heard a pin drop.

The smile slipped from my face as I winced, trying to maintain my composure. "I just graduated, top of my class, and I earned my spot here—"

One of his hands ran through his hair, messing up the perfect strands. And maybe I shouldn't have noticed how large his hands were, but I couldn't help myself.

"That doesn't change the fact that I'm about to embark on a five-year journey with someone with about as much experience as a *toddler.*"

"Captain, I—" I opened my mouth to protest, because that wasn't fair. I *had* earned my spot here, hadn't I? Just like the rest of them, I had to believe I was here for a reason, too.

"Call the Vice Admiral," Captain Kellar instructed her, ignoring me. "Tell him to send someone else." He turned his eyes back to me. "*Anyone* else."

"But—" I started, not knowing how to fix this.

"You're dismissed. Everyone else, settle in tonight, we leave at 0800 sharp tomorrow. I'll see you all on the bridge in the morning."

And then he was gone, the doors closing behind him, leaving me open-mouthed like a fish.

That certainly hadn't gone the way I'd hoped.

Not at all.

FOUR
SYLAS

SHIT. I pinched the bridge of my nose between my thumb and forefinger. Nothing was going the way I'd planned. How did everything get so colossally screwed up?

Aurelia Callisto. On my ship. Serving in my crew.

How could I *not* recognize a name like that?

She was young. Too young to be serving as an officer. I'd asked for the best of the best, had handpicked everyone who would serve under me. And yet... How had I missed this? The manifest of officers hadn't been updated, or I would have noticed last week.

Her father was the most famous pilot of the last century. He'd gone missing during his last voyage, and the federation had renamed their flight school after him. The flight school that his daughter had just graduated from.

That was the first thing I'd noticed. Not how beautiful she was, or how young she was, or—*fuck*—the way her eyes twinkled like gemstones. Because noticing any of those things was wrong. I was her captain. She was a part of my crew. Then there was the fact that she was ten years my junior.

For so many reasons, I needed to get her face out of my mind.

Off-limits. She was not for me. Besides, she shouldn't have even been here, so why was I still thinking about her? She was a temptation I couldn't afford to have around.

A snort came from behind me and I whirled, finding my sister standing there with a disapproving look on her face.

"What?" I narrowed my eyes at my younger sister, who plopped onto the seat across from me, resting her heels on my desk. "You're supposed to be on the bridge." Never mind that the mission hadn't actually started yet. We'd have to adjust to one of us always being there soon enough.

"You were a *bit* of an asshole."

"I'm the *Captain*, Ky. If they can't handle it, they shouldn't be here."

"Still." Kayle inspected her nails, like she wasn't giving me the time of day. "Probably could have been a little nicer to her."

I looked at my sister, frustration leaking into my tone. "She doesn't belong here. This girl's barely even gotten her feet wet, and I'm supposed to trust her to pilot this ship?"

My sister shrugged. "Look. Rist obviously picked her for a reason. I know you wanted Vitto, that you two go way back from college, but you're going to have to make the best of it for now. It's a little late to get a replacement."

"We can just delay by a day or two. I'm sure if we contact the UGSF, they'll—"

"Sylas." Her voice was quiet. *Subdued.* I hated when she used that tone on me, all gentle. Like she was about to tell me something she knew I didn't want to hear. I knew my sister well enough to know all of her moods, and whatever she was about to say definitely would not make me happy.

"What?" I crossed my arms over my chest, feeling every bit the grumpy asshole people liked to claim I was. Maybe they were right. Maybe I was becoming a grumpy old man.

"I know you want everything to be perfect, but..." Kayle shook her head. "I think you should just ride it out. See how she does *before* you judge her? Besides, I don't think the higher ups will be too pleased if we delay setting out just because you don't like her." Her face said *please don't fuck this up for both of us.*

"It's not that I don't like her."

"What is it then?"

I clenched my jaw. How did I explain my apprehension? That I didn't like not being in control? She was my sister—she knew me better than anyone. After thirty-plus years together, I was confident that she'd always have my back. "Look. You know who her father is."

"So, you're accusing her of what... *nepotism*? Because her dad was a famous pilot, she must have only got this job because of him?"

I scowled. *Maybe.* But I kept my jaw shut, shaking my head slightly. "I don't know." I thrust my fingers into my hair. "Everything needs to be perfect. I need this mission to go well."

"So don't let this ruin your chance just because you're worried about one person. The rest of the crew will help her assimilate. You remember *your* first commission, don't you?"

"Unfortunately." My first assignment had been a colossal mess. And not just because I was an inexperienced crew member. But because my captain had it out for me, and he hadn't let me slack off for one minute. We all hated him.

· Was I doing the same thing now? I closed my eyes, exhaling deeply. I needed a drink.

No matter what she said, I needed to figure out how to get a new pilot aboard—*ASAP*.

"THERE'S OUR CAPTAIN," Wren said, slapping a hand on my back and steering me towards the open couch in the officer's lounge. Thankfully, it was just the guys and me here, saving me from another lecture from my first officer. Even if she was younger than me, my sister really knew how to dole it out.

We'd all gone way back, both from college and our time serving in the UGSF together. I'd served on other starships with each one of them over the years as well, though never in a position where I was in charge of them.

Leo held up a glass with amber liquid in it. "Care for a drink?"

"Yes," I muttered, going over to the bar and fixing myself one. It was quickly tossed back, and I poured another few fingers before settling onto the couch.

"Rough day, Sylas?" Orion asked in that polished British accent, running his finger around the rim of his glass. "Is the stress getting to you already?"

Exhaling through my nose, I shook my head. "You all witnessed that colossal shit-show earlier." I'd already gotten this from Kayle—did I really need it from them, too?

A smirk spread over Leo's face. Handsome bastard could get any girl he wanted in college just from that one look. "And what a show it was." He crossed his knees, resting the arm holding his glass on top. "You really have no clue how to talk to women, do you?"

Another scowl formed on my face.

"Careful, or that'll turn permanent," Leo snickered.

Wren chuckled from my side. "I think it already is."

Ignoring both of them, I stared into my glass. "Was it that bad?"

Orion frowned. "I heard she was crying afterwards."

My heart stuttered, but I forced my face to remain passive. "What?" Further evidence that she shouldn't be here. If she couldn't toughen up, she needed to get out. Except... why did hearing that she'd cried make me feel *bad*? I wasn't supposed to feel sorry for her.

"Listen, Cap. Did you ever think that maybe that girl had worked her whole life to be here, and you were kinda raining on her parade?" Wren interjected, and I had to take a moment to think about it.

"No." I was going to need a third drink if these assholes kept on berating me about this. Because I hadn't thought about that. I'd assumed she was just handed the position on a silver platter.

Except, she'd mentioned she graduated at the top of her class, hadn't she?

Don't go down that line of thinking, Sylas. I scolded myself. No good could come from it.

"Can't we talk about anything else?" I market out. "We're leaving for a *five-year* mission tomorrow, and the last thing I want to do is talk about work all night."

Never mind that work was about to be a twenty-four seven thing around here. Even when we were off, we still had responsibilities. A trip to the gym could be interrupted at a moment's notice if something went wrong. That was one joy of being in charge.

With such a state-of-the-art ship, and it being her maiden voyage, I hoped we wouldn't experience too many issues.

"Anyone have anything new to share?" Leo joked. "You know, besides the mission we're currently on?"

Wren settled back in his chair. "No news to report. But the new digs are great, man. You really outdid yourself getting us all assigned to this ship." He looked at me, curling his tattooed hands around his glass.

"You're telling me." I snorted.

I'd been gunning for this post from the day it was announced, making my interest in Captaining her known from the beginning. After serving as First Officer onboard another vessel for the last few years, it made logical sense that I would have my own command, and I'd more than proved myself.

Now, she was all mine. My ship, my crew, my voyage. The brand new captain's chair was ready to perfectly mold itself to my body. Because I was the only person who'd ever sat in it. I planned to keep it that way, too.

Orion nodded his head in agreement. "This entire space is spectacular. And the rec floor?" He flexed his arm muscles, the dark skin rippling with the motion, like any of us needed a reminder of how tightly toned he kept his body. "Damn. You're going to have to pull me away from those machines."

I'd spent most of my first day in there. At first, I'd wanted to break it in—work off the excess energy, sweat out the nerves— but after that, I'd fallen in love with the gym. It even had a pool connected to it, complete with a sauna to relax sore muscles. We all had to stay in tip-top shape, especially while we were on a mission.

I could already foresee a lot of nights spent swimming laps after a long shift on the bridge—and working off Chef Gregori's meals.

"Wait until you taste the food. They got one of the best chefs on the *planet* to agree to come on board."

Leo looked excited. "Really?" The man loved food. "How'd they manage that?"

"Apparently, it only took a *little* bribery. He brought his whole family with him. Plus, the promise of fresh ingredients via the greenhouse only sweetened the deal."

Though civilians used to be forbidden on starship voyages, with a mission like this, it made sense. They'd set up a school for the children and teenagers, as well as a daycare service so crew members could work and know their children would be taken care of. Since none of us had to pay for room or board, it was a pretty good deal. Especially considering how expensive housing was getting back on Earth.

"*Mmm.*" My Chief Engineer's eyes flew shut. "I can already taste it now."

"You're hopeless," Orion muttered, giving him a sidelong glance.

"And starving," Leo confirmed, patting his flat stomach.

Wren pulled up the schedule on his communicator. "Don't worry, I think you're saved. Dinner's only a few hours away."

The small devices we all carried were the modern version of cellphones, the antiquated pieces of technology that only lived in history museums now. Communication systems had come a long way in the last thousand years. Plus, there was a chat function on them that allowed us to ping other crew members with important messages.

"Great. You all introduce yourself to the Chef, and I'll go get the rest of this paperwork done so we can leave on time tomorrow."

After we pulled out of dock at the space station, we'd have to travel at near-light speeds for over a month before we'd reach our intended star system, farther into space than any human had ever traveled before.

The guys frowned at me as I stood up off the couch. "You're leaving already?"

I grunted. "I have to see if there's anyone else they can send."

"And if not? We're supposed to leave the station tomorrow."

"Then one of the assistant Pilots can fill in."

Leo frowned. "Seriously, man?"

"Look, I can't work with her. I just..." I grit my teeth. I couldn't tell them I couldn't work with my pilot because she was too pretty. They'd all think I'd gone mental. "This mission is more important than her *feelings*. If she's upset, she can pack her stuff up and go while she has a chance."

Five years. We'd be spending five years together. Five long years with the daughter of Samuel Callisto.

Five years with the ultimate temptation.

Relationships with the other officers were strictly forbidden. I rubbed a hand over my face, cursing internally. *Get it together, or your entire crew is going to watch you fall apart.*

"See you in the mess hall," I finally said, grabbing another scotch for the road.

I got a ding on my communicator from Kayle.

Her file. Thought you might like to look at the girl you've dismissed without even giving her a chance.

Fuck, she wouldn't let this go, would she? I clicked on the data file, figuring it couldn't hurt to know exactly what my head pilot had been up to the last few years.

FIVE
AURELIA

EVERYONE WAS STARING AT ME. *Shit.* My knuckles were white, the tray clutched in my hands.

Word couldn't have traveled that fast, right? I sucked in a breath, heading to an empty table in the middle of the mess hall. *So much for a good first day on board.* I could still turn this around, though, couldn't I? I'd get him to give me a chance. To realize I was more than just some kid who knew nothing.

Sighing, I took a bite of the pasta dish they'd prepared. At least the food was *good*, since it was all we'd be eating for the next few years. Compliments to the chef, because I'd definitely be going back for seconds. I'd never shied away from eating, even if it added a few extra pounds to my hips and thighs. The cheesy pasta was worth it.

Maybe I'd run a few extra laps around the track that I'd seen earlier, around the fifth level—it went in an entire loop, the recreation center in the middle of it. A good run would help me clear my head, and I'd rather that if people were going to stare at me all night.

"Hey, Aurelia." A soft voice brought me to attention, and I looked up to find Astrid—the Chief Medical Officer—standing in front of me, having changed out of her uniform and into a plain jumpsuit, only her badge showing her rank and the white stripes on her arm showing her position.

A familiar, friendly face. Maybe this wouldn't be the end of the world. "Astrid. Hi." I grinned at her.

She set her tray down, sliding in across from me. "Hey. You all alone?"

I looked around at the empty table and dropped my voice to a whisper. "Yup. Feels like I have a big scarlet letter painted on my back."

"Earlier was…" She made a face. "I'm sorry."

"Yeah." I winced. "I didn't know what to expect from my first day, but *not that*. God, day one and he already hates me."

Astrid gave me a small frown. "I'm sure he doesn't *hate* you. He just seemed… surprised, that's all."

"Oh, good," a third voice said, popping up next to our table. It was the girl with the dark hair in double buns, also an officer —*Violet*. "I was worrying I wouldn't find anyone I knew in here." She sat next to Astrid and then gave me a sympathetic smile.

I waved her off. "If you're going to tell me it wasn't that bad, don't bother."

She laughed, her brown eyes full of warmth. "No, but at least you have a sense of humor about it." Violet reached across the table, laying a hand on my arm. "My first day was rough, too. Don't worry—it'll get better."

Fixing a smile on my face, I stabbed another noodle onto my fork.

"There you three are," the ginger girl said as she sat down with us. Finley. She'd pulled her hair back out of her face with two green hair clips, which made her eyes stand out. "Weird vibes in here."

I sighed. "I think word got out about what happened on the bridge. Everyone's been staring at me since I came in." The crew members who had been in the bridge must have gossiped. God, this was mortifying. What were we, high schoolers? "Definitely don't feel like I'm getting started on the right foot on the ship."

"So let's start over." Astrid's face broke out into a smile as she twirled one strand of electric blue around her finger. Then she stuck her hand out to me. "Hi, I'm Astrid. I'm twenty-seven and I'm one of the youngest Chief Medical Officers in the federation." She shrugged her shoulders. "When I first got my position, everyone doubted me because I was young, and I look like *this*." Astrid gestured to her hair. "As if the color of my hair affects my work."

"Really?" I frowned. "What changed?"

"Me." She laughed. "But I guess... I proved them wrong. And I reminded myself why I was here. Not for them. For me."

Finley nodded in agreement. "I'm twenty-six now, but I'll never forget my first assignment when I was mistaken as an intern and asked to go fetch coffees for the researchers. I don't put up with that shit on my crew." She opened her mouth like she was going to say something else, but then closed it.

"Sometimes people *still* ask me to get coffee. As if I'm some sort of over-glorified secretary as the Comms officer," Violet chimed in, rolling her eyes. "I joined the federation directly out of college. With a communications degree and a computer science background, it just made sense. But there's a lot more to all our jobs."

"You're right. I didn't come here just to turn around with my tail tucked between my legs." Biting my lower lip and worrying it into my mouth, I tried to think about what advice my dad would have given me if he were here. "But what can I do?"

As I stared at Astrid, the answer was obvious. *Start over.* But would it work if I marched myself back to Captain Kellar, explained that I wasn't going anywhere, and that I had a right to be here? To tell him I'd earn my spot here, just like the rest of them.

I just needed time to prove myself.

The conversations in the cafeteria came to a halt, and a few seconds later, I realized why.

A tall, brooding presence stood in the entryway.

He was here.

I leaped to my feet, not fully thinking through what I was going to say. I'd figure that out once I got started. After people got to know me, they always liked me.

How different could it be with this man?

"Captain—" I started, but he brushed past me like I had said nothing, taking his food to the other end of the room. God, this guy really was an infuriating *grump*, wasn't he?

I sat back down, feeling defeated.

"What…" I frowned at the other girls as he took his own seat, as far away from us as possible. "Did he just *ignore* me?"

"I'm sure he didn't mean…" Violet frowned, looking between his table, now surrounded by men—and his sister, Kayle.

"Guess the rumors were true." I sighed, stabbing at my food with my fork before muttering under my breath. "Gorgeous and an asshole." *What a combination.*

Finley snickered under her breath.

Astrid grimaced, giving me an apologetic look. "That was cold. Even for him."

"Have you worked with him before?"

She shook her head. "Not directly. But I'd met him before, and I never got warm fuzzy vibes. He respects hard work, though. Once you prove yourself, I know he'll come around."

If I got the chance.

That was the only thing I could think of through the rest of dinner, even as the conversation around the table lapsed, everyone eating their food. After we'd all finished eating, everyone shared stories of back home, of their childhoods and what it was like when they'd first joined the UGSF.

Maybe no one had as rough of a first day as mine, but I enjoyed hearing some misfortunes they'd gotten into over the years.

Finally, with a yawn, it was time to head to bed, since we would all be up and ready in the early morning. I said goodnight to the rest of the girls and retreated to my quarters.

THOUGH MY SLEEP had been lacking, I was ready, dressed in my flight suit and ready to go before 0800 the next morning. I'd pulled my hair back in two tight braids, and my shiny new badge rested over my heart. *Ready.*

I placed my ID card on the sensor to open the door to the bridge and waited.

Beep. A red light flashed.

Frowning, I removed my card and tried again.

Beep. Another red light. I blinked.

Did I… not have access? I tried a third time before confirming my hunch.

I didn't have access to the bridge. Was it an error, or had that asshole really *locked* me out? How was I supposed to do my *job,* the whole reason I was on this ship, if I couldn't even access the bridge?

Biting back my frustration, I hit the button on the intercom and waited.

Violet's voice came through on the other side. "Lieutenant Callisto, how can I help you?"

I cleared my throat. "My access has been removed from the bridge."

There was a pause, and then she came back. "That is correct."

"Why?" A sinking feeling settled in my gut. "I can't do my job if I can't access the bridge."

"You've been, um… dismissed." There was a wince in her voice.

"*What?*"

His words from yesterday came back to haunt me. *You're dismissed.* Shit, apparently he really meant them.

"Then who is going to be piloting the ship?"

It wasn't Violet who responded this time. "Assistant Pilot Holmes has taken over your responsibilities." That statement, spoken in his deep timbre, would haunt me until the end of days. He wasn't even going to give me a chance.

"But—"

"You're excused, Miss Callisto."

No way. This wasn't happening. My cheeks heated, embarrassment flaring through me.

What was I supposed to do? Get off the ship before it departed? It was already too late for that. Hope that the UGSF would understand and give me a new command? Because they wouldn't.

I'd be the laughingstock of my entire graduating class.

I'd never be able to show my face in the federation again after getting dismissed from my first job. No way.

At least I hadn't cried. That was the only thing that kept my head held high as I walked away. *No tears, Aurelia.* Not today.

AFTER RUNNING off my excess anger on the treadmill in the gym, I'd only reached a simmer instead of a scalding boil. Still, this would not work for me. There was no way I could sit here and let someone *else* do my job while I sat around.

Showering, I let that rage fill my body, not bothering to pull my hair back as I dressed in my jumpsuit and affixed my officer's pin to it. After deciding I looked the part, I headed towards his office.

I could only hope to find him in there instead of the bridge, since I'd been hastily locked out of there.

Smashing my hand against the sensor to open the door, I marched inside the room, and the captain's head shot up from where he sat behind the desk.

"Sir." I didn't give him a chance to tell me to leave.

"What are you doing here?" He grunted. *Actually* grunted.

"Why won't you let me do my job?" I asked, instead of answering his question.

Captain Kellar looked relaxed, like the picture of carefree arrogance as he leaned back in his chair. "You're not qualified to do it."

"I'm *not*?" I repeated, though it wasn't a question. Because I knew I was. There wasn't a doubt in my mind about that. "My degree from the Flight Academy says otherwise. That I was number one in my class and logged more hours of simulator time than anyone else does, too. Sure, I didn't get any actual time in space, but newsflash, asshole—*no one does*. Not until they get their first position."

His brows furrowed.

Shit, had I just called him an asshole? This so wasn't going well.

"You can't fire me. Not until you give me a chance."

SIX
SYLAS

THE MUSCLES in my jaw clenched as I stared up at my pilot. Or, I should say, my *former* pilot, the woman I'd essentially fired this morning. It would be better if she'd gotten off the damn ship last night, but she'd stayed.

Of course she had. She was a spitfire, a feisty little thing.

You can't fire me. Not until you give me a chance.

Her eyes were bright, and from this close up I could see that each one was a different color, pale blue and green. Beautiful. That fact was undeniable. Those strands of reddish-brown hair were damp, spilling down over her shoulders like she'd just gotten out of the shower.

The sweet smelling scent of her shampoo wafted over towards me, and I did my best not to inhale it. God, now I was picturing her in the shower. What was that scent? I shut my eyes, willing myself not to imagine it.

I was her superior officer, for fuck's sake. There was no reason I should think about her like that.

This girl had balls, too. I would give her that. Not just anyone would show up in front of their captain to plead their case. Even if she had called me an asshole in the process.

"Did you really just call me an asshole while *begging* for your job back?" I almost smiled, feeling surprisingly amused by the whole situation.

"I wouldn't say I was *begging.*" Aurelia's lips curved down. "But I will do whatever it takes to convince you." She was wringing her hands like she was nervous. Her eyes were a little red, and there was a knee-jerk reaction in me. "I'll even log extra hours, spend more time at the console, pick up other duties—"

I thought back to what Orion had shared yesterday. My lips tugged down into a frown and I interrupted her. "Have you been crying?"

"What?" Her face looked incredulous.

"You just..." I let out another grunt. "Never mind." Thrusting my hands into my dark hair, I pulled at the strands. What was wrong with me?

The truth was, I'd been standing on unsteady terrain ever since I first saw her. And reading her file... *damn.* She was an exemplary cadet, an incredibly motivated student. No one had done so well during simulation trainings since, well... *me.*

Her scores were incredible. So why was I telling her no?

"Please." Her pleading eyes almost took me out. "This is everything I've worked for my entire life. I can't just sit on this ship and do nothing."

Then leave. That was what I should have said. Because there was no way I was going to be able to work with her under my skin. The moment I'd set eyes on her, I knew she would be.

"Fine." I ran my hand over my short beard. I normally kept it cropped, because it drove me crazy when it got too long.

"Sorry, what?" Her eyes widened, like she hadn't heard me correctly. I wondered what her irises look like close up, if I took the time to admire them. They were so intriguing, the different colors swirling around.

"I said fine." I cleared my throat, tearing my eyes away from her face. "You don't have to do nothing."

"But I—"

"You want to prove yourself to me?" I asked, cutting her off. I knew I was being an asshole, but I couldn't bring myself to stop. Not when she looked so vulnerable, standing in the middle of my office. Not when her scent was overriding my senses, clouding my judgement.

Aurelia chewed on her lower lip before nodding. "Yes."

"Then do it. Show me what you can do."

"Is this a joke? Are you being serious right now?"

Quirking an eyebrow, I kept my face devoid of emotion. "I don't joke, Aurelia."

Her gaze met mine, and she didn't look away. One beat, two —I was ensnared by her beauty. Enraptured just from the feeling of her full attention on me.

"Thank you, sir. For giving me a chance. You won't regret it, I promise."

A grunt slipped out from my lips, breaking the spell as I looked out the window. I was going to get this attraction under control. I wouldn't let my new pilot distract me from my mission. No matter how pretty she was, or how soft her lips looked.

Fuck. I shut my eyes, focusing on something else. Anything else.

"Is that all?" I huffed out.

Her brows drew together before she gave me a nod. "Yes, Captain. That's all." Aurelia dipped her head in a small bow, taking a few steps away before turning back to me. "You'll restore my access to the bridge? And we won't have any other…" she trailed off, like she was trying to settle on the right word, "problems?"

"As long as you do your job, we'll be fine, Lieutenant Callisto."

Something flickered through her eyes, and then she was gone, taking that scent with her. What was it? Floral and sweet, yet pleasant to my nose. Huh.

I looked at the map in front of me, with the carefully plotted out plans all laid out in front of me. The mission would be fine.

Five years would fly by, and I was sure I'd get used to her presence eventually.

Hopefully.

LATER IN THE DAY, I settled back down in the captain's chair, noticing that Aurelia was now sitting at the Pilot's console.

It was hard to miss her and her bright energy. She looked at home on the bridge—clearly having assimilated well to her new surroundings in just a few hours. A big smile was spread across her face as Orion leaned over, showing her something on the screen, and I felt a flicker of irritation at my navigator being so close to her.

Which I *shouldn't*. Because she was nothing to me. Especially after I fired her. *Almost fired her,* I mentally corrected myself.

"She's good," my sister murmured. "It took less than fifteen minutes until she'd familiarized herself with the system. Most people who are new to the bridge fumble for a few days, at least."

I remembered. Even simulators didn't quite compare to having an actual helm at your fingertips.

"Good." I glanced at her, rolling my eyes at her shit-eating grin. "What? A good captain can admit when he was wrong."

Kayle patted me on the shoulder, her voice low. "You did the right thing."

"Shut up," I muttered under my breath, wishing my younger sister didn't have to be right in this instance. I wasn't a man who liked to be wrong, but giving her a chance was better than kicking her off the ship.

She hadn't done anything wrong, regardless. It wasn't her fault I couldn't look away from her.

A laugh sounded from the navigation console, and I narrowed my eyes.

"Status report," I barked out, gaining the attention of everyone on the bridge.

Aurelia sat up straight, her eyes finally leaving the man at her side as she looked at me. Giving me her full attention. *Good.*

"All systems are online and fully functional, *sir*." That came from Leo, who gave me a grin. Bastard. If he wasn't one of my best friends, I would have called him out for not respecting me. But I knew he was just doing it to fuck with me. To get under my skin.

Orion's eyes met mine. "We're approximately twenty thousand kilometers from the warp point, Captain. Just a few more hours, and then we'll be on our way towards the targeted system."

"Perfect. Lieutenant Alastair?"

"Comms are all optimal and there's nothing unusual to report. Everything is running smoothly from my end," Violet reported. "We'll be in satellite range for a while longer, and then after that…"

I was still focused on my pilot, who had said nothing.

What did I want from her? I growled under my breath at myself. *Nothing.* There wasn't a single thing I needed from her. At least that was what I was going to keep telling myself. But wanting and needing were two different things, and I knew that all too well.

"Good." I nodded to myself after a moment. "Commander Kellar?" I addressed my sister.

"Crew all seem to be settling in to their roles well, and everyone is ready to get this maiden voyage underway." My sister looked at me, a little smile creeping onto her face. "*Captain.*" I could practically hear the snicker in her voice.

My eyes connected with Aurelia's, who glanced up at me from her console, those dazzling eyes distracting me from what I'd been about to say.

"Lieutenant Callisto."

"Yes?" she asked, her chair swiveling to face me fully. Her face was filled with surprise, as if she hadn't expected to be called on.

"How are you settling in?" I cleared my throat.

"Oh." She looked embarrassed by me calling her out individually. "Good. Thank you for giving me a chance, sir."

I dipped my head in response. "I expect you will not disappoint me."

It briefly occurred to me that I hadn't asked for her report. How she felt flying the ship, but when all of the faces in the room looked back at me in surprise, my brows furrowed. "*What?*" The question came out as a bark.

Kayle elbowed me from my side, her voice barely a whisper. "You good?"

A slight nod was my only response.

What else was there to say?

"Captain." Orion cleared his throat.

"Yes?"

"I believe you were about to give us our orders."

I smoothed a hand over my face. "Right."

Redirecting my attention, I quickly barked out commands to everyone before settling back in my chair.

It was going to be a long five years.

LEAVING Kayle in command of the ship later that night, I went in search of dinner before heading back to my office to fill out paperwork. No one told you how much of being in charge was just filling out mindless loads of forms and records until you were in the role—and then it was too late.

At least I had time to update my captain's log about everything that had happened over the last few days.

Unfortunately, my moments of peace were always short-lived on this ship—something I'd have to get used to. Leo, Orion, and Wren crowded into my office, piling onto the couch and chairs that were across from my desk.

"Who's on the bridge?" I asked, quirking an eyebrow. Sure, it could auto-pilot itself, and after a certain point in the night, no one *really* needed to be in there—there were plenty of fail-safes in place to assure nothing would go wrong even if disaster was imminent.

That didn't mean I wanted them all in my office, though, either.

Leo grabbed a green apple from my table, taking a big bite of it. "The girls."

Yup, eyebrows were still raised. "The *girls?*"

"Relax," he said, waving me off with the hand he held the apple in. "Your sister is in charge, and the ship won't explode or anything." There was another crunch of the apple, and he looked contemplative. "Probably."

"So why, exactly," I started, waving my hand to close the documents I'd been working on, "are all of you idiots in my office?"

Orion barked out a deep laugh. "They say you should never work with your best friends."

"Who says that?" Leo frowned, pausing his munching. "We're great."

"Dude," Wren rolled his eyes. "*Everyone.* Have you met yourself?"

My blond engineer flashed a pearly-white smile. One that I knew would have women's panties melting, which made me thankful it was just us guys here. "Of course I have. I'm fantastic."

"Shut up," I groaned, wishing I had something to lob at them. Maybe I needed some pillows handy. Or something harder. "I'm trying to get paperwork done, not listen to all of you bicker."

"Sure." Wren crossed his arms over his chest. He'd rolled up the sleeves on his gray jumpsuit, exposing more of his tan, tattooed arms. "*Paperwork*. Definitely not hiding from anyone, huh?"

"Hiding? I'm the captain of this ship. Who would I need to hide from?"

"I can think of a few people," Leo muttered under his breath.

Orion piped up with, "One of them sits right next to me."

I narrowed my eyes, balling up a piece of paper and throwing it in the waste bin behind my desk. "I'm not avoiding Lieutenant Callisto, if that's what you're implying."

"Hey, you said it, not me." Wren moved over to my drink cart, pouring himself a gin and tonic. If I couldn't even count on my second to have my back, who could I count on?

"She's good." My navigator watched me from the couch. "It would have been a shame if she'd left, you know." His fingers danced over his leg, like he was playing an invisible beat.

"Kayle won't let me forget it," I grumbled. I needed a drink myself.

"What changed your mind?"

I rubbed my forehead. There was honesty, and there was, well—telling them to get the hell out of my office. For once, I chose the former. "She came barreling in here, telling me I had to give her a chance. So I did. That's all there is to it."

"Mmm. Sure, sure." Wren gave me that look—the *I see you* look. He'd known me for too long for me to hide much around him. "So it has nothing to do with how gorgeous she is?"

A growl slipped from my lips. Damn, I really needed something to throw at them. I eyed the paper I'd thrown in the trash.

Leo's eyes widened.

"You know I can assign you extra duties, right?" I scowled. My Chief of Security really wasn't making me want to go easy on him right now. "I heard that scut duty is really fun." Not that I could actually do it.

"You'd know," Wren remarked, looking too cool and confident. "Since you spent half of our years as cadets with it."

"I gave her a chance, and that's it. Nothing more."

Or at least, that was what I was telling myself.

Even if it was a lie.

Because she *was* gorgeous, and no part of me should think that way. Not when she was my officer.

Not when a romantic entanglement was the last thing I needed on this voyage.

SEVEN
AURELIA

MY FEET POUNDED on the treadmill underneath me as I worked off my frustrations. The gym had large glass windows on this side, looking out into the endless adrift of space. Music blared through my in-ear speakers, the loud beats of the music matching my stride. This was my new routine, and I was growing used to life aboard the *Paradise*.

Well, mostly.

Over the last week, I'd grown more determined than ever to prove Sylas Kellar wrong. To show him I could *do* this. It didn't escape me how often he looked towards my console, a frown etched into that handsome face, or a scowl that made him look grumpier than usual.

Damn him. Sure, he'd let me resume my post, but that was the basic common decency that he should have afforded me in the first place.

My playlist moved into my cool-down music, so I slowed to a walk before finally stepping off the pad entirely.

Grabbing a towel, I wiped my face before dropping it into the laundry basket. After a quick shower, I'd report back to the bridge for my shift. And make some more small tweaks to the flight route, like I'd been doing bit by bit over the last few days.

I looked back out the windows for a moment before heading to the door.

"Oh," I squeaked, coming chest-to-chest with my captain.

My *sweaty* Captain. It should have been illegal, all of those rippling muscles contained underneath his black t-shirt. He'd clearly had the same idea as me, to get up early and take advantage of the empty gym. I hadn't even noticed anyone else in the space with me, though the treadmill's location in the gym made it easier to miss.

I averted my eyes. "Sorry, Captain Kellar."

I tried not to focus on his forearms, all muscular with veins running up them. Had I ever noticed a man's arms before? My mouth felt dry. His gym shorts were short, that tiny inseam showing more of his thighs than I'd ever expected to see. Was it hot in here?

"Lieutenant." He cleared his throat. "My apologies."

"No," I said, shaking my head. "Nothing to apologize for."

He draped a towel around his shoulders, though Sylas didn't take a step back to put distance between us. His eyes darted down to my lips.

"Um—" I tightened my ponytail, not sure what to do with my hands. "Did you need something?"

He shook his head. Paused. Then asked, "How's the ship treating you?"

I blinked in surprise. "Good, I guess. In some ways, it's not all that different from the academy." A slight wince escaped me. I didn't enjoy reminding him I was brand new at this. It brought back memories of that first day, the one I was so desperate to move on from.

"I suppose not." Sylas tightened his grip on the towel, massaging the back of his neck with his other hand. "I should go."

"Right." I waved my hand. "Back to the bridge. Captain stuff."

A snort slipped from him. "Captain stuff. Right." He shook his head.

"So, uh, I'll see you." I gave him a mock salute before interlacing my hands behind my back.

"Wait."

I froze. "Yes?"

"Listen, we're all going to get together tomorrow night. All the officers. In the lounge." Was it my imagination, or did he seem… nervous? "You should come."

"I should?" I raised an eyebrow. Was I being invited to team building events now? "I thought I was too young and inexperienced." Seeing his face, I added a small, "Sir," on the end.

"That's not—" He frowned. "You are an officer, aren't you?"

"Right." Because I *was*. "Of course I am." I couldn't stop myself from nodding, though I felt a bit like a mindless robot. "I guess I'll be there, then."

"Okay."

"Okay." I gave him a weird look. How had we gone from him trying to kick me off the ship to inviting me to *hang out* in only a week? "Bye."

"Goodbye." He didn't smile, and I mentally berated myself as I turned around, heading out of the gym.

Stupid. So stupid. What did I expect? *Him to actually be nice to me?* I'd sooner expect to see pigs fly in space than that.

I turned back to say something else, but—the Captain's eyes were glued to my ass. *Huh.* Maybe he wasn't as grumpy and unaffected as I thought.

"Enjoying the view?" I asked him, raising an eyebrow.

Sylas's brows drew in, and he scowled at me. "No."

"Sure."

He stomped away, leaving me speechless—and trying to figure out what just happened.

"That was odd," I muttered to myself, heading back to my room. I didn't understand Captain Sylas Kellar—and I wasn't sure I wanted to, either.

I STILL HELD my breath when I pressed my ID against the door sensor of the bridge every time, though I doubted he would try the same trick again. After this morning, it felt like maybe I'd made some progress with my captain, though I doubted we'd ever be friends.

At least begrudging acceptance was better than nothing. If he was inviting me to do things with the rest of the officers, I couldn't really complain. At least, not to his face.

"Good morning, Violet," I beamed at my friend as I passed her.

Though it didn't really feel like morning when we were surrounded by eternal darkness. On board, we operated under *Earth Standard Time*, a twenty-four-hour clock based on Green-wich Median Time, just to keep us on a routine. It was strange, given that there were obviously no signs of day or night in space, to even consider a period *morning* versus night. But it felt a little like working the night shift had during college. You slept when you slept, and life went on.

Thank goodness for the artificial sunlight in the gardens that simulated the eco-systems of earth, and the sun lamp in my bedroom, otherwise I wasn't sure I'd have any concept of time.

"Morning," Violet said from the comm's station, flashing me a small smile back.

Sylas wasn't in his chair after our gym run-in this morning, which was perfectly fine with me. I much preferred his sister to him anyway. At least she didn't seem to harbor any grudges against me for being here. Plus she didn't scowl as much.

I settled in at my station, next to Orion, who was having a quiet conversation with one of the crew members who served on the bridge.

Ignoring them, I pulled up the star maps of our intended

system where we were headed. We still had a few more weeks of travel, given that we were heading beyond the reaches of explored space. Which meant that *my* intended destination— where my dad's ship had last been seen—was much closer.

But it also meant I needed to get to work a lot sooner, and I hadn't exactly figured out how I was going to manage that when the bridge was always full of officers and crew during the day. Everyone—save Captain Kellar—was friendly and loved to talk.

The good thing about working on an incredibly high-tech spaceship was that we didn't need to do much to run it. Besides jumping through key points in space—which required all hands on deck—we mostly were just there as backup. Or in case we ran into any hostile ships.

The United Galactic Space Federation had been formed when we had first modernized space travel on Earth, when every country was fighting for the right to explore the galaxy and look for signs of life in space. After a war almost broke out, truces were signed, and the UGSF was the result.

That didn't mean that there weren't still civilian crafts out there, though. But the only ones that could compare to government crafts were ones with ample funding, which meant it was only the top zero-point-one percent who ever actually saw space flight.

Still, things were different now. We'd colonized Mars. Taking a shuttle to one of the space stations in our solar system was a daily occurrence, and thousands of people worked on them.

But who knew what was out there? Space pirates, disgruntled ex-federation workers, aliens... I was really hoping for aliens. Which was crazy. I'd seen the movies, starting back in the twentieth century. If they were right, aliens were no laughing matter.

But what if they *were* like us? What if somewhere, at the very ends of the galaxy from us, there was another race of beings who could communicate? Who also felt alone in this vast universe? A shiver ran through me. The prospect was more exciting than I could properly express.

My dad and I used to talk about what it would be like to find another civilization before his disappearance. Maybe part of me still hoped that if that happened one day, I'd feel like I was sharing it with him.

Sitting back, I left the star map of our current system open on my terminal as I looked out at the stars.

"What are you thinking?" Orion's thick British accent intruded my thoughts. His dark hair was cropped close to his scalp, and even though he was gorgeous, with his warm, dark skin, there was no spark of attraction. My heart didn't race when I looked at him. Not like earlier at the gym.

Why couldn't any man other than my grumpy captain be the one that I felt this irresistible pull to?

I shook my head, laughing. "Oh, it's stupid." I waved him off. Even if plenty of people on Earth shared my views, I didn't feel like sharing that part of me with anyone else. Not yet.

Not when I was still finding my place within the crew *and* figuring out my place on this ship.

"If you ever need someone to lend you an ear," Orion said, giving me a small nod. "Just know that I am here."

"Thank you." I didn't need to hide my genuine smile. I *was* happy to be here, happy performing my role. Just being a pilot set my heart alight, and it was easy to get lost in it. Being in my element made the day fly by, and I'd often look up from my terminal to find that hours had passed instead of mere minutes.

It helped that I was getting comfortable around everyone, too. Astrid and the girls always invited me to sit with them during meals, which I appreciated. Without them, I probably would have eaten alone in my room most days. Even though I considered myself to be pretty extroverted—bubbly and outgoing and just happy to be around other people—I withdrew into myself when I was in a situation where I didn't know anyone else.

But Astrid, Violet and Finley hadn't given me that chance. They'd practically wrapped me in their arms the first day, welcoming me into a little girl group I'd so desperately needed and craved.

Even my first officer, Kayle, gave me a warm smile and reassuring words.

It was only the Captain where I was struggling to find my footing. But we didn't need to be friends. We couldn't be.

"This isn't what I expected, you know."

The navigator looked back over at me. "What isn't?"

"The crew. All the officers being so close." I shrugged. While I'd observed some of my professors in college who developed deep bonds, but it was nothing like the friendships that this crew seemed to share. "I guess I didn't expect it to feel like this so quickly."

"Oh, yes, well." He cleared his throat. "Sylas did his best to keep us together. It's nice to have a captain who was willing to fight for us." A frown covered Orion's handsome face. "It's probably why he was so disappointed when he learned about Vitto's replacement. They were buddies, too."

It had been obvious watching the guys interact that they were all friends. Which made me feel even shittier, because I was the only one who he acted like this to.

"That doesn't mean I deserved how he treated me," I said, feeling defensive.

"No." He chuckled. "But I hope it's an insight into our Captain. He cares about his people. Sylas Kellar fights for those that he loves."

"Huh." I couldn't imagine him loving anyone. Sure, it was clear he cared for his sister. But that was different. She was his own flesh and blood. Plus, he didn't scowl at her.

He'd never so much as smiled at me.

"Don't look now," Orion whispered.

"Why?" I turned, but then thought better of it.

He winked, but didn't explain further.

"He's standing right behind me, isn't he?" I whispered. I could feel his presence at my back, the warmth radiating from his body.

Orion just nodded. "Afraid so."

Shit. Had he overheard us gossiping about him? I hoped not. I needed a *win*, not for him to think I was just gossiping instead of doing my job.

"Lieutenant Callisto."

"Yes?" I asked, blinking up innocently from my station.

"Status report."

Groaning internally, I went through my updates with him, hoping no one else would notice the blush on my cheeks, and how affected I was by the close proximity of his body.

Not when I was still thinking about the way he looked this morning, dripping in sweat with all of his muscles on display. *Damn.*

"AURELIA!" Astrid's face split into a grin as she waved at me, and I breathed a sigh of relief. Sylas wasn't here yet, which felt like a godsend.

"Hi," I said, brushing my hands onto my pants. Attire was casual, which meant I had to dig through the very few personal effects I'd brought with me to wear my own clothes, which I'd hardly done since I arrived. It was strange how seeing everyone outside of their designated uniforms made them all seem that much more human. Like they were real people, and not just their jobs.

Huh. Maybe that was the whole point of this.

Astrid was wearing a cropped graphic shirt and had twisted her bright blue hair into another double bun updo, but instead of looking young, she looked gorgeous. I wished I could pull that off.

For once, I'd left my hair down, running my fingers through the waves and hoping I looked acceptable enough for this get-together. We'd done events like this during college and my time in the academy, but I'd been too busy studying to ever party for very long.

Now, though, everything had changed. There would be no escaping, no excuse of homework that I could give. Not even the nagging thought in my mind of what I needed to work on was going to pull me out of here.

I had to prove I was a team player to Captain Kellar. That I wasn't some baby-faced, fresh-out-of-school pilot who would leave when she got uncomfortable.

Thankfully, I had the girls.

"You look amazing," Astrid commented, inspecting my outfit. I'd thrown on my favorite pair of black pants and the blue top from my closet that everyone always told me made my eyes pop, even if they were two different colors. With my heterochromia, I always felt like people noticed I was different, so those kinds of compliments always made me feel good.

"Thank you," I tried to hide my blush, before gesturing to her outfit. "I love this. One day you'll have to show me how you do your hair."

"Oooh, let me do yours sometime," she begged. "It's *so* gorgeous. I could do something fun. Next time you come down to MedBay, I'll fix you right up."

"Deal."

I'd have to go by soon for my monthly fertility blocker shot, anyway.

All the unmarried crew were on it, which was probably smart. Unplanned pregnancies and a starship didn't seem like the best idea. And it wasn't like they could prohibit people from having sex, either. I'd already heard rumors of plenty of crew members hooking up. Though celibacy was working just fine for me at the moment. I'd gone this long without having sex... what was a few more years?

The energy in the room changed, and when I looked up, I realized the reason why.

His large frame filled the doorframe, a presence that was impossible to ignore. Not with his broody glare or those captivating, ocean blue eyes. I'd seen them up close today, and *wow.* Nothing did them justice.

It was like he'd sucked all of the oxygen out of the room. Or maybe just from my lungs.

Sylas Kellar was here.

EIGHT
SYLAS

WHY THE FUCK *had I told her we were having a get together?*

In all my time serving on a UGSF ship, we'd never had a mandatory officer gathering. Except in the course of the last day, that was exactly what it had become. I'd convinced everyone to show up, lest Aurelia thought I was doing it for some nefarious purpose.

I wasn't. Not really.

Now we were all sitting in the officer's lounge, the guys sitting at the bar, and the girls were all crowded around the couch, laughing and smiling. I hated it.

Mostly because she smiled at everyone but me.

"This was a terrible idea," I muttered under my breath. Leo was sitting at my side, nursing a scotch, his eyes focused on the other side of the room. "Stop making moon eyes at my sister," I grumbled.

"I'm not," he said, giving a scoff. "Besides, that would never happen."

"She's strictly off limits. Especially to you." I pointed a finger at Leo's chest. "Don't even think about it."

Because I knew Leo all too well. He went through women faster than most people went through socks. Which was to say—

a *lot*. I'd never seen him in a single committed relationship all the way back to our college days. Not that I had room to talk.

I scowled at him before returning my attention to the girls, sipping on my whiskey. My sister was sitting next to Aurelia on the couch, and I strained my neck, wondering if I could hear whatever they were talking about from where I was sitting.

Everyone was wearing casual clothes, which was the first time I'd seen most of them out of their flight suits or officer's dress. Seeing all these people who would live and work together for the next five years gathered around, all chatting... it felt strange, and yet so *normal*. Like there wasn't anywhere I could imagine us but here.

"Hey, have you seen Finley?" Wren asked, looking around the room for the redheaded Chief Science Officer. He'd tucked a dark gray Henley into a pair of dark denim pants, the top buttons undone just slightly, the hint of a tattoo peeking out.

"No." I frowned. "She'll probably be here soon, though."

He mumbled something under his breath, but I didn't catch it. I couldn't worry about his problem when I had one of my own.

Aurelia looked over at me, and I knew she'd caught me watching her, just like she had at the gym. She'd worn black pants and a pretty blue blouse that made her eyes even brighter. Not that I should be noticing. Just like I shouldn't have noticed how good her ass looked in those tight spandex pants she'd worn to the gym.

I knew I needed to ignore this attraction to her. The pulsing thrum in my veins that happened any time she was around. She was *enchanting*, magnetic, drawing me to her like a moth to a flame. Like you couldn't help but look at the stars each night.

Orion settled into the other seat next to me, elbowing me to divert my attention.

"Hey." I frowned. "What was that for?"

He shook his head, his dark skin standing out in stark contrast to his white button up. "You're staring."

Crossing my arms over my chest, I turned my full attention to him. "Was not." Ugh. How old was I? I sounded like I was twelve, not thirty-five. "Sorry. I don't know where my head's been at lately."

He patted me on the shoulder. "I will say, it's strange adjusting back to life on a ship. I thought this life was behind me, but now…" Orion massaged the back of his neck with his hand. I knew he had gone through a rough divorce this past year, and I didn't blame him for choosing to return to the federation after that.

"I'm sorry about Ilya, man." His ex-wife had really done a real number on him.

"We were just too different, you know?" He ran his finger over the glass rim. "And being away on missions, we just grew apart."

It was one reason I'd vowed never to commit myself to anyone, let alone get married. Leaving behind a wife, a family… I could never abandon anyone the way my parents had abandoned Kayle and I.

"Well, you have us now," I said with a grin, looking at Leo—and Wren, who still had his gaze locked on the door.

It finally slid open, the slender redhead barreling in, out of breath.

"Sorry I'm late," Finley said, her Irish accent coming through. "I had some problems and—" she quieted, realizing everyone in the room was looking at her. "Hi, gang," she squeaked

"It's all good," Kayle called from the couch, patting the spot next to her. "Come join us! We were just talking about this trashy reality show we've all been watching."

"Which one?" Finley's lips curled up into a grin. "I love *all* of those shows."

Aurelia's face lit up as Finley sat next to her. "*Love Out of this World*. It's like one of those dating shows, but it takes place in space."

"Of course," I muttered under my breath. Of course they'd all bond over some silly show.

Despite my hopes of speaking with my pilot, the girls held her hostage all night, smiling and laughing while swapping stories from back on Earth.

When the clocks read 2200, I finally gave up, calling it a night.

And I didn't look deeper into the reason I was so disappointed I hadn't shared a word with her all evening.

DAYS PASSED, and though I glimpsed flashes of purple with that beautiful shade of reddish brown hair all over my ship, it was always in passing. Even on the bridge, I'd hardly shared two words with her.

But she seemed brighter. Happy. Adjusted. She had all the girls now, even my sister, who sat with her at dinner and watched stupid television shows together at night.

And I had… no one.

Maybe I was a grumpy bastard, because my only friends were the ragtag group of guys I'd known since college, and had all but coerced into serving on this ship with me. I knew for a fact if they hadn't all been single, there was no way I'd have been able to talk them into a five-year mission, anyway.

It was a long time to be away from your friends and loved ones. But the only person I loved was my sister, and she was here with me.

That was the thought that stuck with me as I did the rounds, too antsy to sit on the bridge while we were still en route to our final destination. That was the thing about traveling across the entire galaxy: even with the most advanced technology on our ship, it took a while to get there.

My hand connected with the entrance pad for the ship's artificial gardens. Our crops grew on the same level, and it was the reason we would have fresh fruits, vegetables, and other goods throughout our voyage.

There was no real reason for me to check in here, but I couldn't resist the urge to go inside. It was peaceful inside—quiet. Something I'd been severely lacking lately. I'd only been in here once before when I'd first boarded and they'd given me the tour of the entire ship, but I'd liked it.

The smell of flowers drifted into my nose, sweet and pungent. It was an incredible greenhouse, simulating the look and feel of Earth itself. Even the ceiling above us was programmed with familiar blue skies and fluffy clouds, while the sun lamps brought a warmth to the place.

My stroll was calming and relaxing, and I wouldn't have even realized someone else inside except... There she was.

Aurelia.

Her long, wavy hair tumbled down her back as it caught the light, making it appear even more red than normal. Last night had been the first time I'd seen her have it down since she'd burst into my office that first day, since she normally wore it up.

She had her head tilted up towards the artificial light, a small smile brightening her entire face. I was entranced, unable to look away. I shouldn't be here, shouldn't be watching her, but there was something so effortless in her being that I couldn't look away, either.

Fuck, what was I doing, staring at her? I stepped back, but my foot caught on a small twig, which cracked underneath my weight.

Her eyes fluttered open. "Oh. It's you." She blinked, adjusting her stance. "Sorry, I didn't expect to see you here."

Before, she'd seemed so open. So... free. Now she was guarded. I hated I did that to her. After all, this was her home now, too.

I cracked a smirk, trying to look nonchalant. "It is my ship, after all." Shoving my hands in my pockets, I resisted the urge to reach out towards her.

Aurelia gave a slight chuckle. "I suppose it is, Captain. I just… forgive me if I'm overstepping, but I haven't seen you in here before."

"No?" I raised my shoulders. "Maybe I should remedy that, then. Do you come here often?"

I liked the idea of her spending time in here, among the flowers. Beautiful—just like she was.

Her cheeks were the slightest shade of pink. *Adorable.* "Sometimes. It helps me think. Feels like home."

"Did you have a garden at home?" I couldn't help asking the question, because I wanted to know her. Wanted to know all of it. Her childhood, what her life was like growing up —everything.

She shook her head. "No, but my dad loved taking my mom to the rose garden. When I was little, we'd go all the time. As I got older, well…" Aurelia frowned. "Things changed. You know how it is."

Did I? Even before they'd abandoned us, my parents had never done a thing like that for Kayle and I. "I don't know that I do."

Her eyes turned to me in surprise. "You don't…"

I didn't like her looking sad over me. Didn't want her to feel bad about me, period. Because I wasn't worth her pity. "We didn't have any gardens where I grew up. But that's okay. I wouldn't have appreciated them, anyway."

"And now?"

I raised an eyebrow in question. "Now?"

"Do you find the view beautiful, Captain Kellar?" Aurelia's hand brushed over the open petals of a purple lily.

"Very," I replied.

But I wasn't looking at the flowers.

"Ah." Another smile curled over her lips. "Well, that's good then. I should…" She looked around. "I should go."

"Don't." The word slipped out of my lips before I could think better of it. "You were here first, anyway. I'll go."

"Or…" My breath caught in my throat as she looked up at me, so much hope in her eyes. "We could both stay. Just for a little while."

I said, "Okay." Settling onto a bench in the middle of the ship's garden, I copied her position from earlier, tipping my head up like I was absorbing the rays of the artificial sun. It wasn't quite the same as the real thing, but suddenly, I didn't feel so alone anymore.

She sat next to me, neither one of us quite touching.

"The other night," Aurelia finally said, breaking our silence. "When you had everyone get together for the officer's night…" she trailed off, before finally settling on, "Tell me the truth. Did you really plan that for me? Because I heard…"

I looked up at the ceiling at the fake sky above me. *Dear Lord,* this girl.

A grunt escaped my mouth. "No. Of course not." She looked hurt, and I hesitated. How did I smooth the situation over without revealing all my cards? "I thought it would be good for everyone. To get closer. We have a long mission left, after all." Crossing my arms over my chest, I kept my eyes straight ahead.

She looked contemplative. "That's true." Aurelia made a humming noise, and then said, "Your sister is really nice, you know."

I could read between the lines here. "Yeah, yeah. She's better than me in every conceivable way. Don't worry, I already know that." I scowled, and her face softened, her hand resting on my arm.

"That's not what I meant."

"I know." I smoothed a hand over my face. "But it's true. I'm an asshole, and she's the most caring person I know." Keeping my face straight ahead, I continued. "We both went through the same stuff, but she didn't come out of it all broken. Not like I did." *Fuck,* why did I just admit that? "I don't know why I just told you that," I said, voice rough. "Sorry. Didn't mean to dump on you."

Aurelia frowned. "It's okay."

I shook my head, standing up and shoving my hands in my pockets. "It's not. But thanks for the company." I dipped my head at our surroundings. "You're right. It's nice here."

"Any time," she mumbled as I waved goodbye, pacing away before she could say anything else.

I didn't know what it was about her. I was attracted to her—of course I fucking was, I had eyes—but there was something *more.*

She was everything good in the world—like a shooting star, lighting up the night sky—and she didn't deserve to have my darkness taint that. She deserved someone better. Someone younger, who would be by her side through all the upcoming stages of her life. Marriage, kids, a happy life—she deserved all of that.

Something that I could never give her, because those things weren't in my future. All I had was this job. This ship. Being the captain of the S.S. Paradise was my future, and I was okay with that. Love wasn't for me.

Maybe other people could believe in love, but they didn't know what it was like to be abandoned. To lose *everything* and not know what you did. How much it hurt to be left behind. To have to wonder what about you was so fundamentally wrong that no one wanted to stay.

It was why I'd sworn off love. It wasn't for me. I rubbed at my forehead.

She wasn't for me.

NINE
AURELIA

TWO WEEKS HAD PASSED since I'd boarded the S.S. Paradise, and I finally felt like I had my groove. Work was *good*, I had a group of friends, and I'd found spots on the ship that felt like mine.

Like the garden, earlier, where I'd run into Sylas Kellar.

I frowned, thinking about what he'd said. That he was broken. What had happened to him and his sister to make him feel that way? Part of me wanted to dismiss it.

After all, what he said was true. He was an asshole. Mostly. *Sometimes.* At least, that was what I'd originally thought. Now... I didn't know what to feel.

"I think the Captain's mood has gotten *worse*, if that's possible," Violet said, her thoughts somehow aligning with mine. "Know anything about that, Aurelia?"

We were all squeezed onto the two couches into the officer's lounge, turning on the large screen to watch a recording of our favorite trashy dating show. Thankfully, the ship was backed up with thousands of different programs, because it wasn't like we got anything new in space.

Love Out of this World was basically the same as any of the other 31st century reality romance shows, pairing people up and making them compete in couple's challenges, but it was set in *space*. They'd used an old, retired starship, locking the contestants on board for the months when the show filmed. There was a whole whopping fifteen seasons we could watch, too, which meant we could binge to our heart's content.

I pulled my eyes away from the screen to look at her. "Why would I?"

Ever since he let me back on the bridge, things had been better, but it wasn't like we were *friends*. In fact, besides a few moments, he'd hardly even talked to me. Still, I couldn't help but think about him in the gardens, with his head tipped up towards the light, an almost smile on his face...

He seemed peaceful, and I'd never seen him look like that before.

Maybe that was why it stuck with me. No other reason.

She looked over at me with a sly grin on her face. "I see him looking at you all the time."

I snorted. "He does not."

There was *no way*. Sylas was... *watching me?* Why? Was I doing something wrong? Except... I couldn't be. I knew I was damn good at my job. And based on Orion's reassurances, it wasn't that.

Except... there'd been that time at the gym. How his eyes dropped to my lips. And when I'd been walking away, I'd caught him staring at my backside. A warmth crept into my cheeks.

"No, she's right," Finley added, tossing a piece of air-popped corn into her mouth. "Every time I see him, he's staring at you. Though he might be glaring, too. I couldn't quite say."

Glaring sounded right.

"Yeah, I think he hates me." I frowned, waving them off and munching on the popcorn myself. "Why are we still talking about *me*, anyway? My life isn't as remotely interesting as you're making it out to be. Let's just watch the show."

We'd discovered our mutual love for this show last week,

and had all decided to watch it together. Which I was grateful for, because at least we had something else to talk about, keeping the focus off of *me*. I wanted them to like me, not speculate that something was going on between me and our captain.

Because nothing was happening, not now, and not in a million years. No matter how vast this galaxy was, there was no way Sylas Kellar and I would ever be together.

The rest of the girls went back to the screen, watching this couple going out on an organized date on the show, and the blue-haired medical officer sitting next to me shifted closer.

"You okay? How are you adjusting? The first month is the hardest. At least, that was my experience." Astrid gave me a small smile as she nudged me slightly.

"As good as I can be." I laughed. "This is all still so *surreal*. I mean, I'm on a freaking starship, right? I can't complain." My eyes drifted away from the screen and back to her. Astrid gave me an unconvinced look.

Sure, maybe there were things I could complain about—my grumpy captain hating me, for example, but I was choosing not to focus on them. *It's going to be amazing,* I reminded myself of the mantra I'd vowed to keep at my graduation ceremony.

"It's really something, isn't it?" Violet chimed in, a look of wonder in her eyes.

A smile lit up my face. "Sometimes, I feel like I'm going to wake up back in my bed at home, and all of this will just be one crazy dream."

If only my dad could see me now.

Kayle chuckled. "I've definitely felt like that more than once during my time with the Federation. I don't think you ever quite get used to it, but it feels normal eventually. And then every once in a while you have to stop, and be like, *my god, I'm in fucking space right now,* just for a brief reality check."

"Well, this is what I always dreamed of. Ever since I was little, I knew I wanted to fly a ship one day." A happy sigh slipped from my lips. "What did you all want to be when you grew up?"

Violet looked out the window, a serene look of longing filling her face. "I actually wanted to be a dancer."

"Really?" That surprised me, considering she'd ended up here working on comms, of all things. "What changed?"

"I grew up." She gave me a sad smile. "What about you? How did this all start?"

"Well, when I was a kid, it didn't matter what role I ended up in. It was just being in space that excited me," I answered honestly, hugging my knees against my body. "But the older I got, the more I wanted to be like my dad. To follow in his footsteps. When I lost him…" It was like I'd lost a piece of me. But no matter what happened, I always felt closer to him when I looked up at the sky. And now, I was really here. I shook my head. "Somehow, I feel closer to him now." Like he was here with me. Even if it was just in my heart.

"That's amazing, Aurelia." Finley gave me a warm smile. She looked a little distracted, holding her communicator tightly in her hand. Was everything okay? "I know I speak for everyone when I say we're so happy to have you on board."

Dipping my head, I tried to hide my blush. "Thank you. What about you? What's your story?"

Finley opened her mouth, but then a ping interrupted her, and she stood up. "Sorry. Gotta answer this."

"I'm getting a drink," Kayle called out, standing up abruptly. "Anyone want anything?"

"Sure," I called. All of this talk of the past had me feeling emotionally drained, and something to drink sounded like exactly what I needed to get back into the spirit of tonight.

"Anything specific?"

I shook my head. "Whatever you're having."

She darted over to the bar, bottles and glasses clinking as she mixed drinks.

"I'm glad you're adjusting better now." Astrid squeezed my wrist. "You know I'm here if you need anything, right?"

I nodded. It wasn't like I could complain about the Captain's treatment of me—especially with his sister and my first officer in the room. *It'll get better, Aurelia,* I scolded myself. *Just give it time.*

Kayle settled onto the armchair next to me, placing a drink in front of her on the coaster and handing me one. "This show is so stupid," she whispered as we watched two women fighting each other over a man.

I rolled my eyes at their antics. "Yeah. Definitely not what I would want my group of friends to look like."

She let out a burst of laughter, one that instantly made me like her more. "No," she finally agreed. "Decidedly not."

I knew in my gut that I liked Sylas's sister. She was kind, and I envied her calm demeanor and confidence. She was effortlessly gorgeous, with that dark brown hair and her ocean blue eyes—I didn't think she even had to try to look good each morning. Plus, her legs were a million miles long. I was five seven, and even I was envious of her stature.

"I heard what they were saying before," she said, taking a sip of her drink. I looked over at Astrid, Violet, and Finley, but they were all once again enraptured, eyes glued to the television.

"About?" I asked, swallowing down my guilt over everyone gossiping about our captain. Her brother.

Kayle gave me a warm smile, and it felt like she saw right through me. "I know he's not the easiest to deal with. But give him time."

"Time?" I raised my eyebrow. "You know he—"

"Tried to fire you?" She grimaced. "Yeah. *Not* his finest move. But even if he's thirty-five, sometimes he still acts like a dumb boy." Part of me wondered if she had anything to do with that— him rehiring me. It felt like she did. Kayle shook her head. "Just don't give up on him."

"Okay." I whispered the word, wondering what there *was* to give up on. We weren't friends. He didn't like me. Until our conversation in the garden today, I hadn't even thought about him like that.

He was my *captain*. Despite the asshole exterior, he'd given me a glimpse inside, but I wasn't going to find out anything more.

No matter how gorgeous I found him, I wasn't here to find love.

I was here to find out what happened to my dad. To solve the mystery that had been plaguing me for the last thirteen years. It was too late to save him, that much I knew, but I wanted to have closure.

To move on.

AFTER LAST NIGHT with the girls, I was feeling better. Maybe it was because it felt like I'd found my place. Whatever the reason, I felt more confident today. Maybe there was something in the recirculated air. Maybe it was space. For whatever reason, when I'd pulled on my dark purple dress uniform this morning, it hadn't even felt like I was playing dress-up anymore. It felt like I belonged here.

"Morning, Lieutenant," one of the crew members said to me.

"Morning," I responded, sitting down at my console.

I kept thinking about what Kayle had told me last night. That Sylas wasn't the easiest to deal with. That I should give him time. I thought about the way I'd seen him smile at his sister, throwing his arm around her shoulder and pulling her in tight. I wondered what it would be like to have that expression pointed at me. To see a true smile on his face.

But how many weeks would it take before he stopped being infuriating?

Infuriatingly handsome.

I started to punch in coordinates on my screen, checking the path the ship was flying, but something was off. Frowning, I backed out of my system, running a full diagnostic on it. Surely, this was an easy solution.

Except when it came back with a ding, I immediately knew what it was. *Shit.* I smoothed a hand over my face, looking around the bridge to see who else was around, before moving over to one of the machines in the back of the room.

No one had paid attention to me getting up, so I was safe. I breathed out a sigh of relief as I began to work.

Except a shadow fell over me, and I froze.

"What do you think you're doing?" A deep, commanding voice.

It was easy to forget how *tall* he was until moments like this, seeing him up close. Sure, I was taller than the average female, but he still towered over me, which was more intimidating than I'd like it to be.

Probably why standing up to him that first day had been as nerve-wracking as it was. Still, it had worked out. He'd agreed to let me work in my position, and I'd gotten to stay on the ship. Problem solved.

I slapped the machine twice. It might not have been my terminal, but everything on the bridge affected the crew. "Fixing this. It's reading wrong."

"No, it's not." He narrowed his eyes at me.

Except... I *knew it was.*

I'd taken a *good* deal of advanced engineering classes in college for my degree, that had seen me working on ships on the back end. All of that was before I'd ever learned how to fly a starship.

"Yes. It is."

"This isn't your job."

My mouth dropped open. "But I can fix it."

He just shook his head. Leo wasn't even around—dealing

with some minor problem in Engineering—and this would only take me a few moments.

Was he really telling me no?

"I learned about this in college. If the calibrations are off even the tiniest amount, it can throw off the entire ship's warp and navigational systems. And I *know* how to fix it. You haven't forgotten that I graduated at the top of my class, have you?"

We were chest to chest now, and that felt too intimate. I tried to take a step back, but it was just machinery behind me.

"You *can't* be serious."

Crossing my arms over my chest, I frowned at him. "Of course I am. Just watch."

He didn't move, and I quirked an eyebrow, giving him a *scooch* motion with my hands.

Sylas said nothing, just furrowed his brows as he watched me work.

A few minutes later, the system rebooted itself, and the numbers on the screen were in the correct range.

"There," I said, pointing at them. "Now it's fixed. See?"

"That's…" He looked up at me. "How?"

"I know what I'm doing." I clicked my tongue in my mouth. "Now, if you'll excuse me, I'll get back to the helm."

He huffed something under his breath, but didn't respond. Instead, he just stared at me.

"Would you like me to pull up the equipment manual and show you?"

"*No.*" He grit his teeth.

"So… am I allowed to get back to work now?" I asked, jutting out my chin towards him.

Sylas waved me off, heading back to his chair.

A smile spread over my lips.

I win.

Score 1 Aurelia, Score 0 Captain Kellar.

If only the rest of the mission would have been so easy.

TEN
SYLAS

STRETCHING OUT MY ARMS, I let out a deep exhale. The ship was right on track, and we were inching closer to our final destination.

So why did I still feel so fidgety? Like there was something I needed to do, somewhere I needed to go?

I couldn't talk about it with the guys, either. Leo would just tell me I needed to get laid.

Which was probably true, however... I wasn't interested.

No, that wasn't right. There was just only one woman on my mind, and I couldn't have her. She was strictly off-limits. *Forbidden*.

Aurelia was feisty, didn't hold back, and wasn't afraid to tell me when I was wrong. And I *was*. Somehow, it was becoming a theme with her. Normally, it would have driven me insane that she could put me in my place.

But with her, I was fascinated. What was it about her? I'd been around plenty of gorgeous women before, and they'd never affected me like she did.

Her eyes twinkled with mischief as she bantered with me, and it made me hard.

Goddamn it, I was *fucked*.

"You need to get it together," I muttered to myself.

I'd drank more in the last two weeks since boarding the ship than I had in years, though I'd avoided the absinthe again, no thanks to my sister's help.

What's one more drink? I asked myself, changing in direction towards the bar on the recreation floor.

The ship was divided into separate living areas: the very top deck housed the observation room, which was like a solid glass dome where you could see *everything* surrounding us. Right below it was the bridge and captain's quarters—where I spent most of my time.

Heading down the ship on the turbo lifts, you could find the officer's floor, with enough rooms to house everyone, plus the lounge and a few other living spaces. The following levels after that were larger, common areas of the ship: the recreation floor housed the gym, mess hall, and a variety of spaces to hang out, including our own personal bar.

The ship also housed an entire floor of greenhouses and agricultural growing spaces, helpful for both not feeling like you were traveling on a tin can through space *and* for feeding the crew. There were also two levels of crew quarters for all the other residents on the ship, including larger multi-room family suites for those who'd brought their loved ones along, plus a classroom, daycare, and nursery.

The Paradise was fully decked out—which it had to be, since we'd be gone for so long. No one wanted to go on such a long mission with no amenities, especially when most of our time would be confined to this space.

Even if we visited the surface of another planet, there was no guarantee of oxygen, and most of my crew would never set foot on alien soil.

That was the thought lingering in my mind as I entered the bar, seeing a familiar head of reddish-brown waves with her back to me at the bar.

I should have left. That would have been the proper thing to do. Except, when had I ever been proper? When I saw her sitting at the bar all alone, I couldn't stop my feet.

"Fancy seeing you here." I slid onto the stool next to her, letting my gaze sweep over her. She was still in her dark gray jumpsuit, but it was getting harder for me to ignore just how it hugged the curves of her body. No one else captured my attention like she did, and damn if that didn't drive me crazy.

Aurelia's cheeks were light pink, a warm haze over her features and a half-drunk glass in front of her. "Captain. Hi."

"Why are you all alone?"

She shrugged. "You know how it is."

I did. But also... "I thought you and the girls had been hanging out? Watching that show?"

"*Love Out of this World*?" She laughed. "We were. Are. But Astrid's working late, and Finley had something come up, and Violet, well... I don't know. Didn't seem like as much fun without everyone."

I nodded. "Makes sense."

"What about you? Why are *you* here alone, Captain?"

God, the way she called me my title all the time shouldn't be as alluring as it was, but I couldn't help it.

"Shifts over. Thought I'd come here and think." I waved over the bartender, ordering a glass of the finest scotch we had.

Probably needed to pace myself, since there was no replacing the alcohol once we'd run out. They'd stocked the ship with the finest we had, but that didn't mean there was an endless supply.

"Mmm. And what does our oh-so-great captain have to think about?" She took another sip of her drink, and my eyes were glued to her glass, the way her tongue flicked over the rim, catching the extra drops of the purple drink.

Wait. What had we even been talking about?

Right. *Thinking.*

"The usual, I'd suppose. *Life, liberty, and the pursuit of happiness.*" I quoted a document that was over twelve hundred years old, like it wasn't the most blasé statement I could make when the real thing I'd been thinking about was *her*.

Her damn hair. How pretty she was. How much had I had to drink? I wasn't supposed to be thinking about how pretty she was.

She just blinked. "Now I know you're really pulling my leg."

"Am not." I lied.

Aurelia let out a giggle, her eyes crinkling at the corners. "No one says that kind of shit and takes themselves seriously." She poked a finger at my chest. "Tell me, Captain Kellar. What ails you so?"

You.

"So dramatic," I muttered instead, swirling the alcohol around in my glass before taking a drink.

Aurelia hummed softly, taking a sip of her drink.

I said the first thought that popped into my mind. "Has there ever been something you really wanted but couldn't have?"

"Sure. But why *can't* I have it? Surely, if I work hard enough, it would be obtainable, right?"

"You'd think." My tone was dry. "But no. No matter what you do, it'll always be out of reach."

"Huh." She frowned into her cocktail. The purple almost matched the stripes on her flight suit, which somehow suited her just perfectly. "I guess that is something to think about, isn't it?" She ran her finger around the rim. "But I guess I know what you mean. I have something like that too. Something I'd give anything to have, but it's gone." Her tone was full of sadness, and I instantly hated that this world had taken something away from this woman. That she ever knew pain. "And I can never have it back."

A deep sigh came from my lips. "But that's life, isn't it? Sometimes it sucks, and then you die." Now I really knew I was drunk, because what sort of asshole said that to a woman who was clearly grieving something?

She looked out the large windows behind the bar. From

where we were seated, you could see the stars shining and the outline of a large, gas-based planet. It definitely wasn't one we could explore.

"Or maybe it's the opposite. That loss makes life worth living. Because isn't it better to have loved and lost than to have never loved at all?"

I frowned, thinking of my parents. They'd never loved my sister and I. If they had, they wouldn't have been able to leave us so easily. But I knew that I'd give anything to have protected Kayle from that pain. "I don't know."

A pretty blush exploded on her cheeks. "I'm sorry. I'm so overstepping." She picked up her glass. "This is really strong. Wow." Aurelia took another drink, draining it to the dregs. "Should I go? I should go." She stood up, not meeting my gaze.

"No." I placed my hand over hers, trying to ignore how much smaller hers looked. "Stay. Please." It was an echo of what we'd said in the gardens the other day, but I wouldn't look into that too deeply.

Aurelia let out a little hiccup, seemingly thinking about it for a moment, before nodding. "Okay." She finally returned her gaze to mine. Her brilliant eyes were sparkling as she looked over at me.

Was it obvious that I was just using this as an excuse to talk to her? That I didn't care what we talked about? But she was thoughtful, contemplative, and insightful.

And I was just a grumpy bastard who was greedy for her time.

"My mom would hate this," she finally said, another giggle tearing through her frame. "Knowing that I was up here, moping. Like I've done all this, but why doesn't it feel like I'm really *living* yet? Half the time I'm in awe that I'm really here. That we're in space. That I made it. But the other half of the time, I just can't help but feel like something's missing." She shook her head. "It's stupid."

I waved the bartender over and ordered us another round of

drinks. She got another one of those purple beverages, the alcohol shimmery and swirling in the glass.

"I know what you mean," I said, swirling my finger around on the top of the bar. "About feeling like you still want more. I mean, I'm the youngest captain in the fleet, and I still can't help but feel like I haven't achieved enough. But when does it end?" No matter what I did, it wouldn't be enough for them, anyway.

"But you're *Sylas Freaking Kellar.*" Her eyes were wide. "Do you know how many people talk about you in the academy? How many people look up to you?"

I scoffed.

"No, it's true. When I found out I was assigned to this ship, that I was placed under you, I was a little intimidated. After all..." She gestured to me with one hand, the other wrapped around her glass. "Look at you."

I puffed up my chest a little at that. That she was intimidated by me. I mean, fucking look at *her*. "And then?"

She laughed, and the sound was like an arrow to my stomach. A shock to my system. Because I was quickly becoming greedy for her laughter, and her smiles. I wanted to hoard them, all to myself. "And then I found out you really *were* a grumpy asshole." Aurelia patted my shoulder. "I'm going to regret saying that tomorrow, aren't I?"

I nodded, hiding the subtle upward quirk of my mouth behind my glass. "Probably. Just be glad I can't put you on scut duty."

Though, sober or not, I'd never punish her for it. Not when it was the truth. Maybe if she called me a grump or an asshole enough times, it would finally stick in my head that she didn't want me. Then this attraction running through my veins would go away.

She wrinkled her nose. "Is that really a thing?"

"Used to be."

"You sound like you speak from experience."

"I do." I sipped the scotch, savoring the taste of it on my tongue. "It wasn't fun."

"Mmm. I'll keep that in mind." Her shoulders shook, and I was surprised at how fun and easy this was. This banter between us wasn't arguing anymore. It felt natural. I didn't want it to end.

"Good. I'd hate to lose one of my officers to cleaning duties, after all." I winked at her.

She gave an exaggerated gasp, her hand flying over her heart. "You *wouldn't*."

"No," I agreed. "That would really cement my grumpy asshole status, after all. I'd rather force everyone to get dinner with me instead."

"I never said thank you for that."

"Why would you have to thank me?" Surprise lilt my tone. I hadn't told her I'd done it for her. In fact, I'd said the exact opposite, scowling and denying her claims.

"Hmm. Because even though you don't like me, you got all the officers together and made everyone bond."

"I didn't do that for you," I grunted.

"Sure," she said, but there was a twinkle in her eye.

Shit, she was on to me.

And even though that thought crossed my mind, I didn't stop talking. Not even when the clock passed 0400, and I knew we should both be asleep.

I didn't want this moment to end.

I WAS TOO old for hangovers.

Groaning, I rolled out of bed, second guessing why I'd had a second drink last night. And the third. Aurelia and I had sat in the bar until the late hours of the night, talking about nothing—

and everything. It was strange, because it was one of the best nights I'd had in a while.

And it was all because of her.

The conversation had flowed, a teasing banter back and forth forming between us. It was exciting talking to her. Hearing her thoughts about the world. Getting a small look into her brain.

"You look like shit." Kayle snorted as I sat next to her in the Captain's chair.

I huffed out a breath of air. "Just love getting shit from my First Officer first thing in the morning."

My sister gave me a teasing grin. "Sorry, Cap."

"What's the status report?" "All systems are running smoothly. Nothing unusual going on."

I looked over the officers working in the bridge, surprised to find that Aurelia wasn't here yet.

I'd expected to find her in that chair first thing, lighting up the room with her brilliant smile she seemed to give everyone but me.

"Good." I leaned back, shutting my eyes. "Smooth sailing ahead then."

I couldn't stop thinking about how last night she'd laughed for me.

That I *made* her laugh. Grumpy asshole, who? A chuckle slipped from my lips just thinking about it. Maybe people said that you couldn't teach an old dog new tricks, or that people didn't change, but I liked to think that slowly…

She was changing me.

ELEVEN
AURELIA

REMIND *me never to drink again*, I thought to myself as I looked into my eyes the next morning. Luckily, I didn't have a hangover, and I was mostly just dehydrated.

But the things I'd said to Sylas—*my Captain*... I groaned. He was definitely going to ban me from the bridge again. Even if it was just for a week.

"I totally crossed the line."

He was my boss. My superior officer. I had no business flirting with him in the bar.

Even if he was the most handsome man I'd ever met. His perfectly chiseled jaw was covered in dark stubble, those deep, ocean blue eyes. That dark brown hair was longer on top than it was on the sides, and I wanted to run my fingers through it. Would it be soft?

His hands were *enormous*, making the glass of amber liquid he held look tiny. I'd thought about them all night, and long into the morning. Wondering what they'd feel like on my skin, especially after he'd rested one over mine. Asking me not to go.

Damn horny thoughts. Now wasn't the time. I had a job to be doing, and it wasn't to pine after Sylas freaking Kellar.

I groaned. Maybe I was still drunk. I'd been drinking those

violet cocktails all night, and as delicious as they tasted, it had probably been a bad idea. I needed something to soak it up. Pancakes? Surely, the mess hall's breakfast would make me feel like a person again.

Throwing on a gray crewneck sweatshirt—it had my last name in big letters on the back, and the UGSF's logo on the front —I headed to find food.

Maybe with a full stomach, I'd be able to face seeing him again.

THAT WAS A LIE. I'd been lying to myself all day, and I'd known it.

Because Sylas Kellar in the light of day was just as gorgeous as he'd been last night, in the dim lighting of that bar. He'd joked with me. He hadn't *quite* smiled, but still. I knew I'd see it if I worked hard enough.

And damn, did I want to see it.

I'd held my breath all day on the bridge, looking back at him more than normal. Because I had so many thoughts running through my mind.

What kind of person was he, really?

Why was he alone last night? Did he not have anyone to spend time with? He was close with the other male officers, and he had his sister. And yet, he was perfectly content spending the entire evening sitting next to me.

I could still smell his cologne. I'd expected him to wear something spicy or musky, but he just smelled clean. Crisp, like the night sky, and yet... all man. Part of me wondered if I could get away with burying my nose in his shirt and taking a deep inhale.

Surely, he wouldn't think I was crazy if I did that, would he? No. He definitely would.

"Aurelia, hey." A voice knocked me out of my stupor. *Astrid.*

I shook away my thoughts. They were bordering on inappropriate, and I needed them to go away before they got any worse.

"Hi, Astrid." I grinned at her. "What's up?"

I'd decided to take a book to the lounge this evening and read. Better that than risk another bar run-in with Sylas Kellar.

A man who I absolutely should not *still* be thinking about.

"We were talking about grabbing dinner. If you wanted to come." She pointed at her data-pad. "I sent you a ping, but I didn't hear back."

"Oh." I pulled the slender device out of my back pocket. "I have it on silent. Sorry, I didn't even hear it." If I went to dinner with them, I could make it back and still have time before I needed to make my way to the bridge. Except... "I already ate," I said, offering her a frown. "I think I'll just stay here and read before I head to bed. I've been extra exhausted lately."

She nodded. "Of course! No worries. Space can do that to you," Astrid joked, wrapping a finger around a strand of her blue hair. "Make sure you stay hydrated, though. And come see me if that sluggishness turns into something more."

"Of course." She didn't need to know I'd been more tired than normal lately because I was barely sleeping. "Thank you, Astrid."

She gave me a nod before heading out, letting me sink back into my book.

TAKING A DEEP BREATH, I looked into the hallway. It was quiet, and the motion-detected lights were currently off. Both were a good sign for me.

I'd spent the last week sneaking into the bridge each night, doing research and trying to come up with answers where I can.

What I discovered was there was only a narrow window of time where no one else was on the bridge. When no one would question what I was doing.

I had to wait until the evening crew left and be gone before the morning crew could arrive.

Glancing at the timepiece on my wrist, I exhaled. *Go time.* I had a few good hours of time before I needed to get back to my quarters.

Yawning, I tightened my ponytail as I snuck through the empty hallway, down the lift to the bridge, and tapped my ID card on the scanner to let myself in.

My station was powered down, but all it took was a few taps and I was in.

I input the coordinates I'd been looking at. We were still far enough away that I had time, but If I waited too long, we'd overshoot it and I'd miss my chance entirely.

And I needed to find answers.

When my dad had disappeared all those years ago, they'd never found the ship, or his body. We'd buried an empty casket. Now, all I had was the coordinates of his last flight, the last estimate of where they'd lost contact with his vessel. Though I shouldn't even have had those—it was only thanks to Anderson Baliss that I did.

When I'd found out that the Paradise's route would go along that same star system… I'd leaped. It was the only thing I'd written on my placement request, as foolish as that was. I'd banked my entire future on this.

Thankfully, I'd been learning from Orion over the last few weeks, watching his console and asking him to explain little things to me. Enough that I could pick up on the finer intricacies of how it worked. How to locate the right spot on the map, where I could hopefully find a clue. I'd been working on it in secret, little bits at a time, but I couldn't do much during the day. The bridge never seemed to be empty, even when the ship was on auto-pilot, and people got a little suspicious if I was sitting at someone else's station.

My fingers flew over the screen, guiding us off course just slightly. I'd been making micro-corrections every night. If I got close enough, I could see what was there. We had star-maps of this system, but they were incomplete. Had dad found something? What could have caused his ship to disappear in friendly space?

I frowned, staring out the large windows. It was probably too late to find answers, but I had to try.

An electronic chime sounded as someone opened the doors to the bridge. I sucked in a breath. *Not good.*

"Shit." I muttered the words under my breath, sliding from Orion's chair back into mine, pressing a button to clear the screen.

The loud, deep voice I'd gotten to know too well over the last few weeks interrupted, sending a shiver down my spine. "What are you doing, Lieutenant?" Sylas murmured, his voice heavy with sleep.

"I didn't think anyone would be up." I turned to look at him —which was a mistake. He was devastating. The UGSF t-shirt clung to his frame, revealing his toned stomach, and he wore a pair of navy sweatpants.

"No one should be." He crossed his arms over his chest, still standing on the upper platform and staring at me. "So why are you?"

I turned to stare out at the sky. "I couldn't sleep." A half-truth. "Thought I'd come keep an eye on the ship." I patted the metal in front of me, like I was coaxing a pet.

"She *does* fly herself, you know."

A snort escaped me. "I'd hope so, since I'm the one who normally flies her."

He rolled his eyes, taking the steps down to me.

And then he was sitting next to me, sitting in Orion's chair, staring up at the darkness of space. I appreciated his stare wasn't on mine.

Sometimes, when he looked at me, it felt like those dark blue eyes were staring into my very soul. It was jarring, the feelings that awakened in me each time our eyes connected.

"Why are *you* awake?" I asked, unsure why I felt the need to pry.

"I have the bridge set up to ping me when anyone enters it between certain hours. If they're not on duty, it flags me."

"Oh." I sucked in a breath. "I didn't—"

"You're not in trouble." Sylas leaned back in the chair, tapping his fingers on the surface in front of him. "But I couldn't help but wondering what my little pilot was up to."

My cheeks were warm as he raised an eyebrow, turning to me. "Nothing," I said, hoping the word didn't come out as defensive as it felt.

"Mm." He hummed in response, hitting the button on Orion's screen to power it up.

All of my earlier searches were still pulled up on the screen.

"I—" *Fuck.* "I promise I wasn't doing anything that would put the crew in danger. I'd never…" I swallowed roughly. "Please believe me."

"I trust you." His voice didn't waiver, and that confidence surprised me.

All I could do was blink. "You…" The past few weeks, he'd given me no sign if he was even pleased with my performance. "You do?"

His head dipped as he fiddled with the settings on the terminal, carrying on without even acknowledging the dumbfounded expression that must have been on my face. "What are you trying to find?"

"It's going to sound crazy," I whispered, and Sylas spun on the chair to face me.

"Try me."

"My dad, he…" I gnawed at my lower lip. "He disappeared when I was twelve. Thirteen years ago."

"I know."

I blinked, surprised. "You do?"

He nodded. "I know who you are. I knew it the moment you stepped onto my ship. The moment you said your name. Aurelia Callisto. Samuel Callisto's daughter. How could I not?" Sylas shook his head. "I was shocked, and I took that out on you."

"I didn't realize…" I trailed off, not even knowing where to start. "I didn't get this position because of him, you know. I worked my ass off in college and in flight school. There were so many sleepless nights. If anything, my teachers worked me harder, knowing whose daughter I was." Bringing my feet up onto the chair, I wrapped my arms around them, drawing myself in tight.

"I was an asshole."

"You…" I hadn't been expecting that. Somehow, it was more than an apology.

He dipped his head. "I deserved it when you called me out. I wasn't being fair to you by removing you from your post without even giving you a chance. I never apologized for it then. Let me now."

"Why are you being nice to me?" I raised an eyebrow.

His eyes drifted down to the terminal, looking at the screen. "Tell me what you're trying to do."

"My dad's best friend gave me the coordinates for where his ship pinged last, before the communication stopped. I've been tracking it, seeing if I could find any energy signatures or any indication of what might have been around there." I shook my head, showing him my research. "So far, I've come up empty. Maybe I really am just chasing a ghost."

"I'll help you."

My fingers stilled on the screen. "What?"

"I said—"

"No, I heard you. I just…" All I could do was stare at him. "Why?"

He frowned, crossing his arms over his chest. "Why what?"

"Why would you want to help me? You don't even like me."

Sylas let out a groan. "*Aurelia.* I'm sorry. Let me do this to make it up to you."

I grumbled under my breath, but I didn't protest when he leaned over the screen, studying its contents. For one, it felt… nice, to share this with someone. To unload the weight of my secret. I'd been working on this by myself for far too long.

"Okay," I finally agreed, after staring at him for far too long. "Thank you."

He stood, rubbing at his short beard with his index finger and thumb. "Tomorrow night."

I looked up, surprised. "Yes?"

"Bring everything you have to my quarters. We'll go through all of it there. No more staying late at the bridge." He stared me down, expression serious. "Go get some sleep."

"Yes, Captain."

He headed towards the door to the bridge, turning back to look at me when he'd reached the top platform. "And Aurelia?"

My heart fluttered in my chest at the sound of my name. "Yes?"

"We'll find out what happened to him. I promise you that." Those ocean blue eyes connected with mine, and I couldn't help but believe him.

"Okay." I whispered the word, and then the door slid closed, taking Sylas Kellar—and all his confusing self—with it.

TWELVE
SYLAS

A KNOCK SOUNDED at my door. *Aurelia.* She was here. I ran a hand through my hair. Was it normal to be this nervous?

I'd had women in my quarters before. Of course I had—I enjoyed sex. During my time with the federation, I'd had my fair share of one-night stands and casual relationships. Not that you'd know it now. The only company I currently enjoyed was my own hand, and admitting that she was all I saw when I closed my eyes in the shower was highly inappropriate.

But I didn't want anyone else, either.

Her long, reddish brown hair hung loose over her shoulders, the scent of shampoo still clinging to her skin like she'd just gotten out of the shower before coming to see me. I had to shut my eyes and count to ten. To remind myself of all the reasons I couldn't have her.

She wasn't here for that. Maybe my dick needed a reminder as much as my brain.

"Come in," I finally grunted, subtly adjusting myself after she passed me.

Her eyes were wide as she scanned my room. "This place is... *wow.*"

"You like it?" I flashed my teeth before reminding myself that

I *wasn't* flirting. That wasn't what this was. I cleared my throat. "Perks of being the captain." One of which was having the largest suite on the starship, complete with my own enormous bathroom and sitting area.

She moved to stare out the large window. Much like the bridge, I had my private view into the vastness of space. I leaned against the wall, crossing my arms over my chest as I observed her expression. The look of childlike wonder as she stared out at the stars.

"It's incredible." She looked over at me. "I'm not sure I'd ever want to leave."

"Mmm." My lips curled up into a smirk. "I don't." Moving, I sat down on the large plush couch in the sitting area, patting the spot beside me. There was a large screen in front of me—one I used to watch movies and stream shows, though it also boasted the ship's state-of-the-art artificial intelligence system.

Anything I could ever wish to know, all at my command.

"What now?" Aurelia asked, shifting her bag before sitting next to me. She left plenty of space between our bodies, though her scent hadn't left me. Every time I breathed, that sweet smell invaded my senses. I hated it as much as I loved it.

"Start at the beginning," I instructed, draping my hands in my lap. "I want to know everything."

"Everything?" she repeated, eyes wide.

"Mhm. If we're going to do this, I need to know all of it."

"Right." She pulled a flash drive out of her bag, running her fingers over the edges. "How much do you know about my dad?"

Everything. When was it acceptable for me to admit that I'd once had his poster on my wall? That I'd been the biggest fan boy when I was a kid, and her dad had been my inspiration for joining the fleet? When he'd gone missing, I'd felt that loss like I had with my own parents. Not that I'd ever admitted it to anyone.

"Enough," I grunted out.

"Right." She inhaled sharply. "Well, when I was twelve, he was sent out on a mission similar to this one." I nodded. I knew that. Almost everyone did. "It was a small crew, and one of the first ships experimenting with jump technology. Though it couldn't travel anywhere near as fast as the speeds the Paradise does."

"The *Departure*." In its day, it had still been an impressive ship, though technology had advanced vastly since then.

"Right. My dad was so excited. I'd begged for months before the mission to go with him, but families weren't allowed." Her face fell. "He had to leave mom and I behind, because the ship was too small. It was only supposed to be a six month mission, but…"

But he'd never come home.

"Hey." I placed my hand on her forearm. "It's okay." If she'd been on that ship… I couldn't even bear to think about it.

Aurelia sighed, wrapping her arms around herself. "I know that whatever happened out there couldn't have been good. That it's been thirteen years, and there's likely not a single clue left. But I just can't help but wonder. To hope maybe, if I find the ship…" That she'd find her dad. She shook her head before pulling something out of her pocket. "I just want closure. To know what happened. This drive has all the data the UGSF had from the S.S. Departure. Its intended flight-plan, the last location it pinged before going silent, all the communication logs and data transfers the federation had achieved… Everything." Aurelia sat it onto the table in front of us, sliding it towards me.

"And?" I waited for her to continue, even though I could guess where she was going with this.

"There's a reason I'm here, Captain. A reason I requested to be on this ship." Her eyes squeezed shut. "We're following that same path. Albeit, much faster, considering how technology has improved. But when I found out the Paradise would go through the same part of space where my dads had last been detected, I knew I had to be here. Whatever it took."

That explained her eagerness, and how stubborn she'd been.

"What were you going to do if I left you behind?" I pursed my lips. "If I kicked you off my ship before we ever left the station?"

She bit her lower lip. "I don't know. It was a contingency I hadn't prepared for. To be honest, even though I'd heard the rumors about you, I didn't think you'd be that much of an asshole." Aurelia shrank back. "Sorry, Captain."

"Don't apologize. You're right. I was an asshole." My fingers instinctively went to my forehead, where I could feel a small crease forming between my eyebrows. "Probably deserve that."

"Still. I don't know. I would have figured something else out, I guess. Always do."

Without a doubt, I believed that. In the last few weeks, I'd seen her work through numerous problems—often, for things out of her own job purview.

"Anyway, it doesn't matter," she continued, "Because I'm here. And I've been looking on the scanners, checking the coordinates, and, well, you saw what I was working on last night."

"I did." And it all made so much more sense now. "So, you think you'll find the ship?"

"I don't know. For all I know, it could be nothing. Just inconsistencies in space or discrepancies in the data. But it could be something, too. And that's what I want to find out. My dad taught me to be curious—to never stop asking questions. To let this go just feels like I'm dishonoring his memory." Aurelia fidgeted with her hands in her lap. "So I have to try."

I nodded, picking up the flash drive. "Let's see what we can find together, then."

"Are you sure?" She sounded hesitant. "If the federation finds out what I'm doing, using government resources to find out what happened, we could end up in hot water."

"So we won't let them find out." Because now that she brought me into the fold, I wanted her to be successful.

And I didn't want her to have to do it alone. I knew what that felt like too well. At least I had my sister. Aurelia was alone. The only person she had left was her mom, and she'd left her behind on Earth to come on my ship.

"You're not alone anymore, Aurelia," I said, reaching over to brush a strand of hair behind her ear. Something I'd been trying to resist doing all night. Touching her was a temptation, and one I couldn't avoid anymore.

"Thank you," she said as her cheeks pinkened. "You don't know how much this means to me."

I shook my head, not saying anything else. Because I had a feeling I did.

Getting up, I plugged the USB drive into the computer unit and instructed the AI to run the data through its software. Aurelia's eyes widened as everything plotted itself out on the screen, a perfect display of all the data.

"Woah. This is amazing."

A 3-D model of her father's ship was projected from the table, and she ran her fingers through the hologram.

"This technology is something I'd only ever dreamed of working with," she admitted.

"Me too," I said with a chuckle. Becoming the captain of a starship had afforded me more opportunities than I'd ever dreamed of. "I never thought I'd be here, honestly."

"A captain?" Aurelia asked, her gaze darting to me.

I dipped my head in answer. "Don't get me wrong, I worked my ass off for this commission. But if you asked me as a kid if I thought I'd be *here* now, I probably would have told you no."

My childhood wasn't something I wanted to talk about, and it surprised even me that I'd brought it up to her. It wasn't fun to dredge up, let alone linger on. I didn't want her sympathy or pity. It happened. We'd moved on.

"That's fair," Aurelia hummed, not pressuring me for more details.

"What about you? If your father hadn't disappeared, do you still think you'd be here?"

"On this ship?" Her brows furrowed. "Probably not. But working for the Federation? Probably. I wanted to follow in my dad's footsteps." Her eyes drifted shut, a serene expression transforming her face like she was imagining an alternate life. "I always liked to imagine us working together. Maybe it would have made up for all the times he left me behind."

Being left—that I could relate to.

"Hmm." I turned my attention back to the screen.

"What? Did you find something?" Aurelia perked up, turning her attention to the screen.

"Yes, and no." I squinted, looking at the data in front of us. Something was wrong. "See these numbers?" I asked, pointing at the string. "I don't get it. Why were they heading there?" And if the numbers were accurate, so slowly. Something must have been wrong with the ship.

"I don't know. They never told me what the purpose of my dad's mission was. A lot of stuff was classified." She rolled her eyes. "Even now, it's like one giant coverup."

But what were they covering up? I frowned. "That doesn't make sense. There shouldn't be anything there." I pointed at the system where they'd been adrift.

"Unless the star charts are wrong."

"Then why send us on a nearly identical flight path?"

"They adjusted the course, though, just slightly." Aurelia pointed at the line. "We were supposed to go here, but I've been letting the ship drift slightly off track." She winced. "Please don't fire me." A pause as her eyes connected with mine. "*Again.*"

A laugh worked free from my lips. "It's a little late for that, don't you think?" I shook my head. "Besides, I'm not going to fire you. Whatever you've uncovered is bigger than us."

"Really?"

I nodded. "But I think we should keep this quiet for now. See what we can investigate on our own."

Aurelia pointed at the flashing sensor on the map. "These are the coordinates I tagged where my dad's vessel was last seen.

There's a moon close by—Planet *XV30041's*. There's a chance..." she trailed off.

"That they crashed there." I finished. Crossing my arms, I rubbed at my jaw with my index finger. "Yes, it's possible." Her eyes lit up, and I hated to destroy that spark of optimism, but— "There's a chance there's nothing there, too."

"I know." She sighed.

"It could have been a meteor storm, or the ship's engines failed. We don't know if they could have ever made it to the surface."

"But we should try, right?" Her tone was pleading, and I could hear the hope in it. How her heart was set on this. "Please."

This time, it was my turn to sigh. "When we get closer, we'll be able to scan the planet for activity. If there's anything human-made there, we'll be able to find it."

"Okay." She worried her lower lip into her mouth. "What if..."

"Hm?"

"What if I did all of this for nothing?" Her voice was quiet, barely above a whisper.

"Hey." I frowned, sliding closer to her. "You can't think like that."

"I know, it's just..." Her eyes were glassy. "I don't know what I'll do. Maybe coming here was a mistake. I just..."

"It wasn't." The words were practically a growl. "You're a damn good pilot, Aurelia. Even if we don't find out anything about what happened to your father, none of that will change. And I know, either way, he'd be so impressed. Look at what you've done. How much you've accomplished."

She sucked in a breath, rubbing at her eyes. "I know. I know. This is dumb. I'm sorry."

"You don't have to apologize." I reached out, squeezing her hand, wanting to reassure her.

Was it an inappropriate touch? I couldn't find it in me to care, not when she looked so close to tears. She had to know, didn't she? How amazing she was?

She looked up at me, surprise in her eyes.

My eyes darted down to her lips. Pink and full—how soft would they feel against mine? If I slid my hands into her hair, bringing our mouths together, would she let me? Did she want this as badly as I did?

"Aurelia…"

She drew in a jagged breath.

A warning alarm sounded, making me jump off the couch. Fuck, what was I thinking? I couldn't be touching her. Couldn't kiss her, for fuck's sake. No matter how much I wanted it.

"I should go check on that." I muttered, heading towards the door.

"Right." She stood, fidgeting with her hands. "Good night, Captain."

She said the word like she needed a reminder of who I was.

Her captain.

Maybe I needed the reminder, too.

THIRTEEN
AURELIA

THERE WAS no way Sylas Kellar had almost kissed me. My fingers ran over my lips when I finally got back to my room, my back pressed against the door.

I still couldn't believe the events of the last two days. Never in my wildest dreams had I imagined that he'd offer to help me instead of reprimanding me. Especially when grumpy was his natural state, and I caught him frowning nine out of ten times when we were both on the bridge. Either he had a serious resting grump face, or he hated me. I wasn't sure which, but I'd resigned myself to it. That as long as I kept my head down and kept doing my job, everything would be fine.

Until last night. Now I didn't know what to feel.

"Aurelia Callisto," I scolded myself, looking in the small mirror in my bedroom as I got ready for bed. "You are really in over your head here."

He couldn't have wanted to kiss me, though. No freaking way. I had to have been interpreting that wrong. Yep. That was it. I was definitely, *definitely* interpreting it wrong.

You're a damn good pilot, Aurelia. Butterflies exploded in my stomach at the thought. From anyone else, those words wouldn't have been much. In fact, they were hardly a compliment at all.

But from him—the man who was always scowling and growling? They felt like a million credits.

He'd been showing me brief glimpses of who he really was over the last few weeks, and I *liked* what I saw. Which was stupid, because he was my captain. Nothing was ever going to happen between us. No matter how eager he was to help me.

Dammit, I shouldn't have liked it. I shouldn't have liked him. That wasn't what I was here for.

Not for crushing on my superior officer. A man ten years older than me. A man I definitely wasn't allowed to have.

Sliding under my covers, I pretended I would not dream about Sylas Kellar and his gigantic hands that night.

That I *definitely* wasn't thinking about what it would have been like if he had kissed me.

AS I PULLED on my uniform, the events of last night played out again in my mind.

"So freaking stupid," I muttered to myself, tucking my cow plush back into its home and straightening my room before getting ready to report to the bridge.

Would things be different today? Or would the easy rapport between us be lost? I hoped not. After all, things were so different now. I hated the thought of going back to his begrudging acceptance, or even blatant dislike, of me. How would I even survive it if we went back to the way things were?

I was navigating the circular hallways towards the bridge when I heard a huffed out, "*Aurelia!*" shouted down the hall.

Glancing behind me, I saw a blue head of hair set against a bright white uniform bobbing towards me. Astrid.

"Hey," I said, when she finally skidded to a stop in front of me. "What's up?"

"Did you hear?"

I raised an eyebrow. "Hear…"

She let out a sound that sounded suspiciously like a giggle. "Apparently, Captain Kellar has decided that since our officer get-together the other week was such a rousing success, he's going to implement it weekly."

"What?" I squeaked.

Did he enjoy seeing me squirm? Was that the reason he kept insisting on having us in the same room? I already felt guilty accepting his help, and then knowing that all the other officers would be there as well—I was definitely in for it. Secrets had never been very easy for me to keep as it was.

"Yup. We're having pizza tonight."

I quirked an eyebrow. "Is that… all you wanted to tell me?"

"Yes." She paused, looking over at me. "Well… no. But the other constitutes as gossip, so I don't know if I should…"

"Tell me."

"Violet said she saw Sylas smiling and humming to himself last night. And she thought he had a girl in his room."

I froze. "What?" My eyes felt like they were bugging out of my face. Or maybe all the color had leeched from my skin.

"Yeah. Maybe he'll be less grumpy now?" She elbowed me, another laugh echoing down the hall. "You're going to come visit me in the MedBay soon, right? I'll give you the entire tour."

"Oh, yeah," I said, trying to ignore how distracted I was. "Of course. I'd love to."

"Great." She gave me a wave. "Gotta get back to it. Patients to see, and all that."

"Right."

Astrid hurried away, leaving me standing dumbfounded in the hallway.

Girl in his room. Me? Had someone caught us? I knew we weren't doing anything, but I still felt guilty.

Especially because I'd thought about what it would be like if he had kissed me.

"Everything okay?"

"Ahh!" I jumped, not expecting another disturbance. But I looked up, and there was a pair of ocean blue eyes peering down at me with concern. Dark brown hair, and a stubbled face.

I blinked a few times, feeling my vision clear. *Sylas Kellar.*

"Sorry." He frowned.

My hand rested over my racing heart. "Not your fault. I didn't expect anyone else. I was a little lost in my own world." *Thinking about you.* Not that I'd ever confess that to him.

"On your way to the bridge?"

I nodded, crossing my hands behind my back.

"Perfect. Me too." He flashed his pearly white teeth at me, walking in stride with me, matching me step for step.

"About last night," I said, keeping my voice low.

"Hm?" Sylas ran his hands through his hair. I couldn't stop staring at him. His dress uniform hugged his biceps in all the right places, his upper arms looking like they were going to burst through the material. And his chest was—*holy wow.* Then there was the way the blue fabric made his eyes pop—like a deep, endless ocean of color.

I could get lost in those eyes.

"We probably shouldn't do it again." A strand of hair came loose from my bun, and I tucked it behind my ear.

"What do you mean? I told you I'd help you."

I looked around, grateful that the hallway was empty. "Someone could catch us. There are already rumors going around that you had a woman in your room last night." My entire face felt warm.

"So?"

"*So?!*" I parroted the word back at him. "I can't have people gossiping about me behind my back, Captain. Not if they think we're doing something—" I dropped my voice lower. "Inappropriate. The repercussions—"

His eyes sparkled with amusement, and I could tell he wasn't taking this seriously.

"I'm serious."

Sylas crossed his arms over his chest. "And I'm serious about helping you. Fuck them. They don't matter."

"But—"

He leveled me with a glare that made me shut my mouth. What more was there to say?

We reached the bridge, Sylas sliding his palm over the sensor and opening the door. *Must be nice.* I still had to tap my ID badge, because my handprint wasn't programmed into the system.

"Good morning, Captain," I heard Violet say before she noticed me right behind him, her eyes going wide.

"Morning," he said with a grunt, sounding much more like the sullen, moody man that I was used to. Not the one who I'd been basically flirting with back in the hallway.

"Hi, Vi," I said, pasting on a smile I didn't exactly feel.

"You excited for tonight?" she grinned. "You heard, right?"

"I did." I flicked my eyes back to Sylas, wondering what he was up to. "Pizza night."

"Think we can convince the guys to watch the show with us?"

Orion snorted. "Fat chance of this one agreeing to that." He jabbed a thumb in Sylas's direction.

"Hey." My captain—I was trying to remind myself who he was to me—frowned. "I'm not opposed to watching your..." His words trailed off, before he finished with, "trashy reality television."

"Don't call it trashy," Kayle said with a faked gasp, placing her hand over her heart. "Those are real people's lives! They fall in *love*!"

"Real *fake* lives," he snorted at his sister. "How many of them actually even stay together?"

She rolled her eyes, and a secret smile spread over my face. Kayle looked over at me, and I knew she caught me. Busted.

I looked away, vowing not to look back at Sylas Kellar for the rest of my shift. A vow of which I broke about fifty times that afternoon.

Somehow, I had to remind myself of who he was. That he wasn't for me. That I wasn't, under any circumstances, allowed to kiss my captain.

Even if he was a stubborn, irritable, grumpy bastard.

I still wanted to do it anyway, dammit.

WHOEVER CALLED it pizza night had vastly underestimated the entire affair.

This wasn't some buffet you'd find on a random corner back on Earth. This was a gourmet meal, as if every detail of this evening had been meticulously planned.

Had Sylas arranged all of this? And when? Though maybe the better question was *why*.

"This is… Wow," I said, standing next to Astrid, who'd worn her hair down for once. The blue strands hit the tops of her shoulders, brushing over the top of her white t-shirt that read *Space Girl*. I was a little obsessed with her graphic tee collection. Tonight, we'd all dressed casually, uniforms thankfully not required. It was just fine with me. I loved my uniform, but wearing it all day every day could get exhausting.

"Do you think he's trying to impress someone?" Astrid whispered to me, her blue-green eyes shimmering with amusement.

"Oh, I…" Did she suspect something? My cheeks felt warm. Why did I feel guilty when the only thing I'd done was be alone with him?

"Relax," she said, giving me a reassuring smile. "I know it's not like that."

But wasn't it? It felt like it was. Sylas had agreed to help me, and now we were all here.

The door slid open, revealing the man himself—and our First Officer.

"Hey, pretty boy," Kayle said, tossing a sultry smile at Leo.

There was tension between them, and I wondered how long it would take for it to snap. Then again, Leo and Sylas had been friends since college. Maybe he wouldn't want to risk their friendship for Kayle.

To me, though, it seemed like they needed to fuck and get it out of their systems.

Sylas had a grumpy expression on his face as he stomped in, and I wondered what was wrong with him.

His words from earlier rang through my head. *And I'm serious about helping you. Fuck them. They don't matter.* Why did he care so much about helping me? What was he getting out of this?

Suddenly, all nine of us were crowded around the large table in the officer's lounge, an entire assortment of pizzas and side dishes made by Chef Gregori laid out in front of us. The man himself had presented them with a bow and a flourish, before disappearing off to wherever he worked. Everything looked amazing.

Loading my plate up with food, I took a bite, moaning as the flavors burst on my tongue.

I looked up, finding Sylas staring at me from across the table. He had a small smile on his lips—barely there, unless you'd studied his face long enough to know his expressions like I had. I averted my eyes, hoping I could hide my blush from him.

A few gulps of wine and bites of pizza later, and I relaxed. I could do this. I'd just ignore him.

"Okay, I haven't had pizza this good in a long time," Leo remarked. "Like, I could fuck with this pizza. That's some damn good pizza."

Wren rolled his eyes, though I noticed his focus was across the table at Finley. Very interesting…

"You say that about everything," Sylas remarked, then furrowed his brow. "Please don't fuck the pizza."

A laugh burst out of me, and startled, he looked over at me. My hand flew over my mouth. *Embarrassing.*

"Sorry," I murmured, averting my eyes.

"No, it was funny," Leo remarked, flashing a smile. "Sy just likes to mess with me."

Sy. The familiarity there was surprising. That they could joke together, riff on each other, and Sylas didn't even seemed phased by any of it.

I wondered what that would be like. To have someone who you could laugh with through any situation. Someone who knew you so intimately that they got all of your jokes.

And despite my head knowing, my heart was so desperate for that. For a partner. My other half. But I knew that wouldn't happen for me.

No matter what I dreamed about at night, it wasn't in the cards for me.

I certainly wasn't going to fall in love.

FOURTEEN
SYLAS

SHAKING MY HAIR OUT, I ran the towel over my chest, picking up the excess moisture before wrapping it around my waist.

I'd just finished swimming laps in the ship's pool, and thankfully, with the early morning, the locker room had been empty. Living and working on a starship had some drawbacks—namely, being away from civilization for a long period—but I wanted to find whoever put a pool on my ship and shake their hand.

Running my fingers through my damp hair, I looked at myself in the mirror. It was not a stretch to say that my body was a temple—a finely honed masterpiece. The amount of hours I spent working out to stay in shape showed. No one had complained about my abs, though, so I didn't think it was a bad thing.

Still, I let my eyes drift over my frame, wondering what I looked like from someone else's eyes. *Hers,* specifically.

Did I look too old? Would she think I was handsome? Why did I care? I didn't want to admit the reasons to myself.

That maybe I cared because I wanted her to be interested in me, the way I was in her. In those beautiful eyes I couldn't look away from. The long, brownish red hair that I was just dying to wrap my fist around. Those pink, plush lips that looked deliciously soft. Her hips—

"Fuck," I muttered to myself, trying to will the thoughts away. "Stop thinking about her." I pointed at myself in the mirror, like commanding myself would be enough to get me to stop.

It wouldn't, but I could pretend.

How much longer could I hide my budding attraction to my pilot? Spending this much time with her wasn't helping. In fact, it was only making it worse. She had invaded all my senses, clouding up my thoughts with *her*.

Heading to the showers, I quickly rinsed off, eager to start my day.

Because being on the bridge meant I'd see her.

And if I was a damn fool for her, then so be it.

Pulling on a t-shirt and a pair of shorts, I dropped my towel in the bin, heading out of the pool area so I could take the turbo lifts back up to my floor.

Except all of my thinking about my little pilot seemed to have made her appear in front of me. She must have been in the gym, just a room away from me as I'd swam laps.

"Hi."

"Oh." Aurelia looked surprised to see me standing in front of her. Her cheeks were red, breathing rough, like she'd just finished an intense workout.

"We've really got to stop meeting like this, Lieutenant." I chuckled, surprised to find myself in high spirits.

Maybe it was because of the way she'd laughed last night when I'd made that joke to Leo. Maybe it was because I'd sat across from her, and I'd imagined what it would be like for her to smile at me instead. For those eyes to light up with that warmth when she looked at *me*. For all of them to be for me.

She looked around, like she was worried someone was going to catch us.

"What are you worried about?" I asked, my voice dropping

to a low whisper as I held myself back from reaching out and wrapping a fist around her high ponytail. "We're not doing anything wrong."

"Captain." Her voice was breathless. "I—"

A door slammed, and Aurelia jerked away from me, like we were standing mere inches apart versus several feet. She had a guilty blush on her face, which amused me.

What did she think we were doing together? Sure, I wanted to kiss her, but we hadn't done anything.

That didn't mean I hadn't imagined it. Maybe she had, as well.

"We shouldn't be alone together," she said, shaking her head. "Not anymore."

"But what about me helping you?"

Again, she shook her head, turning and heading towards the door. "I'll figure it out alone." Then she slipped out into the hallway of the ship without another look back at me.

Like *hell* she was doing this without me. I growled, catching the eye of a crew member walking by, and shook my head.

I needed to get my head on straight.

Or maybe I just needed her *out* of it.

HOW WAS I going to stop thinking about her when I couldn't even stop looking at her?

I glanced over at Aurelia, sitting at her console with a smile on her face. We'd been spending more time together outside of the bridge, which somehow felt like a torture of my own making. Because now she wasn't just some beautiful officer out of reach.

Now I'd glimpsed at the woman underneath the uniform. I'd begun to know *her*. And she was light. Like pure, bright *starlight*. I'd never encountered another person who made me feel the way she did. I couldn't even describe it, but I just knew I was greedy for her attention. I wanted more of her time.

Her eyes connected with mine, and she gave me a hesitant smile. *Brilliant.*

How could one smile mess me up inside this much? Yes, I wanted her. There was no way to deny that. Not anymore. Physically, at least. She was still a stubborn brat, as much as she was sunshine incarnate to everyone else.

A growl slipped from my lips, and Kayle looked over at me, surprise in her eyes. "Something wrong?"

"No," I grunted. Nothing at all.

Definitely not the woman I'd been staring at all morning.

"The ship is getting ready to pass through its next warp point, Captain," Orion called out. "All navigation targets are on track."

"Perfect." His comment was a welcome distraction. It quickly had me barking out orders to the rest of the crew. We were almost there. And then the actual part of the mission would begin.

Exploring the unknown.

I had to focus on that, and not the girl I couldn't get out of my mind. This was too important.

SOMEHOW, it felt like my body had developed a honing beacon to Aurelia Callisto's current location. That was the only reason we kept ending up in the same places, day after day. It had to be.

Even though it no longer felt like a burden. Now, I was intrigued. I wanted to get to know her better.

The mess hall was quiet—mostly on account of it being an

off-time for meals, and she was sitting alone at a table, slowly picking at her food.

Part of me knew I should have walked away. I was already spending enough time with her, agreeing to help her with this asinine task. Having her in my room alone was bad enough. Adding to that seemed like adding fuel to the fire.

Still, I couldn't stop my feet. Clearing my throat, I got Aurelia's attention, and then gestured to the place across the table from her. "Can I sit?"

She gave me a brief nod, her fork pushing food across her plate as I sat down, placing my tray on the table. Dropping the utensil, she exhaled and then said, "Hi."

The corner of my lip tilted up in a smirk. "Hey."

"I didn't expect to see you here, sorry." She waved her hand.

"You don't have to apologize for that." I frowned, hating that she was always apologizing to me. Did she truly think I was so horrible? "Is everything okay?"

Aurelia looked over her shoulder, glancing around before turning back to me. "Yes. Of course. I just—" She sighed. "I feel like I'm not getting anywhere. Like I'm failing my dad. I just…"

"You're not." I reassured her immediately. "You've already gotten farther than any federation member who had this information."

I couldn't believe they'd sat on it for over twelve years and found *nothing*. They'd declared the ship as destroyed, and the crew dead, but other than that… No one had ever seen the wreckage. Never found out what happened. And that was the thing about me. Once I was curious about something, I couldn't let it go.

I was damn curious about this.

And about Aurelia Callisto.

"I guess that's true. I just…" A groan slipped from her lips, and she rested her head against the table. "I don't know what it's like to fail. I've always excelled at everything. No matter what I did, it made sense to me. It came easily. This is…"

"A whole new ballgame," I said, nodding. "That's why you have to bring in the experts. New coaches."

She laughed, the motion making her eyes crinkle at the corner. "Is that what we're doing? You're my new coach?"

"Well, you are looking at a man who graduated with a computer science degree. If there's anything on there, I can find it."

A strange expression formed over her face, and I knit my brows together. "What? What is it?"

"I guess I just… Didn't think about that. You having something you were good at."

"Okay, *ouch*."

"That's not what I meant. It's just… You're the *Captain*. You tell everyone else what to do. It's strange to imagine you underneath a piece of machinery, trying to fix it. Or redoing a piece of code so a program could run. I don't know." She giggled.

"I think everyone should experience what it's like, you know? To understand the struggle of every crew member. Hard work is important to me. So is humility."

A snort left her mouth, and I glared at her. "Sorry. It's just you and *humble* don't belong in the same sentence."

I crossed my arms over my chest, glaring at her. "You don't even know me." Not really. She only knew the man I presented to the rest of the crew. And maybe that was my mistake.

"No," she agreed, resting her elbows on the table and placing her head in her hands. "But I think I'd like to." Aurelia fluttered her eyelashes. "Right now, you're one big mystery."

I hummed in response. It was easy to forget that while I had her file, every piece of information stored in the federation's system about her, she didn't have mine. "What do you want to know?"

She leaned close, staring at my face for a moment. "Why are you doing this?" Aurelia murmured, low enough that no one else around could overhear us. "Helping me?"

"Am I not allowed to do something nice for you?" I quirked an eyebrow.

She snorted, giving me an eye roll. "You know what I mean."

That was the question of the hour, wasn't it? Why did I want to help her? Was it those enchanting eyes that had me under their spell since the first moment I'd set mine on her? Was it the stubborn determination in her face, the way she wouldn't give up?

Or was it something else entirely? Something I shouldn't be feeling.

Her captain. That's what I was. Nothing more. And I couldn't be anything more.

I sighed. My actual reasoning felt too personal. So as much as I wanted to share it now, it wasn't the time. I rubbed at my face. "Because someone helped me when I needed it, and I want to return the favor now." It was as much as I could offer.

She dipped her head in response.

"Why Captain?" She leaned back in her chair, satisfied that she could now interrogate me freely.

I shrugged. "It wasn't my original goal, but once I joined the federation and started rising through the ranks, I quickly set my sights on getting my own ship."

Some of my mentors called me obstinate, uncompromising. They assumed that I didn't like to take orders. I might have been headstrong, especially in my youth, but I didn't mind being told what to do. As long as those orders made sense. Sometimes people got so stuck behind red tape that they never took risks— never took a chance at actually living. I didn't want to operate like that.

But have you *really been living?* Some part of my brain pestered me, and I didn't have a response. Maybe having more responsibility made me see things differently. Because now, I wasn't just the Captain of a starship. I was also the one entrusted with the safety of every passenger aboard.

"And you did it. Youngest captain in the fleet."

"I did." I nodded. "When they told me she was mine, I…" I shook my head. "I didn't believe them. Thought they were pulling my leg. Maybe some sort of ritual. But no. They really entrusted me with a multi-billion credit project." I swallowed roughly. Honestly, I tried not to think too much about that. About how much rested on my shoulders.

If I did, the weight would be overbearing.

She asked me more questions about my life. Growing up with Kayle. What kinds of things I liked. I answered as honestly as possible, not wanting to dump my personal problems on her. But I shared with her my favorite sports. That I'd once stayed up all night in college trying to beat my personal best on a video game. How I'd learned to code, and realized I was good at it. I didn't tell her about the only reason I'd been able to go to college. How every year before that had been a struggle to survive.

I was dying to ask her my own questions, but this was for her. And I hoped there would be time for that in the future.

"It's getting late," I said, looking up at the clock. We'd spent two hours sitting here, and the mess hall was essentially empty now. Our empty trays sat in front of us, food long since finished.

"I should get back to my cabin," she said, her voice quiet. Like maybe… she didn't want to go, as much as I didn't want this to end.

"I'll walk you back," I offered. It was the gentlemanly thing to do, even if it was secretly selfish.

"You don't have to do that."

"I don't," I agreed. "But I want to. So let me."

"Okay." The word was a concession, but I didn't miss the way her lip tugged up into an almost smile.

We walked in a comfortable silence from the mess hall to the turbo lifts, taking the short ride back to the officer's floor.

She turned to face me as we reached her door. "Thank you. For tonight. For… answering my questions. I appreciate it."

"Of course. I'll always tell you whatever you want to know." That was a promise.

Aurelia stepped closer to me, close enough that I could feel her body heat. The top of her boots pressed against mine, and all I wanted to do was to eliminate those last few inches between us.

Her eyes dipped to my lips and then flickered back up to my eyes. It was impossible not to do the same to her. They were the most beautiful shade of pink, and I wondered if they were as soft as they looked. How she'd taste. Sweet, like the drinks she always seemed to sip on?

I reached out, cupping her cheek with my hand. Running my thumb over her cheekbone. *Touching her.* She was like forbidden fruit, and I wanted to take a bite.

"Aurelia…" I murmured, tracing a finger over her lips.

I wanted to kiss her so badly. *Fuck,* but it was wrong, and yet… there was no denying this attraction between us. That she yearned to be kissed as much as I longed to kiss her.

But we shouldn't. We *couldn't.*

"Captain…" she said only, her voice husky, more breath than anything else.

"Don't look at me like that."

"Like what?" Aurelia fluttered her eyelashes.

"Like you want me to kiss you."

She bit her lip, slowly letting the pink lush skin run through her teeth. "Goodnight, Captain."

"Goodnight," I finally responded.

The door closed behind her, and I knew no matter what I did, I'd never be able to get the sight of her out of my mind.

FIFTEEN
AURELIA

THE OBSERVATION DECK was empty when I opened the door, slipping inside to stare at the stars unfolding around me. Leaning against the metal railing, I let myself get lost in the swirling colors of the galaxies as a small smile curved over my lips. What was out there? How many things would we uncover? I'd always loved asking those questions to my dad. Speculating, dreaming—imagining worlds so vastly different and unlike our own.

"Do you think I'm doing the right thing?" I asked, out loud, knowing that he couldn't hear me. But wishing I could talk to my dad, anyway. "Or was coming onto this ship a mistake?" I shut my eyes, trying to imagine his response. I could barely even remember the sound of his voice anymore. Even the memories were slipping away from me, one by one.

Would he be proud of me? For looking for him? For trying to find out what happened to his ship? I hoped so. I liked to believe he was here with me. That ever since I'd set foot on the space station, I'd been closer to him. A single tear dripped down my cheek.

I'd carry him in my heart, always.

"For what it's worth, I think you are," Sylas's deep voice

rocked me out of my moment of introspection. He cleared his throat. "Doing the right thing, I mean."

I reached up to wipe away the wetness from my face before turning around to face him. "How long have you been there?" I asked. "I didn't hear you come in."

"You looked like you were lost in thought. I didn't want to interrupt."

I hummed in response, turning back to the stars. "I was."

"About?"

Everything. "My dad, mostly. If this was the right decision."

He joined me, leaning onto the railing next to me. "Maybe the better question is, if you weren't here, what would you be doing? Would you be happy?"

I instantly knew the answer to that. "No. I'd have always wondered *what if.* What if I'd gone? What if I'd found—" I shook my head. I couldn't let myself hope. Not for that. I cleared my throat. "It's only been a few weeks, but I already love this ship. It feels like it could be home, you know."

"I'm beginning to think I do," he said, but when I looked over, his eyes weren't staring outside. They were on me. "It's a good crew."

"The best," I agreed. They'd become like my family. Even the guys, who I'd spent more time with lately, made this ship feel less like a job and more like fun.

Sylas included. Last night, talking over dinner had been different. Sure, he'd offered to help me, but this felt like the first time he really opened up to me. And he was patient, letting me ask as many questions as I wanted without trying to ask anything back. And I could see in his eyes that he wanted more.

But everything was changing, and I didn't know how to feel about that.

I didn't know how to feel about last night.

If he'd asked me if he could kiss me, I knew I would have said yes.

Without thinking, I would have let him. Because when I

stared up at him—at that handsome face, the chiseled jaw covered in stubble, those deep blue eyes that reminded me of the ocean in California, I lost all rational thought.

Maybe it was a proximity thing. That I'd been spending so much time with him, late in the evening, as we poured over maps and data files stored on that hard drive. I could blame it on that, surely? That and my lack of orgasms lately. With flight school and everything, I hadn't had a regular partner in awhile, and my body seemed to know that.

Yeah, I could blame this attraction on that. It was just *need*. Nothing more. It would happen to anyone.

Except I knew, deep down, that it was just him. The way he carried himself. The way he kept finding ways to spend time with me. It was all confusing my heart.

I needed to remind myself why I couldn't stand him. How he'd tried to fire me.

"Lieutenant..." His voice was rough.

The doors to the observation deck opened, causing us to spring apart. It was just a member of the crew, who quickly left when he saw us standing together at the railing.

"I found something," I said, changing the subject. I needed *something* to distract myself from his face. "It's a solid lead, I think."

The trackers I'd installed to monitor the dataset I'd received had pinged last night, when we'd reached our current system. It meant I was getting closer. It also meant I needed to put the next phase of my plan into action. But would he go along with it?

I explained to him what I'd found. "What do you think?" I asked, hoping he couldn't see the hope in my eyes.

His eyes roamed over my face. "Hmm." Sylas seemed to ponder it for a moment. "I'll have to look at it."

Last night, we'd parted ways because I'd known exactly what would happen if we were in a room alone together. So I hadn't invited him inside. He was my *captain*, for fuck's sake. If everyone found out that we were *fucking...* I winced at the idea.

125

Though I had to admit the idea of sleeping with him—just once, to get it out of my system—was appealing.

He stepped closer to me, and I let my eyes wander down his body, a blatant perusal.

"Captain, I—" I opened my mouth, but he shook his head, stepping closer.

He was so close that I could feel his body heat through my flight suit, his head angling down towards mine. Could he see the heat in my eyes? The desire burning deep within me?

"What am I going to do with you?" Sylas murmured the words, and a shiver ran down my spine. He reached out, his finger tracing over the angles of my face.

Yes, I could blame it on the proximity, but I knew no one else could affect me the way he did. I needed barriers. Without walls to keep my heart safe, to keep me protected, I'd fall. And I couldn't let myself do that.

I crossed my arms over my chest as his body leered over mine. "I thought you couldn't stand me, Captain. That you didn't like me."

"Maybe…" he muttered, curling his finger around a single strand of my hair. "Maybe I just can't stay away from you."

"That still doesn't solve our problem," I said, shaking my head. Wishing I could pull away, not long for his embrace.

"Doesn't it?"

"*No.*"

But then why were my hands clutching onto his collar?

My eyes fluttered, wondering if this was it. Every part of my body cried out, begging for him to kiss me. To know how those lips felt against mine. To know what it tasted like when Sylas Kellar smiled. I wanted all of it.

I really wasn't picky about what order it came in.

"*Aurelia,*" he murmured, tilting up my chin to bring our faces level.

"Sylas," I whispered, wanting so badly to know what his name tasted like on my lips. *Needing it.* It was better than I could have imagined, especially the way his eyes sparkled. "The other night in your room…"

"Mhm?" A hint of mischief shone through his expression.

"Did you want to kiss me?"

He groaned. "More than anything."

"And yesterday, if I'd have said yes…"

"*Yes.*"

I smirked. *Fuck it.* I didn't care anymore. Not about the consequences. Not when he was looking at me like that.

"Then why haven't you kissed me yet, Captain?"

He growled, pinning me in place against the railing.

Sylas's hand wrapped around my neck, and before I could taunt him again, he pulled my body against his. There was hardly an inch between us, and then his lips were on mine.

And holy shit—Sylas Kellar was *kissing me.* It was like a lightning bolt to my system. It wasn't a soft kiss. No. It was the result of weeks of build-up, of longing looks and lingering glances. Of every time our eyes had dipped down, eyes drawn to the other's lips. His were warm and soft and oh-so-kissable.

It was only him and I, in our own little bubble as he coaxed my mouth open, not even coming up for air. I clutched onto the railing behind me to keep myself upright, feeling my knees buckling from the heat of his embrace.

Who was this man who had lost all self control? Anyone could see us. Anyone could walk in right now and find me pressed up against the glass by Sylas's body. There was no mistaking what we were doing in this compromising position, and yet—I wanted more.

My hands wrapped around his neck, fingers curling into the hair at the nape as I let him devour me. His tongue slipped into my mouth, and I barely gasped before I was giving it back, matching him breath for breath. Inhaling him like he was the air I needed to breathe.

Tightening my grasp, I pulled him down deeper into me.

Relished in the groan he let out into my mouth as his tongue lazily swept over mine.

We kissed like we were starved. Like it was the first and last. Which was a damn shame, because my captain knew how to *kiss*.

It made me wonder, if he was this good at kissing, what else would he excel at?

My cheeks were warm at the sudden onslaught of thoughts, but I couldn't stop my spiral. Not when every bit of his hardness was pressed against my soft body, and I moaned—

He pulled away, his hand cupping my face, fingers brushing through my hair. "Fuck." Sylas's breathing was rough.

I ran my fingers over my lips. "Wow."

"You're…" He shook his head.

I expected him to say it was a mistake. That we shouldn't have just done that. But when I looked up into those deep, ocean blue eyes, all I saw was hunger.

"Aurelia, I…"

"Kiss me again," I murmured. "I don't want to think anymore. Not about this. Not about…"

He brought our lips together again before I could finish that thought. And then he was lifting me up, my legs wrapping around his waist, my back pressed against the glass.

Fuck, yes. I let my mouth say everything words couldn't. He sucked my tongue into his mouth, and I ground down against him, feeling his hardness press against me. Gasping at the feeling, I clutched at him tighter.

"*More,*" I begged as he pulled away. "I need—"

He swallowed roughly. "We shouldn't—"

Placing my pointer finger over his lips, I shook my head. I didn't want him to finish that sentence. Not if what came at the end of it was rejection.

"Don't tell me this is a mistake," I whispered. "I can't…"

"I know." Sylas smoothed my hair back before setting me back down on my feet softly. "I know."

He pecked my lips again, pulling back, breathing rough. I leaned my forehead against his chest, unsure if it was possible to calm my racing heart.

But what did he know? That I would give up everything I'd worked for, just for one night? How I would have let him fuck me right here, on the observation deck, without a care in the world for if someone came in and found us?

Because I'd let lust cloud my system. Put my own needs in front of my mission. My goal. And I couldn't do that. Not again.

I groaned into my hands as he kissed the crown of my head and then walked away without another word.

What had I just done?

SIXTEEN
SYLAS

I GROANED, thinking about taking her mouth with mine. How good it felt. How she'd buried her fingers in my hair and kissed me back just as passionately.

We *both* wanted it, and fuck, if that wasn't enough to have me half-hard.

Sylas. I imagined her moaning my name, and I couldn't resist wrapping my fist around my dick as the warm water sprayed over me. How it would feel, having her underneath me. Burying myself in between her thighs, making her come with my tongue, my fingers, my cock.

Getting myself off to thoughts of her should feel wrong. Because it *was* wrong. She was off limits. Forbidden.

Don't tell me this is a mistake, she'd all but begged. Even though we both knew it would have been.

But I couldn't help myself. Not anymore. Not after knowing what her mouth tasted like, knowing what her little mewls of pleasure sounded like. I wanted more. Wanted to acquaint myself with every inch of her body.

Captain. In my imagination, she batted her eyelashes as she took me into her hand, swirling her tongue over the tip. Those eyes never left mine as she licked and sucked and *squeezed*.

"*Fuuuckk,*" I grunted, the vision too good to hold back. All it took was imagining burying my cock in her tight, wet heat, and I was coming, ropes of thick cum splashing on the tile wall of my large, walk-in shower.

My fist pounded against the tile wall. *What the fuck was wrong with me?* Jerking off to thoughts of my pilot? I grit my teeth, trying to hold my thoughts back.

If the federation got wind of anything happening between us, I'd be fired. There was no way they'd want to keep a captain on who had slept with one of his officers. It violated our contract, the code of ethics we'd agreed to when we'd sworn into the federation at graduation.

But was that what this was? Or was it something deeper, unexplainable?

What if? I wondered.

What if we gave into the temptation?

What if she wanted me the way I wanted her? I was pretty sure she did. The way she ground her pussy over my aching cock, her little gasp—she would have let me fuck her right there on that deck.

And it would have been a mistake.

Because that wasn't what she deserved.

No. I watched my release circle down the drain, letting my hand rest over my heart. It wouldn't be some cheap hookup, a mindless fling. Not with her.

And maybe that was what had me taking a pause. Because it was obvious that whoever Aurelia Callisto ended up with was one lucky son-of-a-bitch.

Even more so, because I knew it wouldn't be me.

Whoever she chose would put a ring on that finger and seal the deal before she could flutter away. Give her everything she ever wanted, and more.

A house, a life. Kids, if she wanted that.

And from me… I shook my head. I couldn't give her any of that.

All that was in my future was loneliness, and I'd have to learn to be okay with it.

A KNOCK SOUNDED on the door, and I looked up from where I sat in my small recliner chair, a pair of reading glasses on my face as I thumbed through one of my favorite novels.

Not that it could keep my attention. I'd been distracted all day with thoughts of her. And we still hadn't even talked about our kiss.

That kiss. *Fuck.* It had left me undone.

Leaving the book and glasses on the side table, I padded over to the doorway, pressing onto the pad to slide the automatic door open.

It was like I'd summoned her. *Lovely.* She hadn't been on the bridge earlier, which, at the time, I'd been grateful for. I still felt guilty after my... activities this morning in the shower. But it wasn't like I could apologize for it, could I?

I said nothing. Because I couldn't stop myself from staring at the beauty at the entrance to my room. Finally, I cleared my throat, but she beat me to it.

"Captain." Aurelia's voice was low as she brushed past me, coming into my room. "My lead from yesterday, well... There's something else."

Her scent filled my lungs as she brushed past me. A combination of something sweet and... *violets?* That must have been her body wash, or her perfume. Whatever it was, it was intoxicating. The smell that lingered with me, even long after she was gone each day.

Clearly, we weren't going to talk about the kiss. Fine by me. If we did, I wouldn't be able to think about anything but doing it again.

I shoved my hands into my pants pockets to avoid touching her. "There is?" Blinking, our conversation from yesterday came back to me. *Right.*

She nodded, plugging her tablet into my display, letting something load onto the large screen.

"You know, I've been working on tracking for any sign of my dad's ship. And I found something on this planet. Well, two things, really." She got all the words out in a rush, like she couldn't even pause for breath.

"Slow down." I sat on the couch, looking with rapt interest. "What did you find?"

"Look," Aurelia said, pointing at the thermal imaging scans of the moon of a large gas planet. "There's something down there."

I squinted, watching the little shapes move. *Damn*, she was right. "Aurelia—" I said, hesitating. This was an incredible discovery, but… "You don't know what that is."

"But it's *something*. We should go check it out." She crossed her arms over her chest, a stubborn pout on her face.

"Or it could be dangerous, and I could be sending you down to a suicide mission."

"But—"

I stood my ground. She might hate me for this, but I'd never forgive myself if something happened to her. "We should send the team. Finley and the researchers have been training their whole life for this."

"But…" she repeated, her mouth formed into a solid frown now. "It's down *there*. The tracking signal. That's the other thing. If I could just go down and find it—"

I fixed a glare on her. "No. Absolutely not. It's not safe," I repeated, pointing at the moving things. Some sort of alien creature, I assumed, though I had no idea of what variety.

"Dangerous? Look at them. How big do you think they are? It's not like they're lion sized or something crazy."

We had no reports of this planet. Surely, at the edge of

explored space, someone had found these before. If her dad's ship had flown this path, why hadn't they found something? Though, maybe our scanners had advanced that much more in the last dozen years. Either way... I rubbed at my beard. "Something's strange here."

"See!" Aurelia exclaimed, a proud nod. "That's what I think, too."

"But... I still think we should wait. We'll be close enough to it we can send them down tomorrow, and then—"

"This is my *only* opportunity. And you want me to *give* up on it so you can send a team down first?"

I winced at her tone. Had I given her so little reason to trust me? "You're not giving up on it. I'm just asking you to give me an extra day or two." Crossing my arms over my chest, I scowled at her. "It's proper protocol. You know, those procedures you *love* so much? I'm trying to follow those."

Damn, I was a hard-ass. But couldn't she see it was for her safety? She was impulsive, stubborn, and had a personal stake in this. If this was a federal investigation, she'd be taken off of the case entirely for being emotionally involved.

"They'll find it, and whatever is on there, I won't even have a chance." She sounded defeated.

I stepped up behind her, wanting to wrap my arms around her and comfort her, but how could I? All I needed her to do was to see reason. "I won't let them do that. Not to you."

She whirled on me. There was anger in her eyes, but it burned out quickly. "I let you *in*," she whispered, her eyes full of hurt.

"Aurelia—" I said, not knowing what to say.

"I didn't ask for your help. You volunteered. You..." A choked sob slipped from her lips. "I can't do this. I can't be here. I have to go."

Don't go was what I wanted to say. What I should have said. Instead, I just reached for her hand. But she slipped from my grasp, heading out into the hallway alone.

And I let her go.

Even though I had a damn good idea exactly where she was heading.

SEVENTEEN
AURELIA

THIS WAS IT. My golden opportunity. I couldn't pass it up, even if Sylas thought it was too dangerous. Maybe he was right —that I was being reckless. There was a chance that nothing was down there. But what if there was something?

Something was down there. Besides just the heat signatures, the signal that my device had picked up was definitely man-made. Human made. Which meant that maybe, just maybe… it had come from my dad's ship. A long shot, probably.

But not one worth giving up on, even if I had to do it alone.

Sylas would understand, right? That I needed to do this. Why I needed to go alone. Finding my dad was my mission, my purpose, and I didn't need to involve the ship or the crew any more than I already had.

I'd already pulled on my flight suit and boots, and the supplies I'd borrowed were stashed in a pack under my bed, which meant all I needed was a portable breathing unit. It was the only hesitation I had.

For all I could tell, the planet shared a similar composition to earth, though the surface was much rockier. But was the atmosphere identical—breathable? If I couldn't breathe on the planet's surface, I'd be limited to the oxygen tank in the specially designed helmet, which meant I'd have a lot less time to survey and track down the signal before I had to head back to the ship.

Hopefully, I wouldn't be gone for too long. I tried not to worry too much about how I'd explain all of this to my fellow officers. Where did I even begin? I'd been keeping this from them for so long that now it felt like I was barely keeping myself afloat.

I closed the door shut to the transport shuttle, breathing a sigh of relief at not getting caught as I moved to the console, powering it up. Hopefully, I could get to the signal and back and inspect it before anyone even noticed I was missing.

The display lit up as the lights flickered all around me, and I flipped a few more switches before sliding into the pilot's chair. *I could do this.* Closing my eyes, I pictured my dad's face. He would probably think I was being reckless. And the truth was—I *was.* This was insane. But the flashing coordinates on my data pad were *there,* close enough to almost be within reach, and I couldn't let this opportunity pass me by.

"Lieutenant." The voice startled me out of my thoughts. The deep, growly voice that I heard in my dreams. The one I'd begged to kiss me. "What do you think you're doing?" I shivered, his breath brushing against my neck.

"Captain, I—" I didn't turn around. I couldn't. How could I look at him? Knowing I'd taken advantage of his trust, the way I was starting to care for him—it was all too much.

And so was the way I couldn't stop thinking about that kiss.

My data-pad beeped again, and then it was wrenched from my hands.

"What is this?" He spun the chair around, the motion bringing his face within inches with mine.

I didn't answer, worrying my lower lip in between my teeth.

His face was furious. If I'd thought he looked grumpy before, well... I'd never seen him so serious. He'd pulled on his own flight suit, and his dark hair was combed back. *Hot.* Even angry, he was the most attractive man I'd ever seen. It was almost unfair, really, how gorgeous he was, like he didn't even have to try.

Though if he was ready, and as prepared as I was, maybe I hadn't been as sneaky as I thought.

"I'm going down there," I said, jutting out my chin.

"No." Sylas grit his teeth. "Absolutely not. I told you, we don't even know if it's safe. Let Finley or one of the other researchers—"

It was the same argument we'd been having. To let them go down first. Explore the surface. Bring back samples, and then we could go down with a larger group. But I couldn't risk that.

"I have to do this. Me."

He rubbed at the crease in his brow. "Fuck, Rae. You're the most stubborn person I've ever met."

"I hope you looked in the mirror," I said, smirking at my little quip.

He just glared at me. "I can't talk you out of this?"

"No."

"Fine." He plopped in the seat next to me, crossing his arms over his chest. "Then I'm going with you. I can't let you go alone."

A frown formed on my face. "I can do this without you. I don't need to be babysat."

Sylas cursed under his breath, taking my face in between his hands. "Is that what you think, Aurelia? That I'm *babysitting* you? Or that I don't trust you?"

My eyes darted away from his. "Yes," I said, my voice a low whisper.

"Fuck." When I finally looked at him again, his gaze was fixed on my lips. "How can I get you to get this through your head, little star?"

"What?" I asked, feeling a little dizzy. *Breathless.* And it wasn't even from the lack of oxygen yet, because we were still fully enclosed in the ship's air system.

"When I kissed you, did it feel like I did it out of pity? Or some sense of duty?"

"No."

His thumb brushed over my cheekbone. "Then why can't you believe that I'd be here because I want to be? That I want to make sure you're safe, too?"

"But your job…" I swallowed roughly. "Your duty is to the officers of this ship. Not just me. You're the captain. You can't just leave."

"Kayle's perfectly capable of running the ship for a few hours while we're gone. I trust her."

But he didn't trust me. Not really. Because if he had, he would have been on board with my plan from the beginning.

"Okay." I whispered the word. Trying to ignore the fact that he was still cupping my face. Looking at me like I was *precious*.

Like he wanted to kiss me again.

"We should…" I tilted my head towards the console to point to the ship. *Go.* We needed to go. Otherwise, I'd want to kiss him, and that was a mistake I couldn't let happen.

Not when everything I'd been working towards was on the line.

"Right." He pulled his hands away, strapping himself in to the seat. "Let's take her out, then."

It was strange to see him here, sitting like he was my partner, not my superior.

On the *Paradise,* I never could have imagined him on one of these tiny ships. There was only enough space in them for a small crew, and Sylas took up much of that room with his enormous frame, and those broad shoulders I'd dreamed about running my hands all over. When we'd kissed, I'd felt those muscles under my skin.

A shiver ran through me.

"You good?" Sylas asked, clearly not understanding the thoughts running through my brain. Which was good. He didn't need to know what I was thinking. How much I'd enjoyed that kiss.

How much I wanted to do it again.

Warmth blossomed to my face as I nodded, wishing my hair was down to hide my face, instead of up in its usual bun.

Familiarity and routine had always grounded me. It made me feel safe, the repetitiveness of my schedule keeping my anxiety at bay.

I was throwing all of that out the window now. In a way, I'd left it all behind the moment I'd stepped foot on the ship to the space station. And again, when I'd boarded the S.S. Paradise.

Goodbye, familiar life.

Hello, alien planet.

I'D FLOWN these smaller crafts thousands of times during simulations, but it was different having the real one underhand. Because before, there was always a small part of me that knew it was a game. That if I crashed into something, it wasn't game over. I wouldn't be damaging millions of credits of government or federation property.

Now, though? I felt all that pressure. This wasn't a simulation. I really was flying through space, opening the airlock and leaving the safety of the starship behind.

"What are you waiting for?" Sylas asked, an eyebrow raised when he looked over at me.

"This is just…" I let out a breath of air as the ship's docking bay closed behind me. "Surreal." A smile slipped onto my face. How could it not? "I'm flying a ship in space right now."

"What would you call what you've been doing the last two months?"

I wrinkled my nose. "That's different, and you know it."

A snort left Sylas's nose. "Sure, okay."

Flipping the switches and pressing the required buttons on the dash, I slipped my hands into the steering mechanism.

Just like riding a hover bike, Aurelia. Except that crashing a hover bike meant you'd end up with a scraped knee and a disappointed parent. Crashing a ship like this? I didn't want to think about it.

"Nice and steady," Sylas murmured, pressing buttons on his side of the ship as well, easily slipping into the navigator role. "Where are you planning on landing?"

The planet's moon stretched out in front of us, and I pointed at the dot on the screen. I'd already loaded the coordinates in from my data pad. They were also programmed onto my communicator, since that was more portable for carrying around. "This is where the sensor pinged. I was thinking of setting down a few kilometers away, since the ground doesn't look too stable. Then we can walk on foot."

"And the heat signatures?"

I let out a breath. Talking was good. Did he realize he was helping to ease my anxiety? Maybe that was why he was asking me these questions. Maybe he knew me better than I'd thought.

"They're small, but scattered along the surface. There seems to be a high concentration of them here—" I pointed to a spot on the map as I flew the ship towards my intended area. "But I'm not sure if it's more than one species or what they are, even."

"What do you think they're surrounding?"

It probably would have been helpful to have Finley here, but I knew my way around reading geographical maps.

"It seems like water."

"What?" He looked over at me, surprised.

"I know it's crazy. This planet seems habitable. And considering the last location of my dad's ship, I can't help but wonder…" But hope was painful. I couldn't let myself think that way. I shook my head.

Sylas reached over, placing a hand on my arm. "If there's anything here, we'll find it."

"Thank you. For everything. You didn't have to offer to help me, and you certainly didn't have to—" I didn't have time to finish my statement, though, because the display flashed with warning lights.

"Shit." My eyes flashed to his.

"I thought you knew what you were doing, flying this thing?"

"I did. I mean, I do. It's just… I've never flown one outside of simulations. And maybe I calculated something wrong with the atmosphere of this planet. We're coming in too fast." My eyes flashed to Sylas, a look of worry spread across his chiseled face. "We have to slow down."

"How?"

I shook my head. "Do you know what happened to space-ships back in the twenty-first century? Assuming they'd make it into space in the first place?"

He brushed his fingers over his trimmed beard, a line forming on his face. "Yes. They'd burn up upon reentry."

"Exactly." I tried to ease off the throttle, but it was no use.

"So slow us down."

I hummed. "Great plan. Except, I can't."

"What do you mean?"

It felt like my heart was in my throat. "If I don't slow us down, we're going to overheat. These engines won't be able to take it."

"Aurelia." Sylas's voice was rough. "You can't mean—"

"I know it's crazy. Yes, there's a chance it won't work." A forced laugh escaped my lips, a feeble attempt to ease the pressure weighing on my chest. It didn't. "But I have to try."

There was a large cluster of boulders—though they were so big that classification barely applied. I pointed at them. "There."

"You're insane."

"Probably." I shrugged. "If I hit them at the right angle, it should slow us down without destroying the ship. Hopefully."

My captain groaned. "My life is flashing before my eyes."

I could only hope that wasn't the truth.

That what I was about to do wasn't going to get us both killed.

EIGHTEEN
SYLAS

"WELL, THAT WAS..." I surveyed the damage, wincing at the state of the small ship. We'd pulled on the helmets to keep us safe outside, especially since I didn't trust the air here yet. Something still felt strange about this place.

Luckily, the engine was still intact, and though it was pretty crunched up, the damage to the transport vehicle was mostly cosmetic. At least from what I could see. She was the one with the engineering background, not me. There were a few places where the rocks had punctured the outer hull of the ship, but it could have been much worse.

"If you'd let me have the team check this place out first, none of this would have happened. We wouldn't be stranded here until we figured out a way back." I wrung my hands, staring out at the unfamiliar landscape.

"Or they would have had the same thing happen, and they wouldn't have been able to re-maneuver the ship."

I gave a sigh of exasperation, pacing away from the ship a few paces while Aurelia tinkered with her technology.

The planet's surface was exceptionally rocky, covered in dark black stones that looked like lava rocks. Had there once been active volcanoes on the surface? I could only wonder about the environmental development of it. Until our researchers were down here, wondering was all I could do.

What would we need to survive on this planet? I'd need to grab some equipment from the ship before we set out in search of whatever Aurelia thought was down here. Making a mental list in my mind, I turned around to find Aurelia with her helmet off, ponytail whipping around her. She must have redone her hair while I was surveying the land, because it was up in a bun before.

"Air's breathable. I checked with the machine." She used her thumb to point behind us. "It's not quite the makeup of oxygen on earth, but the levels are compatible with human life."

Oh. So that's what she'd been doing. "Great." I took my helmet off, holding it in the crook of my arm. "This place isn't what I expected." I'd been on plenty of other planets before— Mars, for starters, visiting the colony there—but each had their own unique set of challenges.

This unnamed planet in the hardly traversed edge of the universe was completely unlike those. And that didn't even include the thermal signatures we'd captured from the ship.

She winced, rubbing at her neck as she looked at the ship, then to the sky. "So much for getting back easily."

Understatement of the century. I kicked a piece of metal that had fallen off the ship.

"Fuck, Aurelia. This was so reckless. Do you even realize how dangerous this was?"

She whirled on me, her eyebrows narrowing on me. "What was I supposed to do?"

"Wait for me!" I exclaimed, throwing my hands up in the air. "We were supposed to be working on this together. How can we be a team if you're just doing stuff on your own, not consulting me?"

"It's *my* dad!" Aurelia yelled back. "I had to do something. I couldn't just sit there and wait. Not when this was my only opportunity."

I couldn't dispute that. However… "You should have let me fly it."

Aurelia stepped up to meet me, toe to toe, even though she had to crane her neck up for her gaze to meet mine. "I'm the pilot. This is my responsibility."

"And I'm your Captain. You're *my* responsibility. So is making sure you don't get hurt."

She rolled her eyes, crossing her arms over her chest. "So I am your duty."

"That is *not* what I said." I growled out the words. Dammit, how did she not know this by now? I didn't think of her like that. In fact, I thought of her in ways I shouldn't. Highly inappropriate. Forbidden. She was off-limits, but ever since that kiss, it was all I could think about.

"Aurelia—" My voice was rough.

She frowned, staring down at the communication device in her hand. "I can't get a message out to the ship. *Shit.* Our comms are down."

"Great." I rubbed at my forehead, muttering under my breath. "This was a terrible idea." I should have shut the whole thing down the moment I realized what she was doing.

Instead, one look at her, and I caved. Ever since I first set eyes on her, it had been like this. Something about those eyes, and that I couldn't stand seeing her upset.

Which was why we were here now.

She ignored my comment, looking up at me with those big, captivating eyes. It was like all the fight had melted out of her. "How long do you think it will take them to realize we're missing?"

"Considering it's the middle of the night on the ship, and we're supposed to be in our quarters, *sleeping*, it'll be a few hours until anyone even realizes we're gone." No one would report to the bridge until 0600, and by the time they discovered the shuttle was missing, they'd have to turn around and come back. "Hopefully, the whole damn tracking system isn't messed up."

She gnawed on her lower lip, not saying anything. "I'm going to go check on our supplies. Maybe there's something we're missing," Aurelia mused. "Should we explore?"

I frowned. "Maybe it would be safer in the morning. It's going to get dark soon."

She waved me off. "It'll be fine. Besides, we can just come back to the ship when it is, right?" Aurelia fidgeted with her hands, rocking on the balls of her feet. "I'm too antsy to stay put."

"Fine." I couldn't hold back my chuckle. "Okay. Hand me your communicator."

"What?" She glanced back at me, clutching it to her chest like it was her lifeline.

"I'll lead," I explained. "That way, if there's anything dangerous on this planet, I'll spot it first." Her brows furrowed. Did she really think I didn't trust her? A sigh left my lips. "I trust you. I just want to make sure that you're safe. Can you believe that?"

Aurelia gnawed at her lip, appearing to deliberate my words. "Yes," she finally admitted, dropping the device into my hand. "But you know how much this means to me."

"I do." Tapping on the screen, I looked at the approximate location of the ping before turning back at her. "And I promise you, Aurelia. I'm not going to give up on this." *On you.*

"Okay." She sighed, her posture relaxing. "I believe you."

Good. I hefted the pack onto my shoulders.

Then we headed out into the unknown.

IT FELT like we'd been walking for hours. But maybe that was because the surface of this planet all looked the same. Black rocks, as far as the eye could see. Large formations existed at random intervals, the only sign that we weren't just going in an endless circle.

I couldn't see our ship behind us anymore, and the sky was growing darker. If we weren't careful, we'd be out here at nightfall. I thought about the thermal sensor readings she'd found. Maybe we didn't want to be caught out here unaware at night.

"We should hurry," I muttered. Who knew what sort of beasts were lurking under the surface?

"How far are we from the tracker?" Aurelia asked, reaching over and grabbing it from me.

She walked ahead of me, her eyes glued to the communicator device. She was barely paying attention to the ground.

"Be careful—" I said as her foot connected with a rock, and she went down. I caught her by the arm, my other hand sliding around her waist, and we froze like that.

"Captain," she whispered. Still keeping that barrier between us. I slowly returned her to her feet.

"Are we ever going to talk about it?" I muttered, my hands still on her body.

She swallowed roughly, and her eyes darted to my lips. "About what?"

"The kiss, Aurelia."

She looked away, and I let her slip out of my arms.

Guess that was a *no*. I didn't know why that stung so much.

"Watch where you're walking," I said instead, snapping at her. I knew I was harsher than I should have been, but I was too frustrated to care.

"I know," she muttered back.

If I'd been in front of her, I would have bet every credit to my name that she'd rolled her eyes.

I smirked at the thought. She was a giant ray of sunshine, but with me, she was stubborn as all hell. A brat. Was it bad that I liked how she pushed back against me? Few people had the balls to stand up to me, but this five foot seven spitfire did.

The largest formation of rocks I'd seen on this entire godforsaken place appeared in front of us, almost like a mountain. Huh.

"What do you think?" She asked, turning around. "I think we should go in."

"In?" I leaned down to look at the screen.

"Look. There's a cave." Aurelia pointed at the space in between two of the shiny black rocks.

Well, fuck me. She was right. There was an opening there.

"Maybe we should come back. Explore in the daytime. We could spend the night on the ship."

She turned to look at me, a frown painted over her beautiful face. "We can't give up now. We're *so* close." Aurelia gave me puppy dog eyes, and something clenched in my chest.

"It could be dangerous—"

She fluttered her eyes. "That's why I have you to protect me, Captain."

Pinching the skin between my eyebrows, I gave an exasperated huff. "You're unbelievable."

"And you're *impossible.*"

"Ask me why, Aurelia."

She jutted out her chin, arms crossed over her chest. "No."

I grit my teeth. "Ask. Me. Why."

Why I'd been in knots when she'd left my room. Why I'd thrown on this flight suit and followed her down here. Why I couldn't let her do this alone.

Why I was still thinking about that damn kiss.

Yes, she was unbelievable. But not in the way that she thought I meant.

"I. Don't. Want. To." Aurelia's eyes narrowed.

Fuck, why did she look so hot like that? Her hands propped on her hips, staring me down like *she* was the one with an extra seven inches of height and an additional hundred pounds of muscle, instead of me.

"Stubborn brat." I flicked my tongue across my lower lip.

"And what does that make you?" She poked at my chest. "A grumpy, domineering *asshole?* It's no wonder you're alone."

I was too stunned to say anything.

What sort of weird, fucked up foreplay did I think that was where it felt like we were *flirting?* But she didn't turn around.

Aurelia stormed off into the cave opening, and I let her go, her words hitting a wound in my chest I hadn't even realized were still there.

NINETEEN

AURELIA

"AURELIA!" Sylas's voice called after me again.

But I wasn't listening.

Squaring my shoulders, I kept marching forward. I knew it was irrational—that he was *right*, and I was the one who had endangered us. But he'd agreed to help me, hadn't he?

I couldn't do this right now. Not when he was looking at me like that.

He wanted to talk about the kiss, but I couldn't. Not now. Maybe never. Because the sinking feeling in my gut told me exactly what he was going to say.

I was too young. Too immature. Too reckless.

A mistake. How many times had I heard that? Had I felt that? In past relationships, when I felt like I was a burden, that I was too much, I drifted away. *Self sabotaged*, as my best friends said. Because it was better to leave than be left. Wasn't it?

"The signal is coming from in there," I said, not looking backwards at him. I knew with one look of those piercing blue eyes, I'd fold. And right now, I didn't want to give him what he wanted.

Following the signal to what looked like a cave on a strange moon probably wasn't the *best* idea, but it was the only lead I had. There was no way I was ignoring it.

Sylas stepped up to my side, a large silver flashlight in his hands lighting up.

I blinked. "When did you have time to grab that?"

He adjusted the pack on his back. "When you were busy getting off the ship, I grabbed some supplies, too. I wasn't sure what we would need."

"Oh." I bit my lip. "Thank you. I—" My cheeks felt warm. Hopefully, the darkness of the cave would hide my blush.

"You don't have to thank me. Not for this." His tone gave no room for argument, so I just nodded.

The darkness swallowed us whole as we moved into the cave, the light from the outside quickly becoming only a speck. We had only the light from my communicator, the little red flashing light from the trace, and Sylas's flashlight to see.

"This is eerie," I whispered, my voice echoing back slightly. "What do you think is down there?"

I could feel Sylas step closer to me. Like he was ready to protect me. "I don't know, but hopefully nothing that wants to eat us."

A shiver worked its way down my spine, and I resolved myself to stay optimistic.

"We haven't spotted any creatures yet. I mean, we don't even know that there is any life on this planet. The thermal scans could be wrong." I was pretty sure they weren't, but that was a separate problem.

The walls were narrowing as we followed the caves deeper and deeper, the sound of dripping water echoing from somewhere beyond. When it got to where we could no longer walk side-by-side, I moved in front of him. Thankfully, the light of his flashlight was still shining in front of me, lighting our path.

"Do you think they came here for this?" I asked, my voice a low whisper. "Water is a precious commodity on any planet."

It was something the UGSF had been searching for over the

last thousand years: planets that could sustain life. And if there was water, that was the biggest indicator.

Since the two-thousands, space travel had advanced tremendously. Back then, it used to take eight to nine months to get to Mars. Now, we could fly halfway across the galaxy in the blink of an eye. Technology was incredible, and there was no doubt in my mind that we'd be able to traverse the entire depths of space within the next hundred years.

"They might have. Or there's a chance something happened. But how would they have flown the ship down here?" In the dim light, I could barely make out Sylas shaking his head. "It makes no sense."

"Maybe it's not the ship at all," I said, though I could feel my heart sinking at the thought.

My foot caught on something, and a muscular arm wrapped around my waist. *Again.* Ugh, could he stop doing that?

"Careful," he gritted out into my ear. "The ground isn't stable in here. Hopefully, the whole thing doesn't come down around us."

"Right." If I hadn't been blushing before, I was now. Thanking the stars that he couldn't see my face, I kept going, watching my footing as we climbed through the narrow passageway. The walls opened up, but with the darkness, I missed the drop. I stumbled, my foot catching on a rock and sending me spiraling onto the surface, before finally landing on my hands.

"*Ow,*" I cried out, a sharp pain radiating from my ankle as I rolled over.

When I looked up, Sylas looked, well... he looked pissed. Of course he did. Because I was a *stubborn brat* who had gotten herself hurt. Even after he'd caught me. Twice.

My eyes squeezed shut, embarrassment quickly making its way through my veins. *Dammit.* That hurt. I'd scraped up my hands and elbows too, which stung. How was it possible that I was this clumsy?

"Fuck." His voice was rough. Was he... worried about me?

I'd thought he was angry. "Are you okay?" The concern was evident in his eyes as I looked up at him.

"Yeah. I don't-I don't think it's broken." Wincing, I ran my fingers over my tender skin. "I think I just twisted it." Hopefully, I hadn't sprained it. It wasn't like the shuttle had a medical bay inside of it if it *was* broken. Either way, I'd gone down hard.

"Do you think you can walk?"

I tried to stand, but the weight on my ankle made my legs buckle. "Maybe not." I bit my lip. "You should go back to the shuttle for the night. I'll only slow you down." I tried to give him a smile, but failed. "We can start again tomorrow."

Maybe that made little sense, but nothing really did to my brain right now.

"Aurelia," Sylas practically growled. "I'm not leaving you alone here, for fuck's sake. Get on my back and I'll carry you."

My chin trembled. "You don't have to do that."

"I do."

"Captain—" I shook my head, trying to hold back the tears. *Fuck,* it hurt. Damn rocky planet surface.

"We'll get you back to the ship," he promised, his voice soothing. "Everything's going to be okay. You'll be fine."

I almost laughed, but it came out more like a choked sob. "It's not like I'm *dying* from a busted ankle. Of course I'll be okay."

But our comms were down, we were stuck in a series of caves, and who knew what sort of creatures might exist down here? If the sensors were right, there was life on this planet, which meant there could very well be a strange alien species in this cave. I'd hate if we ended up as a tasty snack.

Even if I'd told him they probably weren't lion size. I wasn't exactly an expert in forensic scans. My advanced engineering degree and pilot's school hadn't focused on biology that much.

He frowned at me, crossing his arms over his chest.

"It's getting dark," I started. "You should go back, in case the

Paradise comes looking for us. If they track the signal of the ship before it crashed—"

"Rae." Sylas's murmur was pained. "I'm not leaving you."

As if in demonstration, he bent down, scooping me up into his arms.

There it was again. *Rae.* I liked the nickname more than I could explain. My friends growing up had often called me Lia, so this one felt special.

Because he gave it to me.

I needed a distraction. Something to rid the warmth lingering in my chest. Maybe I should have gotten on his back instead, because then I wouldn't have his face so close to mine. So focused on me as he continued walking down further. It all felt so intimate. Like there was something more between us.

"You shouldn't even be down here. This is all my fault." He mumbled the words under his breath.

"No," I shook my head. It wasn't his fault that I'd stolen the shuttle and come on an un-sanctioned mission. "It's mine for thinking this was a good idea."

"I should have said no."

Even though I hadn't given him the chance to. He'd practically had to force his way onto the transport as it was. "Captain —" I started to dispute his comment, but he cut me off with the shake of his head.

"*Sylas.*" His voice trembled as his hand cupped my jaw. "Call me my name, just this once."

"Sylas," I whispered, closing my eyes as I let my face rest against his shoulder.

"That's my girl," he said with a slight chuckle.

His girl? Why did I like that so much? My chest warmed, a part of me feeling claimed like I never had before. I'd never been anyone's, other than my own.

Part of me felt like I should have argued that I wasn't his. But at that moment, I didn't particularly care. I wasn't thinking about the kiss, or our argument, or even the pain that was slowly fading.

I let the motion of him carrying me lull me into a warm, drowsy sleep, one where I was unencumbered by the events of the day.

SYLAS SETTING me down in a cavern of glowing rocks was what finally awoke me, and I drowsily yawned, trying to blink the sleep away before I would believe my eyes.

"They're glowing," I said, stating the obvious.

He chuckled. "They are."

"It's wonderful. Beautiful." I'd never seen anything like it. Even when I'd been in caves on earth, I'd never seen one with such magnificent minerals. "What do you think they're made of?"

"A substance we don't have on earth," Sylas observed.

"Thanks, Captain Obvious," I muttered. Then silently high-fived myself, because I should have been using that the whole time.

He was moving around—unpacking, I realized. While we didn't have much, we were way more prepared than I would have been if I'd have set out alone.

"Are we safe in here?" I whispered.

"There's an underground stream not far from here, and hope-fully with the filtration system in the canteen, it's drinkable. But there's only one entrance and exit into this place, so if anything enters, I'll know." His eyes were sharp—detecting.

"Come here," he said, spreading out a blanket on the ground. "Let me look at that foot."

I hobbled over to him, not putting weight on it. Luckily, the distance was minimal, and then I was sitting on the soft blanket,

Sylas kneeling in front of me. He untied the laces of my boot before tugging the shoe off entirely.

The flashlight nestled in between his legs—giving him light —as he removed my sock. I thought about making a joke, but his face was too solemn, too serious, and I still caught a flash of that anger from before.

My ankle was red, and definitely swollen, but I rolled my foot around without too much discomfort. "I'm fine, see?" I said.

He grumbled something under his breath, unzipping his flight suit and shucking the white t-shirt he had on underneath over his head. Tying the sleeves around his waist, he left all of his glorious, bare chest visible in the dim lighting of the cave.

I was too busy ogling his abs to notice him ripping his shirt into strips until I heard the fabric.

"What are you doing?" I gasped. "You need that."

"We need to wrap this up," he responded, all matter-of-fact, before his eyes met mine in a sexy smirk. "You didn't think I was giving you a show for no reason, did you?"

My face was warm as I stared at him, mouth agape. "No. I just—"

His hands lightly massaged my ankle, a frown covering his face as I winced slightly. Slowly—almost torturously, he wrapped that long strip of white fabric, binding my skin tightly.

"How's that?" Sylas asked, adjusting the makeshift wrap after he'd tied it off.

"Great," I barely croaked out.

He looked up at me, and the sudden realization of how close we were—how intimate of a moment this was—wasn't lost on me. My heart was beating a million miles in my chest.

Sylas Kellar, on his knees for me. Shirtless, on a strange planet that was millions of light years away from home. He was my captain, and yet—

"Aurelia."

My eyes darted to his. The way he said my name undid something inside of me.

"I'm sorry," I whispered, trying to ignore the way the tears were springing to my eyes.

"For what?" His voice was calm—soothing.

"For getting you into this mess. Getting hurt. I took your attention away from the ship, and I never should have. This is all my fault."

"Little star," he murmured, voice pained.

"Forgive me."

"There's nothing to forgive."

I shook my head. "That's not true. I've been a pain in your ass since the first day. You don't have to deny it. You didn't like me at first."

"No." Sylas shook his head as his hands slid up to my calf, massaging as he went. "That's not true. And I'm a damn fool for letting you think that for this long."

I raised an eyebrow. "No? What do you call it then?"

"You've never been anything but a temptation."

His palms rested on my thigh, and my entire body was warm. Burning.

And even if I shouldn't, even if he was my captain, I wanted him. In a way that I knew would change everything between us. But I didn't care anymore.

"Sylas," I whispered, the sudden emotion in my chest flooding my system. Clawing it's way out. The way he took care of me today—carrying me, tenderly checking on my ankle, making sure I was okay—it was more than I knew how to handle.

Careful not to put any weight onto my sore ankle, I pushed him back into a sitting position and then climbed into his lap.

"You're the most beautiful thing I've ever laid eyes on," he admitted. "Too good for me. Too young. Too bright."

My hands reached up, cupping his cheeks between them. "You don't see it, do you? How good you are. How warm and gooey you are on the inside. You try to hide it, but I see you. How you interact with the crew. How much you care about your sister." He grumbled, but I kept going. "You're *good*, Sylas Kellar. And you can't convince me otherwise."

It was the first time we'd been like this—*really* touching, for anything other than necessity. My hands slid down his bare chest, running my fingers over the defined muscles he got from his many hours at the gym each week. I couldn't complain.

His deep blue eyes were all I could see, the feeling of his warm, hard body underneath mine all I could feel. I scooted forward, pressing my chest to his.

"Aurelia," he groaned. "What..."

"Shh," I said, leaning down my head to press a kiss to his collarbone. "Let me take care of you now."

I continued my exploration, kissing up his neck, just light presses of my lips against his skin. I moved to his jaw, the side of his lips, before his patience ran out.

Sylas wrapped his hand around the back of my neck, bringing our lips together, and then he was kissing me. *Really* kissing me, like he had that day on the empty observation deck. But this was different. This was full of heat and passion, of desire and lust. Temptation in every sinful way possible.

And when the object of his desire brushed against my core, I gasped. Rocked against him, the hardening evidence that he wanted me the way I wanted him creating the perfect friction against me. But we both had too many clothes on.

I needed them off *now*.

TWENTY
SYLAS

AURELIA'S EYES were clouded over with heat as she reached down, cupping me through my flight suit.

A groan slipped from my lips, and I nipped at her neck. "What do you think you're doing, little star?"

"I told you I'd take care of you," she whispered. "So let me."

But I shook my head. Tried to put some space between us. "You don't have to do that. Not to repay me. Taking care of you is…" I trailed off. *All I've ever wanted.* It was right there, on the tip of my tongue, but I couldn't force it out.

"What if I want to?" She looked up at me through her lashes. And *fuck*, those eyes would be my undoing. Aurelia stroked my cock through the fabric of my pants, and I had to shut my eyes, clenching my teeth. It had been so long since a woman had touched me. Longer than I wanted to admit. "I want you," she breathed out.

It was a siren's song to my heart, and I couldn't say no to her. I'd never been able to. Since the very first time she'd barged into my office, demanding to keep her job, I'd always caved.

The truth was, I wanted her too badly to stop.

Running my fingers through her hair, I pulled out the elastic that secured it into a ponytail. She almost always wore her hair

160

pulled back, but I wanted to see those reddish brown strands hanging down, to feel the strands between my fingers.

Keeping my hands tangled in her hair, I brought our lips back together, letting my tongue say the things I couldn't put into words. How much I wanted her. How beautiful she was. Our mouths were fused together, each stroke into her mouth bringing me closer to ecstasy. Kissing her was better than I could have ever imagined. Even that first kiss on the observation deck was nothing compared to this furious, sloppy, couldn't-get-enough-of-each-other kiss.

"Tell me to stop," I said, my hand fisted in her hair when we finally pulled apart. "Tell me you don't want this."

"I can't," she whimpered. Those beautiful blue and green eyes flecked with gray—like stars—looked up at me with so much emotion. "Don't stop." Her breath was low, and I brought my lips to her neck, kissing again as she let out a little breathy moan. *"Please."*

She didn't need to beg me.

I grabbed the zipper pull of her flight suit, dragging it down her body slowly, stopping when I reached her waistband. She shrugged out of the sleeves, leaving herself just in a black, simple bra that showed off the luscious swells of her breasts.

"Beautiful," I said, entranced. "But I need this off." I shifted our positions, spreading her out on the plush blanket before moving down her body, carefully maneuvering the pants over her wrapped ankle—one I intended to keep her off of, even if it was only a slight pain.

I told myself it was to make sure she wasn't hurting, but really, it was because I was a selfish asshole and I couldn't stop touching her. Carrying her fulfilled some primal part of me I couldn't explain, but I *liked* it. Turns out humans had evolved little from our caveman days.

Dropping her flight suit onto the ground beside us, I sat back, resting my bodyweight on my ankles so I could appreciate her form.

Her hair was spread out around her on the blanket, and she bit her lip as my eyes tracked down her body—like I might memorize each freckle, each curve and dip. If only I looked long enough. That plain black underwear set shouldn't have been sexy, but on her, it was.

I knew that there would never be enough time to appreciate her body, especially if this night was all we had. That was the thought that did me in. I hadn't even had her yet, and I already knew that she was going to ruin me. That there would be no going back after this. She was already in my veins, ingrained down to my very core. And I hadn't even touched her yet. Something I planned to remedy immediately.

She was so breathtakingly gorgeous, not even trying to hide her body from me. Her left shoulder was covered in little stars, a constellation all of her own. I traced my fingers over it before placing a soft kiss on her skin. "This is beautiful."

"Thank you," she whispered. "I got it for my dad. We loved looking up at the stars together."

My throat felt tight. It was the reminder of what we were doing, why we were here—stranded on a strange planet in a system worlds away from Earth.

"But I don't want to talk about him right now," Aurelia said, reaching over to undo the front clasp of her bra. "Not when I have you in front of me." She let the black cups fall open, her luscious tits spilling out, before shrugging the entire thing off and shucking it to the side.

"Fuck, baby." I leaned down, pressing a kiss to the top of each swell. My hands crept down to her waistband. "May I?"

"Such a gentleman," she grumbled, and then gave me a slight nod.

Ignoring the comment—though I planned to address it later, *fully*—I ran a knuckle over her slit, greedily enjoying her little gasp of air as I pressed against her clit. "You like that, don't you? Needy little thing."

"Yes," Aurelia groaned as I peeled back her underwear,

sliding them torturously slow down her leg. When she was bare to me, her hands slid over her body, her eyelashes fluttering. She looked suddenly shy, and I sat up.

"What is it?" I asked, hoping I didn't do something wrong. "Is everything okay?"

But she let out a warm laugh, the sound echoing through the cave, filling my chest with warmth. *"Is everything okay?"* Aurelia repeated, winding her arms around my neck so she could pull me down on top of her. "More than. I was just thinking that I was supposed to be taking care of *you*."

A smile curved my lips. "But I like taking care of you." Wanted to take care of her in ways I'd never wanted to before, which frankly, scared the shit out of me.

I was thirty-five years old—I shouldn't be feeling like a teenager all over again over a woman. Especially not one ten years younger than me. But I couldn't help it.

Not with the girl in front of me, who gleamed like every star in the sky every time she smiled. And with the glow of the rocks illuminating her body, she looked like a goddess.

"What happened to my grumpy captain?" she teased.

"You're a brat, you know that?"

Her tongue darted out, swiping over her lower lip. "Maybe. What are you going to do about it, *sir*?"

Fuck, the way she said it messed with my brain. I draped my body over hers fully, pressing my erection against her opening. If I ever got her in a bed, I'd enjoy spanking her. Making her beg me for it.

But tonight was it. And something unspoken passed between us, the acknowledgment that this was all we could have.

"Sylas—"

I kissed her again, nipping on her bottom lip as I pushed my tongue into her mouth. It was sloppy, both of us losing ourselves in it as I devoured her. This time, there was no reason to hold back. No crew or ship to pull us apart.

Because down here, on this planet's surface, we weren't a

captain and his pilot. There was no ten-year difference, no reason we couldn't be together. We were just Aurelia and Sylas, and I liked that more than I should. It made me hope, and I hadn't done that in years.

"Need you naked," she said when we finally pulled apart, rocking her hips to press against me deeper. "Want to feel you."

I couldn't agree more.

Climbing off of her, I moved just enough so I could get the flight suit off, shimming my pants down my hips. The tight boxer briefs I wore left nothing to the imagination.

Aurelia sat up, her eyes tracking the motion as my underwear joined the pile on the floor with my clothes, the remaining scraps of my t-shirt, and my shoes.

"Wow." Her eyes widened as she reached out, sliding a finger up my length. I shuddered at the unexpected contact. I could see her mentally puzzling out our size difference. "You're..." I felt smug as she took in my cock. "Big," she finally finished.

I'd always been confident in my *male prowess*, but not just because of my size.

Aurelia wasn't *small*, not by any means—maybe seven inches shorter than me, total—but I could rest my chin on the top of her head. And I knew I was larger than the average male.

"It'll fit," I promised, kissing her to reassure her as I cupped her breasts, thumb rubbing over her nipples. Finally, she relaxed against me, and I pulled away.

She didn't look confident, but I was patient. I knew how to put my credits where my mouth was. A smirk crossed my face, thinking about where exactly I wanted to put my mouth to use.

All in good time.

"Now..." I swatted at her bare ass. "Are you going to be a good girl for me?"

She nodded, biting her lower lip. "Yes, sir."

"Good. Now lay back, so I can get you nice and wet and ready for me."

Aurelia laughed, and I liked that. How this wasn't just sex. It was also… fun. Once she'd laid back on the blanket, I gripped her thighs, pulling them apart to bare her pretty pink pussy to me.

"Look how wet you are for me," I mused, unable to tear my eyes away from her. "*Dripping.*"

Her giggles stopped the moment I thrust my tongue inside of her, her taste exploding on my tongue. *Fuck.*

"Sylas." She squirmed underneath me, my hands on her thighs the only thing keeping her pinned down. "You don't have to—"

I peeked my head up from between her thighs. "Don't have to what? Make you come on my tongue?"

Her cheeks were bright pink, and she squeaked out a quick, "No," before burying her hands in her face.

My fingers tightened around her skin. "Tell me," I murmured, sensing there was something she was holding back from me.

"I just…" Aurelia hesitated. "You don't have to do that." She repeated her words from before. "I know most men don't like it."

"Boys, baby." I pressed a kiss to the inside of her thigh, and then repeated it on the other side. "Boys don't want to go down on their women." Was that what she was to me? *My woman?* That possessive, caveman part of me liked that. "I, on the other hand, can't get enough of you." I swirled my tongue over her clit, licking up her juices.

"Oh." She let out a little squeak as I kept her spread apart with my legs, needing my hands free to make sure she was ready for me. Teasing her clit with my thumb, I spread some of her wetness around before finally slipping a finger inside.

"Fuck," I groaned. "You're so tight." Her insides were clamping down around me, warm and wet, and I knew I wouldn't last long once I was finally inside of her. She was too much. Temptation and everything good all swirled into one.

"Don't—" She grit out the words. "—tease me."

I worked my finger in and out of her, doing just as I promised —getting her nice and wet, loosening her up for me. When I added a second finger, Aurelia's head dropped back, a light moan slipping from her lips.

She liked that. My chest filled with male pride, and I continued pumping my fingers into her, crooking them to hit just the right spot, before I bent my head back down, swirling my tongue around her clit as I fucked her with my fingers.

Her juices soaked my fingers, and I didn't stop—not even as her breaths got louder, those moans filling the entire cavern, and I could feel her tightening around my fingers, getting closer to her peak.

I wanted it. Craved it. Wanted to make her come in ways no one ever had. Wanted to treat her right, because it was increasingly obvious to me that no one had ever put her pleasure first. But I always would.

"Sylas," she moaned. "I'm so close."

"Come for me," I urged, not stopping. "Soak my fingers. I want to taste you on my lips."

I groaned, flicking my tongue against her bundle of nerves as she gushed around me. Continuing my steady rhythm even as she climaxed, I finally pulled my fingers out as her pulse evened out.

"That was—" she started, breath rough. "*Wow.*"

I quirked an eyebrow as I popped my fingers into my mouth, licking the taste of her off my skin. "I could spend forever between these thighs and not tire of doing that," I mused.

Leaning down to kiss her, I let her taste herself on my tongue, and Aurelia wrapped her hand around my erection, pumping it as we lazily made out. Kissing had always felt like a chore before, but with her, all I wanted was to have her mouth on mine.

"Shit." I stilled her hand with mine, clenching my teeth.

"What?" She gave me an innocent expression, giving my dick a squeeze.

"I need to be inside of you," I groaned, burying my face between her breasts and kissing the spot there.

There was a cheeky grin on her face as I looked up at her, rubbing my stubble against her breast. "So what's stopping you?"

"Mmm." I pressed my nose into her neck, inhaling her scent.

I didn't want to rush this. That's what was stopping me. But I couldn't hold back, either. Not when her taste was still in my mouth, and all I could see, feel, and hear was *her*. My senses were completely overrun, and I never wanted to get her out.

Guiding myself to her entrance, I coated my tip with her wetness, teasing, driving her mad.

"Please," she whined.

"Wait." I groaned, desperate to be inside of her but unable to turn that nagging part of my brain off. "We don't have any protection." Even if the entire crew was on fertility blockers, not using anything was always a risk.

She seemed to grasp where I was going before I could elaborate.

"I'm all clear," Aurelia reassured me. "I had a physical before I came on the ship, and I haven't been with anyone in... awhile." Her blush crept down her throat, her whole body the loveliest shade of pink.

"I—Same." *I haven't even looked at another woman since I met you.* That wasn't an admission I wanted to make, though. Not when I couldn't be sure she felt the same. I cleared my throat. Physicals were standard practice—though the celibacy wasn't. "There's been no one else."

"Good." A flash of possession flashed in her eyes as she wrapped her arms around my neck. "Do it."

"You're sure?" I asked, poising myself at her entrance. "Because once I start, I won't be able to stop."

"Yes. Please fuck me, Sylas."

Fuck, hearing my name on her lips instead of *captain* or *sir* made me even harder, if that was possible.

I pressed the tip inside, just an inch, and watched the little "*o*" form on Aurelia's mouth as I pushed inside.

Part of me wanted to rut into her, to fuck her like a beast, a madman, to take her and ruin her—but I held back. Because this was about more than sex, something that was becoming all too apparent to me.

How much I wanted her, needed her.

"You feel so good," she mewled, nails digging into my back as I pushed inside of her, inch by inch.

Her eyes rolled back into the back of her head as I pulled out, pushing in farther the next time.

"Oh *God*," she groaned. "You're too big."

My eyes focused on the spot where I entered her. She was impossibly tight, perfectly wrapped around me. Like her insides were hugging my cock. I wasn't even all the way in yet, and I already knew I wouldn't be able to last.

Aurelia moaned as I continued to stretch her.

"Are you okay?" I asked, nipping at her neck before pressing a kiss to the soft, tender skin there. I went slow, not wanting to hurt her.

"*Yes.*"

"Do you want me to stop?" Stilling myself inside of her, I waited for her answer.

"*No.*" She growled the word. "If you do, I think I'll kill you."

"Think you can take the rest?" A smirk covered my lips as I slammed my hips into her. "You can," I rasped. "You can take it. Gonna bury my cock in this sweet pussy."

"*Fuck.*" A gasp flew from her lips. "Holy shit. I've never been so full."

I had to hold myself still for a moment, squeezing my eyes shut at the pure bliss of being seated fully inside of her. Heaven —or the closest thing I'd ever come to it.

"That's it," I praised, my eyes unable to leave the spot where we were connected. "Look how well you're taking me. Every—" I snapped my hips. "Fucking—" Another thrust. "Inch."

"Yes. Yes. *Yes,*" she cried, drawing the word out as her hips rose in time to meet mine.

"Such a good girl for me," I crooned.

And then we were both lost in it, in the unrelenting rock of my hips, in the glorious slide of her wet heat, in each other and everything and nothing. It had never been like this for me before. So good that I'd been able to forget everything else but the woman in front of me.

I felt so much, and I knew I was fucked. Because there was no way I could go back to whatever I'd experienced before this. When sex had been meaningless and *boring*. This was explosive. Passionate. Both of us moving in tandem as we learned the other's body. It was incredible.

Sucking her nipple into my mouth, I kept up my brutal pace until I felt Aurelia's insides contract around me, and then I followed her down into oblivion.

"MMM," I hummed, nuzzling further into my cozy pillow. The ground was a little lumpy, and I was pretty sure there was something sticking into my ass, but I was warm and content, even with the slight ache between my legs.

"Good morning," a deep voice chuckled as my pillow moved.

Not a pillow at all. *Right.* I'd slept on Sylas's chest. We were all curled up in each other, still naked after the events of last night.

My cheeks were burning red when I brought my eyes up to meet his gaze. "We fell asleep?"

"Sure looks like it," he muttered, glancing around the cavern. There was a stream of light coming in from the ceiling, where there must have been a crack in the cave that led to the upper surface of the planet.

"Shit." I rubbed at my head as I sat up. "At least we can confirm there are no critters in the cave system, right?" I was pretty sure we would have known by now if something was climbing over us in the middle of the night.

"If that's our only positive right now, I'm not sure we're doing very great," he muttered, his eyes scanning the cave.

"How's your ankle?"

"Fine." I probably wouldn't be running any marathons right now, but I didn't need to tell him that.

He frowned, like he didn't believe me, so I changed the subject. "Do you know where my communicator is?" I rooted around in the pile of our stuff for my bra and underwear, suddenly very aware of his eyes on me.

Last night had been *amazing*, but it was a line we shouldn't have crossed. I knew it all too well, and I was already mentally preparing the walls around my heart to protect myself when he pushed me away.

Because he would, and those tender touches, the way he'd looked at me as he buried himself inside of me... It all felt too precious.

He wrapped his arm around me, placing a kiss on my neck. "Where do you think you're going, missy?"

"We have to follow the signal." I turned my head to look up at him. "Otherwise, all of this was for nothing."

"We'll find something," he promised, smoothing my hair back. "I promise."

"Don't make promises you can't keep, Captain Kellar."

He gave me a playful swat on my ass as I stood up, stretching my arms as I stepped into my underwear. But Sylas's eyes never left my form, making me all too aware of how my nipples were pebbled, of the marks on my hips from how he'd gripped them last night. The heat in his eyes was too much. Turning around, I pulled on my bra, latching it closed in the front. At least in my underwear, I felt a little more protected.

Maybe I needed to build those walls a little higher.

The sound of a Sylas's zipper distracted me for a moment, and I turned to see he'd covered up those broad shoulders and magnificent forearms, too. *Good.* I didn't need the distraction of his body, either.

"Listen, last night—"

"It didn't mean anything, right?" I said, turning away from

him to pull on my flight suit. "We just needed to get it out of our systems. Won't happen again." I zipped up the front, keeping my hands busy so I wouldn't be tempted to touch him.

"Aurelia—" He frowned as I found my hair tie on the cavern floor, pulling it back up into a tight ponytail.

"Captain," I addressed him, needing the distance between us.

He stood up, capturing my wrists with his hands. "*Sylas,*" he corrected. "Don't do this."

"Do what?" I swallowed roughly. "I'm just trying to complete the mission, sir."

Sylas growled, and the noise went straight to my core.

I shouldn't be getting turned on right now. Not when I was still deliciously sore from last night. Not when I could still feel him *everywhere.* The way his beard scraped against my inner thighs, how he stretched me impossibly full—

He guided my hands to the back of his neck, melding our bodies together before his mouth was on mine. There was no preamble, no warning, and he was *kissing me.* Like there was no one else in this entire galaxy. Just him and me.

When we finally pulled apart, breathing heavy, he rested his forehead against mine. "You can't just run away from this. Not after last night."

"But—"

He silenced me with another kiss.

"Okay." I finally agreed. Maybe I shouldn't have, but I couldn't resist him, and I knew it.

AFTER SYLAS and I had eaten the meager meal bars that were in the bottom of the pack, we packed up our things and headed deeper into the cave system, following the blinking beacon on my screen. Sylas was in the lead this time, though he'd slid his hand into mine, and I liked the feeling far too much to argue with him or pull away.

We elapsed into a comfortable silence as we journeyed deeper and deeper into the planet. Part of me knew I should have had more fear or apprehension, but something about being here with Sylas made all of that melt away.

Because I did trust him, and I knew he would protect me.

The narrow cavern widened out, and there was a small underground lake, lit by the same luminescent crystals as the cave we'd spent the night.

"So there's the water I could hear," Sylas mused, crouching down onto his knees to inspect the surface of the water.

"Do you think it's safe?" I asked, bending over next to him.

"Only one way to find out." He looked over at me, dipping his hand down into the water.

I smirked, toying with the zipper on my suit. "I *could* use a bath." Washing the sweat off—and other things—from last night sounded like an amazing idea. Pulling my ponytail free, I let my hair fall down past my shoulders.

Quickly shedding my clothes, as well as the wrap on my ankle, I dropped them on the bank, dipping my toes into the crystal clear water. When nothing happened to my skin—like a strange chemical reaction, I decided it was okay. The water was chilly, but it felt good.

No going back now.

I turned around, legs half submerged, his eyes were glued to my backside. "Are you going to join me?" My voice sounded sultry as I waded out deeper into the pool, going in till the water covered my entire body.

The temperature of the water felt great against my aching muscles, and I let out a low moan.

Sylas had stripped out of his suit as well, and I took the moment to really appreciate his body in all the ways I hadn't been able to last night. His muscular chest. Those delicious forearms. Even his cock, which rested half-hard against his thigh, was a spectacle. I couldn't look away if I tried.

It was like he'd been sculpted from granite, made in the images of my finest imaginations.

I could see him doing the same thing to me, and I cupped my breasts, biting my lip just to toy with him.

"Fuck." He wrapped his arms around me. "You're evil."

I pressed my wet, hardened nipples against his chest as I coiled my body around his. "I can't help it. You're the most handsome man I've ever seen." His chest puffed up, and I knew he liked that.

"Even the stars pale in comparison to you, Aurelia." He pressed a kiss to the stars I'd had tattooed on my shoulder when I turned eighteen. It was my tribute to my dad, and normally I hated talking about it with other people.

But he never showed me pity. No. Instead, he made me feel seen. Heard. Like he *cared*.

Maybe that was why I'd been so open and honest with him yesterday.

"No more running," Sylas said, and I knew what he meant without him having to explain.

"No more running," I repeated back, his lips finding mine.

Our bodies were tangled together, water all around us, and somehow, even with last night, it felt like the most intimate moment of my life.

"We're never going to find the signal if we keep getting distracted like this," Sylas murmured, his voice low. *Pained.*

I sucked on a spot on his neck. "It's not going anywhere," I whispered. "And besides, when else can I touch you like this?" I dragged a finger up the length of his cock, which now pressed against my hip.

Wrapping my hand around his shaft, I pumped him. My fingers didn't even meet in the middle, he was so large, and it made it hotter.

His eyes closed as a strangled noise slipped from his lips. A drop of pre-cum pooled on his tip, and I ran my thumb across it, licking it off my finger.

Sylas groaned, and wetness pooled between my thighs. How was it possible I was *this* turned on?

I wanted him inside me. Now. Fuck the consequences. I said I wouldn't run away, and I meant it. But now, I just wanted him.

Something brushed against my leg, and I froze.

"Sylas?"

"Hmm?" He asked, his lips focused on their current mission of kissing their way down my neck and across my chest.

"That wasn't you who just touched my leg, right?"

He gave me a stern look. One that said, *really?* Because his hands were cupping my tits, and his erection was pressed against my stomach, and I knew it wasn't his foot.

"Maybe we should get out," I whispered, an ominous chill running down my spine.

"Wait." Sylas's hand stilled me. "Look."

We huddled together, his arms wrapped around my back as the strange alien creatures swam through the water, climbing up onto the banks, clearly oblivious to our presence.

"What are they?" My eyes widened.

"Well, I think we can confirm that the heat signatures were, in fact, lifeforms." Sylas muttered, both of us watching the small mammal-like creatures play on the bank of the underground lake. They must have lived in the rivers of the underground caverns that we'd been passing through.

"They almost look like a cross between a dog and an otter." One of them climbed onto the bank, shaking off its fur. "They're *so* cute." They had little speckles on them, the coloring like a blue merle puppy—no two of them looked quite the same. With short little legs, floppy ears, and an otter-like tail, they were clearly accustomed to life in the water.

"Be careful, Rae." He grasped my wrist as I took a step forward in the water. "They might not be friendly."

I rolled my eyes. "Look at them. They're like little puppies, playing with each other."

There was no part of me that wanted to ignore the impulsive thought of *pet the cute alien animals.*

"Wait. Look at that one. She's hurt." I frowned, staring at the little alien creature who was looking up at me with a pair of gigantic eyes.

"How can you tell?" Sylas snorted. "Maybe it's just trying to make you feel sorry for it, and then it's going to attack. Protect its territory and all that."

"Or... she's limping."

"How do you even know it's a female?"

"Just a hunch. Look." I pointed at the paw that it wouldn't put weight on. The animal made a whimpering noise.

He chuckled. "Just like you."

I rounded a glare at him, not pleased to be compared to a wounded animal. Even though I'd certainly let him carry me like I was one, just last night. My cheeks burned, and I was glad there was minimal lighting.

"Do we have anything left in the pack?" I asked, wading towards the edge.

"What, like food? You can't seriously be considering feeding a wild animal, Aurelia."

I frowned, extending out my hand.

The little creature waded over, giving me a chirp and tilting her head before nuzzling against my palm.

"See?" I whispered to Sylas. "Friendly."

He looked amused. "I think she likes you."

Now that I was closer, I inspected her paw. "She's bleeding." The pad of it had rivulets of dark blood dripping.

"Maybe it cut itself on a rock?" Sylas trudged out of the water, pulling on his boxers before finding the remains of his torn shirt and tossing it over to me. "If it's not too deep, it'll probably heal on its own in a few days. Like a paper cut."

Still, I tore a strip off his shirt, bandaging up the paw to keep it clean from any other rocks. I didn't want it getting infected, but this was all I could do with limited supplies.

"Is that better?" I asked, getting another chirp from the animal, who brushed its little fuzzy head against my arm. "You're so cute." Scratching at her head, I looked over at Sylas, finding him still watching me. An amused smile curled up on his lips.

"Wonder what they eat," I said, watching the little thing run around in front of me. It was chirping away, the cutest little sound that made me want to pick it up and snuggle with it.

"Don't get attached," he warned.

"I'm not." I jutted out my chin. "It's not like I'm dumb enough to keep it as a pet."

My toes were feeling prune-y, in the way they did when you stayed in the water too long, which was the moment I realized I was still standing there, stark naked.

I crossed my arms over my chest, hiding my nipples that were still pebbled from the cold water, moving back to the shallow end where we'd gotten in. Man, a towel would be great right now.

"This seemed like a great idea earlier," I muttered, grabbing my bra off the edge and hurrying to get re-dressed.

But I felt better. More optimistic, somehow.

The fact that we'd discovered a race of mammals on this planet was huge. Sylas was right. We definitely should study this place more. My stubbornness had kept me from looking at the bigger picture.

I sighed.

"What?" Sylas looked over at me.

"I hate admitting it, but you were right."

He looked smug. "I know." Then raised an eyebrow. "About what, exactly? Because I'm right about all sorts of things."

I shoved my palm over his mouth to stop him from talking. "About Finley's team coming down here. They should really study this place. Them." I waved at the otter-like creatures.

"We can discuss that more after we find the source of the signal."

I nodded. "Good idea."

Finally, we were both fully dressed again, and it was easy to forget how just twenty minutes before, we'd been flirting and making out in the pool.

"No more distractions," I mused, heading for the back of the cave. It split off into two different passageways, and I looked back at Sylas, who had my data-pad. "Which way?"

"Left," he said, before slipping his hand back into mine.

And he didn't let go.

TWENTY-TWO
AURELIA

"WE'RE on top of it now," Sylas said, his faced focused on the small device in his hands.

"I don't see anything—" I started, shaking my head.

He clicked on a second flashlight, handing it to me. "Look." He whispered the words, and my eyes found the spot he was pointing at.

"What is that?" I could feel my eyes growing wide.

It wasn't a ship, but it was clear it was human made. There was a hum to it, common with technology.

Brushing my hands through the dust that had collected on the metal, a gasp slipped free from my lips. "But how?"

"Maybe the creatures found it on the surface and brought it down here." Sylas squinted, looking up at the cave ceiling above us. "Or maybe it shifted down here over the years. Who knows?"

It was a piece of the ship, the letters *Departure* faded, but there. "You know what this means, right?" I looked up at him. "They were here. My dad was *here.*"

But where did he go? I frowned, because the fact was—there were no humans on this planet. Right? We would have been able to see that. But this piece of the ship had to have some sort of clue, right? The universe couldn't have led me all the way here just to find *nothing*.

"Help me lift it away from the wall," I said, already trying to get leverage on the giant hunk of metal. It was almost as big as me, and there was no way I'd be able to budge it alone.

Sylas smirked, flexing his muscles, and with his help, we moved it to the center of the room without too much effort.

A small chirp sounded behind us, and the little creature from the lake popped up, winding around my legs. It had followed us all the way here?

I looked at Sylas, my eyes wide with surprise.

He sighed. "So much for not disturbing the native wildlife."

I picked her up, scratching under her chin. "What about your family?" I asked her, getting another coo instead. "Did you leave them behind?"

"I think she bonded with you."

"Huh."

Holding the pup in my arms, I circled the hunk of metal. "Do you think there's more somewhere else? Or could they have left this behind so someone knew they were here?" It was wishful thinking, but maybe that was what I needed right now. *Hope.*

A FEW HOURS LATER, sweaty and dusty, we finally emerged to the mouth of the cave, data chip from the hunk of ship in hand. I didn't know what we would find on it, but it was something.

Another clue. This all just felt like one giant scavenger hunt. But what was waiting for me at the end? Sylas had been quiet, and I wondered if he was thinking the same thing.

That I was doing all of this just to find out what I already knew. That he was gone. There was no way he'd been alive for the past thirteen years and hadn't come home to me or my mother. No matter what happened, I believed that. He would have found a way back to us.

"You have to stay here," I instructed the little creature. "I can't take you back with me." She whined, scratching at the dirt with her little paw. I reached down, scratching her ear. "I'm sorry."

We began to walk away, and her little ears drooped. "Go find your family," I said, waving my hands. "I'm sure they're missing you."

Sylas wrapped an arm around my waist, like he could sense how enamored I was with the little beast after only half a day. It was the right thing to do, but she was so cute. Her little dabbled gray coat, the soft fur that I wanted to bury my face in. Her little tail, just like an otter's, so she could swim easily through the underground rivers. Even those gigantic eyes had me under their spell.

"Are you crying?" He murmured, kissing my forehead.

"What?" I wiped under my eyes, removing the evidence of my tears. "No."

Turning me around, he walked us back to the ship, never once removing his arm from my body. It was the warmth I needed after the last day on this planet.

"I still can't believe all of this is just... *rock,* and down there is..." Beautiful. There were no other words for the glittering crystals or the animals below.

"Makes you wonder if the other crew never made it here, or if they wanted to hide it," Sylas mused.

He was right, though. What would humans do to this place? We *could* colonize it, build an outpost here as we expanded our reaches of the universe, but... I thought of the little creature who'd followed us. What would happen to them if we did?

I sighed, burying myself deeper against Sylas's side.

"Should we go home, Rae?"

"The crew's probably missing us by now," I said, giving him a small smile.

"You, maybe. Me, not so much." He furrowed his brow. "Don't even try to deny it. They all like Kayle better than me, don't they?"

A laugh burst out of me. "Maybe if you weren't such a grumpy asshole..." I winked.

He grumbled, but I knew from the way he didn't tense up next to me he knew I meant nothing by it.

Our ship came back into view, the *S.S. Paradise* painted on its side, only bearing a few scratches from our rough landing.

It was crazy to think that my first big adventure was almost over. We'd barely gotten here, and now it was time to go back.

We set our stuff inside the cargo hold, me tucking the chip safely into an empty small box where I knew it wouldn't get lost, before I headed to the cockpit.

"What are you doing?" Sylas asked, leaning against the doorway. I'd left the electronic door between the cockpit and the ship open, so I hadn't even heard him approach.

I popped my head up from underneath the terminal. "Fixing the ship."

He raised an eyebrow. "You could have done that the whole time?"

"Well..." I fluttered my eyelashes. "I *do* have an advanced engineering degree, you know." Crossing my arms, I turned around to look at him, but a look of awe was spread over his face. "What?" I stood up, taking the few steps towards him.

"Fuck, you're amazing," Sylas said, wrapping his arms around my waist and pulling me in tight against his body.

I opened my mouth to say something, but he crashed his lips against mine, capturing my mouth in a fierce kiss. There was only me and him—no desolate planet, no ship, no team of people waiting for us—nothing.

"I never should have doubted you."

I laughed. "No."

"You're never going to let me live down how much of an asshole I was, are you?"

"*Nope*," I said, popping the p for emphasis.

He rolled his eyes playfully, dropping another kiss to my lips. "I'm sorry I ever did."

I cleared my throat. "We can try contacting the ship now. I think I fixed it." I'd always planned on doing it after we investigated further, but that was a fact that I didn't feel like I needed to mention now. The important thing was, we'd survived an alien planet, found an unhostile species of mammals, and recovered information from my dad's ship.

Even with my rough landing and the transport ship being a *little* banged up, it was a win.

Okay, it was more than just a little banged up. I'd definitely taken the landing harder than I'd hoped, and I wasn't sure I could get the shuttle airborne if I tried.

Sylas stepped up to the console, fiddling with the buttons before pressing the line to open the communications channel.

"S.S. Paradise, this is Captain Kellar. Do you read me? Over." He released the trigger button of the comm, and we waited.

A moment later, a familiar voice came over the speaker. "Captain Kellar, this is Lieutenant Alastair. I read you, sir. Loud and clear." *Violet*. A grin spread over my face.

"Thank fuck," Sylas muttered to me only, before pressing the comms button once again. "I have Lieutenant Callisto with me. We're requesting an immediate pickup. Transferring our location to you now. Transport is wrecked, but salvageable. We're on planet XV30041's moon." Most of the unexplored, unnamed planets just had a code assigned to them, which made it easy for them to pinpoint our exact location.

Short, sweet, and to the point, but I understood his efficiency. We could explain why we were down here to the team later.

"Can she fly, sir?"

He looked over at me, and I shook my head. "Better not," I mumbled.

"Negative, lieutenant. Ship was damaged upon entry into the planet. Fly slow and take it easy. The atmosphere will burn you up otherwise."

I nodded, giving him a thumbs up.

"Anything else?" He asked me, and I shook my head.

"Coordinates have been received, Captain. The Paradise is en route. We didn't go too far once we realized you two were missing. Hold on tight."

He gave a brief nod, transmitting one last message to let Violet know we'd be waiting, before he turned the comms channel off entirely.

Turning to me, he pulled me into his arms.

"Sylas," I murmured, resting my forehead against his chest. There was no trace of my grumpy captain as he looked down at me. All of his emotions were visible on his face. "Everything is about to change, isn't it?" I whispered the words.

He brushed a hair off my forehead.

"I'm afraid so," he said, tracing my jaw with his index finger before tipping it up to bring our eyes together. Deep ocean blues looked back at me, and I wanted to drown in them.

There were two bright suns setting in the sky when we headed back outside, so lost in our own world that I barely even noticed when our transport finally arrived.

All I wanted was one more kiss. One more minute.

TWENTY-THREE
SYLAS

FUCK, she was incredible. I couldn't stop replaying the moments from the past twenty-four hours in my mind. Her look of surprise when I praised her. Clearly, I needed to stop underestimating Aurelia Callisto, because she was determined to blow my mind in every way possible. Why had I ever doubted her place in my crew? She was exactly what I needed. Her smiles and her laughter filled a void in my being that I hadn't even known existed before.

The shuttle door opened, and I reached for her arm, to pull her back and tell her—what? That she was perfect, and I was a fool? That I wanted more? I couldn't have those things, and I knew it.

I shook my head, letting her walk back onto the ship, into the arms of the other officers who'd become her friends.

"Welcome back, Captain," Leo said, clasping an arm on my shoulder and squeezing.

My sister stood at his side after a moment, and there was a worried expression on her face. Before I could reassure her I was fine—really—she threw her arms around me, pulling me into a tight hug that we hadn't shared in years. "You worried the shit

"I won't," I promised. But looking over at Aurelia, at the warmth in her face as she embraced the other girls, I knew I would take it back in an instant if something happened to her. "I'm sorry."

"When we couldn't reach you, I just—"

"Did exactly what you needed to do. And we're back in one piece."

She dipped her head in a nod, letting out an exhale. "Right."

Leo and Kayle shared a look. I wondered if something had passed between them. She'd normally rolled her eyes at him at least once by now. The two had never hated each other, but there'd always been a fire between them. They'd rile each other up like no one ever had.

It was amusing, but I also meant what I'd told him before. If he fucked around with my sister and broke her heart, there would be hell to pay.

"Captain—" It was Wren, this time, who spoke up. "What happened? We need to know."

"I know," I said, unable to pry my eyes from Aurelia. "We'll give a full debrief soon."

First, I wanted to talk to Aurelia alone.

They stood in a line, faces formed into disapproving lines. I knew they didn't understand what had transpired. I barely understood it myself.

But if they thought that this was just an excuse for us to sneak off alone, they couldn't have been more wrong.

Even if that was *exactly* what had happened.

Orion cleared his throat. "Three hours, on the bridge?"

I nodded. That time would be helpful. At the very least, we could clean ourselves up. And I could check in on Aurelia, who'd been quiet. "See you then."

Everyone else funneled out, clearly dismissed.

"Aur—Lieutenant Callisto," I called, trying my best to ignore my slip-up over calling her by her name.

"Yes, Captain?" She looked up at me from underneath her

lashes, and I stood close enough that if I moved just an inch, we'd be touching. God, how I wanted that. To memorize every curve and sweep of her body. To really know her, intimately, inside and out.

"Good job out there." My throat felt dry. Was this really how we were going to leave things? "You were... exceptional."

The rest of the crew finally vacated the room, leaving just her and I standing in the hangar bay.

"Thank you." She dipped her head, worrying her lower lip into her mouth. I wanted to smooth that furrow between her brows. Longed for our time back on the planet's surface, because there was no chance of prying eyes.

My voice was hardly above a whisper. "What's on your mind, little star?"

"I..." Aurelia smoothed a hand over her uniform, looking up at me. "I don't want to go back to the way things were before. Between us."

"No?"

"No." She shook her head. "Things feel... different now."

I shifted an inch, so the tips of our boots were touching. "Different how, Aurelia?"

Her skin turned that beautiful shade of pink. But she didn't hold back her tongue. "You know how, *Captain.*"

"Brat," I muttered, loving that mouth of hers. Wanting it back on mine. We'd shared one last kiss before the ship came into view, under the setting sun on the rocky surface of that strange planet.

If it was the last one we'd ever have, at least we made it count.

Her hands came up, clutching onto my jumpsuit. "Rae..."

My voice was low. A warning. Anyone could walk in. Anyone could catch us.

"I don't want this to end," she murmured, her lips only a breath from mine. "I don't want that to be the only..."

"I don't either," I admitted. And though I thought it would

cost me something to admit, it didn't. What had passed between us was too good to limit to one time. If she thought it would get her out of my system, she couldn't have been more wrong.

"Sylas."

Fuck, the way she said my name. It undid me. Brought me to my fucking knees. What I wouldn't give to have her say it every day. To look at me like *that*.

"Mmm?" I rubbed by nose along her neck, inhaling her scent.

"We can't," she said, her breath low. "The crew—"

"Who cares?" We were too close together, but I couldn't bring myself to move away. "Fuck them. They don't matter. Only we do."

"But—"

A large metal clang sounded, and we sprung apart.

Aurelia winced as she settled on her ankle.

I scowled at her injury. "You should head to MedBay. Get that checked out."

"I'm fine." She jutted out her chin. "It's not even bothering me, really."

I ground my teeth together. "You're *not*." Looking around, I scooped her up into my arms. "We're going. End of discussion."

"Sylas." My name on her lips was soft. Her voice was light, but it was impossible to miss the tone of worry in it. "We're going to get caught."

"I'm just helping my officer who's in pain," I said, though really I just needed an excuse to touch her. "If anyone asks, that's what we'll tell them."

"Okay," she whispered, relaxing into my hold as she finally wound her arms around my neck.

I liked how perfectly she fit in my arms. I'd thought the same thing back on the planet's surface, too. That holding her like that felt right. It should have been jarring. Should have left me on unsteady feet, like the ground was crumbling underneath me. Instead, all I could wonder was why... Why hadn't we done this sooner?

Heading towards the MedBay, I kept my gaze in front of me, not making direct eye contact with any of the crew in the halls. Luckily, it wasn't too busy, and we made it with no effort.

"Aurelia," my Chief Medical Officer rushed out, as I set my pilot back down on her feet. "Are you feeling okay?" Astrid wrapped an arm around her waist, guiding her onto one of the sterile examination tables.

"I'm fine. I just twisted my ankle or something. Sy—" She cut herself off, clearing her throat. "The Captain wanted me to get it checked out."

Astrid gave me a look, and I nodded. "She couldn't walk on it. Took a pretty nasty fall, too."

"Any cuts?"

"Mostly just scrapes," I interjected. "We got them cleaned off."

Aurelia's cheeks had a faint blush to them. Her eyes connected with mine before looking away quickly. Was she thinking about our time in the underground lake too? She gave me a look as Astrid stepped away to grab her equipment.

"What?" I asked.

"You're acting like an overprotective—"

I narrowed my eyes. "Watch how you finish that statement." My head dipped low, my lips brushing against her ears. "Or I'll find a way to put that mouth to better use."

"Sylas." My name was a whine released from her throat.

I stepped back as Astrid came back into the room, her medical tablet and a tray of tools in her arms. A male MedBay nurse was at her side, ready to assist.

The thought of someone else touching Aurelia, another man's arms on her smooth skin, almost had me seeing red.

But I shook the thought away, because I had no right to jealousy. We'd slept together *once*. Though there was no doubt in my mind if it hadn't been for the furry friend who'd taken a liking to Aurelia, I would have fucked her in that lake, too.

And even if what she said earlier was the truth—that she

didn't want whatever was between us to end—I couldn't help but worry about losing her.

She was too young for me. Too pure and warm, and everything I didn't deserve. Eventually, she'd realize that too. And then she'd leave. Just like they always did.

"Let me get you all checked out, and then you can go."

"Thank you." Aurelia dipped her head.

Astrid turned to me. "Will you be staying for my exam, *Captain*, or do you have somewhere else you need to be?" She raised an eyebrow.

"Right. Err." I felt the full weight of both women's stares as I turned around. "Let me know how she's doing, Commander Loxley."

"You got it, Captain," Astrid agreed with the dip of her head.

I left the room, wondering exactly how fucked I was, because there was no way I was going to get Aurelia Callisto out of my mind.

TWENTY-FOUR
AURELIA

"ARE you sure everything's okay with you?" Astrid asked me as soon as the door slid shut, Sylas disappearing out into the hallway.

I watched his muscular form for a beat longer than I should have, but who could blame me? His glutes were fantastic, even more so knowing what they felt like under my hands. Whew. I resisted fanning my face.

"Aurelia?"

I blinked at her, trying to focus on what she'd asked me. "Of course. Everything's fine." On the outside, that was what I was pretending, at least. On the inside, I was freaking out.

Because I'd told him I wanted more. That I didn't want things to go back the way they were. Because things were different now. And they were *good*.

"*Suuure*." She dragged out the word, making it clear she didn't believe me. "Is your ankle actually bothering you, or was that just an excuse for Captain Muscles to carry you into my MedBay?" *Captain Muscles*. I'd have to add that one to my mental repertoire.

I flushed. "Oh, you saw that?"

Astrid muttered under her breath something I couldn't make

out, and then, "Pretty sure *everyone* on board saw that, Aurelia. How could they have missed it? He came storming in here, that cross expression on his face…"

"Oh." Was it possible for my face to be any hotter? I didn't think so. "Well. He was just taking care of his officer. It's his duty as a captain, you know."

"Oh, his duty, hmm?" She wiggled her eyebrows.

"Shut up," I muttered, looking away. "And my ankle's fine. Really. I took a wrong step and twisted it on some rocks, but it doesn't hurt now."

"I'm still going to do some scans, just in case."

Nodding, I gave her permission. Mostly because I wanted to avoid her stare for a few more minutes. "Can't hurt."

Was it just an excuse for him to touch me? The way he'd doted on me after I'd fallen had felt good. There was no way I could lie about that. But now…

Astrid came back with the equipment to scan my ankle, and I looked out the window. I could still see the planet from this side of the ship, and it was surreal to think I'd just been down there.

How would I go back to life as usual after that? The rush of excitement, the exhilaration of stepping foot off the ship… I knew this mission would have countless more opportunities for it, and I couldn't wait. Maybe this one would always have a special place in my heart, but I was glad to have explored it with Sylas—alone.

"Everything looks good," Astrid said, patting me on the ankle. "If it's bothering you, you can always wear a compression sleeve for some extra support." She plopped a bottle of painkillers in my hand. "And take those if it's causing you pain. But not too many." My blue-haired friend tapped the label.

"Okay."

"Do you want me to give you your monthly shot while you're here? It's coming up in the next few days anyway, so…"

"Oh. Ah…" I stared up at her, wondering if she could read

my mind about what I'd been up to last night. "Yes. That'd be great." I shot her a smile.

Two months. I'd already been aboard the S.S. Paradise for two entire months. Where had the days gone?

"Titus!" Astrid called, her assistant MedBay nurse popping up. His dark black hair was shaggy, practically falling into his face. "Can you grab a FBS out of the cooler for me?"

"Of course." He gave me a small smile. "Hi again, Aurelia."

"Hi, Titus."

We'd only met in passing a few times—normally when I was eating dinner with Astrid—but it was nice to see him again. He was handsome, in the way popular boy band members were— pink, full lips, that smooth, clean-shaven face, and beautiful brown eyes—but for whatever reason, I felt nothing when I looked at him.

Because the only man who made my heart race anymore had sapphire blue eyes, the color of the ocean, and a dark stubble that covered his jaw and neck. That soft, dark brown hair and broad shoulders. His hands that cupped my breasts with such care, fitting perfectly in his palms.

Sylas Kellar. My grumpy Captain.

The man I'd slept with last night. The man who I thought hated me, but now had me questioning everything I'd ever known.

FINALLY, after being given the all clear from Astrid—and one fertility blocking shot later—I headed back to my cabin. I lugged my bag back to my quarters, frowning at its weight as I finally plopped it onto my bed.

Had it been this heavy before?

The top flipped open on its own, and a chirp sounded. I knew that noise.

"Oh." I gasped at the little fuzzy head that poked out of the pack. "You little stowaway! How did you get here?" She wiggled out onto my bed, pouncing on me like a puppy whose owner had just returned home from work.

It was the same creature who had followed us through the caves—her little spotted coloring gave her away. I rubbed at her ears, which were small but yet slightly floppy. Her bright blue eyes shone up into mine. She had to have been a baby, given her small size.

"God, you're so adorable." She yipped in excitement as I scratched at her tummy. "How's that paw?" I lifted her foot, finding the scratch fully healed. Huh. Maybe they healed faster than humans?

"I'm going to be in so much trouble if anyone finds out you hid in my bag, little girl," I said, wondering what to do with her.

I couldn't exactly keep an aquatic animal in this small bedroom, could I? I didn't even have a bathtub, just a shower. Surely, she needed to swim and be around the water. And taking her into the ship's swimming pool seemed like a great way to get caught.

Glancing down at the time on my data-pad, I winced. I had to shower and then report to the bridge for Sylas and I's recap on what happened down there.

But could I leave her alone? I didn't even have food for her, let alone somewhere she could sleep. But maybe... she curled up on the edge of my bed, staring up at me as I paced back and forth.

"Right." I addressed my new pup, feeling like a crazy person for continuing to talk to a wild animal, but it seemed like she understood me. "I'm going to shower, and then we'll figure this out." I paused, stopping in front of her. "Do you need food?"

She yipped, her nose sniffing in my bag.

I dumped out the contents, finding empty wrappers for the

meal bars I'd had in there. "Well, at least you're not starving. Maybe I can find you some fish from the mess hall."

God, they were going to think I was crazy if I tried to carry raw fish out of there. But what else did a creature like this eat? There were no other animals that we'd come across on the surface, nor were there plants that covered the river banks, which meant fish or other organisms must have been in the underground rivers and lakes. Right?

She gave a few joyful barks, wagging her otter-like tail. "Okay, okay," I laughed. "I won't let you go hungry, I promise."

The little thing pressed her wet nose into my palm, and I placed a kiss on her forehead before shucking my clothes off, dumping them into my laundry basket. Heading into the bathroom, I turned the water on, the familiar hiss a blissful sound to my ears after the last twenty-four hours. The lake had been refreshing, but there was nothing like being truly clean.

After turning the water on, I came back to find the little creature curled up on my bed, resting her head on her front paws.

"You wait right here," I said, petting her head. "I'll be right back."

Getting in the shower, I washed my body, moaning a sigh of relief as the heat relaxed my back muscles. I heard a whine and opened my eyes to my new companion scratching at the glass door.

"You want to come in?" I asked, turning the water down slightly so it wouldn't burn her skin. She yipped, hopping up and immediately sat down under the stream of water, licking it and playing in the puddle that had collected on the floor.

I laughed, letting her play as I washed my hair, using my favorite shampoo that smelled of violets before going through the rest of my hair routine. My hair wasn't quite curly, but it wasn't straight, either, so if I did nothing to it, I just had a frizzy mess on my hands.

When I stepped out of the shower, towel drying myself, my little friend tilted her head, shaking dry before rolling around on the bathmat, clearly enjoying the fuzzy warmth. I chuckled, watching her as I wrapped the towel around my body.

"Are you going to be okay if I leave you alone?"

A bark. Shit. What if someone heard her? This was so not going to go over well.

Leaving her to run around the bathroom like a maniac, I pulled on a clean pair of underwear and my dress uniform before smoothing out my hair with some product.

"Good enough," I muttered to myself after swiping on my usual minimal makeup routine. Some concealer, eyeliner, mascara, a bit of blush, and my favorite nude lip were all I had the energy for most days. It would have to do.

Scooping my now mostly dry animal back onto the bed, I booped her nose. "Be a good girl and stay here, alright? I'm gonna go get you food."

She gave a little whine, but laid down on the bed, resting her head on her palms again.

Checking my watch, I hurried towards the mess hall, hoping I could keep all of this together long enough for our meeting.

And hoping no one would find out about my little stowaway.

At least long enough for me to figure out what to do about her.

TWENTY-FIVE
SYLAS

SHOWERED and back in my dress uniform, it felt like nothing had changed when I stepped foot back on the bridge a little over three hours later.

Except, in the span of less than twenty-four hours, *everything* had changed. There was no going back. I wasn't the same man that I'd been before we'd left.

"Captain." I received a few nods as I settled back into my chair. Aurelia's spot was still empty, which I hoped didn't mean something was wrong, and she was still in the MedBay.

I held my breath until the door opened once again, the rest of my officers sliding into their posts. Aurelia was the last to enter the room, her long, reddish-brown locks hanging damply over her purple dress uniform.

Stunning, even like this.

I inhaled a deep breath. We had to tell the rest of the crew what happened—minus our time in the cave. There would definitely be a few key details we'd leave out. *Forbidden.* I squeezed my eyes shut. *Not for you.* What would they think if they'd known we slept together?

Normally, everyone in the bridge would bustle about

focused on their own assignments and at their stations. Now, it was so quiet you could hear a pin drop.

I cleared my throat. "Thank you all for gathering here. I know this was… unexpected."

"You mean you two absconding to another planet without so much as a peep?" Leo chimed in, giving me a smirk.

I ignored him. "Two nights ago, Lieutenant Callisto made a surprising discovery about an object on the surface of that planet." I waved my hand out the window. We were still close enough that it was in full view of the large glass windows.

"Why were none of the rest of us informed?" Kayle asked, swiveling in her chair to look at me.

"That's on me," Aurelia said, piping up.

"No." I crossed my arms, furrowing my brow. "You're my responsibility, so it's on me, Lieutenant." I turned back to my sister. "I made an executive decision as this ship's captain to investigate the lead. While it might not have been proper procedure, I did not expect the complications we faced after entering the planet's atmosphere." I quickly explained what happened, though I was light on the details, especially since my sister was glaring at me.

"Reckless," she muttered.

"It was," I agreed. "But had it not been for Lieutenant Callisto's discovery, the moon of planet XV30041 would have remained undiscovered." We probably needed to give it a name, but that wasn't in my purview. "And had we not gone down there, we never would have found that it's true beauty lies beyond the surface. In fact, my plan tomorrow is to send a crew of researchers down to study the animal life and bioluminescent crystals that we stumbled upon in the caverns." Finley's eyes lit up, and I gave her a confirming nod.

Aurelia was at the edge of her seat, her eyes searching mine. *You're not going to tell them the real reason we went down there?* She seemed to ask.

I gave her the slightest shake of my head. It wasn't my place. It was hers. But I also wouldn't punish her for trying to uncover answers about her father.

"There's something else," Aurelia added, her voice quiet. Like she was making herself small. "We found a piece of wreckage from the *S.S. Departure.*"

"But that ship…" Leo started, scratching his head.

"Went missing thirteen years ago," I finished. "Yes."

"Wow. That's an insane find," Orion said, turning in his chair to look at my girl.

My pilot, I corrected myself. Because we might have been sleeping together, but was she really mine? Not yet. We hadn't had a chance to really talk.

"It was the ship my father was on when he went missing," Aurelia admitted.

"And? What did you find?"

"The piece of ship had settled inside the underground caves, though it's not clear how it got down there. But there was—"

"Nothing." I hastily cut her off. "There was nothing on it."

That chip sat in Aurelia's pocket even now, but I knew the moment she admitted to having it, there was no chance of us discovering whatever information it possessed without everyone else getting involved. And I wanted her to have that opportunity to have closure. Even if it was just knowing what happened to the ship.

"Any other questions?" I asked, running my fingers through my hair. I was exhausted after spending the previous night sleeping on the floor, especially considering I'd spent the better half of the night awake, worried something might sneak up on Aurelia and I.

Plus, part of me hadn't been able to believe she was in my arms. That if I fell asleep, I'd realized it was all just a dream. But the way she'd climbed on my lap, how we'd connected… even now, the intimacy was startling. It had never been like that before. Not for me. I shook off the thought, crossing one leg over my knee.

After Aurelia and I answered everyone's questions—to the best of our ability—I announced my intentions to head to bed, lugging myself off the chair.

I already knew it would take me a long time to get to sleep that night.

LESS THAN HALF AN HOUR AFTER I returned to my room, a beep sounded—alerting me to someone at the door. Instantly, my heart sped up at the thought that it was Aurelia. Had she come to see me, knowing that I was thinking about her? Wondering how things would go now?

She'd taken off her dress uniform, pulling on a pair of pants and a loose t-shirt, and in her hands was—"Aurelia." I froze, staring at the creature in her arms. "What's that?"

"Don't be mad." She bit her lip.

Looking around the hallway, I urged her into my room, hoping no one had seen her.

All I could do was gape at her. "Please explain to me why, exactly, you brought an alien life-form—one who may or may not be dangerous—onto my ship?"

"Oh, *relax*, Captain Grumpy." Aurelia scratched the top of the little beast's head. "You know as well as I do that she's perfectly friendly. And it wasn't exactly *intentional*." I raised an eyebrow, and she continued. "She must have followed us onto the ship as we were leaving. I didn't even realize she'd smuggled on board until I got back to my room. I opened my pack, and she'd curled up inside of it."

The little beast leaped up onto Aurelia's shoulders, curling around her neck like a scarf.

"She'd eaten the rest of my meal bars, too." She let out a laugh. "I guess my telling her to go back to her family didn't work."

"No." I reached out, scratching underneath its chin. The little thing had probably been abandoned by her family, just like I was. I had a soft spot for that. "We should probably tell the crew, though."

"Do we have to?" Aurelia pouted, her hand resting over the creature's head. "I don't want to freak her out with so many humans around."

"I won't let them take her from you," I said, smoothing a hand down her arm. "But they should know that you have a... pet inside your cabin, Rae. You can't exactly keep her hidden forever."

Fuck, this was *so* against federal regulations. Keeping a wild alien animal as a pet would be highly frowned upon, but I was right before. The animal had bonded with Aurelia. Clearly, there was no keeping them apart.

"Oh. You're right." Her face morphed into a beaming smile. "She needs a name, don't you think? That way, we don't have to keep calling her *it*."

"Mmm." I couldn't disagree—the creature needed a name. But what...

"Her eyes are like aquamarines. And we found her in the water..." Aurelia clicked her tongue. "Maybe Aqua?"

I shook my head. A unique creature like this deserved a beautiful name. "She's like your little protector," I mused, watching them. "You helped her, and now she wants to take care of you, too."

Aurelia gave her some head scratches, smiling as she deliberated over name options.

Something clicked in my head. "What about Brina?"

"What does that mean?"

"*Defender*." I grinned, sticking a hand out towards Aurelia and getting a low hum of disapproval from the creature. I switched my hand to pet her instead, and she let out a satisfied chirp in response. "See? She barely even wants me to touch you."

Though that wouldn't stop me. Not when I craved the woman in front of me like I'd craved no one before.

She was mine. Even if she didn't know it yet.

"Brina it is," she said with a smile. "What do you think, little Brina?"

The animal chirped again, a low, almost-purr rumbling through its chest.

"She likes it," I confirmed.

"It's weird to think that we stumbled upon a completely new species of animals. They don't even have a name."

"That we know of," I said, watching as she sat on my bed. Brina curled up next to her, wrapping her tail up and setting her nose on top of it.

"*Canis lutra.*"

"Huh?"

"Animals all have scientific names, right? *Canis lupus familiaris*—that's what we call a domesticated dog. And *lontra canadensis* is a river otter. So… Canis lutra." Maybe it was dumb, but that was the first thing that had popped into my mind.

"Dog otter?"

"Do you have a better idea?" I asked, quirking a brow.

"No." She huffed out the word. "How do you even know all that, anyway?"

"I have my ways." I didn't want to admit that I'd been looking up their scientific names earlier, because I couldn't get the little beasts out of my mind. *Lutra* meant otter, and Canis belonged to the genus family that dogs were in. It just… fit.

"We should probably just leave the naming to the science division, anyway." The words were muttered under my breath.

"Speaking of… I don't want them to poke and prod at her. Sure, they'll study them on the surface, but…"

"I know." Clasping my hand over Aurelia's, I threaded my

fingers through hers as she relaxed. "She'll be safe here." I'd make sure of it.

"Thank you." Aurelia wrapped her other arm around my waist, hugging me tight without dropping our connected hands. "For everything."

She didn't let go, so I didn't either, simply swaying us back and forth. It almost felt like we were dancing. I leaned my head down, pressing my cheek to the top of her head and inhaling her scent. *Violets.* She always smelled so sweet, and I thought I could get hooked on it.

"Of course, little star." I kissed her forehead. "Anything for you." I didn't bother telling her she didn't have to thank me again. That she never needed to apologize. Though both were true.

"I better get to bed," she murmured, glancing at Brina, who was sound asleep on my comforter. "Probably should be responsible, since I'm basically a mom now." She winked, stepping back to scoop up the pup.

My mouth went dry, and my heart beat a strange tempo in my chest. Why was that so alluring? Thinking about Aurelia with a child?

Our child. The thought was there and gone in an instant. It wasn't like that between us. We might have been sleeping together, but that was all it was. She'd given me no sign that she wanted anything else from me besides sex. I knew that, and yet I couldn't help but wonder.

She stood on her tiptoes to press a soft kiss to my cheek. "Goodnight."

"Goodnight," I muttered back, feeling frustrated at the sudden urge of possessiveness that was pulsing through my veins.

I didn't want her to leave. I wanted to ask her to stay here. To sleep in my bed. To curl up beside me. To let me hold her, like I had last night. But I couldn't.

I was frozen in place, watching her leave, taking that sweet scent and her little creature with her. Leaving me all alone once again.

Anything for you. That was the thought that remained in my mind, long after Aurelia and Brina had left for the night. That I'd do anything for her.

I'd do anything to *keep* her.

Fuck, I was down bad for this girl. The one girl I never should have wanted. And yet, how could I not?

"CAPTAIN."

I rubbed my eyes.

Aurelia was standing in front of me, wearing a tiny black nightgown, her tattooed constellation on her shoulder on full display.

"What are you doing here?"

"Can I come in?" Her voice was low as she glanced around the hallway.

It was well after 0200, so the likelihood of someone being up on my floor and catching us was slim, but we couldn't be too cautious. Not when the chances of being caught were so high.

"Of course." I let her slip in past me and closed the door, latching it shut. My door required my ID card to open it, but the extra layer of security made me feel better. "Are you okay? What's wrong?"

She shook her head. "I couldn't sleep. All I could think about was *what now*? Where do we go from here?"

"What do you mean?" I asked, holding my breath.

The words she said earlier echoed in my mind.

I don't want to go back to the way things were before between us.
I don't want this to end.

All night, I'd been tossing and turning, the same thought

flicking through my mind since she'd left me. I couldn't bear to part with her either. Not when I knew what it felt like to be inside of her. When I was so desperate to have her again.

I wanted everything with her. And I was going to take it, if she offered.

"We shouldn't be together," she mumbled the words.

"Probably not," I agreed, stepping closer to brush a strand of hair off her forehead. "I'm your captain."

"You're my captain," she repeated. "Being in a relationship with your superior officer is forbidden."

"But."

"But..."

I threaded my fingers through her hair, letting my palm rest against her cheek. She closed her eyes, like she was absorbing my touch for a moment.

"But I can't ignore this thing between us, either."

"So what are we doing, little star? I'm at your mercy here. Whatever you want, I'm yours."

Aurelia reached for my free hand, interlacing our fingers. "I want *you*."

"Thank fuck," I muttered, cupping the back of her neck to bring her mouth to mine.

My kiss wasn't soft. It was hard—demanding. Taking. Swiping at her lower lip, I coaxed her mouth open with my tongue, kissing her deeply. It was everything. It wasn't enough.

"Where's Brina?" I asked, my eyes flicking down the length of her body.

"Asleep on my bed," she whispered. "I don't think she'll do much harm."

"If she does, it's okay."

"Yeah?"

"Mhm." I nuzzled my face against her neck. "Because you can just stay here."

"Oh, I can?"

"*Yes,*" I said, lifting her up into my arms. "My bed. My room. *My woman.*"

Aurelia wrapped her legs around my waist. "Yes," she agreed. "I am. I'm yours."

"Good." I dropped her on the bed, loving the way her hair spread out around her like a halo. An angel in the heavens.

My star in every galaxy.

TWENTY-SIX
AURELIA

PART of me still couldn't believe how he'd defended me, taking the downfall for the whole thing. It was my fault, and yet... he'd protected me. Even going so far as to keep me from revealing the chip that was currently hiding in my dresser drawer.

And how he'd promised to keep Brina safe? It melted away the last of my resistance, the stubbornness in my system rapidly fading. How could I continue to keep him at arm's length when he was so determined to force his way into my heart?

It was why I'd shown up to his room in the middle of the night. Because I couldn't deny how I felt anymore.

I needed him.

"Did you wear this little thing for me?" He said, his voice so low it was almost a growl.

I fluttered my eyelashes as I ran my hands over the sheets on his bed. "Yes." It was a black nightgown with tiny little straps—adorned with lace on the top and a little bow in the center.

Rubbing my legs together, I let out a needy whimper.

He stood over me, looking larger than life. All six feet and two inches of him made me feel small. *Dainty.* Sylas's knee nudged my legs apart, and I already knew what he would find

I was helplessly turned on, and the expression in his eyes only made me wetter. Damn him.

His fingers crept up my body, dancing under the short hem of the little nightgown.

Truthfully, I'd only packed it in case I wanted to wear something that made me feel pretty on this long voyage. My personal clothes were slim to none—my dad's old jacket, a few pairs of jeans, my favorite tops, and a few lacy underwear I couldn't go without. The rest was pretty standard federation issuances—sweats and t-shirts. I didn't even have a dress hanging in my wardrobe.

"Sylas," I whispered as he wrapped a hand around my upper thigh, pulling me down to the edge of the bed.

He pushed the bottom half of the nightgown up, torturously slow, and he groaned. "No panties. *Fuck me.* Did you come all the way up here like this? Knowing anyone could see you?"

I nodded, biting my lip as he drew circles on my inner thigh —not where I needed it. He was torturing me, driving me wild with need.

"Am I going to find you wet for me, Rae?" The words were a rasp, a sound that went straight to my core.

"*Yes.*" A whine slipped free from my throat. "Touch me. Please."

In response, he ran his knuckle over my slit. "*Fuck.* You're drenched."

Squirming under his gaze, Sylas finally gave me what I wanted, dipping one finger inside of me. His thick, long finger stroked my insides, and then he added another one. Even just from that, I felt impossibly full. And it was nothing compared to the feeling of his cock inside of me.

"Are you sore?" He asked, placing a kiss on my neck. "From yesterday?"

"A little," I said with a gasp as his fingers hit just the right spot. "But I can take it."

Normally I rolled my eyes at the idea of *Big Dick Energy,* but damn, Sylas Kellar had it in spades. And he knew what to do with it, too.

"Of course you can," he said, a smirk on his face. Like he knew I wouldn't back down from this.

He pumped me with unrelenting focus, and I couldn't hold back my voice, letting out a series of breathy moans that only spurred him on more.

"That's it," he encouraged. "Coat my fingers, baby. Give it to me. Nice and wet, so you can take me."

Holy shit. Was it possible I could come from his fingers alone? Normally, I needed more stimulation, but I'd never felt this worked up before.

The wet sounds of his fingers as he fucked me with them were downright obscene, but *filthy* and delicious. Sex had never been like this before. So dirty and rough, yet solely focused on my pleasure. On getting *me* off.

My back arched off the bed as I shattered, coming on his fingers, my insides squeezing around him as I came down from it.

I propped myself up on my elbows as he pulled his fingers out of me, bringing them up to my lips. "Open," he instructed, running them over my lower lip, spreading my juices there. I did, letting him slide those two fingers into my mouth. "Suck."

Obeying his words, I tasted myself on his skin, sucking until his fingers were clean. I pulled off with a *pop*, finding a darkened expression on his face. One day, I wanted to see what face he made while I went down on him.

His thumb rubbed over my lower lip before pulling it down. "Such a good girl," he murmured. Leaning down, he lazily kissed me, letting our tongues tangle together. He cupped my breasts, rubbing the hardened nipples through the silk fabric, and I let out a moan.

I eyed the pressing matter in his boxers, wondering if I could return the favor now. "That looks painful." I reached out, brushing against his erection with my fingers.

He grunted in response, stilling my hands.

"Need this off," he said, tugging the nightgown's material up over my head as he guided me into a sitting position, giving himself full access to my breasts.

"God, these tits," Sylas muttered. "I'm fucking obsessed with them."

His hands were large enough that he could cover them completely, and I didn't think I'd ever found hands so attractive before. Especially when he massaged them, thumbs running back and forth over my nipples, driving me wild.

Then he bent down, taking one breast into his mouth, licking and sucking on the peaks, that sinful tongue of his doing wicked things to my body. He nipped at my nipple, brushing his teeth against it, and the sensation sent a jolt of pleasure through me. As if sensing the pleasure, he repeated it on the other side, licking and sucking, biting and soothing. It was everything.

It wasn't enough.

"Sylas," I moaned. "I need you."

"You have me, baby. You have me." He groaned.

God, he was so effortlessly handsome. His dark scruffy beard, that soft hair I wanted to run my fingers through. His bare chest and boxers. I liked all of it.

I looped my finger through the waistband of his tight boxer briefs, pushing them down his hips until his cock sprang free. A bead of pre-cum sat at the tip, and I reached out, capturing the drop with my tongue.

This time, I had time to explore. In the caves, it had been a frenzy. Now, I wanted to make him feel the way he made me. *Wanted.* Cherished.

I swirled my tongue over his tip, each strangled sound he made serving as a means of encouragement. Dragging my fingernail up his shaft, I felt him shudder beneath me.

"Like that?" I gave him an innocent smile.

"You're such a brat," he said, wrapping my hair around his

wrist and giving it a slight tug. "You know exactly what you do to me."

I flattened my tongue, repeating the motion with it, before wrapping my lips around his head and sucking.

"I don't want to come in your pretty little mouth, Aurelia."

I gave him one last lick before he slid free.

"No?" I fluttered my eyelashes. "Then where do you want to come?"

He groaned, lifting me up into his arms and pulling me down on top of him. His cock, hard and heavy, was pressed between us, resting against my stomach. "You know where. In this tight little pussy." Sylas kissed my neck. "Is that what you want, little star? For me to fill you up?"

I rocked my hips, desperate for it.

"Yes," I said. "Please." My hands cupped his cheek, rubbing over his short beard. God, I loved the feel of it. Even more so when he'd been between my legs. The way his scruff had rubbed at my thighs, leaving the skin reddened. It was all too good.

He guided his tip into my opening, pushing in just an inch, the stretch already impossibly good.

I'd definitely feel him tomorrow. But maybe that was what he wanted, too. The reminder of whose I was. They were just words in the heat of sex, the haze of pleasure, but I couldn't deny the way they made me feel.

Planting my hands on his chest, I worked myself onto his cock, sliding down an inch at a time. It was a tight fit, and I was stuffed full of him. But I loved the bite of pain, the slight burn, and the way it all melted into endless pleasure.

"You're too big," I groaned. "I'm so full."

When he was fully inside me, I could have sworn I climaxed just from the sensation. From this angle, I could feel him everywhere.

Sylas's hands were at my waist, and I rolled my hips, needing more friction. I rocked back and forth, a little gasp escaping my lips every time my needy clit ground down against the base of him.

"You feel like you were made for me," he grunted. "The perfect fit." He moved his hand, resting it over my stomach, pressing down just slightly. The pressure doubled the sensations, and I cried out. And when he thrust up from underneath me? I was a goner. There was no chance of surviving this.

"Come for me, baby." Sylas's lips were at my ear as he pulled me against him. His free hand snaked down to my entrance, where his eyes were focused. Like he couldn't stop watching the slide of his cock into my opening.

He pressed his thumb against my clit, and that was all it took. I came, stars exploding in my vision, and I instantly knew that it had never been this way before. And it would never feel like this again. Not with anyone else. Not when Sylas made me feel this *good.*

He took over for me, helping guide my hips up and down his length as my body clenched, the pulsing sensations still running through me when I felt him get harder inside of me.

"*Fuuuck,*" he grunted, and then let go, pouring his release inside of me. I wanted to throw my head back, to lose myself in the sensations, but I couldn't. Because watching the face he made when he came was more important to me.

Gorgeous. My hot, alpha-male, overbearing captain was the most handsome man I'd ever seen. Orgasm face or not, he could pull anyone on this ship easily. With that amazing body—one I wanted to touch, always—sometimes I still couldn't believe he was with me.

I ran my fingers over his abs, appreciating the muscles.

"Like those, do you?"

"About as much as you like my tits," I said, placing a kiss on the scruff on his neck.

He flashed a cocky grin. "So a lot."

"Mmm."

"Worth every hour in the gym." Sylas winked at me.

He was still inside of me, our bodies pressed closely together. He brushed a sweaty strand of hair off my forehead and then dipped his lips down to my lips. "But I'm pretty sure I love your tits more."

I felt his cock soften inside of me, and I went to slide off of him, but he caught my wrists, stilling me with a kiss. "Not yet."

"Mmm." I wiggled against him, pressing down deeper on him.

"Evil." Shifting us so we were both laying on our sides, his arms wrapped around me, I almost fell asleep like that. I was warm and comfortable, and something about having him still inside of me was almost... nice?

Finally, he pulled out, and I felt the loss immediately.

Sylas's eyes were focused on the spot where his cum dripped from my body. He dragged his finger through it, pushing it back in. And oh, fuck, I liked that—too much.

Was I going to have some weird kink for it now? Thank god we were both on fertility blockers, because otherwise, this would be dangerous. *Too* dangerous.

No matter how I felt, having a baby right now was not something in my plans.

But, what if... I shook the thought away. Now was not the time. Not when I had a baby animal snoozing away in my quarters, one who I barely had any idea how to take care of. When we weren't even in a relationship, not really.

And yet...

"Aurelia."

"Mmm?" I asked as he ran his nose over my neck.

"How are you feeling?"

I yawned, stretching out my arms. "Like I could float away on a cloud." Sure, I was a little sore, but mostly I felt incredible. I wasn't worrying about the future, about things we couldn't control. And his bed was the most comfortable thing I'd been on in months.

He chuckled. "Good thing there're no clouds in space."

"You know what I mean." I pushed at his shoulder playfully.

"Gonna clean you up," he murmured, nipping at my neck.

Good idea. He pulled me into his arms, and I didn't complain, just wrapped my legs around his waist and let him carry me into the shower. I was all too aware of his already-hardening cock as I clung to him like a koala cub.

If he made me feel like *this* every day, I certainly wouldn't say no to climbing him like a tree.

"Mmm," I said, enjoying the warm water as it ran over my skin, the soothing circles from Sylas's soaped up hands as he rubbed at my inner-thighs.

It wasn't inherently sexual, but it was the most sensual experience I could have imagined, as he washed every inch of my body with his body wash.

Deep and masculine. I liked the idea that I smelled like him. He ran his hands over my nipples from behind, cupping them as he soaped them, and then he tilted my head back, making sure I didn't get water in my eyes as he dampened my hair.

And... Sylas Kellar was shampooing my hair. *Goddamn.* His strong, capable fingers dug into my scalp, massaging slightly, and I let out a moan that had nothing to do with the heat pooling between my legs already. It was pure satisfaction, like he was rubbing all the tension out of my skull.

We didn't speak, other than his quiet commands. *Close your eyes. Tilt your head back. Does that feel good?*

I loved wearing my hair up, but my thick hair gave me a headache when I had it in a bun or ponytail for an extended period.

After he'd finished rinsing out the shampoo and rubbing conditioner into my ends, I turned, intending to give him the same treatment.

Partially because I wanted to touch him like he'd just touched me. But I also wanted him to feel cared for. Appreciated. Like he deserved.

"Aurelia." He groaned as my hands brushed up his torso.

"Let me," I whispered. "Please."

He nodded, and I filled my palms with soap, rubbing down his broad shoulders and thick forearms. I didn't appreciate them enough. Maybe because they were constantly covered up by his uniform. It should have been illegal to hide these perfect specimens from the world.

Before I could run my hands over his straining cock, he let out a low growl. "Don't start something you don't intend to finish, little star."

"But what if I intended to finish it?" I ran my thumb over the tip, collecting a bead of pre-cum.

In a flash, he'd let the rest of the soap wash off, and then turned the water off. He pulled me out of the shower, dried me off with a soft towel, and then threw me over his shoulder.

Carrying me back to bed.

No complaints here. Especially not with this view I had of his ass that just wouldn't quit.

God, how did I get so lucky to find myself all wrapped up with this man?

It was the question I hadn't been able to stop asking myself.

Maybe I never would.

TWENTY-SEVEN
AURELIA

I YAWNED, stretching out on my blissful cloud. Sylas's chest rose and fell beside me, and Brina was sleeping at my feet. Though I would have been content to fall asleep in his arms after our glorious shower, I'd felt guilty leaving her alone in my room for the night.

She was like a little puppy, all too happy to just be around her humans. We'd also stolen a pad for her to use and some more fish from the kitchens, which meant we were all stocked up for our little alien otter-puppy hybrid.

"How am I supposed to sneak out of here?" I whispered, glancing at the time on the clock. "I need to go get a fresh uniform."

Sylas wrapped his arm around my waist, pulling me to his chest. "Don't leave." He buried his head in my hair, inhaling deeply. "I like you in my bed."

A little smile curled up on my lips.

This was so, so wrong, but I couldn't help myself anymore. It felt right.

"I like your bed too, Captain Kellar." He swatted at my bare ass, and I poked at his chest in retaliation. "It's much more comfortable than mine."

"Captain's perks," he said, a smirk dancing over his lips.

"Oh?" I crossed my arms, letting them rest on his bare chest, and rested my head on them. "What do you call this, then?" Leaning down, I pressed a kiss to his lips.

"Mmm." He hummed, like he was thinking about it, wrapping his hands around my hips. "*Mine.*"

I laughed, pushing him off and trying to get out of bed.

"Do we really have to get up?" He groaned the word, throwing his forearm over his eyes.

"*Yes.*" I poked at his chest. "Because you're the captain, and you're the one who planned this planetary research mission for today."

He grumbled under his breath, sitting up and running a hand through his hair.

"I have to take Brina to my room, too." It wasn't like she was going to live *here*, in Sylas's room.

Except I was pretty sure she was in *love* with his bathtub. We'd filled it up with a few inches of water, letting her splash around and use that powerful tail to swim around. Hopefully, I'd get the chance to use it myself at some point.

He sighed. "I know."

"I should take her back," I whispered. The thought had only just occurred to me. We *were* taking a transport ship back down to the surface today. It would be the responsible thing to return her to the wild. To her home. But... I was already a little in love with her.

Sylas brushed a hand over my hair, like he knew what I was thinking. "If you want. But if she doesn't want to go, then we'll find a way to make it work."

"Really?" I looked up at him, my heart swelling in my chest.

Oh, this was dangerous. *He* was dangerous.

Probably for my heart.

MY PLANS TO keep Brina a secret were quickly foiled that morning when Finley asked, "Aurelia, what were those noises I heard coming from your room last night? Because it sounded like barking, which is weird, because no one has a dog on the ship."

Shit. Guess the walls weren't as thick as I hoped.

"About that. I..." I winced. "I sort of had an additional passenger come along yesterday."

We were all in our flight suits, ready to board one of the larger transport shuttles down to the planet's surface. Most of the officers were staying behind, but Finley and a few of the head researchers—including Zaria and Ryder, who were twins that looked uncannily alike—were accompanying us.

"What?" Finley's eyebrows were practically at her hairline. "You..."

Yeah, I could see how this didn't sound good.

"I had a stowaway. Syl—" I quickly caught myself. Dammit, I couldn't keep slipping up like this. "Captain Kellar and I came across an injured native animal and I, uh, assisted it." A sheepish smile crossed over my face. "She somehow got into my bag, and I didn't realize it until we were already on the ship."

"She?"

"Brina. Ah—the creature. It's a girl." Something I was like 90% sure about, assuming their anatomy was at all similar to creatures on Earth. If not, I was calling her a girl, anyway. I was simply too stubborn to admit when I was wrong.

"You named it?"

"Yup. Well, the Captain did, technically."

"Sounds like you two have been spending a lot of time alone together." Finley raised an eyebrow.

I blushed. I couldn't help it. "It's not like that."

But it was. It was so like that. And I was dying to tell someone about it, but who could I tell? Our relationship was strictly forbidden. He was highly off limits. If anyone knew, they should technically report it.

Which meant I couldn't confess to my best friends about all the sex I'd been having. Good sex. No—amazing sex. A smile slipped on my face as I thought of Sylas this morning. How he'd tried to keep me in his bed.

But we had a mission. This ship wasn't just here for vibes alone. And we had landed on a geological wealth of a planet.

Even if I had this unsettled feeling in my gut that my dad had found it, too. But why hadn't the federation known about it? Or if they had, why send us on this same path? Something didn't add up.

"Aurelia?"

"Hm?"

"You ready?" That was Kayle. Sylas was staying behind, partially because of the whole captain of this ship thing, and also because we couldn't afford to get caught if someone noticed we were always in the same place. But mostly because I needed to pilot the ship, to make sure we had a safe and smooth landing. Given that I'd already flown into this atmosphere once, I was the smartest person for the job.

Plus, I could show everyone what we'd found in the caves.

"Yes." I settled into my seat, strapping in before going through the process to boot up the ship. At least I couldn't fuck this up as badly as I did before.

The motions took over, fingers flying on the console as I set our flight path, adjusting the variables slightly based on yesterday.

I looked out of the cockpit, finding Sylas standing there, a proud expression on his face. The warmth flooded in my system, just from his small smile. That show of belief and support he could only communicate in one way.

And to think, two months ago, he'd tried to kick me off the ship.

I snorted, and Kayle looked over at me, her face showing obvious amusement.

"Shut up," I mumbled, not wanting to explain the train of thoughts that led me there.

Then, with a few pushes of buttons and flipped switches, we were ready to go. Sylas disappeared with a wave, and the airlock was open.

Time to fly.

"GOOD WORK TODAY, EVERYONE," Kayle called as everyone filed off the ship. "See you back here tomorrow, bright and early!"

The ship was abuzz with excitement, mostly because Finley and her researchers couldn't believe what we'd stumbled upon. Not only the native creatures; but also the crystals that seemed to *glow.*

Ryder seemed to think the energy stored within them could be harnessed somehow. I found that blasphemous, but then again, we were on a starship millions of light years away from earth.

What did I know? I had an engineering degree, not an advanced geology degree. Sure, I knew a lot about a wide variety of topics, but I certainly wasn't an expert on rocks or crystals.

"How are you feeling, Aurelia?" Kayle asked, watching as I rubbed at my shoulder muscles.

"Good." Sore. I was a little tense, too, but there was no point in mentioning that. "Just tired. Sleeping on that cave floor the other day really did a number on my back.

"Hmm."

"What?" I raised an eye at her.

"Nothing." She gave me a sweet smile. "I wanna meet your little creature, though. Think she'd be up for it?"

I shrugged. "Maybe?" I had no idea how Brina would be with strangers. So far, it had only just been me and Sylas. Would she bite? If she was going to cause problems, I'd have to take her back. And I really didn't want to have to abandon my new little friend. Especially when I'd bonded with her. "I don't know…"

"It's okay." She gave me a small smile. "I'm just curious."

A laugh burst out of me. "You and everyone else on this ship."

"Can you blame us? Those little guys are so cute!"

"What's cute?" came that deep voice I knew without even looking up. Sylas. My body relaxed as he walked up, standing behind me. We weren't touching, and more than a foot of space separated our bodies, but it still felt like his body heat radiated to me.

"Brina." I turned back to him, having to tilt my chin up to look at him. Holy tall. Sometimes, when I wasn't in his presence for an extended period, I could forget how tall he was, and then he would stand over me like this. A shiver worked its way down my spine.

A genuine smile lit up his face. "She is pretty cute. I was just on my way to find you, actually."

"Oh?"

He nodded, running his hands through his hair. "She's in my room."

I quirked an eyebrow. "Why?"

"I—" Was it just me, or did Sylas look nervous? "I felt bad about her being all alone all day. So I rescued her."

"You…" My jaw dropped. "You went into my room?" My voice was so low it was practically a whisper.

"Don't worry, Lieutenant. I didn't see your stuffed cow."

My cheeks were definitely on fire now. "I—"

"I let her splash around the bathtub for a bit. She's a very happy pup."

Kayle looked between the two of us like we'd grown two heads. "What is going on here?"

I frowned. "What do you mean?"

"You're acting like pet parents right now." She whirled on Sylas. "And since when do you smile?"

His face dropped. "Since always." He was messing with his hair again. I liked that it was his nervous tell, because it meant I knew when he was feeling out of control.

It made him feel more human, especially compared to the larger-than-life grumpy captain I'd once thought him to be.

Now he was just... Sylas. The man I cared for, more than I wanted to admit. The man who was helping me care for a strange alien animal like she was our beloved pet. The man who delivered more orgasms in bed than I'd ever had before.

"It's no big deal," I said, trying to brush his sister off. "We found her together, so it only makes sense that she likes both of us."

"Right." Sylas nodded. "I can't exactly abandon the little bugger, now can I?"

I held back a giggle at his words, and Kayle looked at the watch on her wrist. "Shit. I gotta run. I, uh... have somewhere I need to be."

Sylas and I shared a confused glance, but when she said nothing else, we both waved goodbye, watching her sprint away.

His hand rubbed at his beard, his jaw working. "That was... weird."

"You don't think she suspects something, do you?"

"Of course not." He turned his body fully towards mine, and the smell of his cologne hit my nostrils. God, I loved the way he smelled. Like the night air. I wished I could bottle it up. Or better yet, sleep with that scent on my pillow.

Because it wasn't like I could bury my face in his chest every night. *Right?*

He pinched my ass, causing me to glare at him. "What was that for?"

"You had this look on your face."

I crossed my arms over my chest. "I did not."

He smirked, but I knew the exact face he had seen. *Lust.* I inhaled deeply. Fuck. Me.

"Are you coming to my room tonight?" Sylas asked, the words so low that even if anyone else was around, they wouldn't be able to hear.

I glanced around before pulling him into an abandoned supply closet. The dim blue safety lights flickered on, and then I was in his arms, my body pressed against the wall as he kissed me.

"What are we doing?" I asked, pulling away from his mouth long enough to get the words out.

He pressed his lips against my neck. "What do you mean?"

"We're not like…" I struggled to find the words. "In a relationship or anything. Right?"

I wanted him to say *yes.* That this was something more. That he wanted to be with me—fuck the rules.

"If anyone catches us—" I started again.

Sylas silenced my protests with another kiss. "They won't."

"How can you be so sure?"

Because whenever people were convinced they were really being sneaky, people around them already knew what was going on. A few too many of his flirty smiles or heated stares in my direction, and the entire crew would know.

And that would be *mortifying.* I didn't want people to think I was sleeping with my captain. Not after we'd gotten to such a rocky start at the beginning of the mission.

"Because it's us." He ran his fingers through my ponytail, undoing the elastic so it would fall around my shoulders.

"Because this is *good*. And it can't be wrong if it feels like this, right?"

Sighing, I rested my forehead against his chest. "I don't know. I'm worried your sister will figure it out. She's too perceptive."

"Maybe. But she won't tell on us, Rae."

"She's legally required to."

"She's my sister," he insisted. "And she's all I have."

My hands were still wrapped around his collar. "What about me?" My voice was soft. "And Brina?"

"Fuck. Little star—"

I shook my head. "I'm just wondering if we're in over our heads here, Sylas. We're not supposed to be together. You're my Captain, and you're—"

"Too old for you." He groaned. "I know."

A giggle burst from my lips. "That's not what I was going to say."

"No?" He raised an eyebrow.

"I don't care that you're ten years older than me, Sylas. I care about what kind of man you are. And all you've done is show me that, day after day."

He frowned. "I'm just a grumpy asshole who doesn't deserve someone like you."

"I think the opposite is true." I pressed my lips to his cheek in a soft kiss, brushing my face over his stubble. "I think you deserve someone exactly like me."

TWENTY-EIGHT
SYLAS

I THINK *you deserve someone exactly like me.*

Did she know what those words did to me? I grabbed her hand, interlacing our fingers. "Come on. Let's go check on our kid."

She let out a strangled laugh. "Don't call her that. People are going to get the wrong idea. Besides, it's not like we have joint ownership."

"Don't we?"

I pressed the button to open the closet door and then looked down at our joined hands. She dropped them, looking away guiltily as we exited, the automatic mechanism closing it once again once we were back in the hallway.

"After you, Captain Kellar."

I nodded, clearing my throat. I hated this. Why did I hate it? It should have been fine. But I wanted her to call me Sylas. Wanted her teasing remarks, her laughter and her smiles. I wanted everyone to know she was mine, dammit.

Hiding made me feel like there was something to be guilty of. Besides being her captain, there was nothing else to keep us apart. We were both legal, consenting adults. So who the fuck cared if we were together?

Leading the way to my quarters, I was all too aware of Aurelia behind me. We might not have been able to hold hands, but every once in a while, her hand brushed mine, and that was enough.

It would have to be.

"Oh." Aurelia's hand flew over her heart after the door slid shut behind us. "Sylas. You did all of this? Today?"

I nodded, suddenly unable to find my voice.

I'd made a little habitat for Brina in the corner of my room, pushing my small table and chairs aside. There was a little bed, a blow up pool—don't ask me why someone had it on my starship, but I wasn't complaining—and a fuzzy blanket spread out on the floor. Part of me had wondered if we should install a gate, like you would with a house training puppy, but Brina was smart. As soon as I'd told her it was her space, she'd been content.

Plus, I'd taken her to the gardens and let her run around this afternoon. The fish in the hydroponics section hadn't been amused, but I hadn't let her eat *too* many of them.

Just kidding. Mostly.

"I wanted her to have somewhere she felt safe."

As if in response, Brina poked her head out from underneath her blanket. Somehow, she'd rolled herself in there like a burrito.

"This is amazing. Thank you."

"You don't have to thank me." I shook my head, taking her hand once again. "Not for this." I kissed the top of her hand, not letting go.

"You're incredible."

"Nah. I'm just trying to make her like me more than you."

Aurelia cracked a smile. "Impossible." She walked over to Brina's new habitat, getting down on her knees. "Hi, little girl."

Brina perked up, wagging her tail and letting out a series of adorable yips.

"You're never going to want to go back to my room, are

you?" She barked, and Aurelia sighed. "I guess daddy is going to have to deal with me being here more often, isn't he?"

Fuck, but if that statement didn't have me hard. I didn't even *like* being called Daddy in bed, but her saying it did something to me.

I rubbed at the spot on my chest that felt tight as I watched them. Brina crawled onto Aurelia's lap, rested her head on her knees, and gave a contented sigh.

You know, the way an animal sighed that made you go, *what ails you, you adorable little freeloader?* Yeah. Precious as fuck. Even I wanted to snuggle that thing.

Her paws and tail were like an otter's, with the snout of a little puppy and these half-floppy tiny ears. Plus those bright blue eyes, and she should have been freakish, but no. Adorable.

"We're going back down again tomorrow."

"I know." I blew out a breath. My sister and I had already discussed it.

"I think I'm going to take Brina with me this time."

"Why?" That surprised me.

"Because it's her home. And I hate to leave her again." Aurelia's face was downturned, and I knew there was more on her mind.

"You just mean you don't want me to become her favorite."

Aurelia stuck out her tongue at me. Then she sighed, snuggling the creature. "I know we both want to keep her, but I just keep wondering… is this the best place for her?"

My heart sunk. What could I say? "I know."

Because I was pretty sure Brina had bonded with her that first day, and now, well… I'd bonded with her, too. Even if she wasn't committed to staying by my side, I was quite fond of the little thing.

I'd never had a pet before. Growing up, I'd wanted a dog, but my parents had refused. And then, when they were gone, it was all I could do to keep Kayle and me clothed and fed. There were never spare funds for a pet.

It was all as well, because once I'd joined the academy and become a member of the UGSF, there was no time for a dog. Especially not on long space missions. The only animals on board were typically service dogs, and they had their own private space for when they were off duty or to relieve themselves.

Still, what did I know about being a responsible pet owner? Nothing. I highly doubted in my ability to keep any being alive, let alone myself. But for her, I wanted to try. Because I didn't want to see Aurelia sad.

And if this strange creature made her happy, so be it. It was part of the crew now. It could have a home. I'd find it somewhere to swim and eat and whatever else it needed.

No problem.

"I'll take her back with me tomorrow," Aurelia finished, a sad tone to her voice.

"Okay," I agreed.

Sitting next to her, she leaned on my shoulder, and I smoothed my hands over her hair before rubbing soothing circles down her back, soaking up her presence.

BRINA WAS RIDING on Aurelia's shoulders, not willing to part with her newly-acquired human, as Finley and her team worked around us, collecting samples from the planet.

I'd convinced Kayle to stay behind today and have command of the ship, mainly because I couldn't bear to be apart from Aurelia.

"She really doesn't want you to leave her," I observed, scratching her head as she remained on her perch, her little tail practically wrapping around Aurelia like a scarf.

"I know." She sighed. "I know I'd be sad if she left, but I just feel like she's leaving her entire life behind. Her family. Creatures that are like her."

"But isn't that what we did, too?" I asked, stepping close and dropping my voice. "Maybe that's why we understand her. Because we're the same."

"It's not—"

"Sure, we still have human surrounding us. But our family? The people who were supposed to love us? They left us."

"Sylas." She whispered the word, her hand brushing against the back of mine.

"And we... We left in pursuit of something different. Can you say she's making a different choice?"

"No." Aurelia leaned up, petting Brina, who let out a series of happy chirps. "She's too smart for her own good."

"Maybe the other alien otters ostracized her for being such a smart girl, huh?" I scratched under her chin. "That's why she wanted to come live with us."

"Okay, *daddy*." She snorted.

"Aurelia." I groaned.

"What?" She battered her eyes, looking all innocent.

"Don't call me that."

A smirk curled over her lips. "Or what?"

"Or later, when we're alone, I'll make you regret it."

She sucked in an inhale of breath. "Do you want me to beg, Sylas?"

I was caught in her spell. Entranced. Totally fucking taken by this brazen woman who was sunshine incarnate and yet the biggest brat I'd ever met. Talk about duality.

"Stop making me hard." The words were a rasp. "Fuck."

Aurelia winked, spinning away to go talk to Finley.

I stood awkwardly by the ship, willing my body to cool down.

Tonight, I wanted to show her exactly how badly I wanted to see her beg. To have her squirming under me, needy and pleading.

"AURELIA." I cursed under my breath, berating myself for forgetting that half of the officers were also on this vessel. "Lieutenant Callisto."

"Yes?" She looked over at me, an innocent, coy expression curled over her face as she clicked on her safety restraints.

My girl stared up at me, like she was expecting me to ask a question. The problem was, I didn't even have one. I just wanted her to look at me. Wanted her undivided attention.

"I have to fly the ship now," she murmured under her breath, low enough that only the two of us could hear.

"This place is fucking insane, man," Leo was saying to Orion behind us, and that was the only thing that brought me back to reality.

I forced out a chuckle as I listened to their conversation.

Orion wasn't as easily excitable as Leo—who sometimes just acted like an overgrown dog—but you could still see the wonder in his eyes. "And just think about how many places out there are undiscovered? Places we can only dream of..." He trailed off as Aurelia finished the last steps of her takeoff routine, bringing the ship into the air.

Unlike an airplane, we had to reach the upper atmosphere and then keep going, and it took precise calculations and immense skill to do it as flawlessly as Aurelia did.

Fuck, why had I ever underestimated her? She was brilliant. Amazing. In every single way, she was constantly blowing my mind. I'd promised myself to give her a chance, and that had paid off in more ways than one.

Though I'd never expected how she'd worm her way into my heart by letting her stay as my pilot. Now, she was so deep; I didn't think I'd ever get her out.

Not that I wanted her to be. I rubbed at my chest, wondering if the ache would ever go away. Or if loving her would always feel like this.

Was that was this was?

No. It couldn't be. It was too soon.

No matter if my whole body lit up with every single precious smile of hers I was lucky enough to get.

I was a selfish bastard, and I would be keeping them all to myself.

TWENTY-NINE
AURELIA

ONE NIGHT in his bed turned to two, and then three, and suddenly, I'd blinked, and I couldn't remember the last time I'd so much as showered in my own quarters. I'd even brought a backup of both sets of uniforms to his room, meaning I didn't have to sneak back to my room at the crack of dawn anymore.

Now I just had to sneak out of his *without* people realizing where I'd stayed all night.

Brina was content in her little corner, enjoying all the attention she got from following me all over the ship. I was pretty sure she was going to be plump and fat quickly, considering how much food she conned out of unsuspecting crew members.

I'd joked about putting a bed under my console on the bridge, and then the next day, there had been one. Sylas's eyes had sparkled with mischief when I looked back at him, and I didn't think I'd ever had a man care for me like this before.

All the officers had now been down to the surface of the planet, and though Sylas and I had kept the exact location of our cave a secret, everyone had seen the underground beauty that it boasted. Both of us had an unspoken understanding, though. We'd have to leave soon.

And I hadn't touched the chip in my room. It was still in the same little locked box where I left it. Part of me was afraid to look at it. I wasn't sure what I was more afraid of, though—finding nothing, or finding everything? What sort of data in those last moments had they protected?

So, instead of facing the things that were hard, I'd decided to just live in this little bubble with Sylas. Here, in his room, none of the things that kept us apart mattered. We were just Aurelia and Sylas. Not a captain and pilot, not in a forbidden relationship.

We flourished at night, speaking with our bodies the way we never seemed to do with our words. I felt it in every action of his, the way he was always making sure I came twice before he did, touching me so gently, so tenderly. It was everything. But was it enough?

"Mmm." I nuzzled against his chest.

"Are you awake?"

"No."

He laughed. "Aurelia."

Was it possible to notice a change in someone like this? He seemed lighter. Happier. The bags under his eyes weren't as deep, and he laughed more. And maybe... that was because of me. Because he was happy with me.

We'd still never clarified what we were to each other, even though I already suspected how he felt. Not that I was very far behind him.

He brushed his finger under my chin, bringing my gaze to his.

"What?" I asked, pulling the sheet tighter against my body as I turned to face him fully.

He traced a thumb along my cheekbone. "You have stars in your eyes."

Oh. My heart.

Didn't he know sweet nothings like that weren't good for it? Because if I wasn't careful, I'd give him my heart. I was having a hard time reminding myself *why* I couldn't do that, why I wasn't supposed to trust in this.

He cupped my face, bringing our lips together in a soft kiss. "Little star…"

"Why do you call me that?" I whispered the words I'd held back from the very first time he'd uttered the nickname.

His hand stilled. "It's dumb."

"No." I took his face between mine. "Tell me. Please?"

"I can't hide anything from you," he said with a sigh. "It's because you're brighter than any star in the sky. Because I look at you, and all I want to do is orbit around your presence. Because you're my star, Aurelia Serena Callisto. And I never want to look away."

"Oh." My eyes were filled with unshed tears, and I tried to blink them away. Because his words were so sweet, and all I wanted to do was cry. "My dad used to call me that. *My star*. He said…" I shook my head, the lump in my throat getting bigger. "He said as long as I continued to shine, he'd find his way home to me." Tears were falling now. Big, fat ones. "It was so cheesy, but I love it." I let out a strangled laugh. When was the last time I'd truly let myself cry?

I couldn't remember.

Sylas wrapped me in his arms, letting me sob into his chest. He'd put on one of his soft t-shirts that I absolutely loved. Probably why I kept trying to steal them. Sure, they weren't any different than the federation shirts in my closet, but his were way bigger. I liked how baggy they were against my slender frame. And that they smelled like him.

"I miss him," I said with a hiccup as my tears finally slowed. "I miss him so much that it hurts. You know? Because he's gone, and he's not coming back. No matter what I do, he's gone."

"It's okay," Sylas murmured, stroking the back of my head, over and over. Soothing me through it, just like my dad used to when I was upset. I didn't even remember any of my reasons for crying back then, just how my dad had been there for me.

I shook my head, not saying anything. "I just can't help but wonder."

"Wonder what, baby?"

"What he would say if he was here. If his hug would feel as good now as it did when I was twelve. If this pain will ever really stop, or I'll miss him for the rest of my life."

"You don't have to wonder."

"Huh?" I scrunched up my face.

"I know what he would say. I…" He took a pause. Gave a shaky breath. "Don't be upset with me. I looked at the chip we salvaged off the ship, and I found something on it. Your father's files. I know I should have told you before but I… I just wanted to keep you to myself just a little bit longer." Sylas's hand weaved through my hair, like he was combing through it.

Nervous. He was nervous. It was cute.

"Okay?" I whispered the words. Because what else was there to say?

Sylas kissed my knuckles before standing up, still in that damn-sexy white t-shirt. The one that stretched over his abs and pecs, and I definitely did not spend the rest of my night sighing over it.

"The flash drive you gave me had files embedded in it. Some were corrupted, but I think I figured out a work around."

"You did?"

He winked at me. "I did. And it didn't even take much. Just a little bit of tinkering, but the files on the chip from the ship were encoded in the same way."

I nodded, the words caught in my throat. It wasn't too crazy, since it was all federation technology from the same time period.

"They're video diaries of your dad's." He smoothed his hand over his jaw. "Ones where he's talking to you."

"What?" I was floored. "They're really…" I trailed off, not finding the words.

The fact that Sylas had thought about it, spent time to find a way to make the clips playable... It all melted my heart. "You did that for me?"

Did he really think I'd be mad that he touched the chip? Because I knew that I would have avoided it for months. The same way that I knew as much as I needed the closure, it would hurt, too.

"Of course." He brushed my hair off my shoulder, pressing a kiss to the stars. I noticed that he liked to do that, and it was just another thing that warmed my chest. "I would do anything for you, Aurelia."

Climbing onto his lap, I cupped his face between my hands. "Thank you. You have no idea what this means to me."

He shook his head. "You don't have to thank me—" But I cut him off with a kiss.

Pressing soft ones all over his face, until he groaned, taking my mouth with his and kissing me deeply. His tongue swept over my lower lip, seeking entrance, and it was all I could do to let him in.

Just like I'd let him into my heart.

He tugged my nightgown over my head, his eyes darkening as he took in my naked body on top of him. No matter how many times we did this, he still had the same reaction. Pure and unrestrained lust. The man worshipped my body any chance he got, and he never failed to make me feel sexy. *Beautiful.* Desired.

Tonight was no exception.

SYLAS WAS ASLEEP, his dark brown hair falling onto his forehead, the gentle rise and fall of his chest making me feel at peace.

I shouldn't have been this comfortable with him. Not with

everything at stake. But being here, in his giant bed, wrapped in his arms each night, just felt… *right.*

Untangling myself from his arms, I brushed the strands off his forehead before pressing a kiss to his stubbled cheek.

He grumbled, stirring awake. "What are you doing?"

"Just going to go get something to drink. Go back to sleep."

Sylas sat up, frowning at me as I grabbed his shirt where he'd taken it off last night. His eyes flared, and there was something about the way he was looking at me, knowing that his last name was written across my back, the soft cotton hitting my thighs that made me feel invincible. Like I could do anything.

Maybe that was why I stuck my hand on the door pad, opening up his door.

He tilted his head, an interested smirk crossing his lips.

"Are you coming?" I asked, curling a loose strand of hair around my finger.

Before I could blink, he was out of the bed, pulling a pair of sweats up over his hips, and throwing a plain white t-shirt on over top.

I slipped out into the hallway before he could reach me, carefully evading his grasp.

The ship was quiet—thankfully, considering the late hour, and that this was a relatively unoccupied floor, even during the day. *Captain's perks.* I wouldn't complain if that was what kept the rest of the officers from hearing me scream each night.

"Little star," he growled. "Where are you going?"

"I'm thirsty," was my only reply, as I tiptoed through the hallway, feeling his presence right behind me, knowing he had a full-view of my bare legs.

"Someone's going to see—" He protested.

"No one's awake, Sylas. You need to loosen up." I shimmied my shoulders, and his eyes dropped to the hem of my shirt. *"Live a little."*

Reaching the refresher, I filled a glass of water, looking up at him from under my lashes as I drank half of it, before offering it to him.

He placed his lips in the same spot I had, finishing it off, before caging me against the wall. "Now what?"

I ran my finger up his chest. "Now I think I'm hungry for something else entirely." I winked.

"Brat." His arms pinned me in place, and I could see the desire flaring in his own eyes. The sweatpants he wore did nothing to hide his erection, and I giggled.

Slipping under him, I opened the door to the bridge, thankful that I didn't have to use my ID card anymore. The room was empty, though I knew at least one officer was on standby in case any alarms went off, which meant we had the whole place to ourselves.

I could hear him follow me in, the padding of his footsteps against the tiled floor, and when the door slid shut behind us, I couldn't resist the devil on my shoulder.

Swaying my hips in a way I knew would drive him crazy, I waltzed over to his chair, settling against the soft leather before I could convince myself it was a bad idea.

"You're in my chair." Sylas raised his eyebrow as he crossed his arms over his chest, even more delicious than usual sans his jumpsuit.

Biting my lip, I fluttered my eyelashes at him. "I am. And what are you going to do about it?"

I knew that we shouldn't have snuck out here at night, but there was something about the way he was looking at me, with those sweatpants slung low on his hips and t-shirt tight across his muscles that made my heart race.

Just like I knew sneaking around like this was wrong, that dating a superior was strictly forbidden, but... I didn't care. Not anymore.

He slapped his hand on the control panel across from me, giving him access to the ship as I rubbed my hands over the arms of the chair. "Lock down the bridge," he commanded, his voice rough.

The ship's AI beeped back, confirming the request, and I heard the door locks bolting us in.

Sylas stalked towards me.

"Captain..." I shifted my position, knowing that his shirt would ride up, showing more of my skin.

He let out a pained groan. "Aurelia." Sylas gripped the arms of his chair, effectively pinning me in place once more as he nudged his knees in between my legs. "You're on thin ice here, little star."

"Hmm?" I ran my tongue over my bottom lip as his fingers dug into the leather. "I don't know what you're talking about, *sir*."

A guttural noise left his throat. "You're killing me. Do you even know? What you do to me?"

I shook my head. "Show me."

He didn't say anything else, just spread my legs apart and kneeled before me. His eyes were focused on that spot between my legs, where I knew he would find me already wet for him. Sometimes it felt like all it took was one look, and I was burning for him.

Fuck. "*Sylas*," I moaned as his tongue entered my slit. He repositioned my left leg, pulling it up to give himself better access as he gripped the outside of my thighs.

"You look so perfect sitting here in my chair. Like it was made for you." The words were a rasp against my skin.

It was hard to ignore the fact that I was sitting in *his* chair, and he was worshipping me like I was a queen on a goddamned throne.

"Always so sweet for me," he mused, rubbing his stubble against my inner thigh, giving me the most delicious burn.

I dug my fingers into the arm of his chair as he licked me thoroughly, plunging inside of me with that talented tongue of his. I'd never enjoyed a man going down on me before—maybe it was because they'd been doing it wrong. But maybe it was because they hadn't been Sylas. His beard scraped against my inner thigh, and the burn was so good that I didn't even care.

He ate me out like a man starved of thirst, like I was the first drink he'd had in months.

A moan slipped from my lips, and I clasped my hand over my mouth.

"Let me hear you," he rasped, looking up at me with my release glistening in his scruff. "Let the whole fucking ship know whose you are."

Oh, God. He was going to ruin me. No—he already had. Definitely. How could I ever move on after being with a man who talked to me like that? His filthy words elicited a reaction in me like never before, and I didn't even want to try.

I buried my hands in his hair, pushing him back against my aching clit.

Resuming his ministrations, Sylas added his thumb to my clit as his tongue fluttered inside of me. He rubbed it just the right way, providing the most glorious pressure, and I couldn't hold back my whimpers of pleasure.

That, and a string of oh's, and *don't stop's* and *right there*—and I was exploding, seeing stars—literally, since the galaxy stretched out in front of me. Sylas's rough grip kept me in place as I screamed his name, my insides clenching around his tongue as he eagerly lapped up my release.

I freed my hands from his hair, a smug satisfaction rolling through me at the way I'd messed up the strands.

My eyelids drooped, feeling satiated, and a little drunk with pleasure as he licked his lips.

"I'm never going to get over that," he said.

"Making me come on your tongue?" I asked, breathless.

"No." He smirked. "You saying my name."

Pushing at him with my foot, I tried to hide my blush. He caught my leg, kissing my ankle.

"You're way too smooth." I pouted. "Where did my grump go?"

But his smile didn't fall. "Maybe you fixed me."

A laugh burst out of me. "No, that's not it."

He scooped me up into his arms, ignoring my sounds of protest, before sitting back down in his chair, me in his lap.

I leaned my head on his shoulder, looking out the window. "Does it ever get old?"

"Honestly?" His voice was low. "No."

Humming, I snuggled into his side. "I hope it never does."

A yawn slipped from my lips, and it didn't take long before my eyes were growing heavy. Especially with Sylas's warm chest as my pillow.

"Let's get you back to bed, little star," he murmured, adjusting his shirt on my body to cover me before standing up.

I was asleep before we were even back in the room, feeling safe and comfortable in his arms.

There was nowhere else I'd rather be.

THIRTY
SYLAS

I HAD *the girl* asleep in my arms. My girl. Life was... beyond my wildest imaginations. Never had I expected this. But now that it was here, I didn't want it to end.

Aurelia hadn't talked about what we'd found on the planet. Besides Brina, it was like she was ignoring the chip and piece of her dad's ship entirely. Until last night, she hadn't brought it up in days. And as much as I loved the sex, it was clear she was using me as a distraction.

Which was why I'd told her about the videos I'd uncovered. I'd never meant to hide them from her in the first place, but I'd been waiting for the right moment. Well, this was the moment.

Sliding into my room, the door closed behind me, and I breathed a sigh of relief. I couldn't imagine parting from her. But how could this end in anything other than disaster? What if everything fell apart? There were still almost five years left of the mission. Who knew what would happen during that time period?

And yet I trusted her. Implicitly. Deeply.

The attraction hadn't diminished. Not one bit. And yet it had morphed, too.

I laid her out on the bed, her lithe form draped out over my sheets, my t-shirt large on her frame. Brina chirped, jumping up on the bed next to my girl and curling up in a little ball. She made another little sound at me, looking up at me with those strange blue eyes, before laying her head back down on her tail.

"What are you doing to my heart?" I murmured, unable to drag my eyes away from her. She was making me want things I'd never wanted before. Things I'd decided I didn't want or need.

But now...

"Come back to bed," Aurelia murmured, her eyelids fluttering as she peered over at me.

"Okay, little star," I responded, sliding underneath the covers and pulling her tight against my body, wrapping my arms around her.

Within moments, I was fast asleep, with my entire world in my arms.

SHE ZIPPED up her purple uniform top, covering up her creamy skin. Thankfully, they also hid whatever marks we left on each other, which was probably for the best.

I wrapped my arms around her stomach, looking at both of us in the mirror. She fit so perfectly in my arms. My chin rested on the top of her head, her entire body cradled by mine.

She let out a deep sigh, and I frowned, squeezing her hip. "What's wrong, little star?"

She turned to face me, biting her lip. "It's just..." Aurelia squeezed her eyes shut. "This sucks, you know? Not being able to go out. We're together, but we can't *be* together. Back on earth, we'd be going on dates. Doing couple stuff." I could hear the disappointment in her tone. "But you're the captain, and we *can't*."

"Rae…" I breathed out, brushing her hair back over her ear. I knew what she meant. It was hard keeping it a secret from everyone. Being with her, but not really being with her.

I'd never wanted a relationship, but now that I had her… I wanted everyone to know she was mine. That we were together.

Off-limits. That's what she was. Off-limits to everyone but *me.*

"You're mine," I said, bringing her lips to mine. Kissing her lightly. "You know that, right?"

She blinked up at me, those dazzling eyes—one blue, one green, with little flecks like stars—gazing up at me. "I mean, I hoped so." Her lips curled up in a little taunting smile.

"There's no one else. There's been no one else."

Aurelia rested her forehead against my chest. "For me too," she mumbled.

"Good." I played with the ends of her hair, letting her stay against me. "Because I don't intend to let you go."

She gave me a smile, though it didn't quite reach her eyes.

Reporting to the bridge that morning was strange. For one, because I'd gotten so used to the same familiar view each day, and now we were back, moving deeper into space. Our first target planet was still two weeks away, but the knowledge that we'd left behind a place like that ate at me.

I'd had the remnants of her dad's ship lugged out of that cave system one day without Aurelia knowing, and now it sat in the research bay. We'd found a few other pieces of the ship as well, but not the entire vessel.

And as much as I wanted to continue to search for it, we had a mission. So I had to keep going. There were few decisions as the captain that I'd had to make that had been harder than this one.

I watched her out of the corner of my eye all day at her console. Wondering if she was really okay after my revelation last night. Wondering if she was ever going to talk about it.

My confessions from earlier sat in my mind, but I didn't know how to make sense of everything that I was feeling.

"What really happened down there?" Kayle asked me, quirking her eyebrow as she looked at Aurelia. Damn, it like she was reading my mind. I hated how perceptive my sister could be.

I shrugged. "It's not my place to talk about it."

"But she won't talk to *me*, either. Or Astrid. Or Violet. It's just..." She sighed. "You know I'm not good at this. Being friends with girls. But I like that they included me." My sister gave me a small smile. "I enjoy hanging out with them. But Aurelia's been pulling back, and—"

Aurelia *was* withdrawn. I knew that. When was the last time she'd even hung out with the other girls? I hadn't meant to keep her all to myself, but maybe I was a selfish asshole and I'd been taking up all her time.

"Maybe you should plan something. A girls' night out, or something."

She quirked an eyebrow. "You realize the only place we can go *out* on a starship is to the bar, right? It's not like there's a club on board."

"Is that what young people do these days?" I asked, teasing her. "You'll have to fill me in, baby sis."

"I'm only two years younger than you," Kayle said, rolling her eyes. "And you know what I mean. We're not exactly a ship prioritized for *fun*."

But fun was exactly what my girl needed right now. A distraction.

"If you think you can set something up, I'll get her there."

She raised an eyebrow. "You?"

"I'm the Captain," I said, crossing my arms over my chest. "Do you think I can't tell one officer where to report without it being suspicious?"

"Well, when you put it that way..." Her lips curled up in a knowing smirk. "Then yes. I do think that."

I groaned, holding my head in my hands, trying to figure out how the hell I'd gotten myself into this mess in the first place.

MY SISTER WAS A GENIUS. Her and Lieutenant Alastair had turned the simple bar into something resembling a dance club back on Earth. They'd all gotten dolled up, wearing tight dresses I wasn't even sure where they'd found, with their hair curled and makeup done to the nines.

Aurelia looked beautiful. Gorgeous. They played hit pop songs from the last century, and the girls were moving their hips to the rhythm, dancing and swaying in the neon glow of the lights.

And I sat, sipping whiskey neat at the bar, because I couldn't touch her in public. Because no one else knew that we were together. Because we couldn't be together, not really, and I knew that fact was wearing on both of us.

But her comments from earlier had me thinking. We couldn't be together out in the open, but... that didn't mean we couldn't do things together.

After all, there was nothing wrong with a captain spending time with one of his officers. Alone, in a dark room... I shut my eyes, trying not to groan at the thought when a familiar scent made me perk up.

Aurelia. She was standing in front of me, her purple body-con dress hugging the curves I'd traced with my tongue, the skin I'd kissed practically every inch of.

"Thank you." Aurelia's cheeks were flushed with happiness, her eyes bright. "How did you know I needed this?"

"Just a hunch." I swiveled on my barstool to face her more fully.

Aurelia stepped between my legs and then seemed to remember how many people were around us. I stopped her from pulling away.

"We shouldn't..." Her voice was low.

"They're all drunk. No one's even paying attention."

She looked around and then gave me a nod when she realized I was telling the truth. No eyes were on us. Almost all of my officers were here, drunk off their asses. Tomorrow would be *fun*.

"Sylas…" Her words were low.

"Come on, baby," I said, wrapping an arm around her thighs. "Let's go to bed."

"But…" Aurelia's cheeks were pink. *Cute.* I wanted to kiss her so badly. But not like this.

Not in front of them. Not when I hadn't figured out how we were going to make this work yet. How we could be together without breaking every one of the federation's rules.

Still, she slid her hand into mine, letting me guide her back to the room that was feeling like *ours*, not just mine. Her scent was on my sheets, my pillow, her stuff was in my closet, and I was beginning to think she'd begun occupying a space in my heart, as well.

PLACING A KISS ON HER NECK, I unzipped the tight purple dress, stripping it off her body.

"Whose is this?" I asked, my voice rough. "Tell me you're not giving it back."

"Violet's," she responded, gathering up her hair as I flicked open her bra, letting those luscious tits spill free. I held one in each hand, massaging them lightly. "I won't." She let out a little moan, and I pressed myself against her ass, enjoying her little gasp as she felt how hard I was.

"Feel that?" I asked. My eyes met hers in the mirror, and she nodded, her eyes half-lidded. "Feel how hard I am for you? From seeing you in that little thing?"

"Yes," she gasped. I pinched her nipples, playing with them as I watched us through the reflection.

"Do you like this? Watching us?"

Aurelia nodded, and I pressed my lips to her pulse point, sucking it into my mouth. She was writhing, grinding against me, and I let my hand dip down to her black panties, creeping underneath her waistband.

"What do you want, little star?"

"Touch me," she begged. "Please."

I ran my finger up her slit before pressing it inside. *So wet.* "Were you thinking about me all night?" I asked, teasing her with the lightest of touches. "Dancing on the floor with your girls, dripping wet for me?"

"*Yes.*" She wiggled her hips. "Sylas," Aurelia moaned, her hand gripping my wrist as I rubbed circles over her clit, getting her nice and wet for me. "More, I need—"

"That's right, baby," I crooned, dipping a finger inside and stirring her up. "Get all messy for me."

With my free hand, I unzipped my pants, pulling out my cock and pumping it with my fist.

Aurelia gasped as I added another finger, pumping her roughly, crooking them to hit the spot inside that I knew would make her see stars. "I'm so close," she panted, her hips rocking against me as I fucked her with my fingers.

"Do you like that?" I asked her, my lips against her ear. "Coming undone on my fingers? Coating them with your cum?" Her pussy clenched down around me, squeezing my fingers. I felt like the luckiest asshole on any planet as she came, her head dropping back onto my shoulder and a low moan slipping from her throat.

"Just like that," I murmured, pulling my fingers out and licking her taste off of them. "Fucking delicious."

Quickly shedding my pants and boxers, I moved us in front of the mirror. "Hands up," I instructed. "Keep your legs closed for me."

She obeyed, still too lost in her orgasmic haze to be a brat. I slipped my length between her legs, knowing each time I pushed forward, I would brush against her clit. Her juices coated my dick, making it slippery.

"*Fuck.*" I grit my teeth. Why did this feel so good? I wasn't even inside her yet, and I was already so close to spilling my load. But as much as this sensation felt amazing—my cock nestled between her thighs as I thrust my hips, relishing in the smooth slide of her skin—I didn't want this to be over yet.

"I need you inside," she groaned. "I'm so empty, *please.*"

Pressing a kiss to her bare shoulder, I worked her higher and higher. "Beg me."

I groaned as she tightened her legs, pressing her thighs together more. My vision went white, and I almost came right then and there. Each time I passed over her clit, she gasped, and I added to that friction.

My lips dropped to her ear as I nibbled on her earlobe. "Where do you want my cum, my star? Your needy cunt or should I get you all sticky? Mark you up, rub it into your skin so everyone knows you're mine?"

She answered with a whimper. "Please, please, I need it. I need you."

"Where do you want me?"

"Inside. I need your cock, Sylas. Buried in my needy pussy. *Please.*"

"Good girl." Grabbing her chin, I turned her head just enough so that I could kiss her lips, our tongues entangling in a sloppy kiss.

Then I helped her arch her back, pushing her legs apart with my knees, and positioned my tip at her entrance.

"Are you ready to take me, Rae? Every inch of this cock you love so much?"

She moaned as I pushed in, burying myself inside of her. My hands wrapped around her waist as I let her adjust to my size. Her warmth surrounded me, and fuck me, she was so wet. I was already coated with her release, which made the glide in even smoother. There was hardly any resistance, like she was sucking me in.

Fuck, this position was insane. I groaned, feeding her inch by inch as I watched her pretty pink cunt swallow me. I gripped her hips, burying my fingers in her soft, curvy ass.

"I'm obsessed with your body," I muttered, massaging it. "I can't get enough."

Holding tight to her, I slammed in the rest of the way, sheathing my cock in her tight cunt.

"And here I was," she started, letting out a series of sharp breaths as she arched her back further. "thinking you were a tits guy."

Nipping at her ear, I practically growled out, "Baby, with you, I'm an everything guy."

She hummed, wriggling on me to force me in deeper.

I laughed, smacking her ass lightly, a low moan slipping from her lips. *Hm.* I raised an eyebrow, smacking the other side, a sharp gasp slipping out from her lips. *Fuck,* I liked that.

"My brat likes to be spanked, does she?"

She looked back at me, eyes filled with lust and heat. "Yes," she said with a groan.

Picking up my pace, I pumped inside of her, wanting her to come again before I did.

"Are you close?" I asked, the sound guttural.

Could she tell how close I was to losing control? That being inside of her like this was the best I'd ever had? There was no comparison. It was like she was made for me. We fit perfectly, and I knew that there was no one else in the universe I would feel like this with.

She gasped as I rocked into her again. "Almost."

"Touch yourself," I murmured, wrapping my arms around her stomach to keep her upright. "Feel the way I'm fucking you."

"Oh my god," she groaned, reaching down with her fingers

spread, and I watched her eyes in the mirror as she slid her fingers over the spot where I entered her. "You fill me so good. So *deep*. I can feel you everywhere."

Moving my hips, I felt her fingers rub on my shaft, sending me closer to the edge. I could feel myself growing harder inside of her, my balls tightening.

"Rub that clit for me, baby. Make yourself come."

That was all it took. She exploded, her inner walls milking my cock, squeezing it for everything I was worth. And I followed right behind her, keeping up with that steady rhythm, withdrawing before burying myself to the hilt once again. Once I was as deep inside of her as possible, I surged, letting my orgasm rip through me, the blissful feeling spreading through every inch of my body as I poured rope after rope of cum into her body.

Pulling out, I watched as it trickled down her entrance, dripping onto her thighs.

I was hyper-aware of the fact that I was quickly growing addicted to this. That without the fertility blockers, we would never have been connected like this.

But was it the caveman in me who liked the idea of filling her up? Flooding her womb with my seed? I groaned, kneeling down and pushing it back in with my fingers.

"So fucking hot," I said, entranced.

Aurelia's legs wobbled, and I scooped her up into my arms, carrying her back to bed.

"I think you've fucked any rational thought right out of me," she said with a yawn. "Not sure I'll be able to walk tomorrow."

"Good." I pressed a kiss to her shoulder. "Then maybe the other guys won't look at you."

"Possessive."

I growled. "Damn right I am. The only man who should look at you is me."

"Down, boy. They're not looking at me, anyway."

"What do you call Orion constantly leaning in close and always talking with you?"

"Sylas." Her laugh was melodic, and it eased some of the ache in my soul. "He's the navigator. I *have* to work with him. Besides, I think he has eyes for someone else."

"You do?" I raised an eyebrow. I hadn't noticed Orion spending any extra time with anyone... Had I?

"Mmm. But I was sworn to secrecy. Sorry."

"Not fair." I rolled on top of her, caging her in with my arms. "I'm the Captain. That means I should know about this."

She gave me a secret smile, her cheeks flushed with exertion. Aurelia extended her arms out for me in a hug.

"Come 'ere," she mumbled, her eyelids fluttering.

I could tell she was close to sleep, and even though I knew we should clean up first, I couldn't help but pull her into my arms, letting every inch of our naked bodies press together.

Tangled up in each other, we both fell asleep before either of us could say goodnight.

THIRTY-ONE
AURELIA

SYLAS HAD TOLD me to report to the movie theater on the rec floor after my shift on the bridge, which had surprised me. What exactly did he think we were going to do?

And how was I supposed to dress for an occasion like this? It wasn't a date, was it?

Oh, God. I'd complained the other night that we couldn't be seen in public together. What was he up to? After last night, well… everything was different between us.

Because it was the first time I'd wanted to say *fuck it*. To forget the consequences, and claim him publicly. When I'd stepped between his legs at the bar, I'd known exactly what I was doing.

I'd left with him, not caring if anyone else saw us.

What was all that different about this?

I dipped inside the theater, spotting him in one of the back rows, sitting low so no one would notice him. Not that anyone could miss him. He had the energy that commanded the room. Domineered any situation he was in.

And that was the same magnetism that drew me to him, like a moth to flame.

Maybe it was dangerous to feel this way. Like he was the sun, and I wanted to orbit around him, just so I could be in his gravity.

Ugh. Even my analogies were bad. I needed to get it together.

"What are you doing?" I hissed out, feeling my eyebrows practically at the top of my forehead.

"Shhh," Sylas said, dipping his head down and slouching into the seat. "The movie's starting."

I blinked, but sat down on the cushy chair next to him. "What are we doing?" I asked again, but this time quieter.

"We're going on a date."

I squinted. "Here?"

He hummed, reaching over and placing his hand on my thigh. "Yes. Here."

My cheeks warmed. But in the dim theater, even if anyone was paying attention to us—which they most definitely aren't— no one could see, anyway. Okay, so maybe it had merits.

"Why are we having a date in the theater?"

He looked over, giving me a small glare. "Because you wanted to do something where we could be a normal couple. And here we are."

"What's playing?" I whispered, not commenting on how... surprisingly sweet that was. My secret softie, showing up once again. Between this and him setting up a space for Brina, I wasn't sure how I was going to survive this without letting him have my heart. Which was dangerous.

I tried to remind myself of all the reasons I said I wouldn't fall in love.

His lips curled up in a smile. "A romantic comedy from a few years back."

Of course, none of the things that played on the ship were new, but I liked that he'd put thought into what kind of movie to take me to. That he knew me.

Because he did. He knew me better than anyone. I'd never let anyone into my life—into my heart—the way I'd let him in.

Sylas Kellar had been slowly breaking down my walls for a while, and I'd been blind to it.

But not anymore.

He squeezed my thigh, winking over at me as the movie started. I leaned my head on his shoulder, watching the picture light up the screen in front of us.

Had anything between us ever felt so *normal?*

And why was this the best first date I'd ever had?

IT WAS TIME. Maybe it was because of Sylas's sweet gestures lately that I finally felt ready. Or maybe it was just that I knew I couldn't put it off any longer. Because I needed closure, and Sylas had handed me a file of videos from my dad.

How long could I ignore them?

Since I wasn't scheduled on the bridge for the day, I'd decided *now or never.*

"Are you sure?" Sylas asked, brushing his hand down my hair. "I can stay…" He trailed off.

I was sitting on his couch, wearing his shirt and a pair of sweats, and Brina was curled up in my lap. He'd all but tucked me into the position earlier with a soft, cozy blanket.

The man had gone so far as to bring me a cup of my favorite tea.

He was lingering, concern for me clear. And it was *cute.* I shouldn't have found it so adorable that a grown man was doting on me, but I didn't care. Maybe that was my heart trying to tell my head something. But I couldn't process that right now.

I appreciated his actions more than words could describe, but I needed to do this alone.

"Go," I said, shaking my head. "You have captaining to do."

He cracked a small smile at my comment, pressing a kiss to my forehead before leaving me in silence to boot up the videos.

I'd been putting this off. I knew it, and so did he. Watching my father's video logs was so many things, but above all, it was like saying goodbye. It meant accepting that this was *it*.

Sylas had been more than patient, even as I'd slowly pushed him away. Sure, physically, everything was amazing. Emotionally, however, I was a shell.

After this, there would be no more dad. No more chances to see him one last time. I'd have to accept it. *Closure.*

That was what I'd been looking for all along, wasn't it?

But I didn't know who I was anymore. Not after this.

"What do you think, Breens?" I asked the alien otter-dog as I slid my hands over her short but soft coat. "Think he'll find out if I put it off again?"

I was pretty sure she could sense my mood. That was why she'd been all over me since this morning, not wanting to be separated from me for one second. She truly was like a puppy in so many ways. At least I had an emotional support animal to guide me through this.

The video clips were already loaded, meaning all I had to do was start it.

I finally hit play, my father's face coming up on the big screen in Sylas's room. I'd almost forgotten his face. How much life he had. For the last thirteen years, I'd only had photos to remember him by. And now…

"My star." He was younger than the last time I saw him, so full of life, even on the screen. "You're eight years old, and I had to leave you behind today." Dad sucked in a deep breath. "You'll probably never see this video. I hope you don't. Because if you do, it means something happened, and I'm gone. I love you so much, baby girl. You and your mom. But…" He looked outside, the porthole from his room visible. It was a smaller set of quarters than mine, reflecting on times passed. How far we'd advanced in the last almost twenty years. "Space is dangerous.

You never know what will happen. That's why I know that every day I have is precious."

He went on, telling me about their current mission. What he was doing. What they hoped to achieve. It was... inspiring. Because I remembered him coming back from that mission. How he'd picked me up into his arms and spun me around, laughing in our backyard till we collapsed on the grass.

My mom had come outside, probably to scold us, but it hadn't taken long for her to join us, too. Those were the moments I treasured the most with my family. The happy times.

He finished talking, and I clicked to the next one. There were more from that same mission, and then the background changed. Dad looked older, too.

"Hi, Aurelia. Guess this is a tradition now, huh? I meant to say no when they asked me if I'd go on this mission. It's not a long one, but it's so hard to leave you behind. But you have school, and your mom, well... she never really wanted to be in space. Not like me. So asking her to leave life behind on earth to come with me seemed like an enormous burden to bear. But I hope I get to show it to you one day. To see it through your eyes. It's amazing up here, my star. You couldn't even imagine the things I've seen."

I let out a strange choked laugh, because now I *could*. I'd seen some pretty incredible things myself.

"The hardest part is knowing how many of your milestones I'm missing, baby girl. I wish I could be there for all of them. Your first softball practice. Watching you win the blue ribbon for your science project. Yelling the loudest of any parent in the crowd when you got all As. But as much as I want to be there, I'm not. Never doubt how much I love you. To the end of the universe and back isn't even enough, Aurelia. I hope one day you'll understand why I left. But also, you'll know why I can't wait to get home. Back to you and your mom." He smiled, kissing his fingers and then pressing it to the screen before signing off.

I flipped through a few more before settling on a video that was date-stamped as being taken the year he went missing. He looked exhausted, like something was wearing on him.

"I've never imagined making a video like this. But the ship… Something's wrong. And I know we won't make it back to Earth. Not without a miracle. We don't have the parts necessary to fix it. We got caught in a geomagnetic storm, and it damaged our communication systems and engines. At this point, we're just drifting through space." He sighed. "I'm the best damn pilot in the federation, and even I can't do anything about it. What good are all of my skills if I can't even use them to come home to you? Honey, I'm so sorry. Aurelia, if you're watching this…" He shook his head. "I'll never get to see you graduate high school. Turn eighteen. Go to college. Fall in love. Get married. I'll never get to be a grandpa. All because I put space first." He buried his face in his hands. "God, I'm so sorry, baby girl. I never should have come on this mission. I should have stayed home to watch you grow up."

Tears were streaming down my face, but I couldn't stop them. All I could do was watch each video, one by one. Where he said goodbye. The days counted down on the ship's counter, and I knew time was running out. He told me what was happening to the ship. Answers to my questions that had been building for years, and even more so the last few months.

"I love you, Aurelia," he said, eyes distant as he looked away from the screen for a moment. "I hope you never forget to stop looking at the stars. Because I'll be here, watching over you." A deep sigh came from his chest. "Callisto, out." The video turned black.

For the longest time, I stayed there on the couch, staring at the final, frozen screen of my dad. His face looked back at me, and I didn't bother trying not to cry. I cried till there was nothing left. Till my eyes were red and swollen, and I was sure everyone would notice how puffy they were tomorrow. But it was cathartic, too, in its own way.

"Oh, baby." Sylas's words were low as he scooped me up off the couch later, pulling me into his arms. "Are you okay?"

I hadn't moved from that spot in hours. "No." I shook my head. *No, I wasn't okay. But...* "I will be, though." I cupped his cheek, even as tears streamed down my face. It was hard to get words out, mostly on account of the hiccups, but I was trying. "Thank you. For this gift. For one last goodbye."

He pressed a kiss to my forehead. "I think I found something more, too. Where the ship ended up. Whenever you're ready."

"Not now," I said, needing time to process this on my own. "But... soon."

"He loved you," Sylas said, like he was reading my mind.

"So much," I agreed. "Everyone always said I was Daddy's little girl. And maybe I didn't realize how much until he was gone. But he was my best friend. Growing up..." I looked out the large window of his bedroom. "Those were some of the best times. Him, my mom, and I. I knew that as long as I had them, everything would be okay." I took a shuddering breath. "But I'm realizing that everything is going to be okay again. Isn't it?"

"Yes." He murmured, pressing a soft kiss to the corner of my lips.

"And everything's going to be okay because I have you."

"*Yes.*"

"Does this make you my boyfriend?" I asked, squinting at him.

He burst out laughing. "That was not what I expected you to ask."

"Needed to lighten the mood somehow," I mumbled.

"Yes, Aurelia. I'm your boyfriend. Or whatever the fuck you want to call me. I don't care, as long as I get to call you mine."

"I'm yours," I agreed.

"Good." He slid his hand in next to my cheek, kissing me tenderly. So soft, my heart ached. "That's all I've ever wanted."

THIRTY-TWO
SYLAS

DOES *this make you my boyfriend?* A smile tugged at my lips as I thought about our conversation from the previous night. It had been on my mind all day.

How I'd come back to find her in tears, and she'd let me hold her. Comfort her.

How it hadn't even been about sex, because after, when I'd carried her to bed, all I'd done was hold her. Stroked her hair and whispered praises into her ear. How strong she was. How brave. How proud I was of her.

How I'd given her words I'd never given anyone else before. The way *I'm yours* slipped from her lips so confidently, like she didn't even have a moment of hesitation. I was too fucking old to be someone's boyfriend, but I'd be whatever she wanted me to be.

How could I have ever wanted anything else?

How could I have ever thought I didn't want her? Because I was a fool. And now, all I could do was stare at her. And wish that I could sit by her side. That I could rest my hand on her thigh and let her babble on about her day.

Her smile lit up the room, and I was completely mesmerized by the sight.

"You're different." Leo tipped his glass back, his eyes appraising me as we sat in the mess hall, eating dinner.

"Huh?"

My chief engineer gave a nod. "I'm just saying. There's something different about you. I can't quite put my finger on it, but…"

"No, he's right." Wren chimed in. "You seem happier."

I crossed my arms over my chest. "I'm the same as I always was. Come on."

There was a twinkle of humor in their eyes as they grinned at me.

"Seriously. *Nothing's* changed." Stabbing at my food, I glared at them.

Certainly not the feisty, stubborn pilot who'd been spending every night in my bed.

The woman who was sitting at the table across from us, currently smiling and laughing with the other female officers crowded around her. It was good to see her smiling again. The last few days had been rough, and I knew she was grieving all over again. But she looked happier, too.

Aurelia caught me staring at her and winked. I looked away, feeling strangely guilty.

"Why are we sitting over here when they're having all the fun at their table?" Leo grumbled, poking at his food.

"Let them have their fun," Orion said. "They have to deal with us all day as it is." He slung an arm over Leo's shoulder.

I gave a noise of agreement, even though I agreed with Leo. I wanted to sit by Aurelia's side. Listen to her stories and to her talk about her day in public.

"Hey, I have a question," I said, getting all of their attentions.

"Hm?"

"Have you ever heard of two officers who were… together?"

Leo's face paled. "What?"

"Like, in a relationship." I ran a hand through my hair. "Or a captain who was with a subordinate?"

Orion raised an eyebrow. "Why, is there someone you wanted to date?"

"No." I exclaimed, a little too quickly. "God no. Of course not. I was just wondering how it worked, that's all. With federation guidelines..." I trailed off. Where was I going with this? Was I just looking for some sort of justification for being together?

"Well, I heard that there was a couple on the *Voyager* who were both officers and they were married. But I'm not sure if they were married before or after they served together." Wren said, smoothing a hand over his stubble. I noticed he'd been staring in the direction of the girls' table, spacing out. *Huh.*

"Anyway, no. You guys know I don't have time, nor the desire, for a relationship. I wouldn't even know what to do in one, anyway. Love isn't in the cards for me."

Even though now that felt like a lie. Still, I wasn't sure I knew how to love. Would I stick around? Or would I be just like my parents and run away when things got hard?

I didn't think I could ever do that to her. Not when just thinking about leaving her made my chest ache.

Well, fuck.

LUCKILY, the guys hadn't harped on my comment for too long, which meant I could slip back into my daily duties without them wondering why, exactly, I wanted to know.

Married. Huh. I scratched at my jaw as I sat on the captain's chair later that night. The rest of the bridge was empty, besides a few lingering crew members who were finishing their duties for the day.

We hadn't even had a conversation about our future. It was like we both knew the subject was too delicate. Five years was a long time. But would she want to be with me after the fact? Was it wrong of me to hope that the answer was *yes?* I didn't know what my path would look like after this. Undoubtedly, I could take another command. Another long, multi-year commission.

But when this ship docked, I'd be forty years old. And I knew, instantly, that if I kept up in the same way I had been, going and going like I had for as long as I could remember, I'd never stop.

And then what? I'd be fifty, sixty years old, single and alone? I'd retire to a cold, empty house. With no one there to spend the rest of my years with. In my imaginary scenario, even Kayle had found someone.

So why was that thought so depressing? It was what I'd always imagined my life would be like. But now...

"Something on your mind, Cap?" Orion's deep British accent brought me out of my thoughts. He was leaning in front of a console on the upper platform where I was seated.

"A lot of things," I grumbled, crossing my arms over my chest. "What are you doing here? I thought you left—" I checked my watch. "—hours ago."

He chuckled. "I did. But your sister said you were still in here, and I thought I'd come check on you."

I rolled my eyes. "Sometimes I think she forgets who the older sibling is."

"You're her hero. You know that, right? She's never forgotten all the things you've done for her. How much you gave up to make sure she had a good life."

I did know. We might have teased each other and given each other shit, but we were close. Close enough that I felt guilty not telling her how I felt about Aurelia. It was like I was hiding part of my life from her, and I never did that.

"She's all I have."

"I'm not sure that's true anymore, though."

"What do you mean?" I froze.

"Sylas." Orion laughed. "I'm not blind."

"Never said you were," I muttered.

But Orion had always been observant. And he worked right next to Aurelia. Had she mentioned something to him?

Fear coursed through my system, before my friend said, "Relax. I'm not going to say anything. I'm just saying. You have a lot more people than you realize. Leo, Wren, me—all of us. You might not have your parents, but we're your family, too. We've got your back."

A lump formed in my throat. "But what if she leaves? Just like they did? And then I'm..." *Alone.* I couldn't get the word out.

He shook his head. "Why are you worried about this now? It seems like things are going well. That you both make each other happy."

"I don't know." I shook my head. "I just can't shake this feeling that something's going to happen, and I'm going to lose her. It's never been like this for me before. There's never been a woman that I cared about this way."

She was everything to me. *Everything.* And maybe that was a red flag. That I wanted to put her before anything else. That didn't change the fact that Aurelia was more important than even the chair I was sitting in now.

I startled. She was, wasn't she? Because with Aurelia, I wasn't alone in twenty years, sitting in an empty house. I was surrounded by love. Life. Laughing, smiling faces. Warmth.

It was close enough to touch, if only I reached out to take it. And I wanted it. So badly.

Orion hummed. "So, what are you going to do?"

"Whatever it takes," I said, meaning every word.

Whatever it took to keep her.

To make her fall in love with me.

MY CABIN WAS empty when I made my way back there, and I frowned.

Brina chirped at me, raising her head up to look at me from her little corner. She'd been sleeping in her fuzzy bed. I crouched down in front of her, rubbing the top of her head.

"Where's our girl, Brina?" I asked her, cursing the fact that the alien creature we'd discovered couldn't exactly communicate with words.

Still, she gave me a few more noises—her vocalizations were a strange mixture of sounds that somehow were cute as fuck, no matter the scenario. I smiled at her, not caring that I wasn't my grumpy asshole self, and then headed back out to search the ship for my girl.

Before I got too far, I dinged her communicator.

SYLAS

Brina looks lonely.

Where are you at?

Okay, maybe I'm the one missing you.

AURELIA

Come and find me, Captain. ;)

Mine. That was what she was. In every possible way. I felt it down to my bones. That giving up on her, on us, would be the biggest mistake of my life.

But it was too early to tell her that, wasn't it? So I'd wait, see how she was feeling. And when the time was right, I'd spill my guts.

A voice broke me from my thoughts. "Captain?"

"Oh, hey, Commander Loxley," I said, nodding at Astrid. She looked like she'd just left the MedBay, still in her white uniform, with her bright blue hair braided on each side of her scalp. "How's your evening?"

"Good." She gave me a small smile. "I actually just finished up with Aurelia. She was back by MedBay last time I saw her."

"Great." I nodded. "Thanks."

I was so focused that I hadn't even thought about the fact that Astrid offered the information on Aurelia before I'd even asked—or how she'd known I was looking for her.

Maybe if I had, I would have thought about the consequences of us getting caught. Would have remembered that no matter how we felt, this relationship was still forbidden.

My ride down the turbo lifts was short, though I barely paid attention to where I was going, letting my feet carry me towards her. At least it seemed like my homing beacon was definitely working.

Aurelia was leaning against the gleaming white walls that led to MedBay when I got there, eyes sparkling with mischief.

Her expression dimmed when she saw me. "What's wrong?" she asked, and I wondered what she saw in my eyes.

"Nothing," I said, wondering why I was feeling so choked up. "Just missed my girl."

"Aww." She held her arms open, and I scooped her up with mine, pulling her into a hug. "You've gone soft on me, Captain."

I didn't pull away. Not until she did. Because someone taught me once that you shouldn't let go until someone else did. You never knew how much they needed that hug.

And well, I needed Aurelia's just as much. I inhaled the smell of her, the sweet violet scent settling something inside of me.

She rested her head against my pecs before finally pulling away. "Thank you. I needed that."

"Me too," I mumbled. "I haven't seen you all day."

She laughed. "I thought it would tip everyone off if I was at your side every minute."

A grumble slipped out of my lips. "They can go fuck off, for all I care." I ran my fingers through the ends of her hair. "I can't explain it. I want everyone to know you're mine."

"You don't have to." Her hand reached up, fingers dancing up my chest.

"Aurelia…" I murmured, running my hand down her back, before cupping her ass with both hands. I gave them a soft squeeze before hefting her up, lifting her into my arms.

A giggle slipped from her lips as I grinned up at her. "There he is."

"Hm?" I asked, walking us forwards.

"Captain Grumpy, my secret softie," Aurelia said with a whisper, leaning down to kiss my cheek.

I grunted in acknowledgment. But fuck yeah, I liked it when she called me that. Enjoyed being her teddy bear. Because all I wanted to do was wrap my arms around her and haul her into my arms every minute of the day.

"Wrap your legs around me, baby," I instructed. She complied, wrapping her arms around my neck at the same time before I pinned her up against the wall.

And then I kissed her. Like I didn't have a care in the fucking world. Because, *again*. Caveman brain. Something about the idea of getting caught made this even hotter.

"Someone could see us," she whispered back, eyes darting around the hallway.

"We can fix that," I said, pressing the panel to open a supply closet door and pulling her inside. "Better?" My voice was pure sex.

God, I wanted this woman. Needed her.

Pressing her against a set of shelves, I took her mouth with mine. Something clattered to the floor, but I was too absorbed in her to pay attention to what it was.

When we finally pulled apart, Aurelia pushed on my chest, and I set her back down on her feet, all too aware of every inch of her body as she slid down my front.

She dropped to her knees, and I was very aware of how little space there was in this tiny supply closet.

"Baby," I spluttered out. "What are you doing?"

"What does it look like?" She said, and even in the dim lighting, I could make out the little smirk on her face as she pulled the zipper down on my pants. "I'm going down on you."

"You don't have to—"

She freed my cock and wrapped her hand around it. *Fuck.*

"I want to." Her tongue darted out, licking my tip, and I groaned. "Let me taste *you.* I wanna suck your cock."

She was going to kill me. That was the only thought running through my head.

"Tell me what you like," she said, flattening her tongue to run it up my length. "I want to make you feel good."

I choked out a, "Tap my thigh if it gets to be too much." She nodded, her eyes half lidded, moistening her lips with her tongue as she pumped me with her hand.

Aurelia's lips wrapped around the tip, and she hummed around me, that tongue swirling around my head.

"Harder," I instructed, grabbing her ponytail and tugging it slightly. She always wore her hair up—unless we were alone. I fucking loved it. That I got to see this version of her that no one else did.

She tightened her grip on my shaft, stroking harder as she sucked my cock deeper into her mouth, her cheeks hollowed out.

"*Fuuuck.* Just like that." A strangled sound left my throat. I was trying to hold back, but her technique was too good. My hips rocked involuntarily, and I slid deeper inside her mouth.

She groaned, the vibrations going straight to my balls. I was already impossibly hard, but *shit.* "That feels amazing, baby."

She looked up at me, those beautiful eyes—one blue, one green, perfectly unique and perfectly her—gazing at me like I was her entire world.

"Look at me fucking that smart mouth."

She reached down, rubbing at her clit through the fabric of her uniform.

"Is this turning you on, hm? Letting me use you like my little slut?"

Aurelia moaned, nodding her head. The motion made her bob on my cock, and I slid in deeper.

"How much do you think you can take?" I asked, running my finger under her jaw. "Will you let me fuck your throat, Aurelia?"

She nodded.

There was no stopping me then. A guttural groan came from my lips as I started pumping inside of her, rocking my hips in and out of her mouth.

Tears formed in Aurelia's eyes, but she didn't tap my thigh. "Is this too much?" I asked, checking in, and she shook her head.

From the little noises she was making, all while rocking against her hand, I could tell she was enjoying this as much as I was.

Pleasure burst through me, and I grit my teeth, feeling my base tightening. "Will you swallow it all, baby? Every last drop?"

She hummed again, pulling back slightly and I let out a deep moan as I poured my release down her throat, rope after rope of thick cum.

I pulled out, and she swallowed before running her tongue over her lips, like she was determined to drink it all. Some primal part of me liked that.

"Fuck." I pulled her up against me, taking her mouth with a burning intensity as I kissed her deeply. I felt her knees weaken as I parted her lips, and I could taste my release on her tongue.

"Hottest fucking thing of my goddamn life," I said, panting roughly as we pulled apart.

She hummed, resting her hands on my shoulders and kneading slightly. Aurelia stood up on her tiptoes to whisper in my mouth, "Take me to bed, Captain."

And who was I to say no to that?

THIRTY-THREE
AURELIA

AURELIA

Captain.

SYLAS

Yes, Lieutenant?

Love out of this world is on.

And?

Do you want to join?

Aurelia.

You really think I want to watch your show?

:(

Please?

Fine.

Be there in fifteen.

AURELIA

Daddy.

SYLAS

Fuck, Aurelia. I'm working.

Brina misses you.

Come for a walk with us? I'm going to take her to the gardens.

I have to finish this paperwork.

Pleeeaasseeee.

You're a brat.

Does that mean you're coming?

...

Yes.

SYLAS

Stop looking over here.

AURELIA

Make me.

You're driving me crazy.

Brat.

Fuck it out of me?

My room. Thirty minutes.

Don't be late.

"YOU SEEM HAPPIER," Astrid remarked, sitting on the couch with a bowl of popcorn between her legs.

"I..." I blushed. Surely, it wasn't that obvious to everyone, was it?

I was still on a high from our movie night, and even if I couldn't talk about it with the girls, it was nice feeling normal for a night. I could almost pretend I was a normal girl in a normal relationship. Not an officer dating her captain, risking everything if they were caught. Somehow, I thought the sneaking around made it hotter. But maybe that was just the sex.

Really, really fantastic sex. Like how I'd gone down on him in a supply closet outside of the MedBay. I'd been so turned on that I'd practically jumped him as soon as we'd gotten back to his room.

But I felt guilty, too. I'd spent so many nights with Sylas lately that I'd been neglecting my friends. Besides the bar the other night, we'd barely done anything together in a while. It was something I'd wanted to remedy as soon as possible.

She leaned in close. "Is that a... hickey on your neck?"

"No." I tugged up my shirt to cover it. Sylas loved to worship my body, and the idea of marking me up had been too good to resist—for either of us. Except I could barely cover it unless I was wearing one of my uniforms, because at least those had a high neck.

Hence, why we were all gathering in the lounge for another binge night of *Love out of this world*. We were almost to the season finale, just a few episodes left until we'd find out which couple had won.

Everyone was already there—except for one redheaded science officer. Finley.

"Do you think everything's okay?" I asked, worrying about

her. Maybe she'd gotten stuck in the lab or something else was wrong. I could only imagine.

We all devolved into separate conversations, Astrid gossiping with me about the MedBay nurses and who was sleeping with who on the ship—which made my eyes grow extra wide, because she actually did know everything that was going on.

I made a mental reminder to myself not to cross her.

Kayle and Violet were seated on the other couch across from us, leaving the smaller love seat open for whenever our last member joined us.

"God, can you believe it?"

"I know. I can't imagine keeping something that important from my best friend. If I was in her place, I'd be upset too."

My stomach dropped. The girl in the show had been in a secret relationship with another contestant. The competitors spent so much time together and formed bonds, so I could understand how upsetting that would be to be lied to.

And fuck, if I wasn't doing the same thing. How would they react once they found out what I'd been hiding from them? I felt guilty about keeping my relationship with Sylas a secret. Especially now that we'd put a label on it. Sure, boyfriend and girlfriend felt like a vast understatement for whatever we shared, but it was more than just hooking up. But what did he want in the future? I hoped we'd have that conversation soon. Because I wasn't just in it for the now. I wanted to be with him. For the long haul.

My lips tilted up in a smile as the door slid open, revealing Finley in a casual top and pants. "Hi, Finley!" I called, patting the spot next to me on the couch.

"Hey. Sorry I'm late. I..." She looked down, and I noticed a little redhead peeked out from behind Finley's legs. "The daycare couldn't keep her any longer, because she had a slight fever, and I..." A wince left her, like she was embarrassed. "I hope it's okay that I brought her."

"Of course it is," Kayle said. "It's girls' night. She's welcome anytime."

She gave us a hesitant smile, like it only just occurred to her we hadn't met the tiny child attached to her legs before. "Everyone, this is my daughter, Kinsley."

I had no idea that she was a mom. Instantly, shame rolled through me. How bad of a friend was I that I didn't even know she had a kid? She'd mentioned coming on the ship to leave an awful marriage behind during dinner once. Which meant she was a single mom, too. I couldn't imagine how hard that would be in an environment like this.

Crouching down, I smiled at the girl, who was still clutching her mom's legs. "Hi, Kinsley. I'm Aurelia. It's very nice to meet you."

"Hi," she said, peeking her head out. She probably was no older than three, and had a little yellow dress on, with bows tied into her pigtails.

Finley sighed. "I'm sorry for bringing her. I thought I had a crew member's wife who could watch her, but schedules got crossed and…"

"It's okay," I said, beaming up at my friend. "None of us mind. Besides, I love kids." I hadn't grown up with siblings, but I'd always enjoyed babysitting the neighbor's kids.

She fidgeted with the hem of her shirt, her voice growing hesitant. "I guess I just didn't want you girls to judge me."

This time, it was Violet who sounded surprised. "Why would we do that?"

"Because I'm a single mom. I know people think it's wrong that I took her away from her father and—"

"No one thinks that, Fin." Violet placed a reassuring hand on Finley's shoulder. "We all love you. And we know you're doing whatever you think is best for your little girl, too."

"Thank you," she whispered, her eyes rimmed with unshed tears. "I just didn't want anyone to think I couldn't do my job because of her. That I'd prioritize her over my responsibilities. It's dumb, I know."

"It's not. More than any other reason, I think it makes perfect sense. You just want to protect her." Kayle offered her a hug, and it was a few beats before they pulled apart. My first officer gave Finley a reassuring smile. "But it's okay. Because we're your family now, and that means we'll protect her too."

"Thank you."

And then, finally, we were all huddled on the couch, blankets tucked around us.

"Is she okay to watch this?" I whispered to Finley, who was sitting in the chair across from me.

"Eh, it's fine. If it gets inappropriate, I'll just cover her eyes."

I laughed. It wasn't like we all hadn't watched a few episodes, and there wasn't any sex on the show. Plus, the foul language had all gotten bleeped out. "Alright. Let the binge begin!"

We all cheered, and I knew that anyone who wandered past us for the rest of the night would have heard laughter.

The perfect distraction from thoughts of Sylas.

And the future I so desperately wanted.

WATCHING someone sleep should have been creepy, but it felt like the most intimate experience of my life. Sylas was shirtless, his usually grumpy expression formed into a single line, and it was taking everything in me not to reach out and touch him.

But I knew from experience what happened when I did. Not that I was complaining. I loved how caring he was, how he held me and made me feel, well… loved.

I knew I needed to end it before I got too attached, before my heart could get broken. If I lost him the way I lost my father, it wouldn't just devastate me. It would end me. But I couldn't bring myself to stop seeing him. Couldn't bear to stop sleeping in his bed, snuggling against his hard, broad chest. He was the perfect pillow. Maybe I just didn't want to give up my restful sleep and all the orgasms he'd been giving me.

Yeah, I *definitely* wouldn't complain about the latter.

And right now, I wanted to comfort him like he'd comforted me.

For the last two weeks, he'd been so patient with me. It might have been forbidden, but I didn't care anymore. I didn't want to lose him. But there was so much he hadn't told me. I'd opened up to him about my dad. How his loss had affected me. About my memories and my life growing up.

I wanted to know everything about him, too.

The pain that I saw behind his eyes when I mentioned my parents. The despair that kept him emotionally closed off.

"What happened to you?" I whispered, intertwining my fingers through his dark hair. It was soft, and I liked the feel of it in between my fingers. "Who broke your heart?"

And was I enough to heal it? To show him how worthy he was? Of every little thing? Sure, at the beginning, I'd thought he was an arrogant jerk. He'd dismissed me without even giving me a chance. But now, I suspected he was trying to guard himself from something, even back then.

Sylas's eyes fluttered open, and he took my free hand, kissing my palm. "Aurelia." His breath was solemn. "Why are you awake?"

"Couldn't sleep," I admitted, still combing through his hair.

He turned to face me. "A lot on your mind, little star?"

I hesitated. Would bringing it up now be too much? Would it push him away? "I just… seeing Finley and her daughter tonight made me realize… I don't know much about your family. You've mentioned bits and pieces, but…"

Sylas stiffened. "I don't like to talk about my parents."

"I know." With a heavy heart, I mustered a smile for him. "But I want to know you. To understand what's going on up here." I tapped his forehead. "To know why you get this devastating look in your eyes sometimes."

"I don't know anything about love," he admitted. "Not from my parents. They abandoned us."

"Will you tell me about it?" I asked, smoothing my thumb over his furrowed brow.

"There's not much to tell. I was thirteen, and Kayle was eleven when they decided they weren't cut out to be parents. They left us in our apartment and disappeared. I don't know where they went. To this day, I…" His voice sounded choked up.

"Oh, Sylas." My eyes filled with water. "You were completely alone."

He nodded. "Just me and Kayle. And I had to be strong for her. I had to…"

"You never looked for them?"

"Why bother?" His tone was harsh. "If they could leave us that easily, I didn't want them back in my life. I don't even know if they're alive. Or if they died. I've just been carrying around all of this anger for years. At them for leaving us. For making me an adult when I should have been a teenager. I had to learn to take care of my sister when I should have been learning pre-algebra."

"I bet that was hard."

Those shoulders I loved moved in a small shrug. "I made it work. And for the first year, it was okay. And then the building manager found out that my parents were gone. I'd been working odd jobs so I could keep paying the rent, dropping the cash off in envelopes so he wouldn't suspect anything was wrong."

"What happened?"

Sylas winced. "He kicked us out."

"Onto the streets?"

"Yeah. Chicago had shelters, luckily. We bounced around between a lot of them until I turned eighteen. Luckily, I'd saved up enough credits by then for a place of our own. Made sure

Kayle made it through high school. I started taking college classes at the community college in the meantime. Turns out, I was good with computers." He grinned. "A recruiter from the UGSF approached me the year after she was out. I was still working to cover our costs, and tuition wasn't cheap. He offered me the opportunity of a lifetime."

I rubbed my finger over his palm. "What did he give you?"

"He saw potential in me. Told me that if I could stay in school, keep my grades up, he'd cover our bills. Kayle's and mine. And when we finished, we could enlist in the federation. Become officers. Go to space. For a twenty-one-year-old, I'd never heard of such an amazing offer. I jumped at it. We both did."

"And then you worked your way to here."

A nod. "Youngest captain in the fleet. But I earned my spot. Every single day, I worked to prove myself. And here we are."

"Here we are," I murmured. "You survived."

He chuckled. "I guess when you look at it like that, I did. And I'd do it all over again, if it brought me back here."

I interlaced our fingers together, wanting to be physically connected with him. "I don't think it's true that you don't know anything about love, Sylas. I think you loved your sister so much, you would have done anything for her. That's love, in its purest form. Putting someone else before yourself. Prioritizing their needs over yours."

"But is it worth it?" Sylas ran his free hand over my bare skin, tracing the stars on my shoulder. "Loving and losing? Living with that hole in your heart?"

My eyes filled with tears. "Of course it's worth it. All of it."

He kissed me softly. "You've opened my eyes to a lot of things, Aurelia Callisto." Sylas brought our foreheads together.

It was hard not to feel the gravity of the situation. This all felt so... important. My heart fluttered in my chest.

"You know, tonight also reminded me of something."

"Oh?" His hand slid down my arm, intertwining our fingers.

"About how much I've always wanted a family," I said, my voice rough. "For a long time, I didn't think it was possible, but now..." Now, it seemed like a possibility. "Maybe it's okay to let myself dream again."

"And that's what you want?" He asked. "A husband? Kids? A white picket fence?"

The last part made me laugh, but I nodded. "Yeah. I think so." I played with our fingers, keeping my eyes focused on them instead of Sylas's face.

I wanted all of that.

But I'd left out the most important part.

I wanted it with *him*.

THIRTY-FOUR
SYLAS

NEITHER ONE OF us had said the words yet, but I wondered if she was feeling the same way I was. Like this was more.

Those little words begged to spring from my lips, but it wasn't time yet.

Not when there were so many things I still hadn't told her.

But I was letting myself hope. That the family she spoke of, the future she imagined... I wanted to be a part of that. So fucking badly.

"Do you remember the story you told me?" I asked her, gathering up a handful of her hair and running my fingers through it. "About how you knew you wanted to follow in your father's footsteps? To become a pilot?"

She nodded. "Of course I do."

"Well, I have a similar story."

"You do?" She blinked up at me, and I pressed a kiss to her forehead.

"When I was little, I had a poster of my biggest idol on my wall. A man I looked up to. One who seemed to have it all. A family, love, the most amazing job on the planet."

"And what happened?" Aurelia whispered, like she already knew how the story ended.

"I grew up," I said sadly. "But long after that poster came off my wall, I knew I wanted to be someone great like him. Imagine my surprise when he'd stood in front of me, offering me everything I'd ever wanted. And when I joined the Federation after college, I shook his hand at graduation. Thanked him for everything he'd done for me."

Aurelia's hand flew over her mouth, tears collecting in her eyes. "You did?"

"I took one look at you when you walked onto my ship and I knew who you were, Aurelia. Even without telling me your name, I knew your face. The daughter of the man whose poster I had on my wall. My childhood hero." I looked away. "When he went missing, I..." I shook my head. "That was when I realized maybe I couldn't have it all. He'd left behind a wife and a young teenage daughter." A strangled curse left my throat. "I never wanted to do that to someone. To risk leaving them behind. I couldn't—"

A hand landed over my arm, and her reassurance flooded through my system. "I know." She shared the same grief. That same burden as me.

Being abandoned. But my parents had willingly left me.

Samuel Callisto never would have willingly left his daughter.

"You met my dad?" Aurelia repeated, eyes shimmering as tears dripped from her eyes. I wiped them away with my thumb, caressing her cheek. "He was the one who helped you?"

"I did." I chuckled, thinking back to the memory. "I owe him everything. Truly. I was twenty-one, completely without a focus for my life. I don't know how he found me, but he saved me. I don't even remember what I said to him. I was star struck. Here was this man who was everything I'd ever strived to be, shaking my hand and telling me I could do it." No one had ever said that to me before. He couldn't have known how much it meant to me to hear it. "When I crossed the stage, I'd gotten *well done, son.*"

Tears were falling down her face rapidly, but she was smiling, too. "I can't believe—"

"Shhh," I soothed, brushing my hand over the back of her head and pulling her tight against my chest.

"I can't believe that you two met. That you idolized my father. I never thought..."

"What?"

"It's silly," she whispered, looking away.

"Tell me anyway." I rubbed my thumb over her temple. "I want to know every thought in that brilliant brain of yours."

Her cheeks turned pink, and she buried her face against my chest. "Don't laugh." The words were mumbled, muffled by my skin. "Part of me was always upset that my father would never know the man I would marry one day. I knew that he'd never walk me down the aisle, but this..." She laughed, more tears leaking from her eyes. "But he knew *you*. And without even knowing, he put us on the path to meet each other. I just..."

It was like we were meant to be. Some would call that fate, us meeting. Maybe it was. I didn't know. I just knew that I was more grateful for that action, that decision that had set me on this path, than she could ever know.

"Oh, baby." I pressed a kiss to her starry shoulder. "Whether or not I'd met your father, he's always going to be here with you. Because he's in here." I tapped her breastbone above her heart. "And he loved you so much." Tears fell freely. "He loved to brag about his baby girl. How smart you were. How beautiful. How kind and caring, even back then. And twenty-two-year-old me was *envious*. Do you want to know why?"

She shook her head. "W-why?" The words were a whisper, punctuated by a small hiccup.

"Because I wanted someone to look at me with that much pride. To love me the way your father loved you."

"Oh, Sylas." She cupped my cheeks with her hands, and I wiped away her tears with my thumbs. "You don't have to wonder. Not anymore."

"Oh?"

Aurelia leaned in, softly kissing the corner of my lips. Once, twice, lightly against each side. "No," she said, her voice husky. "Because you have me."

Wrapping my arms around her waist, I rolled her on top of me, letting her straddle my stomach.

"I'm the luckiest fucking man in the galaxy, Aurelia. To call you mine. To get to…" *love you.* I swallowed back the words.

Not yet, I reminded myself. Not now. I wanted this moment to be special, and I didn't want to ruin it by saying it too soon.

But I did. *I loved her.* And it was worth everything. She was worth anything.

I'd resign my whole damn commission if I had to. There was no protecting my heart anymore. It was hers. Completely. I wouldn't let her go. Wouldn't let her run away from me. Not anymore. Not after this.

And if she fell? I'd be there to catch her.

"I know," she said, scooting back and running her fingers up my erection. I'd crawled into bed in nothing more than my boxers, which clearly needed to come off. Now.

"Brat." I swatted at her ass, and Aurelia gasped, a sharp inhale of breath.

"*Yes,*" she agreed, looking up at me through half-lidded eyes. "And you like it."

I tilted her chin up and brought our lips together. "Yes," I murmured after kissing her softly. Once, twice. "I do."

"Captain," she said, the word barely more than a moan.

"Not Captain," I corrected. "Say my name."

"*Sylas.*"

"Good girl," I praised, feeling her preen from my comment. I liked how she'd tighten when I told her how good she was doing during sex. My little brat and her praise kink. I smirked.

She pushed my boxers down my hips, allowing my cock to spring free before she scooted back, positioning me between her backside.

"What do you want, baby?" I asked, unable to focus on anything but the way she was rubbing her ass against me with her tits in my face.

"To ride you," she said, letting out a little moan. "I want you inside. Need you to fill me up."

I couldn't agree more. "Then put me inside of you," I instructed.

She obeyed, raising up on her knees and guiding my tip to her entrance before sliding back down. There was no foreplay, so it was a tight fit, but I could feel her growing wetter as she worked me inside of her. She was determined to fit all of me, sinking down inch by inch.

"Fuck, baby," I groaned, my hands digging into the meaty flesh of her hips. Her wet heat surrounded me, already feeling like I was planted impossibly deep inside of her.

Aurelia rolled her hips, her hands planted on my chest as she rode me.

"You're so deep," she gasped out. "I can feel you *everywhere.*"

"Good. I want to fuck you so hard that you're ruined for anyone else."

"I already am." She panted, shaking her head.

She rocked back and forth, little shudders spreading through her body each time her clit made contact with my base, and I reached out, cupping her tits and massaging them.

"Sy," she cried. "That's too good."

I raised my torso so I could suck a nipple into my mouth, flicking my tongue over her sensitive flesh. "Do you like that?"

She nodded, and I did the same thing to the other one. I was an equal opportunity boobs kinda guy.

"Are you close?" I asked, watching as her eyes fluttered shut.

"*Yes. Sylas. Yes.*" Her words devolved into moans and murmurings of my name and nonsense as she continued rocking her hips and then began sliding herself up and down.

I felt her squeeze me with her insides, and I groaned. "*Aurelia.*"

"Hm?" She fluttered her eyelashes.

I returned my hands to her waist, helping her move on top of me, willing myself not to come before she did. It would be close, though.

Because this wasn't an urgent fuck. It was fucking cheesy, but this wasn't just sex. Not for either of us. And when her eyes focused on mine, I brought our torsos together to kiss her.

Plain and simple, we were making love. Maybe we hadn't called it that, but the emotions bubbling inside of me couldn't be mistaken as anything but. I felt so much all at once. Every roll of her hips, every time she tightened around me, I was closer and closer to ecstasy.

She cried out as she came, and then froze.

"What was that?" Aurelia's eyes widened as another large banging sound came. Had something hit the side of the ship?

I groaned. "Fuck. Why does this always happen to us?" I rested my head between her breasts, still planted deep within her.

The alarm went off on the ship, a high-pitched incessant beeping. It didn't stop, and I knew the crew were probably already running around like crazy. And as the commanding officer and head pilot, we couldn't exactly ignore this.

"Shit." I adjusted our positions, helping her off of me so I could pull out of her. "We have to go." I kissed her forehead.

"But..." she looked at my cock, angry and oozing with pre-cum.

"I'll be fine." I swallowed roughly. "I can take care of it later."

She gave me a determined nod, already up and out of bed. She rolled her head, stretching out her muscles, before pulling on her uniform. Finally, she wrapped her hair into a tight bun. Perfect. She always looked fucking perfect.

"It'll be fine," I said after I'd dressed, pulling her tight to me and claiming her lips in a quick kiss. "Everything will be okay."

I had to believe that was the truth.

"REPORT," I huffed, running into the bridge without a moment to stare.

"There's an asteroid shower, Captain. Nav's auto-pilot failed, and we're in danger of engine failure if we sit here. The best course of action is—"

"I'm here!" Aurelia said, running in behind me, already heading to her station to take control of the ship. Her chair to the terminal transition was seamless, those fingers already hurrying.

"Can you do this?" I asked her, though I had complete faith in her.

I'd watched her steer a ship so it didn't crash. I'd seen her, day after day, give her all to this crew in her role. She was the best damn Pilot I could have ever asked for.

And to think, you tried to get her fired, a little voice in my mind taunted me. *And then you went and fell in love with her.* No regrets. Not with her. Every moment had brought us here—together—so I was grateful for all of them.

"I was born to do this, *sir.*" She winked at me and fuck, I fell even deeper in love with her. Down bad, and didn't I fucking know it?

I tried to ignore the uncomfortable pressure in my pants, which that little quip definitely wasn't helping.

"Then fly."

She bobbed her head in a nod, facing forward.

Sitting in the Captain's chair, I quickly took over the helm, barking orders at the crew and other officers while I watched Aurelia's hands fly over the screen.

"Helm is under my control, Captain," she said, eyes looking back to connect with mine. "Everyone might want to strap in, though. This is going to get a bit... rocky."

A glimmer of amusement shone in her gaze, and I chuckled.

286

Only she would crack a joke in the middle of a life or death situation.

That's my girl, I mouthed, and she winked at me. Then her body straightened, and I watched in awe as she guided us through the asteroid shower with lethal precision.

The major problem was the large ones, which were likely to do a lot more damage than the small amounts of debris, though it clung to the large window of the ship like some kind of space dust.

My heart was in my throat as I watched her, unable to take my eyes off of her for even a minute.

You can do this, I thought, hoping she knew just how much I believed in her.

THIRTY-FIVE
AURELIA

I'D RUN through simulations of asteroid showers throughout my time at the academy, but I'd never expected flying through one to feel like this. I held my breath, trying to keep my hands as steady as possible, knowing that one minor error, one slip, and we would all be dead.

But no pressure, right?

An hour ago, we'd been tangled up in the sheets, Sylas sharing more about his past than I'd ever gotten before, and now… It was life or death.

I wasn't used to this kind of pressure.

Honestly, the only thing keeping me going right now was the laser focus they'd drilled into me at the academy. The intensity there helped me shut off my brain.

Don't think about him, I scolded my brain. There'd be time for that later. Time to think about the words I'd thought he was going to say to me.

Right now, I just needed to *fly.*

"THAT WAS INTENSE," I said, squeezing my eyes shut as I dropped onto a couch in the officer's lounge a few hours later.

"You were *amazing*, Aurelia. I told my brother he was an idiot for doubting you in the first place."

I chuckled. "But if he hadn't, who knows where we'd be?" I meant it as a joke, but as soon as it was out there, I knew I was serious. Sure, the first few weeks on the ship weren't as optimal as they could have been, but I'd found a place here.

And I'd found *him*.

"You love him." Kayle said, not quite a question, and I stopped twirling the piece of hair between my fingers. Looked up at her and nodded.

I did. Didn't I? I had for a while.

"Have you told him?"

"No." I sighed. "We were interrupted this morning. You know, asteroid shower and all that. This is the first moment I've had to breathe." And Sylas was still on the bridge, overseeing repairs.

Kayle gave me a pat on my shoulder. "Just make sure that this is what you want."

"What do you mean?" I blinked.

"Just... if you're going to leave, break his heart now. Don't prolong this and then leave him broken. I don't think he could survive that."

"I would never," I said, the words bubbling out of my throat. "I'm not going to leave him. Ever." There was more, too, but I wanted to say it to him, first. "How long have you known?"

She gave me a coy smile. "Awhile. You two aren't that subtle, you know? I caught you eye-fucking on the bridge at least ten times a day."

"Oh." My cheeks were most definitely a bright shade of pink. "Why didn't you say anything? Technically, we're not even supposed to be together."

"Superior officers have that rule because they don't want

them taking advantage of their subordinates. But Sylas isn't taking advantage of you, is he?"

I shook my head. "No." No matter what happened, I believed in his feelings for me. That they were genuine. The way he touched me, took care of me, and spent time with me... How could they not be? Someone didn't just fake all of that intensity.

"Good. I think I would have had to kill him if he was. Maybe throw him into the brig."

I froze. "Do we actually have one?" I was pretty sure I'd explored every inch of the ship, but maybe I was wrong.

There was a mischievous glint in Kayle's eyes as she brushed past that comment. "And anyway, he's my brother. The only thing I stand to gain from enforcing the regulations is ruining our relationship and having to take over as captain myself. And honestly, I like my position. Maybe I'll be a starship captain one day, but not of the *Paradise*. He earned this."

"He did." I agreed, nodding my head. "Sylas told me everything. About your parents. How you two grew up. I'm so sorry no one was there for you."

She shook her head, squeezing my shoulder before heading towards the door. "That's where you're wrong. Because someone was always there for me. Him. But I think it's time that someone else is there for him. Do you know what I mean?"

I had a feeling I understood exactly what she was saying to me.

"HEY."

Sylas was at his desk, working on paperwork, and I leaned on the door frame. There was so much left unsaid—on both of our parts. If we hadn't been interrupted earlier, I knew I would have confessed all of it.

He looked up at me, swallowing roughly. "Everything okay?"

I took a deep breath. "Yeah. I talked to your sister."

"Kayle?" Sylas furrowed his brow. "What did she want?"

Padding over to his desk, I slid onto it. "She knows."

"About…"

"Us." I nodded. "Yeah."

"*Fuck*." He cursed under his breath. "How did she find out?"

"Well, apparently we aren't very slick about keeping our eyes off of each other on the bridge, *Captain*." I danced my fingers up his very firm chest.

"And? What did she say?"

I glossed over most of our conversation. We weren't there *yet*. Better to work up to it. "That she wasn't going to report us."

Sylas rested his hand on my thigh. "Oh?"

"She doesn't want to be the captain." I shook my head, emotion suddenly making my throat tight. "But maybe we should think about this. If this is what we really want. To be… together. I don't want you to lose your position because of me. You worked so hard for this, and I…" I swallowed roughly. "I can't be the reason you lose your dream."

"I don't need to think about it. I want you." He moved to position himself in between my thighs. "You could ask me a million times over, and I'd say the same thing. You're my everything, little star."

"Are you sure?" I whispered, my heartbeat practically thudding against my chest.

"Yes." He didn't even blink.

"Sylas," I murmured, my voice low.

"Fuck it," he muttered, cupping my face in between his hands. "I don't want to hide this anymore."

"I don't either," I whispered, feeling the words down to my core. Sneaking around was exhausting. It made me feel like we were guilty of something, and the only thing I was guilty of was how much I cared for this man.

"I'm pretty sure everyone else already knows anyway," he remarked, his lips barely inches from mine. A low chuckle slipped from his lips. "So who cares?"

"I guess that's one way to look at it," I joked. Wrapping my arms around his neck, I slid my hands into the back of his hair. "So, what do we do now?"

"Now, you stubborn woman, I'm going to kiss you. And then we'll figure out the rest of it together."

"Oh you are, are you?" I hummed, running my tongue over my lower lip.

He growled, taking my lips with his before tugging on that same lip with his teeth. His tongue swirled with mine, letting our saliva mix, and he let out a little groan—

A knock sounded at the door, and Sylas didn't move, staying right where he was.

"Not again," he cursed, looking up at the ceiling. "We're cursed."

I giggled, and the door slid open. Kayle rushed in, her eyebrow raising at our position, but she didn't say anything. My cheeks pinked, and I looked away.

"Sylas." She sounded out of breath. "We have another problem."

"Of fucking course we do."

"We need you on the bridge."

"What is it now?" He growled, eyes narrowed. "One of these days, I'd like to finish this conversation without getting interrupted."

"It's fine," I said, running my fingers over the hair that had flopped onto his forehead. "We can finish it later." It was a promise I intended to keep.

He dipped his head, and I hopped off the desk, already heading back towards the bridge.

THIRTY-SIX
SYLAS

TODAY WAS NOT GOING to plan at all. All I wanted to do was to crawl back into bed with Aurelia, but someone had to keep this place running.

Top of the line, brand spanking new starship, and apparently, they couldn't keep it running without us.

My eyes were narrowed, arms crossed over my chest as I stared at my crew. It was so quiet on the bridge, you could have heard a pin drop.

Even the crew members working in the background were completely silent.

"Report."

"Captain," Leo said, turning from his station with a grimace. Like he didn't like what he was about to tell me as much as he knew I didn't want to hear it. "The sensors on the top of the ship are blocked. We're not able to operate the ship at its full capacity in this state."

"So go fix them," I barked out, rubbing my temples.

I was out of patience. Mostly because it seemed like everyone in the galaxy was out for Aurelia and I having the most important conversation of our lives.

Was it so hard to say it? Three words. Eight letters. So simple. And yet...

Leo hadn't moved. "I can't."

"What?"

He cleared his throat. "The ship wasn't designed to have that kind of maintenance while operational. Our center of gravity is too high. One slip, one miscalculation, and..."

"So what you're saying is you're *too tall* to get on the hull and fix it?"

"Yes."

Which meant I was also too tall. Fuck. But... I looked around the room.

"I'll go," Aurelia volunteered, before I could think through a solution. "I can do it."

"No."

"Why not?" she asked, glaring at me. "I might be trained as a pilot, sir, but I also have a degree in advanced aerospace engineering. I could do this in my sleep."

I ignored the way she was still calling me *sir*. Like everyone on this bridge couldn't guess that we were in a fucking relationship.

"Aurelia." I growled. Didn't she see that this wasn't about her skill? I couldn't risk her. "Absolutely not. You can't do this. I won't let you."

"You can't stop me, either." She glared at me. *"Captain."* She added a little emphasis to the last word.

"Don't you *dare*."

She turned to Leo. "Can you walk me through on how to fix and reset the sensors?"

"No," I said again.

"Yes," Leo answered her, ignoring me. "We can tether you to the ship, so there shouldn't be any serious chance of injury."

I knew what he really meant. *Death*. If anything happened to her, I would kill him. I didn't care if he was one of my oldest friends.

"This is insane," I grunted. None of them were even listening to me. "You're really going to send her out there?"

"It's our best option," Wren remarked. "You know it is. If you stepped back and looked at this objectively…"

But I couldn't remain impartial when it came to her. I wasn't rational when it came to her safety. And my lack of being objective was getting in the way of me being captain.

"I can do it, Sylas." Her voice was low as she stared at me.

Whipping around, I didn't hide my unhappiness. "Of course you can do it. I don't doubt that. I believe in you. You're—fuck." I rubbed at my temples. "Commander Kellar," I barked.

My sister's head whipped up. She'd been staring at her tablet, focused entirely on the data in front of her. "What?"

"You're in charge. I can't condone this."

Turning on my heel, I walked off the bridge, trying to ignore the sinking feeling in my gut.

DIDN'T she understand that it wasn't that I didn't believe in her? I knew she was incredible. She was amazing. I'd fallen in love with her somewhere in between her smart wit and that bratty mouth.

That didn't mean I wanted her risking herself.

Fuck it. I meant what I'd said in my office. I didn't care if everyone knew we were together. The rules didn't matter to me. Not when I loved her more than I'd ever thought possible. More than life itself.

"I can do this," she reassured me, now outfitted in a space suit. Turns out my feet hadn't taken me far away from her when I'd left the bridge, because I'd followed her directly to the airlock that would lead her to the top of the hull. The suit's helmet was in her arm, tucked under her shoulder. "If nothing else, believe in my fancy engineering degree." She winked and then grew serious. "Or in Leo and Wren. They won't let me fall."

I turned to glare at them. They were some of my best friends, and I still wanted to throttle them. "They better not." I cupped her face with my hands. "If anything happens to you, I—"

"*Sylas.*" The word was a whisper. A reminder.

Of how much I *didn't fucking care anymore.*

I kissed her, right there, in front of half my officers and whoever else was watching. Kissed her like it was the first time, which in some ways, it was. The first time I was being honest with myself, with all of them.

"I can't remain impartial when it comes to you," I admitted, echoing my thoughts from the bridge. "Not anymore." Burying my nose in her hair, I inhaled her sweet scent. "I'm not rational when it comes to you. I want you too bad."

It was more than want. It was *need.* I needed her, needed her warmth and care and the way she looked at me with so much hope and optimism. Like I was capable of anything.

Because I wanted to be. I wanted to be all of those things she wanted, wanted to be everything to her.

"Me too," she whispered. "I've never felt like this before. It's never been like this before with anyone."

"Even if I have to resign my command. I don't care. It's always been you. It was always going to be you."

Tears filled her eyes. "I—"

"Don't say it," she begged, voice low enough that no one else could hear. "Not now. Not when I'm risking my life."

"You're going to be fine," I reassured her. "Okay? But please, be safe."

"I will."

"Come back to me."

She nodded.

"Promise me." I pressed my forehead to hers. These words were important. Almost as important as the other ones she wouldn't let me say.

"I promise."

She slipped out of my hands, heading towards the airlock. Aurelia didn't look back once. And I wondered who was more nervous: me or her? If she knew just how painful looking back at me was as I did staring at her?

The door sealed, and my knees felt weak.

"Please," I said to no one. To anyone who was watching. To the universe. "Bring her back to me."

I wasn't above pleading.

MY HEART WAS in my throat as I watched her follow Leo's instructions, moving towards each of the sensors. Debris from the asteroid shower had gathered all over the top of the ship, which, from my vantage point, seemed like a legitimate issue.

Still, I didn't understand why Aurelia was the one who had to fix it. Surely, there was someone in engineering who was small and nimble enough for this sort of thing?

It didn't need to be my girl.

But I couldn't look away, either. We were watching from a camera installed on the top and sides of the ship, giving us multiple angles as Aurelia slowly made her way across the top.

"Got the first one," she said, her voice coming loud and clear over the speaker thanks to the microphone that was installed in the suit.

She moved to towards the next one. The tether keeping her tied to the ship was like something you'd use in rock climbing, but I didn't like the sight of it one bit.

She slipped, losing hold of the ship momentarily, her legs flailing in the air before she could grab the line, pulling herself back down to the ship.

"I'm going out there," I said, already pulling another suit off the wall. Fuck if I cared about the reason she was out there. This was too dangerous for her to do alone. I never should have agreed.

"She's got it," Leo said, diverting my attention. "Look."

"I can't watch this," I grumbled, crossing my arms over my chest. It was too stressful. All I could do was stare at the door and will her to come back.

Twenty minutes later, the airlock opened, and there she was. Disconnecting from the cable. Climbing into the pressure stabilizer.

Those twenty minutes had felt like a millennium. They'd probably taken ten years off my life.

I rushed in the moment the light turned green.

"Holy shit," Aurelia gasped, her hand clutched over her chest after the airlock closed. "That was…" I took off her helmet that circulated air, letting it drop to the ground at our feet.

"Fuck." I crushed her to my chest, needing the reassurance that she was here. That she was okay. That I hadn't almost lost her. "You scared the shit out of me."

"I'm sorry." Her eyes were wide, shaking her head.

"I can't lose you. I don't know what I'd do if—"

"I know."

In response, I took her lips in mine. Kissed the everliving fuck out of her. Sucked on her tongue, and inhaled her little gasp into my mouth. All I could hear, see, taste, smell was *her*. Aurelia wasn't just in my senses—she was in my bloodstream. In the very essence of who I was now. I needed her like I needed oxygen to breathe.

When she was breathing roughly, I pulled away. "Let's get you out of this, little star."

She rubbed over her lips with her thumb, like she was a little awestruck that I'd just kissed her here.

But no one was around. Everyone else was inside the ship, not in the small airlock. And hopefully, they were all minding their fucking business.

Turning her around, I dragged down the back zipper. She was still wearing her dark gray jumpsuit underneath it, those purple accents showing.

Her breath hitched in her throat as I dipped my head to press a kiss to her neck.

Finally, I finished the tortuously slow glide of the zipper, and helped her step out of the spacesuit.

Then she was standing in front of me, a little flush to her cheeks, hair looking adorably tousled, lips pink and a little swollen.

"Hi," I said, wrapping my arms around her wrist. I needed her in my arms, so I could reassure myself that she was here. She was safe.

That I had my entire world in my arms.

THIRTY-SEVEN
AURELIA

THE AIRLOCK SEALED tight behind me, and it was just him and me in the chamber. I was still trying to catch my breath, the adrenaline coursing through my body demanding a very different physical activity.

For a while, I'd been holding back my emotions. Because I hadn't known if they were reciprocated. And then, well... because it had seemed like the world would end if I told him how I was feeling and he said nothing back. But I didn't care anymore. Not after we'd just lived through an asteroid shower and I'd gone on a super dangerous space walk.

His arms were still wrapped around my waist, keeping me tight against his body, and I placed one hand over his heart. I could feel how rapidly it was beating.

And suddenly, I wasn't scared anymore.

"Sylas," I said, taking a deep breath. "I need you to know that I'm never going to leave you. That I'm in this for the long run. However long that is... You have me. I'm yours."

He pressed his lips to my forehead, not saying anything for a beat.

"I—" I started, but he slid his finger over my lips.

"Aurelia." His voice was pained. "What you did out there

300

was reckless. It was brave. It was fucking amazing, little star. But none of that matters if you don't come back to me."

"I know," I whispered again.

A ragged breath slipped from his lips. "Do you remember when I asked you if it was worth it?" *Love.* He'd asked me if love was worth it, even if you lost them in the end. I nodded. "And you remember when you said that we should think about if this is what we really wanted? Being together?"

"Yes," I croaked out.

"It is. I never knew what it was like before—loving someone. But now I do. Of course, it's worth it, being with someone who makes you feel like the best version of yourself every day. Someone who burrows themselves so deep in your soul, you don't think you can get them out. Because you don't want them out. You want to hold on to them so tightly that they can't slip away."

My words were barely a whisper. "I won't slip away, Sylas."

A smile slipped over his lips. A big, beautiful, genuine smile. One that was worth every star in the galaxy. One I would do anything to keep on his face for the rest of our lives.

And to think, all those months ago, I'd thought he was the grumpiest man in existence. Now I knew about his secret soft side, the ooey gooey filling that he'd showed me every day. By caring for me, building Brina a home, and every single time he'd gone out of his way to cheer me up.

"I love you," Sylas said, and the words filled a void in my chest I hadn't even realized were there. "You're worth it. You're worth every risk. You said you can't be the reason I lose my dream. But that's where you're wrong, Rae. My dream isn't the federation, or even being captain."

"It's not?"

"No. It hasn't been. Not for a while." He tucked a piece of hair behind my ear. "You're my dream, Aurelia. Being with you is everything I could have ever asked for."

"I love you," I blurted, not able to hold it in any longer. "I

301

don't know when it started, but I do. I know I called you a grumpy asshole before, but you're really not. You're this secret teddy bear. Like you have all this goodness inside of you, but you're afraid to show it to anyone else. You didn't grow up with examples of love, but you love harder than anyone I know, anyway. You're always taking care of everyone around you, and I want to be that person for you. Because you deserve every ounce of love that you give out. How could I not love you?"

He leaned his forehead against mine, that gorgeous smile still covering his face. I slid a hand onto his cheek, running my fingers over his short beard. "Aurelia..." Sylas's voice was low. Reverent.

"I know."

I raised onto my toes and pressed my lips to his. A soft, sensual kiss. But it quickly turned into something deeper. He kissed me like we'd never kissed before. It was something I'd waited my whole life for. To be kissed like this. To feel this much. Our lips meeting, over and over, as we barely came up for air. I didn't need any—he'd be my oxygen supply, for all I cared.

We were in perfect sync. Like our hearts were beating as one. He was the only thing in my orbit.

His erection pressed into my hip as I let out a moan into his mouth.

"Fuck," Sylas groaned. "I need you."

And suddenly, I was wearing too many clothes. "Yes," I agreed. I needed to feel him inside of me, needed to be reassured that this was real. That we were here. Nothing else mattered but the fact that we were here, together.

He slid my zipper down with his teeth, slowly revealing inches of skin.

"Sylas," I whispered. "They're outside—"

"Don't care," he said, helping me out of the sleeves, before peeling the suit off my skin. I was slightly sweaty from my efforts, but Sylas didn't seem to care. He pushed my underwear to the side and plunged two fingers inside me without warning.

I cried out, because the sensation was too good. Too much. I was so full of him. He worked me till I could feel myself dripping around him, and I knew he was just making sure I was ready for him. Like always.

He was still fully dressed, me just in my bra and panties—which, frankly, seemed a little unfair.

"Do you want them to hear?" Sylas asked as his fingers hit that spot inside me that made me see stars, and I gasped.

"I don't care," I cried.

"Good. Let them hear how I fuck my girl. Because you are. You're *mine*."

"Yes," I agreed.

He unzipped his pants, freeing that magnificent cock.

"I'm not going to last very long after earlier," he admitted, cupping the back of my neck with his free hand.

"I don't care." I smiled against his lips. "Fuck me, Sylas."

"God, you're such a brat." He ran his fingers through my wetness one more time, before rubbing it all over his cock.

My eyes widened. That was—my cheeks flushed. Why was that so hot?

"Gonna fuck that attitude right out of you."

Holding my panties to the side, he guided his tip to my entrance, burying himself in my cunt in one stroke.

"*Oh,*" I gasped, seeing stars. I was pretty sure I'd come just from him inserting it inside of me.

Sylas reached down, grabbing one of my knees and pulling it up towards his torso, giving me the most delicious stretch.

"So tight. This cunt was made for me, Aurelia. And I want to fill it up every day."

I didn't even know what he was saying anymore. I was blinded with pleasure as he rocked his hips into me, each thrust sending me towards the edge. He'd said he wouldn't last long, but dammit, I wasn't either.

"Sylas," I cried, my leg resting against his shoulder. I didn't even know what I was saying. All I knew was I was clutching onto him for dear life. Thank god I was pressed up against the wall, otherwise I wouldn't be standing. *"Ohmygod."* My vision went white. I saw stars.

Though some of that might have been the airlock itself.

Sylas grunted, and then I felt his warmth spill inside of me as his head slumped against my shoulder. The rest of his body was still wrapped against mine, and even if we'd just done it standing up—and in the airlock, for fuck's sake—I'd never felt so protected. So cherished.

Something was definitely wrong with me.

He pulled out, our combined releases coating his length, and then adjusted my underwear. I could feel his cum dribbling out of me.

Maybe that was his goal.

"Come on, baby. Let's go back to bed."

I nodded, taking his hand and letting him help me redress. My legs were weak, so I couldn't have done it by myself if I wanted to.

HE CARRIED me back to his room—our room—and Brina came over, shaking her little otter-like tail and yipping at both of us.

I gathered her up in my arms, pressing kisses to her face.

Shit, I felt bad that we'd left her alone in here during all of that. I confessed my guilt to Sylas, who just scooped me up in his arms, pressing a kiss to my forehead.

All the while, our little alien pet curled back up in her bed, letting out a little sigh. I made a mental reminder to spoil her with fresh fish and a long swim later.

But for now, I had someone else on my mind. Our clothes were quickly shed on the floor. His cum was still inside of me, and when he pulled my underwear from my body, I felt a stream trickle down my leg.

His eyes flared as he watched it, and then his eyes met mine. My nipples hardened from his perusal down my naked form.

I didn't know why, but I suddenly felt shy. Not because we hadn't seen each other like this before—we were insatiable. *Thank you, fertility blockers.*

But because this was the first time after we'd said those three big words. *I love you.*

And all of me was laid bare now. My body, my heart. It was all his.

Wordlessly, Sylas brought me back into his arms, picking me up and carrying me across the room.

He laid me down on the bed. "Fucking beautiful." He kissed my ankle. My inner thigh. Then moved up—ignoring where I needed him most. Kissed my stomach. The swells of both of my breasts. My collar bone. My neck.

Then my lips.

And oh, I loved when he kissed me like this. With tongue. Deep. Like he couldn't get enough.

"Sy," I murmured, eyelids fluttering. "Your cum is still dripping out of me."

"Good," he said, a wicked grin on his lips. "I like it there."

His nostrils flared as he took in the heat in my eyes.

"Should we finish what we started earlier?" Pushing him down onto his back, I straddled him.

Guiding his length into my opening, I took him in fully, sinking down to the hilt. I meant what I'd told him earlier—in this position, I could feel him everywhere. I rested my hand on my stomach, pressing down lightly.

"Rae." Sylas's murmur was pained. "I need you to move."

I shook my head, feeling too much. Everything was different now.

He loved me.

I loved him.

For two people who were an unlikely match, a forbidden pairing, everything felt so raw. Real.

Sylas let me ride him for a few moments, before he sat up, bringing our chests together as he wrapped his arms around me.

My breasts pressed against his hard chest, the brush of my nipples against his skin sending sparks of pleasure down my spine.

He kissed me lazily, before rubbing his stubble over my cheek, pressing open-mouthed kisses to my neck. I couldn't help my whimper. It was too much. It wasn't enough.

My legs were behind him as I sat in his lap, his cock deep inside of me, all of that cum making me wetter than normal. One hand wrapped around my back, and his other across my hip as Sylas dropped his forehead against mine.

Tears pricked my eyes at all the emotion, but he didn't say anything.

Instead, he moved inside of me, a slow but sensuous pace. It was everything. It wasn't enough. His hips rocked against mine, helping me to move as he pulled out, leaving only the tip inside.

"I love you," he murmured, kissing my neck as he pushed inside of me once again.

I let out a breathy moan. "I love you."

He didn't pick up his pace, just continued that steady rhythm, and it was simultaneously the most intimate and erotic sexual experience of my life.

"You're mine," he murmured, coaxing me into bliss.

"Yours," I agreed, running my hand over his beard. "And you're mine."

He kissed my palm, and then we were lost in it.

In each other.

In all the love we felt for each other.

I GAVE A SLEEPY, blissful yawn as my eyes fluttered open later. I had no idea how much time had passed, but I woke up to find Sylas's form still wrapped around mine, one of his legs thrown over mine and almost every inch of our bodies pressed against each other.

He sleepily nuzzled his face into my boobs.

"Knew you were a tits guy," I said, brushing my fingers through his hair.

A smile crept over his face as he opened his eyes, looking up at me with those gorgeous deep blues. "You caught me."

I rested my head against his when he finally pulled back.

"Thank fuck no one interrupted us this time," he grumbled. "I thought I was going to lose my mind earlier."

"I wanted to tell you this morning," I mumbled. "How I felt. Before everything happened."

He cupped my cheek. "Me too. But I was worried that you wouldn't feel the same, and I'd scare you away."

I laughed. "If you didn't scare me away after you tried to kick me off the ship, what makes you think you'd be able to now?"

"Touché." A deep chuckle came from his throat. "I'm so fucking lucky you don't listen to me."

"Oh, you're going to regret saying that one day," I said, a wicked grin on my face. He reached down, tickling my skin, and I shrieked, pulling away from him.

Then my mood soured. Because everything was *wonderful.* Amazing, really. But we still had one big problem we hadn't solved.

"What's wrong?" He frowned, brushing my hair back off my forehead.

I sighed. "You know the federation won't be happy when they find out we're together." And as much as I loved the phrase, *ask for forgiveness, not permission,* I didn't quite think that would fly here.

"No. There's one good thing, though." A smile crept up his lips.

"What?" I furrowed my eyebrow. "You know I love the rules. I'm a stickler for them. I practically have the regulations tattooed on the insides of my eyelids." If that was a thing, it would have been extremely useful during my exams.

"We're millions of light years away from Earth. When do you think the soonest they'd receive a transmission about our... *indecent transgressions?*"

"Oh." He was right. Sure, it was *wrong*, but also... We weren't hurting anyone.

We were both adults with fully formed prefrontal cortexes. He hadn't manipulated me into being in a relationship with him.

"You know, I could always resign."

"No." He brushed my hair back, placing a kiss on my forehead. "This is your dream. Being a pilot. Following in your father's footsteps. I don't want you to give that up."

I laughed. "How is it possible that we can both say the same things, and neither one of us listens?"

But he was right. This *was* my dream. And I loved flying this starship. Being a pilot made me feel closer to my dad, but it was also my calling. I was damn good at it. Giving it up wouldn't be true to who I was.

Sure, for the next four something years, we'd be fine. We could finish our mission as captain and pilot and then present ourselves in front of the federation. Surely, they wouldn't find it fit to fire us both. Right? I chewed on my lip, contemplating that thought.

He gave me a grumpy expression, wrapping his arms around my waist and bringing me closer to his body. "I already told you my dreams changed. I want you."

Speaking of my father, a thought came to me. I hadn't been ready before, but I was now. "You said you found where the debris landed from my dad's ship? Where it all ended up?"

He nodded, explaining what he'd found on the flash drive.

"I know we have time, but I think… maybe soon… I'd like to go. To say goodbye. For closure."

"Are you sure?"

"Yeah. Maybe it's strange, but now that I have those videos, I feel like I have a part of him back. And it's time to let go." A little tear rolled down my cheek. "I'll always miss him, but I can't hold on to the grief forever."

Sylas kissed my forehead. "Whenever you need me, or whenever you want to talk about him, you know I'm here."

"Thank you."

He brushed his fingers over my shoulder, tracing a line between my stars. I always wondered what pattern he found. "I think there's a way we can have it all." Sylas was so calm that I immediately looked up at him, letting myself sink into the view of those deep ocean eyes.

"How?" I blinked at him.

"Do you trust me?" He brushed a strand of hair back from my forehead.

"Of course." I buried my face in between his pecs. "I trust you more than anyone."

"Then… I think there's something we can do."

"Anything."

There wasn't a single thing I wouldn't do for—or with—this man.

THIRTY-EIGHT
SYLAS

THE NEXT DAY, I stood on the bridge, facing all of my officers. I had no idea how they were all going to take it. Sure, a few of them—maybe all of them—knew, but this was different. Because it wasn't just about them accepting my decisions or me, it was also about them accepting *her*.

Accepting us together.

Which felt more daunting. But I didn't have to question the reason. I was looking right at it. At her normally smiling face, which was currently worrying her lower lip into her mouth.

"So, you're together," Leo stated, raising an eyebrow before looking back and forth between the two of us.

"Yes." I'd just finished briefing the entire officer team about our relationship status. And maybe none of them had really been surprised that we were sleeping together, but they'd all looked shocked about my revelation on the bridge.

"Like, *really* together?" That was Violet.

Astrid grinned. "I knew it."

Orion rolled his eyes. "It was obvious."

"Thanks for the support," I muttered, letting my gaze drift back to Aurelia.

"But... what will the federation think?" Finley asked, her eyes wide.

I crossed my arms, glaring at all of them. Even if some of them were supportive, they all needed to hear it.

"We're four and a half *years* from being back on Earth. Who the fuck cares what they think? They can fire me when I get back, for all I care." I looked at all of them. "And if you want to vote to remove me as your captain because I'm emotionally compromised, *fine.* I don't care. But I will not change my mind."

"No one's going to do that." Kayle sighed, looking at her nails. "I'm just disappointed you felt like you couldn't tell us sooner."

Internally, I wanted to roll my eyes. Externally, I just exhaled deeply. Because as much as I regretted not confessing all of it to Kayle before last night, I knew she had my back. And she was just playing a role of her own right now.

Aurelia spoke up. "I didn't want you all to think I was getting special treatment. That he was treating me differently. And then with the federation rules..." She shook her head. "I hope you're not disappointed in us."

"You're really going to risk everything, though? For a relationship that's been going on, what... three months?" Violet frowned. "Aurelia, you know I love you, but you know his reputation, right?"

Aurelia winced, and the weight in my pocket felt like a million bricks.

"Don't talk about her like that," I growled. "Like she's nothing to me. She's my *wife.*" I ground the words out between clenched teeth, and the entire crew looked between her and I, dumbfounded.

"Your... *wife?*" Everyone was stunned into silence.

Aurelia twisted the new band of steel around her finger. "It's true. We're married." She looked up at me with the most dazzling smile, and I knew what those eyes were saying.

I love you.

My wedding band sat in the pocket of my uniform, and I slipped it on too. We'd both agreed to keep them off until we told the crew.

Well, the cat was out of the bag now.

"Besides," my new wife said, gaze focused on Violet, who she gave a soft smile. "I know he's a little grumpy. And sometimes he comes across as an asshole. But that's not really who he is. And I love him anyway." One side of her lips tilted up. "Even when he's a big ol' grump."

Ridiculous, I mouthed to her.

Secret softie, she mouthed back.

I cleared my throat. "Any other questions?"

The entire room exploded into discussion, and Aurelia slid up to my side, interlacing our fingers together.

Leo was looking at Kayle with a confused expression, and she just shook her head in a *I'll tell you later* kind of way.

Late last night, after we'd discussed it at length, we'd gotten dressed and went and found my sister.

See, the Captain and their first officer were granted the authority to sanction official documents and ceremonies on a starship. Like… a wedding.

Because what Wren had told me about the *Voyager* having a married couple both serving as officers, had me digging into the specific regulations about internal fraternizations or affairs. And while those relationships *were* frowned upon, especially between a captain and his subordinate, it wasn't explicitly forbidden. The likelihood they could actually fire either of us for being in a relationship was low.

Aurelia had spent two hours combing through the regulations.

And then we'd said *I do.*

Because at that point, neither one of us could imagine going another moment without being married. We were already linked together inexplicably. And I knew she was the only woman I'd want. Forever.

It wasn't a big ceremony—just my sister and two crew members to serve as our witnesses.

Maybe it was insane. Maybe we should have waited. But it felt right. And her wearing my ring on her finger—the ring I'd had melted down from scrap pieces of metal in the engineering room—satisfied that primal part of my brain that wanted to claim her.

"Do you think we can sneak out of here with no one noticing?" Aurelia whispered into my ear.

"It seems unlikely. Especially since we clearly weren't very subtle about being together in the first place."

"Oops?" My girl gave a little half-hearted shrug. "I'm just glad no one's upset."

"Why would they be?" I frowned.

"I don't know. I just didn't want to lose their friendships because I was sleeping with the captain. It's not like I want any special treatment. I never asked for that."

"I know you didn't." I ran a thumb over her cheekbone. "And I'm pretty sure they all do, too. Sometimes, it's hard to see from our own positions just how much support we have. But this crew…"

I looked at each one of them. They all were special to us. The girls had brought Aurelia so much support. Friendship when she needed it. And now, they practically had a sisterhood.

And the guys, well… They were my brothers. I'd never said those words to them, but it was true. These people, this crew— they were our family.

"Turns out we're exactly where we were supposed to be all along." I kissed her forehead. "Thanks for finding your way to me, little star."

"I love you," she murmured.

"I love you too," I responded, tipping up her chin to press a soft kiss to her mouth.

"Get a room!" Leo shouted, and everyone burst out into laughter.

As if I didn't plan to do exactly that.

THE DOOR to my office slid open, and I turned to find my sister standing there. Everyone else must have still been on the bridge, or back to their everyday lives. Aurelia was checking on Brina, probably taking her out for a walk or a swim.

"Hey."

"Hi."

She joined me on the couch, leaning with her back against the arm.

"I'm proud of you, you know."

I raised an eyebrow at my sister. "What?"

She sighed, crossing her legs in her lap and sitting like she had since she was little. "I worried about you for a long time."

"You never told me that."

"Of course not. Because you were my big brother. It was your job to look after me. But someone had to make sure you were okay, too."

"I never minded taking care of you after mom and dad left us."

"I know. That's just the kind of man you are, Sy. *Selfless*." She reached over, patting my arm. "But you didn't grieve. Not like I did. The first few months they were gone, I cried myself to sleep every night."

I'd known. Of course I'd known. What sort of big brother would I have been if I hadn't heard her cry?

I cleared my throat. "I didn't—"

She shook her head. "Let me get this out." Kayle took a deep breath. "I missed them like crazy, but you just trudged along. You made sure we ate. That we got to school. That we had a roof over our heads. I fell apart, and you kept us together. For *years*."

"Of course I did," I grumbled.

A tear fell from her eye. "But no one took care of you. And you were so closed off. You didn't open up to me about the stuff that really mattered. At one point, I figured as long as I had you in my life—my big brother, my best friend—it didn't really matter. But all I wanted for you was to find someone who would love you like you deserved. But you brushed off relationships, and I knew you had the guys, but… How much did you really let them in?"

She was right. They were my best friends, but I'd never been as open with them as I should have been.

"And then… Aurelia came along."

Some of the tension melted out of my body at the sound of her name.

She laughed. "You were so stubborn, insisting that she had no place on your ship. Because you *liked her.*"

"Shut up," I grumbled, shutting my eyes.

"You totally were crushing on her, and it was so obvious. Who forces everyone to hang out just so they can be in the same place as the girl they like?"

Grunting in response, I let her continue without interrupting.

"But then… I watched how she blossomed, too. How she opened up to you. How your expressions became more open, your personality less guarded. Our parents might have been selfish jerks who abandoned us, but you never were. And seeing her melt that grumpy persona you built?"

I crossed my arms over my chest. "It's not a persona."

"I've never seen you smile as much as you do with her."

Maybe that was true. In fact, I knew it was. I couldn't deny a single thing she was saying, so I didn't try.

"I really do love her, you know." I looked at the wedding ring on my finger. "And I know marrying her like this was reckless, but—"

"I don't think it was reckless at all. Not when you care for her this deeply."

"It felt right. And if the federation tries to say anything, I'm the one who will take the blame. Not her."

"I know." She gave me a hopeful smile. "That's who you are."

"Thank you," I said, pulling her in for a hug. "For never giving up on me. Even when I was moody and a stupid teenage boy who didn't know the first things about periods and tampons."

She sniffled. "Just doing my sisterly job to prepare you for your future wife."

"I never thought that this would be my life. That I'd get to love someone. To dream of a future where I had a wife. A family. I always thought love wasn't in the cards for me."

"I've always known it was. You love too big, too hard, to not find the perfect woman for you."

"You'll find your person too, Ky. I know you will."

"Maybe." She shook her head, giving me a sad smile.

I wondered if there was something more that she wasn't telling me. If it had anything to do with all the times I'd caught Leo staring at her.

We sat on the couch for a while, talking about stupid sibling shit. And about my wife. It was nice to talk like this—out in the open, where anyone could hear. I was so glad we didn't have to hide anymore.

LATER, after the bridge had emptied, I leaned against a railing on the top level, staring out the large window.

The ship was quiet, all diagnostics coming back clear. Everything was running properly. Sometimes, when I was wide awake in the middle of the night, I liked to come down here and check the code. The ship was built on a complex artificial intelligence system, but part of me never quite trusted that.

Settling into my chair, I watched the stars in front of me. The last twenty-four hours had been a complete whirlwind. I fidgeted with the ring on my finger, spinning the metal around and around.

"What's got you thinking so hard?" That soft, lovely voice called out, and there she was. Wearing a t-shirt that had my name on the back.

Her name now, too.

Finally, it was just the two of us.

Aurelia slid into my lap, and I wrapped my arms around her. Her feet dangled off one end of the chair as she sprawled across me.

"Hi." I nuzzled my face into her hair, letting her scent relax me.

"Hey. I thought I'd come check on you. You've been quiet since earlier."

"Just thinking about things, I suppose."

"No second guessing, I hope," she said with a chuckle.

I picked up her hand and kissed her ring finger. "Nope. I told you that you're mine. And now everyone else knows too. So don't even think about leaving me."

"Of course not." Her voice was soft. "And I'm going to make sure you know just how much you're loved every day." She kissed me softly. "Let's go to bed, husband."

"Mmm." I hummed. "I like the sound of that. Wife."

Standing up while keeping her in my arms, I headed back towards our bedroom.

I wanted to show her just how good the rest of our lives looked.

THIRTY-NINE
AURELIA

AS IT TURNED OUT, he needed very little persuading to leave the bridge and come to bed.

His name—the last name I'd taken just yesterday—was spread across my back, and his eyes had burned as he'd plopped me down into bed, practically ordering me to turn around so he could see it.

Which, of course, had ended with him pushing into me from behind, both of us filled with the same insatiable need. He fucked me with his t-shirt still on my body, wrapping a hand around my hair and pulling until I gasped.

After, we'd collapsed into bed, panting and sweaty, with his seed dripping down my legs. After a trip to the bathroom, he'd pulled me back into his arms, holding me tight against him.

I squinted at him as something occurred to me. "You know, I don't even know your middle name."

He leaned his head back and *laughed*. "It's Archer, baby. Sylas Archer Kellar."

"Mmm." I burrowed myself in between his arms. "I like that."

"I like yours more." Sylas ran a finger under my chin and

tilted my head up. When our eyes met, his were filled with so much love. "Aurelia Serena *Kellar*."

I blushed. "You know, I don't think I'm ever going to get used to that."

"Nah." He grinned, brushing his finger over my ring once again. "You will."

Sure, the silver band sitting on my wedding finger wasn't *exactly* what I'd always pictured when I imagined being married one day, but it was still special.

Especially when he'd had them specially made of scrap metal from the *Paradise*. Which meant that, for the rest of our lives, this symbol of our love would also carry a reminder of the place where those feelings had grown.

I hummed, watching as he played with my fingers. I was too comfortable to want to move, front to front, one of my legs thrown over his and his arms wrapped around me. Brina was sleeping at our feet, all too comfortable and used to us at this point.

"Do you regret it?" he asked, a weird look on his face.

"Regret what?" I frowned, interlacing our hands. "Marrying you?"

He shrugged. "Rushing it. Not having a ceremony…"

"I don't need a ceremony," I said. "I just need you."

Sylas picked up our hands, kissing the top of mine. "I was just thinking, it's a shame…" He looked contemplative. "I wanted to see you in a wedding dress."

"That's what you want?" I couldn't keep in my laugh.

"Mhm. I still think about how the dress you wore to the bar hugged your curves." I could feel him hardening against my thigh. "My kink might be you in a dress, Rae."

I was pretty sure he got off on me calling him *Captain*, because it always caused a groan to slip from his lips, but I wouldn't say that right now. Even if I loved being his brat.

"Well, you still can." I rolled my eyes. "When we get back.

We can have a ceremony. Do the whole thing. I'm sure my mom would like that."

A smile spread over his face as he rolled us, pinning us to the mattress. "On one condition?"

"What's that?" I fluttered my eyes, looking up at him through my eyelashes in the way I knew drove him crazy.

"Let me get you pregnant first."

"Sylas!" I exclaimed, laughing as he peppered my neck with kisses. "Have you forgotten we're on a *five-year* mission?"

"Four years."

"What?" I blinked.

"There's only four years left."

"We haven't even *talked* about having kids."

"Sure we did. You want them. I want them. Ergo, we have kids." He kissed my neck. "Easy."

"How many?" I rolled my eyes. "And you think having a baby while on a multi-year space journey is a good idea?"

"Why not? We have some of the best medical staff on board. The entire MedBay is perfectly equipped to handle anything. There's other parents on board, so I'm sure there's an extra crib or two lying around."

"*Two?*"

He shrugged. "You never know."

"I want at least two, I think. Just maybe not at once. This room isn't *that* big." I said, spinning my new metal band around my finger. "But being an only child growing up was pretty lonely. I always wished I'd had someone to play with. So... I'd want our kid to have a sibling."

"I agree. I'd never trade my sister for the world. Sure, she might have been a pain in the ass growing up, but she was also my best friend. And I'd want them to have that too. Whenever you're ready."

"Okay," I whispered. Because as crazy as it was, I wanted that. And I wanted to give it to him, too. When it was time. I traced my finger over his abs. "Is it bad that I want to wait a few months first? And just enjoy us being *together?*"

"Not at all." Sylas laughed, the emotion lighting up his entire face. I loved seeing him this happy. "But a shame. And I was thinking of telling the MedBay to do away with our shots." He splayed his hand over my flat stomach, his eyes focused there. "One day, I can't wait to see you grow our children."

"Sylas..." I blushed.

"With your eyes, I think." He leaned down to kiss my forehead. "What do you think, Mrs. Kellar?"

Humming, I wrapped my arms around his neck. "I think it gives us plenty of time to practice, Mr. Kellar."

His erection pressed against my hip.

"Practice?" Sylas smirked, flipping me on top of him. "I like the idea of that."

Straddling his chest, the fact that I wasn't wearing any underwear was becoming exceedingly obvious.

He pulled off his over-sized t-shirt from my frame. Sometimes, I felt like I couldn't find my own clothes. Then again, I was pretty sure his reaction to me wearing them was absolutely worth it.

Even though I knew all of my clothes were now in *our* room. The one we'd be sharing from now on.

Like I hadn't spent every night here for the last two months.

He gripped my hips. "Come sit on my face, baby. I wanna taste you."

"Oh." I squeaked, as he helped lift me onto his mouth. "Sy."

Hovering over his face, I gasped in surprise as he pulled me down. *How was he going to breathe?*

"*Sit,*" he ordered, digging his fingers into my thighs. "Don't make me ask again, Aurelia."

He slapped my ass, and I inhaled sharply. Spanking never used to appeal to me, but when Sylas did it, all it did was turn me on.

Maybe it was because I knew he would never hurt me.

I let my hands rest against the headboard as I sank down onto his mouth.

And then his tongue pierced inside of me, and I lost all rational thought. There were no words. Not when he was fucking me with his tongue like I was the most magnificent feast, and my hips rocked against him, a little bolt of satisfaction hitting me each time his nose bumped against my clit.

"I've never—" I gasped. No one had ever made me come like this before. When I'd tried it before, it had just been *okay*.

Nothing with Sylas had been just *okay*, though. I should have known this would be no different.

I couldn't stop moving, letting out little gasps and moans as he used his tongue with expert precision, and then when he finally sucked my clit into his mouth, giving it pressure with his teeth and suction, I came.

His fingers held me in place for a few more moments as he lapped up my release, like he was desperate for every drop.

I climbed off of him, rolling onto my back on the bed, and his beard was still shining with my release. I'd soaked his face.

"Damn, baby. I should have done that sooner. If I'd have known how much you'd like it…"

He pulled me to him, bringing our lips together and letting me taste myself on his tongue.

We kissed like that for a few moments, until I was all too aware of his growing erection pressing into my stomach, his need outweighing any desire I had to stretch this out.

Sylas rolled on top of me, pushing a pillow under my hips.

"Gonna fill you up," he murmured into my ear, and oh. *God.* Yeah, I liked that. He grabbed my leg, bending it back till it almost hit my ear, and then slid inside. "Fill your aching cunt with my seed. Do you want that, baby, huh?"

"*Yes.*" The pressure felt crazy, the way he was pushing on my leg, making me tighter than normal.

He'd bottomed out with the first stroke, and I was still sensitive from my first orgasm. Still so wet from his tongue. The wet noises that happened each time he thrust inside of me were borderline obscene.

It was everything.

"God," I gasped. "You're so big. I'm so full of you."

"Gonna keep you stuffed full of me always," he said, bending over to tug on my ear with his teeth. "That way, you don't forget whose you are."

"Yours," I said, devoid of any other answers. No other rational thought came to my brain.

But I was his, and he was mine, and we chased our orgasms together, and it was pretty perfect picture of the rest of our lives.

A FEW NIGHTS LATER, I was ushered to a revival of Sylas's so-called officer *get-togethers*. Didn't he know I didn't need an excuse to hang out with him anymore?

It was sweet, though. That he was still attempting to spend time with our friends now that we were out in the open with our relationship. Now that we were married.

"Surprise!" A loud chorus of voices called out as the door slid open, automatic lights flickering on like they'd been statues in wait.

"What's all this?" I asked, taking in the decorated officer's lounge. Someone had hung a *'Congratulations!'* Banner, and there was my husband, standing in the middle of it all, looking gorgeous in his dark gray jumpsuit.

"Sylas," I laughed. "Did you do all this?"

"Not completely. I had some help. Everyone wanted to celebrate."

Violet was the first one to come up to me, hugging me quickly before pulling back. "I hope you're not upset with me. I know I said some things and made some snap judgements, but I just wanted to make sure you knew what you were doing. That you were happy."

I looked over at Sylas, who gave me a dopey grin. "I am," I replied. "Completely happy."

For once, I'd never been happier.

"Good."

Astrid pulled me aside next. "You're not pregnant, are you?"

"No," I said, laughing. But Sylas's eyes caught mine, and the look he gave me was scorching. "Not yet," I added under my breath.

"Mmm." She winked. "You know where to find me when you want to come off the shots."

I rubbed my thighs together. *Indeed.* Indeed, I did.

Kayle and I had already had our heart-to-heart the other day —before she'd married Sylas and I. She was the extra special icing on the cake to marrying Sylas.

Because now, I had a sister. I'd always wanted a sibling growing up, but my parents only had me. And I knew they loved me enough to make up for it, but this was different.

"Thank you," Kayle said again. "For loving my idiot brother. I know he wasn't the best at first, but I'm so glad he has you."

"Me too." I hugged her tight. "Glad he has you, I mean. That he's so close with his sister. And now he has to share you with me."

She grinned, like she was also already imagining the shenanigans we could get up to. How we would drive him crazy.

"Having fun, baby?" He asked, wrapping his arms around my shoulders, rocking us back and forth to the low music that was playing in the lounge. Everyone was drinking bubbly— courtesy of someone in this room, whose initials I was pretty sure were *S.A.K.*—and having a great time.

"I am," I answered, beaming up at him. "But you didn't have to do any of this. You know that, right?"

"I figured if we have to wait four and a half years to have a real wedding, we might as well celebrate."

"So it wasn't just an excuse to break out the fancy bubbly?" I raised an eyebrow, turning my head so I could see his face better.

"Oh, no. It was definitely that." He smirked. "And I don't want you to ever feel like you're not loved—cherished."

I turned in his arms.

"That's impossible. This *is* you we're talking about, right? The man who created an entire pet sanctuary for an alien creature we'd rescued and all but had me move in with him after we'd slept together twice?"

Sylas snorted, and I patted his chest. "You have no chill, babe. My big teddy bear."

"Only for you," he said, leaning down to kiss me.

I hummed in response. "Good."

We celebrated well into the night, well past any of our usual bedtimes.

I didn't care, because the smile didn't drop from my face—not once.

FORTY
SYLAS

ONE YEAR LATER...

OUR FIRST YEAR on the S.S. Paradise had come and gone.
So far, the second year was shaping up to be the best year yet.
Even if we were only a month into it.

Tomorrow, we would dock at another planet to explore. Each
one was a brand new adventure, an entire world to explore.

None of them would ever be as special as *our* planet. The one
where we'd found each other. I thought about the cave where
we'd come together that first time. Where we'd found Brina. So
many memories.

We'd made even more ever since making it official. It turns
out it was much easier to be in a relationship when you weren't
sneaking around, trying to hide it from everyone.

Aurelia groaned, zipping up her dark gray jumpsuit.

"Need a hand?" I asked, stepping up behind her and looking
at her through the mirror.

"It doesn't fit," she huffed, giving me her best little pout. "I
was supposed to have more time before this happened." Aurelia
buried her face in her hands. "This sucks. Everyone's going to
know."

"Guess we'll have to find you something else to wear." I was perfectly fine if she wanted to wear my sweats all over the ship. Thinking about my crewneck on her lithe form shouldn't have been sexy, but it was.

"Sy." She glared at me, punching me in the shoulder. "This isn't a time to joke around."

"You can't even tell in your officer's uniform, Rae."

She furrowed her eyebrows. "Those pants are itchy. And I don't know if they'll zip, either. It's official. I popped."

She looked down at her belly, that was slightly poking out in her jumpsuit. Her breasts, which had also grown over the last few months.

I wrapped my arms around her middle.

Aurelia threw her head back to rest it on my shoulder.

My *wife*.

And now, the mother of my child.

I'd told her it was up to her when we wanted to start trying, and six months after that, we'd both intentionally skipped our shots. Imagine our surprise when we'd found out that I'd knocked her up on the first try. A late-night visit to Astrid in the MedBay had confirmed it, and we were over the moon.

We hadn't told anyone yet, though wanting to keep it to ourselves for a little while. At first, we'd wanted to get through the first trimester. And now, well...

I flattened my palm against her belly. "We should tell everyone."

She sighed. "Everyone's going to treat me differently, and you know it. They're not going to let me fly anymore. Not the transport shuttle. Which means I'll be left behind."

"I don't think that's true." I patted her shoulder.

Even though it definitely was. I'd been trying to get her to stop flying those shuttles for the last two months.

And she was right. At sixteen weeks, her belly was visible in her uniform.

"Fuck it. I'm wearing leggings." She pulled out a pair of stretchy black pants from the closet.

I wasn't sure where we kept acquiring clothes from—given this was a starship, and it wasn't like we were stopping at a shopping mall on any of our stops—but her closet kept growing.

Luckily, we had an enormous suite, and there was plenty of room. Perks of being the captain, as I always joked.

She pulled on her officer's tunic, smoothing the fabric over her small belly and admiring the curve in the mirror. Her officer's badge glinted in the light, and I threaded my fingers through hers.

"Ready?"

"Do I look okay?" Her eyelashes fluttered.

"You look beautiful, Rae." I never understood that shit about pregnant women glowing—not until now. Because she did.

"You're just saying that because you're my husband," she pouted.

I gathered her hair up, helping to pull it off her neck by braiding it down her back. I'd noticed fairly quickly into her pregnancy that she was getting migraines fairly frequently, and her tight buns and high ponytails hadn't helped that.

"I still think you're the most beautiful woman in the world," I said, kneeling in front of her and placing a kiss on her stomach. "Just as much as the first day I met you. Maybe even more so, now that you're carrying our baby."

"Yeah, yeah, you big sap." She gave me her best puppy dog eyes. "Will you help me put my shoes on?"

ONCE I'D FINALLY GOTTEN Aurelia out of our room and onto the bridge, she'd perked up. Standing tall, you could hardly tell that there was any bump in her uniform top anyway—not unless you were really looking.

"Good morning," she said to Violet as she passed her console, positively beaming.

I settled into my chair, and my sister looked over at me. "Morning."

Orion gave Aurelia a nod of greeting, and she looked back at me, blowing me a kiss.

"You two seem happy," Kayle said, a smile dancing over her lips.

My only response was a hum.

My communicator pinged with a message from my girl.

AURELIA

Now?

SYLAS

Whenever you want.

Okay.

Kayle raised her eyebrow as she glanced at the device in my hands. "Are you two really sending messages when you're only this far apart?"

I shrugged. "Can't help it."

Of course, I left out the fact that it was normally Aurelia who started our conversations. Half of them were flirty, and practically all of them left me hard by the end. She was a brat, through and through. Only for me, though. I liked how she didn't show her bratty side to everyone else. Just me.

She caught me staring and winked at me.

"Hey, guys. Sy and I have an announcement."

I stood up, and she slid into my side, wrapping an arm around my middle.

All eyes in the room slid to us expectedly.

"I'm pregnant." Aurelia rested her hand over her belly.

"Oh my gosh!" Violet squealed. "Really?"

"Yeah. We wanted to wait until I was a little farther along to tell everyone, and well…" Her cheeks flushed as she looked down at her bump. "Surprise. I can't really hide it anymore."

"I was wondering about the pants," Kayle said with a laugh.

"My flight suit doesn't zip anymore," Aurelia pouted. "I'm so sad. I love that jumpsuit."

"I have a friend on board who makes clothes," my sister offered. "I could see if she could make you something more comfortable to wear on the bridge."

I crossed my arms over her chest. "No field suits."

Aurelia sighed. "He's a little overprotective now."

"A little?" My sister laughed, and her eyes lit up. "I can't believe I'm gonna be an aunt." She pulled Aurelia into a hug before turning her attention to me. "I'm so happy for you, Sy. You deserve every happiness in this life and more."

"Thanks, sis." I squeezed her shoulder before we pulled apart. "It's going to happen for you too. I just know it."

She looked over at Leo, their eyes connecting briefly. "We'll see."

Astrid came onto the bridge, screeching loudly. Her blue hair was bouncing when she finally made her way over to Aurelia. "You told everyone, and I wasn't here!"

"Sorry." My wife gave her a guilty smile. "Decided it was time. My pants don't fit anymore." She curved a hand over her little bump.

"Look at you!" Astrid held both her hands, squeezing them. "Damn, you really did pop."

"I thought I'd be able to get away with my jump suit for a few more weeks, but no…" She twirled a piece of hair around her finger.

"Do you know what you're having?" Finley asked. "I found out with Kins."

"No." Aurelia squeezed my hand. "We decided we wanted to be surprised. Boy or girl, I don't care."

"I'm hoping it's a girl, though," I added, my voice a little gruff. A little mini-Aurelia sounded good to me. I hoped they'd get her hair. It was much prettier than the dark brown of mine.

"Awww," Violet said, placing her hand over her heart.

"I think it's a boy, but what do I know?" Aurelia shrugged. "We'll see in a few months."

Astrid had a little smile on her face, watching Aurelia's interactions with the crew, and I narrowed my eyes at her. "You know, don't you?"

"Of course I do." She winked at me.

The guys all patted me on the back, wishing us the best, and I was very aware of the fact that all nine of us that were *supposed* to be running this spacecraft were all just standing around on the bridge.

I swallowed roughly. "Alright. Back to work, the lot of you. Don't let me catch you goofing off."

"Yes, sir!" That was Aurelia, who gave me a flirty little wink. I pinched her ass before she could walk away, and her eyelashes fluttered.

Brat.

"EVERYONE TOOK IT WELL."

She looked around, blushing, but no one else was on the observation deck. It was just us.

I'd made sure to lock it this time.

Getting caught once was enough for me, and we'd scarred the poor crew member who'd come in as I had her hoisted up against the window. I'd been too desperate to be inside of her, and neither one of us had wanted to wait.

Turns out that being off the fertility blockers had made both of us extremely frisky, and I had no problems satisfying my girl whenever she needed me.

Aurelia was standing against the railing, looking out the large windows of the observation deck, one hand resting on her bump.

"I don't know why I thought they'd react any other way."

A chuckle came from my lips. "They love you."

"They're our family, you know? Especially up here."

"Yeah." I wrapped my arms around hers, resting my chin on her shoulder. "And you're *my* family. You and our little space baby."

She hummed, snuggling against me. "It's surreal, isn't it? Knowing that we're doing this, millions of light years from home, and yet I'm completely, utterly happy?"

"Yes." I pressed my lips to the side of her neck. "I agree. But I'm so thankful for you *and* them."

"Sylas," Aurelia whispered, squirming against me.

"Yes, baby?" I asked, continuing to press kisses on her exposed skin.

"I need you," she whispered.

"Here?" I asked, raising an eyebrow. "Or do you want to go back to the cabin?"

She shook her head, rubbing her ass against my already-hardening length.

"So needy," I muttered, creeping my fingers down the stretchy waistband, dipping them underneath the fabric.

I pressed my thumb against her entrance, feeling the wet spot already growing as I rocked my palm against her clit. "What do you need?"

"Your fingers," she said with a gasp.

Pushing back the elastic of her panties, I gave her two, sliding them inside her tight, wet heat. Aurelia wrapped her hand around my wrist as I stuffed her full of my fingers, working them inside of her.

Another side effect of pregnancy: she was insatiable. Not that I was complaining. I'd do whatever it took to keep her satisfied.

Between my fingers working inside of her and the way I was rubbing against her clit, I could tell she was already getting close. A series of little breathy noises came from her throat, and I stilled my movements, delaying her orgasm.

She squirmed against me as I pulled my fingers out, and I tsk'd my tongue against her ear. "Patience."

I pushed the waistband of her leggings down, helping her out of them. Her panties were next, the plain black set, and then those were on the floor, too.

She whimpered as I pulled her uniform top off, exposing the swells of her breasts. Unhooking her bra, it joined her shirt on the floor.

"Fuck. Look at you."

Her nipples were peaked, begging for attention, and I continued my perusal of her naked body. The swell of her stomach, rounded and firm. Aurelia cupped her breasts, rubbing a finger back and forth over her nipples as I stood there, fucking entranced, just looking at her.

Finally, I reached out, placing a hand on either side of her little belly. Our baby was in there.

"You're so beautiful carrying our child," I murmured, caressing her skin.

Splaying my fingers out over her bump, I leaned down and flicked her sensitive nipple with my tongue. Aurelia let out a low moan as I did the same to the other side before running my teeth over them. Her whole body shuddered when I sucked one into my mouth.

"I love how sensitive you are," I said, pulling away.

She ran her hand up the front of my pants, cupping me through the fabric. "Let me have you," she murmured. "Please."

"You know I can't say no to you," I muttered, playing with her hair.

Aurelia unzipped my pants, her small, nimble fingers sliding into my boxers to wrap around my cock, the touch of her soft skin making my brain short-circuit.

Freeing my cock, I let her have her fun for a few moments before I gripped her hips.

"Turn around," I ordered, spinning her to face the window once more. "Grab the railing."

She did, bending over and arching her back just slightly, and turned to look at me.

"Good?" I asked, not wanting to put too much pressure on her belly, and Aurelia nodded.

"Yes. Please. Give me your cock."

"Good girl," I praised, guiding my tip to her entrance and pushing in slowly. I didn't want to be too rough with her, not when she was carrying precious cargo.

She wiggled her ass as I filled her completely, feeding her inch after inch of my thick cock.

"Damn, baby. Look at you taking all of me. The perfect fit."

A moan slipped from her lips as I slowly pulled out, feeling her insides cling to me, before thrusting back in. Over and over, I picked up my pace, not caring about anything but how it felt inside of her.

At some point, I would have assumed it would have stopped getting better. But the more time we spent together, the better it got. *Fucking amazing.*

"Sylas," she cried out. "Harder. I need—"

Moving my hands from her hips, I cupped her belly as I snapped my hips into her, driving us both higher and higher.

"I know," I rasped out. "Let go. Come for me, Aurelia. Let me feel you."

Her pussy contracted around me as she came, my name on her lips, and it pushed me into my own orgasm.

I splayed my fingers across her stomach.

"You're obsessed," Aurelia giggled as she stood up, turning back around in my arms to face me.

"I can't help it. I love your belly."

She hummed, relaxing into my hold.

I pressed a kiss to her forehead, and we stood there, wrapped up in each other, blocking out the rest of the world.

There wasn't a single thing in this galaxy that could draw my attention away from her.

EPILOGUE

SYLAS

AURELIA TOOK MY HAND, leading us off the jet bridge. They were our first steps back on earth since we'd departed on the mission five years ago, and in a way, stepping off the ship—my ship—it felt like nothing had changed.

The sun still shined. Life went on.

And yet, everything was different now.

I looked over at the woman by my side, her reddish-brown tresses glinting in the sunlight.

Everything changed because of her.

My eyes caught on the silver metal band that she wore on her ring finger—one identical to mine. *My wife.* What had felt like an impulsive decision after only a few months of knowing each other ended up being the best decision I'd ever made.

And ever since, she'd shared my cabin—our cabin. I'd never been so deliriously happy. Even the crew liked to make fun of the smile I seemed to have most of the time, though that normally brought a scowl back to my face.

I was happy to not be the grumpy asshole if it meant I got to have her by my side.

Picking up her hand, I kissed her ring, enjoying the blush on her face. Even after all this time, it never got old. I loved making her squirm, just as much as I loved when she mouthed off to me.

"What was that for?" She looked over at me, raising an eyebrow.

"I love you."

"Mmm. I love you too." Aurelia leaned over, softly kissing me in front of all the crew who were also disembarking.

"Get a room!" Leo called, a humorous glint in his eye.

"We're working on it!" My wife yelled back.

I chuckled. "Do you have everything?" I asked, looking back at the small transport bay that had brought us back to earth. Brina was curled up asleep in the small kennel we'd gotten to transport her in, not wanting questions from federal security.

Sure, she might have been an unauthorized transport and an illegal creature we were smuggling in, but she was family now. If people could own raccoons, surely we could have an alien otter-dog hybrid for a pet?

"Well, that depends," Aurelia said, lips curling up in a smile.

"On?"

"Daddy!" a little toddler holding hands with my sister exclaimed, before running over to us. He wound his arms around my legs, hugging them tight.

"Ah, yes." I grinned. "Can't forget the wee one." Picking up our three-year-old son, I ran my fingers through his long, dark hair. He was the spitting image of me, and fuck, I'd never imagined how rewarding it would be to be someone's dad.

Neither one of us had wanted to wait until we were back on Earth to have kids, and though we'd both been on fertility blockers, we'd quickly stopped them after getting married.

Samuel was the biggest blessing, even if having a baby in the middle of a five-year mission in the depths of space had seemed crazy to some of the crew on board. We wouldn't have it any other way. Besides, the ship was outfitted with some of the best and most advanced medical technology of our time, and no one had been more excited than Astrid herself about getting to do Aurelia's pregnancy checkups.

"You just want to leave him with me so you two can have a night to yourself," Kayle muttered, joining us on flat ground.

Aurelia laughed, squeezing my hand. "I won't lie. The thought crossed my mind."

My sister leaned in, pressing a kiss to Sammy's forehead. "It's okay, your auntie loves you very much, little spaceman."

He giggled, tugging on a strand of my sister's hair.

Rae slid her other hand over her barely there bump. The little kernel of pure happiness and joy that we'd been keeping a secret from everyone on board—including my sister.

It was crazy to think about how different it would be this time. We were back, and I had no intentions of taking up another commission soon. I wanted to enjoy my early retirement—at forty, Aurelia loved to tease me how I was an old man—and spend this time with my family before we welcomed another one into the world.

It was time. Time to say goodbye to the officers who had become friends, and then our family, over the last five years aboard the Paradise.

Adjusting our son onto my hip, I wrapped my arm around her shoulders, pulling her in tight as I kissed her forehead. "Let's go home, my star."

Her eyes gleamed with happiness as I tugged her body tight to mine. "There is nowhere else I'd rather be, Captain."

I smirked. "I'm not your captain anymore, Aurelia."

"No? What are you, then?"

"Your husband." I dipped my head down, pressing a kiss to her forehead. "The father of your children. The love of your life."

"Mmm." She gave me a cheeky smile. "Verdict is still out on the last one, isn't it?"

Reaching over, I slapped her ass, delighting in her little yelp. "Oh, you're so getting it later."

"You're going to scandalize our son," she murmured into my ear.

"I fear we've already done that, sweetheart." There was nothing he could see now he hadn't seen before. Especially in tight quarters on the starship.

The number of nights I'd had to beg my sister to take him just so we could have a few moments alone in our room was... frequent.

I was looking forward to having a room with a door that *locked*.

"You know, I have a surprise for you." Her mouth brushed against my ear. "I had Astrid do one last scan this morning. Before we disembarked the ship."

"Oh?" I raised an eyebrow. We normally went to the MedBay for her ultrasounds together, but I guessed it made sense to see her friend in that capacity one last time.

She nodded. "Heartbeats are good. Strong."

"Beats?" I responded. Surely she didn't mean...

"Mmm. Yeah. Turns out there's not just one in there." She gave me a little wink. "Think we can handle two more?"

I laughed, turning back to look at the transport vehicle that was now pulling away. "If we could handle five years in space, I think we can handle anything."

"That's true." Aurelia grinned. "Because I'm probably going to be twice as cranky this time."

Bring it on. I was happy to indulge any craving she had during her pregnancy, to rub her swollen ankles, and wait on her hand and foot. It was how I took care of her. How I showed her how much I loved her.

"I hope we have girls this time," I murmured, kissing her forehead. "And I hope they look just like you."

"I don't know. Those Kellar genes are pretty strong." She pinched my side, and Sammy squirmed in my arms to get down.

A laugh burst from her lips as our son ran down the jet bridge, his eyes wide as he pressed his face against the glass. The high-speed monorail would take us into the city, and then we'd board another shuttle that would take us to the house we'd rented for the next few months. The UGSF had arranged it for us, given that all our belongings had gone into storage before we'd boarded the S.S. Paradise and our leases ended.

We planned to spend the next few months looking for a big house in the country—preferably one with a pool, for Brina, and enough room for the kids.

It was crazy to think in less than a year, we'd have three.

Aurelia breathed a sigh of relief as we all loaded up into the monorail. Our luggage would be driven to our end destination by the UGSF, meaning the only thing we had to carry with us was Brina's carrier and Sammy's stuff.

"I'm glad we'll get a few weeks of alone time," Aurelia said, leaning her head on my shoulder as Sammy rested on my other side, fast asleep. "I don't think I'm going to be able to hide that I'm pregnant much longer from everyone."

"We can tell them whenever you want, Rae."

"I know." She curled a protective hand over her tiny bump. "But I want to keep it to ourselves awhile longer. After we told everyone the last time, they were all over me." She groaned. "Like, didn't they have anything better to gossip about than us?"

I smirked. "It was a small ship. News travels quickly."

Aurelia rolled her eyes. "A little *too* quickly."

"I just can't believe you could hide your morning sickness from the crew for that long."

A groan slipped from her lips. "God, that was awful. I swear, it was ten times worse than with Sammy. I should have guessed earlier that there were two of them in here."

"Are they…" I started, rubbing my hand over my jaw.

"Identical," she confirmed. "My egg split. Which means it wasn't thanks to your super sperm." Aurelia poked a finger at my chest. She'd teased me relentlessly about the fact that the first month we'd been off fertility blockers, she'd gotten pregnant. This time, we'd gotten in a lot more practice.

I wasn't even phased. In fact, I grinned. "This is fucking awesome."

"I can't believe you're so excited about me pushing *two* babies out of me. It was bad enough with him." My wife glared at me. Stubborn, but damn, she was strong.

At five-foot-seven, she wasn't small, but our genes together definitely hadn't warranted a small baby. My six-foot-two frame was probably to blame for his gigantic head.

Something she liked to remind me of daily.

"Sorry." I winced, patting her shoulder.

She sighed. "At least we made a cute kid."

"Hell yeah we did." He wasn't just cute, he was *adorable*. And you'd never seen so much cute in a room as when Brina— now fully grown but still as precious as ever—curled up at his side.

My ovaries are crying, Aurelia used to say, staring at them asleep in his crib.

Well, I'd certainly fixed that problem.

She pushed at me with her shoulder. "What's that look for?"

I shook my head. "Nothing." Dipping my head low, I murmured into her ear, "Just thinking about how hot it was to knock you up."

"Well, you better keep those memories fresh, because this is it. Three's enough."

Mmm. We'd see. I pressed a soft kiss to her lips.

Now arriving…

Our train was pulling into the station, and I stood up, helping my wife up before heaving our sleeping son onto my chest. Aurelia tried to pick up Brina's carrier, too, but I stopped her. I was more than capable of carrying both of them.

"I'm pregnant, not incapable," she said, blowing hair out of her face with a huff of breath.

"Don't care," I said, keeping hold of both of them as we headed out of the station. "You've got precious cargo on board. And I have two arms."

Still, she pouted. "The shuttle is picking us up outside of the station?" Aurelia asked, and I nodded.

"Yup. They'll take us back to the rental." Where I had one last surprise for her. It had been harder to arrange, especially with the long-range communication signals, but as soon as we'd gotten closer to Earth, I'd been able to get in contact with her mom. She'd be waiting for us back at the house.

I might not have parents who cared about me anymore, but I knew how much Aurelia loved her mother. How strong their family bond had been. And I wanted her to feel that now that we were home, too.

Home. The word settled into my heart. Truthfully, home was wherever she was. Where my family was. For a long time, I'd lost sight of that. I'd had my sister, sure, but we hadn't had a *home.*

Aurelia leaned on my shoulder, and I wrapped an arm around her, all too aware that I had my entire world in between my arms.

I'd never trade it, even for the entire galaxy.

After all, I'd found a love beyond the stars. And that was worth more than anything in the world.

EXTENDED EPILOGUE

AURELIA

TWO YEARS LATER...

SLEEP WAS FOR THE WEAK.

That was what they all said, but chasing around a five-year-old and twin two-year-olds really put that statement to the test.

No more. I'd practically put my foot down after the twins. I wasn't having four kids running around this house.

But life was *good.* Sylas and I weren't retired, but we'd taken off the years where our kids were little to just be parents. Luckily, working on a starship paid *well,* especially for a five-year mission, so we didn't have to worry about money. All our credits were stored in our account, accruing interest.

We'd bought our house soon after disembarking the *Paradise* and returning to earth, and even though some days I still yearned for the white walls and the observation deck, I loved my life now, too.

Above all, I loved my family. Being a *mom.* Knowing that my dad was still with me, even now.

Sometimes, when I was missing him, I loaded up one of his old videos and let his love fill me up. My mom had cried when I'd played them for her, just like I'd lost it years ago. But even if my kids only had one grandparent, I knew she loved them beyond words. She'd make up for the lack of Sylas's parents.

I could tell it still bothered him sometimes, the way his parents had abandoned him and Kayle. He didn't even know where they'd gone after leaving them. I didn't understand how a parent could do that to their kids. To abandon them…

There was no way that I could ever leave my babies behind. I'd miss them all too much. Plus, I never wanted to miss out on moments like these.

Sylas was in the living room, wrestling with our three kiddos. Samuel was climbing on his back, like a monkey, while the two girls were content with him tickling them. Anastasia and Adeline had been a surprise in the best way. When Astrid had told me it was identical twins, I'd almost fainted. But now, I couldn't imagine our family as anything but the five of us.

"Daddy! Daddy! Tell me the story of you and mommy in space!"

The twins giggled.

"Again?"

I looked at Sylas, who was sitting on the floor, all our kids gathered on the couch in front of him. He was dressed so casually, in just a basic white t-shirt and jeans, and even now, at forty-two, I thought he was the most handsome man I'd ever laid eyes on.

Maybe I wouldn't be opposed to *one* more…

"What do you want to know, kiddos?" He asked, reaching over and ruffling Sammy's hair.

"Did you meet any aliens?" My son asked. "No! Tell the story about Brina!"

"What about the story about how mommy and I fell in love?" He looked over at me, catching my eyes as I dried off dishes in the kitchen.

"They've heard that one a million times, honey," I said, drying my hands and coming to sit beside him. "Maybe we should share a new one?"

"What about the time you flew the ship through an asteroid shower and got us out in one piece?"

"Hmm. I don't know. What do you think, Sammy?"

"Yes!" He exclaimed, jumping up and then falling back onto the couch cushions.

Sylas looked over at me, an eyebrow quirked. "Do you want to start it, or should I?"

My face heated. Even after seven years together, he somehow knew exactly how to make me blush.

"Your Dad and I were, um, cuddling in bed, when..."

He interrupted me. "Cuddling?"

"Shut up," I muttered. "Do you want to tell the story or am I?"

He kissed my forehead. "All you."

I recounted the story about how we'd woken up to the alarms on the ship blaring and rushed to the bridge to find we'd somehow flown straight into an asteroid storm. Of course, autopilot couldn't handle that kind of rough maneuvering, but luckily Mommy was an amazing pilot and could perfectly fly through such a dangerous storm.

"What happened after that?" Sammy's eyes were wide, his head resting on his hands as he laid on his stomach.

Addie climbed into my lap, nestling her head against my chest.

"The storm knocked some debris onto the ship, blocking the sensors, and Daddy wanted to get out there to fix it, but he was too big."

"Too big?" My son asked, eyes wide.

I nodded, chuckling at my husband's annoyed expression. "Plus, it wasn't safe for the Captain to risk himself like that. But I volunteered."

He muttered under his breath, "Because of course she did."

"Daddy was absolutely terrified as I pulled on my space suit."

"He was?"

I nodded solemnly. "Yup. Because he was in love with me." I leaned over to Sylas, inhaling his scent. After all, I still remembered how I'd felt after that space walk. It had been terrifying. Honestly, I had no business being out there. But I'd been stubborn, and I didn't want us to get stuck there.

The moment I'd gotten back inside, and his arms wrapped around me, I'd known my world was completely changed.

"And your Mom knew that she loved me too." He used his forefinger to tilt my chin towards him, bringing our gazes together.

"I did."

Probably best to leave out how we'd made out as soon as the airlock was closed, though. Little ears didn't need to know about what we got up to. Actually, the kids didn't need any of the details of our sex life, ever. Especially not the things we'd gotten up to on the Paradise.

"What happened next?"

Addie tugged on a strand of my hair as I adjusted her position. Ana had curled up in Sylas's lap, too—because the twins were always determined to do things together—but she'd fallen fast asleep. My husband was rubbing circles on her back, bringing a smile to my face.

"I asked her to marry me."

"You did?" His eyes were wide.

"Yup. It had only been a few months, but I already knew she was the best thing that had ever happened to me. And I couldn't imagine another moment without calling her my wife."

"Awww. You sap. You really liked me, didn't you?" I gave him a coy smile.

"Baby." He laughed. "We're married."

"Still." A smirk spread over my lips. "You had it bad."

"Like you were any better."

"Says the man who built a home for the alien creature I'd brought on board for the sole reason of me spending every night in his room."

"Okay, so I might have done that."

"Or what about when you organized so-called officer get-togethers just so you could spend time with me?" I added air quotes around the term officer 'get-togethers' because those had definitely just been an excuse.

He grumbled under his breath. "I plead the fifth."

"It's okay," I whispered. "I love you anyway."

"You better," he said, a low warning to his voice.

Sometimes, it was still fun to tease him. I liked being his brat. Liked when he was rough with me. It happened less now, sure, especially on account of having three children and limited sleep schedules, but he always knew exactly what I needed.

Sylas leaned over, kissing my cheek. "I love you too." His face had softened, a loving expression in his eyes.

Even Sammy was asleep now. "Mission accomplished," I laughed. "Somehow, we put them to sleep without even trying."

"Who said I wasn't trying?" He gave me a smug grin. "Why don't we tuck them into bed, and then we can reminisce in the bedroom instead?"

I waggled my eyebrows. "Oh, Captain. I like the way you think."

"Little star," he said, dropping his voice in a low warning. "You're on thin ice here."

"That's what I'm counting on, *sir*." I winked, and he took Addie from my arms.

"Alright, I've got these two if you want to tuck him in?"

I nodded. "Sounds like a plan." *Teamwork*. It was what had always made us better. Stronger. We'd always been working as a team, from the moment he'd walked in on me on the bridge and volunteered to help.

He kissed me on the cheek. "See you upstairs."

"Not if I see you first," I sassed back, knowing that he would likely have spanked me for it if he hadn't had his hands full with our daughters.

Ha. A smile curled over my lips.

I win.

Score 531 Aurelia, Score 40 Captain Kellar.

What? I'd been keeping track.

SYLAS

I closed the door quietly behind me, both girls tucked into their toddler beds, and let out a sigh of relief.

Every day was full of new challenges, but we faced them together. A team. Just like we had been, from the moment I'd offered Aurelia my help when I found her attempting to find her father's ship.

Some days, I missed the ship. How we'd traveled so far across the galaxy, exploring new worlds and all manners of fascinating things. But other days, I was content. This life wasn't one I'd ever thought I'd be lucky enough to have.

But I'd never once had the urge to leave them. Unlike my parents, who'd been able to leave without looking back. Aurelia and our three kids were the best thing that had ever happened to me.

This dream was better than being the captain of a starship ever could be.

I slid into our bedroom, the lights still off, and pulled my t-shirt off over my head.

Flipping the light on, I found Aurelia lying across our comforter, wearing a tiny lacy thing.

"Beat you," she said, a little smirk curled over her face.

A rumble sounded in my chest as my eyes trailed over her body appreciatively. "Damn, baby." I mused. "That's quite the getup. Is this all for me?"

She shifted her legs, stretching out. All that gorgeous hair was tousled, spilling down her shoulders, and the ring on her left ring finger glinted in the light.

I loved our rings that I'd had made on the ship, but when it had come time for an actual ceremony, I'd gotten her the gorgeous ring she deserved. The large, round stone was set in a starburst, the entire band a halo of smaller diamonds surrounding the white sapphire stone. *Beyond the stars* was inscribed on the inside, a constant reminder of how we'd fallen in love.

And our original band sat on top, of course. No matter where we went, we both carried a piece of the *Paradise* with us.

Fuck, I loved seeing them on her. Knowing she was my wife.

There was a sparkle in her eye as I climbed onto the bed, caging her body in with mine.

Slipping my finger between the thin strap and her shoulder, I picked it up, letting it snap against her skin. She gasped, looking up at me with half-lidded eyes. Heat swirled in them, and I knew she was turned on.

"If I touch you right now, am I going to find you wet for me?"

"Why don't you find out?" Aurelia fluttered her eyelashes, her eyes crinkling at the corners.

Seven years together, and I still couldn't get over this. How much was between us. How explosive it was, every time. Every time I touched her, her body lit up for me. Aurelia's pleasure was my pleasure, and no one could say I didn't put my wife's needs first. Every time.

I pulled her thighs apart, digging my fingers into her soft skin, exposing her pretty pink slit to me.

Not wanting to wait, I pressed my face against her entrance, giving one long, languid lick.

The taste of her exploded on my tongue, and I groaned. Keeping her legs apart, I dove back in, devouring her like a man possessed. I was dying of thirst, and she was the only one who could quench it. Sucking her clit into my mouth, I kept going as she cried out, a flood of moisture coating my face and beard.

"I fucking love this," I said, fingers playing with the lace. The damn thing was crotchless, those tiny straps attached to lace cups that her cleavage spilled out of, with a little bow in the center of her tits.

"I thought you would," she said, giving me a secret smile. "I know we haven't gotten to spend as much time together alone lately, but I wanted to spice things up."

"You're too fucking perfect for this world," I rasped out. "Out of this damn galaxy."

I kissed her deeply before moving down to her tits, sucking them into my mouth through the lace.

"*Oh,*" she said, her head rolling back with pleasure as I gave her nipples the care and attention they deserved. After all, they deserved it.

Aurelia still liked to tease me that I was a tits guy, and yeah— I fucking loved hers—but I was an equal opportunity guy with this woman. I'd willingly take all of it.

She ran her fingernails down my abs, cupping me through my jeans. "Take these off, husband," she said seductively in my ear, her voice dripping with sex.

I was happy to comply, quickly kicking them off behind me and shedding my boxer briefs. My cock was all too eager to be inside of her again.

"I love you," she murmured as I positioned myself at her entrance, not quite nudging inside.

"I love you, my star," I said, cupping her face and kissing her gently.

And then I lost myself in my wife, wondering if there would ever be anything better than this in my life.

If there was, I didn't fucking care to find it. I was content right here.

In my house with a white picket fence, a wrap-around porch, and the only four humans I'd ever need.

BONUS SCENE

SYLAS

EVEN ALL THESE YEARS LATER, the *Paradise* still looked the same. White, gleaming metal coated the outside, every inch of her gleaming. They'd brought the ship back in for routine maintenance for its twentieth birthday, inviting all the officers from the very first crew back aboard.

"Mom!" Sammy exclaimed out the window, tugging on Aurelia's jacket. "Look at it! That's so freaking *cool!*"

She smiled over at our son. "That was my reaction when I first saw it, too."

He'd turned eighteen this year, and it was officially all our kids' *first time* in space. We were just taking the transport vehicle up to the space station, but both of the girls next to me had their eyes glued to the window, mesmerized. They were both fifteen now, and though they looked practically identical—though it was easy enough to tell them apart if you knew them like we did —they had completely distinct personalities.

It wouldn't surprise me at all if we had three kids who all ended up following in their parents' footsteps one day. Though Addie was a natural born caretaker, she'd been talking about wanting to be a nurse, but I definitely also could see her as a doctor in a big prestigious hospital back on Earth. Samuel was getting a degree in Mechanical Engineering, and Ana, well... who knew with that one? She was naturally curious, always on the hunt for something. Maybe she'd be the one to discover the next planet we'd colonize. Who knew?

And I was so damn proud of all of them. In the people they were becoming.

Even if them getting older also meant *I* was getting older. I'd turned fifty-five this year, a fact that my wife had teased me about *relentlessly,* especially with the salt-and-pepper look I was now sporting.

Meanwhile, my wife still had her gorgeous russet brown locks, and looked just as beautiful as the first day I'd laid eyes on her.

I regretted a lot of choices in my life, but never being with her. Falling in love with Aurelia was the best damn thing that had ever happened to me. Our kids were the best thing that ever happened to me.

Looking over at her, I couldn't help the lovesick smile on my face.

"What?" she asked, raising an eyebrow. "Why are you looking at me like that?"

Reaching across the aisle, I grabbed her hand and squeezed it. "No reason." *I love you,* I mouthed.

Aurelia returned the smile, squeezing back. "Love you too," she murmured.

The ship docked in the space station, and we all de-boarded, walking down the ramp, and then through the well-lit hallways to the boarding station for the *Paradise.*

"This is so cool," Sammy said, voice in awe as we finally walked onto the ship.

It had been a long time since we'd sat foot on the Paradise. At first, we'd taken an extended time off from the Federation—Aurelia had the twins, and neither one of us had been in a rush to get back on a spaceship with one newborn, let alone *two.*

But my wife was a natural born pilot, and I know she missed

flying, even while we were on Earth. After the girls were in pre-school, she'd accepted a post at the flight school she'd graduated from—the one named after her father. Now, she was an incredible teacher and faculty member. Damn, I was proud of her. She still got to fly, though her missions were typically only weeks long now instead of years.

Even if the federation called me every year asking if we'd be willing to take another commission.

I'd ended up taking up a Vice Admiral position, in charge of deployments for our new UGSF starships, sending out missions just like our own to other ends of the galaxy. Even in the last fifteen years, the things we had discovered were incredible. Unknown elements, new materials for building, and planets we were working to colonize. Space stations had been built farther out, allowing for more long-range communication, and we were truly on our way to an entirely new way of life.

"I can't believe you guys actually lived here for five years," our daughter, Anastasia, added. "That's so *long.*"

"Sammy lived here too, you know. He was three when we went back to Earth." I ruffled his dark brown hair. Just like mine. Though he'd gotten his green eyes from Aurelia—and her father. Looking at old photos, he was practically a spitting image of Samuel Callisto.

"*Dad,*" he protested. "I'm not a kid anymore."

He hated when we called him his childhood nickname, but secretly I was always going to think of him as that little boy who had made us parents. The sight of her in the MedBay with that little bundle wrapped up in a white blanket... I rubbed at my chest.

"You okay?" my wife whispered, nudging me with her hip.

I leaned over to kiss her temple. "I'm great. Perfect, actually."

She hummed in response. "You are." Then my wife patted my ass for good measure.

Some people went soft as they got older, but not me. Aurelia liked my muscles too much for me to let them go, so I still spent more hours in the gym each week than I'd liked to admit.

"There she is! Aurelia Kellar." Admiral Eliza Baliss—Aurelia's childhood friend—beamed at her from the middle of the bridge.

"It's so good to see you," my wife answered, as Eliza wrapped her up in a big hug.

"And Sylas!" Jax—her husband, and another high-ranking official for the federation—slapped me on the back. "Thank you both so much for coming today."

They'd both been at our earth-side wedding celebration, which we'd ended up having while Aurelia was about five months pregnant with the twins. Still, it was a fond memory for me. Her dancing with her mom, all our friends flying in from all over the planet to be there... The memory made me grin.

"Of course," I responded. "We wouldn't miss this for the world. It's good to be back." On here, it seemed like no time had passed at all. I still remembered the first time I boarded the ship. Getting my bearings. Learning the ropes, figuring out how to be captain.

And then there were the little things, too.

All the times we'd spent in the officer's lounge. The bar that we'd turned into a dance club on multiple occasions throughout the five years. Walking through the gardens. The entire damn ship being completely enamored with Aurelia's otter-dog.

Finding out we were having Sammy.

All those *good* things that had given me my family. Not just Aurelia, but all of them.

"There's my man!" That was Leo's voice, entering the bridge behind us. "And look at the kids! They've gotten so big!"

"They're all grown up now," Aurelia agreed with a laugh.

"Hi, Uncle Leo," Sammy said, grinning up at the blond former chief of engineering.

"And look at my girls!" My sister's voice now. Ana and

Addie ran into her open arms, both hugging her at the same time.

"Did you bring our cousin?" Anastasia asked, rocking on her heels. Her curls bounced with the motion.

"Course I did." Kayle grinned. "Lyra is up in the observatory. She's waiting for you."

"Yay!" The girls looked at each other, a smile splitting their identical faces. They both shared Aurelia's reddish-brown hair and my deep blue eyes. They looked back at us.

"Can we go up there?" Adeline asked.

It was only one level above us. "Sure," Aurelia answered. "Do you want us to show you the way?"

"Nope!" they shouted. "We'll find it!"

My wife turned to me, biting her lip. I chuckled. "They're fine. How much trouble do you think they can get into on a stationary starship?"

She quirked her eyebrow, as if to say, *do you remember how much trouble we got up to?*

"Besides, Adeline won't let them misbehave. She's too responsible."

The rest of our fellow officers filtered in, many of them with their kids in tow. Finley, with her daughter—Kinsley. She was twenty-three now, all grown up before our eyes. Wren was behind her. Then came Astrid. Orion. Violet.

Everyone was hugging, sharing stories from the last few years. We didn't often all get together, living in all different corners of the world, so it was normally just at weddings and large celebrations that we all got to say hello again.

Leo's twelve-year-old son—Lukas—came up to me, giving me a fist-bump as he said, "Hey, Uncle Sy."

He'd picked up calling me that from my sister. No doubt about that.

When I turned around, Aurelia gave me a sly smile before plopping into the Captain's chair, looking like she fucking belonged there. She was the only one who could get away with that. My little brat.

She slid her hand over my heart. After the twins were born, I'd gotten a constellation tattoo of my own. One big star, and three little ones. Aurelia liked to kiss it each night. It was my representation of them, the people I'd do anything in this world for. The people I loved more than anything.

They let us all wander for a while, kids pairing off and laughing, the rest of us taking it at a more leisurely pace.

Aurelia and I enjoyed a stroll through the gardens. They were even more beautiful now. Like they'd truly grown into their splendor over the last fifteen years.

Finally, we ended up in our favorite spot.

I ran my thumb under her chin, tilting her head up towards mine. "This was always my favorite spot."

"Yeah?"

I nodded. "It's the first place I kissed you."

"Mmm." Aurelia slid her hands up my shoulders. She squeezed slightly, and after all these years, I knew exactly what she was doing with that motion. Feeling me up.

I smirked, and my lips found their way instinctively to hers. Just like we'd done so many times. My tongue traced the softness of her full lips, lingering, savoring every moment.

"Sylas Archer Kellar," she muttered, eyes narrowing. "You're holding out on me."

I chuckled. "Only because I don't want to get caught in here, and if I kiss you like I did twenty years ago—"

My wife silenced me by pulling me in closer to her and giving me a punishing kiss. It was the kind of kiss you could sink into. Forget the entire world, as you consumed your partner's mouth.

"That," she said, her knees wobbling a little, and her face flushed. "That's how you kissed me."

"It's a good thing you have such a great memory. In my old age, I think I'm starting to forget."

Aurelia rolled her eyes, and I spun her around, wrapping my arms around her waist so I could tug her backside against my body.

She hummed, leaning her head backwards onto my shoulder.

"What are you thinking, husband?" Aurelia said, tilting her neck so her eyes could meet mine.

"I'm thinking about how lucky I am, wife," I said, marveling at her. "I love you, little star."

"I love you too, Captain."

I kissed her softly, and she beamed, the smile lighting up her entire face.

Looking at her was like looking at the stars: bright and shining. But she shone brighter than any star in the night sky, and I knew that no matter how many galaxies I spent looking, none would ever captivate me the way she did.

Our love had spanned galaxies, and I knew it would last us a lifetime.

ACKNOWLEDGMENTS

It's crazy to think that, at the time of writing this, I just finished my eighth book. Lucky number eight! It's always been my favorite number, and I might be biased but I absolutely love this book.

There's some people that I absolutely could not have done this without, and I wanted to say one GIANT thank you to them.

First of all, to my bestie and writing partner who always believed in me (even when I was stressed and way behind my deadline, Maren: I love you so so so much. Thank you for being my friend (and letting me spend 75% of Apollycon hanging out with you and your crew) and for taking me under your wing. What would I do without you??

To Sam, who drew this amazing cover for me: thank you so much for bringing Aurelia & Sylas to life. It's absolutely beautiful! I'm so thankful for finding you through Helnik art, and getting the chance to show Cal and Dani your art (including this cover!) this year is a core memory for me.

To my author friends: thank you for keeping me going, for being a source of inspiration, for being the ones I could bounce ideas off of, send art updates to every five minutes, and generally for just being some of the loveliest people I know. I don't have room to list everyone, but you know who you are.

To everyone who beta read: THANK YOU!! I couldn't have done this without you. I appreciate you all more than I can express in words.

And to all of my readers: I wouldn't be here without you. Thank you for taking a chance on my spicy space book. I hope you had fun on this adventure with me.

ALSO BY JENNIFER CHIPMAN

Best Friends Book Club

Academically Yours - Noelle & Matthew

Disrespectfully Yours - Angelina & Benjamin

Fearlessly Yours - Gabrielle & Hunter

Gracefully Yours - Charlotte & Daniel

Castleton University

A Not-So Prince Charming - Ella & Cameron

Once Upon A Fake Date - Audrey & Parker (late 2024)

Witches of Pleasant Grove

Spookily Yours - Willow & Damien

Wickedly Yours - Luna & Zain (coming Fall 2024)

ABOUT THE AUTHOR

Originally from the Portland area, Jennifer now lives in Orlando with her dog, Walter and cat, Max. She always has her nose in a book and loves going to the Disney Parks in her free time.

Website: www.jennchipman.com

- amazon.com/author/jenniferchipman
- goodreads.com/jennchipman
- instagram.com/jennchipmanauthor
- facebook.com/jennchipmanauthor
- x.com/jennchipman
- tiktok.com/@jennchipman
- pinterest.com/jennchipmanauthor